The Flames That Forged Us

The Pyre Song Trilogy Book 1

Gisele Stein

This book is dedicated to my sister.
Some people spend a lifetime looking for a true friend; I've been
lucky to have one since day one.

Prologue

Northern Germany, 1943

The full moon tugged her magic like the tides.

The witch dug her bare feet into the sand, the North Sea wind whipping her coat around her legs. Ocean spray misted her face, mingling with the first drops of rain that cleansed away any detrimental effects the salt might have on her craft. Beneath her toes, the wet sand yielded and reformed with each wave. She swayed in that rhythm, humming from deep within her belly, a primal song echoing the Earth's ancient heartbeat, steady as mountains rising from the ocean floor.

She tilted her head back, and the moon bathed her face in silvery light. People spoke of its dark side as if it were a place of danger, of shadow. But she knew it wasn't dark at all. The side of the moon we cannot see from Earth spends half its time in sunlight, too, but it's a place we never get to glimpse. The dark side, then, is where the hidden forces dwell. Ruth Hausmann — for that was the witch's name — had understood this paradox long before the Reich came calling, long before she traded secrets for power: What others labelled as darkness was merely power they couldn't comprehend or control. And sometimes, one had to venture into those darker realms in order to access true strength.

Her path was *not* a fall from grace — but an ascension, to clarity, to the light.

Magic hummed through her veins as she tuned into that hidden light now, making her stronger tonight than she had been in weeks, or maybe ever. The late summer tide aligned perfectly with the full moon, creating ideal conditions for what they needed to accomplish.

When she turned toward the land, they were waiting.

Twenty-eight witches formed a wide circle on the flat stretch of beach, their faces hollow in the moonlight. Seven among them were from Ruth's own Schwarzmilan Coven, devoted disciples and true believers of the cause. But most of the witches present did not choose to be here. They clung to the old ways, to hiding their magic like embers banked beneath cold ash. They lacked the courage to step into darkness when necessary. Some stood with shoulders slumped in defeat, others with jaws clenched in resentment. None met Ruth's gaze directly.

Beyond them, the dunes rose like a wall between ocean and land, sheltering the temporary structures of the Reich Weather Division on the island of Sylt – a cluster of canvas tents and wooden platforms shaking in the wind. Spotlights cut through the night, illuminating the ring of armed guards that surrounded the witches, the soldiers' breath frosting in the unnaturally chilled air.

"The front is approaching from the northwest tonight," Ruth called out, her voice carrying over the wind. "The British bombers will attempt to reach Hamburg by dawn. You know what must be done."

The tallest witch – Margot Kettering from the Netherlands

– shook her head almost imperceptibly. "Dit is waanzin..." *This is madness*, she hissed.

Need I remind you what is at stake? Ruth's voice pierced directly into Margot's thoughts, employing telepathy, a rare gift even among witches. She made eye contact with the nearest guard, who stepped forward, nodding, his handheld radio crackling with static noise.

"The children remain comfortable, for now," the guard reported after a brief exchange. "But their... comfort depends entirely on tonight's success."

A visible shudder passed through several of the women. They all knew where their children were being held: in the far corner of the tented camp, attended by nurses who could become executioners with a single command.

"Begin," Ruth ordered.

Reluctance gave way to necessity, and the witches raised their arms. Their voices rose in a chant that harmonised with the wind's howl, calling to the approaching storm front. This was the fourth such attempt this month, but tonight they would push further than ever before.

Ruth watched as the air between the witches began to shimmer with Anima. From her vantage point, she could see the energy flowing like luminous currents between the women, pooling at the centre of their circle before streaming upward to the clouds above.

A younger officer approached, keeping a distance. "Standartenführer Meyer asks for a report on progress," he said, unable to hide his nervous glance at the thickening storm clouds.

"Tell him we are intensifying the front as ordered," Ruth replied. "The cold air mass is being sped up. It will collide with the warm front in approximately sixty minutes, directly in the bombers' path."

"And the... magnitude?" The officer's voice dropped, as if

speaking too loudly of such things might invoke them prematurely.

"Beyond anything we've yet achieved," Ruth answered, allowing a thin smile. "The Führer will have his impenetrable sky."

As the officer retreated, Ruth returned her attention to the circle. The witches' chanting had taken on a ragged quality, their bodies swaying with effort. Above them, the clouds churned unnaturally, spinning too fast, compressing too tightly.

She could feel it now, the resistance in the natural system. This was to be expected; after all, weather patterns formed over days, not mere minutes. The energy required to force such rapid change was immense, and the debt it created needed to be balanced elsewhere in the natural world.

In previous workings, they had performed the balancing rituals simultaneously, half of the women redirecting excess energy into the ground in controlled releases. But tonight's orders had been explicit: maximum effect, no delays, no diversion of energy for what the Nazis had deemed "unnecessary caution."

Ruth had argued against this plan, explaining Anima's core principles of magical balance, but had been overruled by increasingly desperate leadership.

Germany was losing the war. Hitler needed results, not excuses.

The storm was forming quickly now. Lightning arced between clouds that, under normal circumstances, should not yet have been charged enough for such displays. The wind picked up dramatically, lifting sand from the beach in stinging sheets.

One of the witches – Gerda, a Schwarzmilan member from the Frisian Islands – fell to her knees, blood streaming from her nose as she forced herself to go on. *Salt.* In her struggle, she'd let too much of it penetrate her pores. The others instinctively moved to compensate, their own burdens increasing.

Stand up! Ruth implored her sister mind-to-mind. *Maintain the circle!*

Guards rushed forward, roughly pulling Gerda back to her feet. The witch's eyes rolled back, showing whites, yet her lips continued to form the words of the chant.

Despite herself, Ruth felt the first tremor of doubt. She had pushed these women before, but never beyond their physical limits.

Above them, the storm's rotation tightened ominously. The clouds had taken on a greenish tinge that reflected off the churning sea. The pressure dropped so rapidly that Ruth's ears popped, and she winced from the sudden pain.

"Fräulein Hausmann!" Meyer himself was approaching now, his greatcoat lashing behind him. "Was geht hier vor?" *Is this development as expected?*

Before she could answer, a bolt of lightning struck the sand not twenty meters away. The guards flinched but held their positions.

"The intensity is... higher than expected," Ruth admitted. "We should really split the group and begin the balancing—"

"Absolutely not," Meyer cut her off. "The ritual continues as ordered. The storm must reach maximum intensity within the hour."

"Standartenführer, ich befürchte das Gewitter ist zu unbeständig." *I'm afraid the system is becoming unstable.* "If we don't release some of the accumulated energy soon—"

"These are direct orders from Berlin," Meyer snapped. "The Reich cannot afford another bombing raid on Hamburg. Your witches will continue until instructed otherwise."

As if on cue, another witch in the circle collapsed. This time, none of the others could compensate. The chant faltered, then resumed with desperate intensity as the guards raised their weapons.

Ruth looked from the witches to the storm and back to Meyer. She had crossed many lines since aligning with the Reich, justified many compromises. But this... this was madness.

"The imbalance really is growing critical," she said, struggling to keep her voice steady. "No natural system can be pushed this far without consequence."

Meyer's eyes narrowed. "Are you defying a direct order, Fräulein?"

Ruth hesitated. Her gaze drifted to the facility on the dunes where other witches' children were held. Then to the circle, where women who had once been her sisters in magic now suffered under her direction.

How had it come to this? She had revealed herself to the Reich believing witches would finally take their rightful place in the world. That magic would be recognised, respected, elevated. Instead, she now stood on a shoreline watching witches being worked to death like draught animals.

But turning back was impossible. The only path was *through*. True power lay on the dark side, she reminded herself. We must embrace it to achieve greatness.

"No, Standartenführer. I am merely advising caution."

"Noted," Meyer said. "Now increase the intensity as ordered."

Ruth turned back to the circle, raising her arms. "Channel deeper!" she commanded. "Draw from the earth beneath you if you must but strengthen the connection!"

The witches obeyed, their faces taut with effort. The storm above grew more violent, its unnatural rotation now unmistakable. The sea began to heave, waves crashing higher on the shore than the tide should allow.

Ruth felt it then. For the first time ever, she could sense the moment when natural forces began to slip beyond control. Magic had its own inherent balance, a cosmic ledger that always required payment. When that balance was pushed too far, systems didn't just fail; they *inverted.*

The first sign was subtle: circles of frost forming on the sand around some of the witches, despite the howling wind. Then came the stillness – a sudden, eerie cessation of sound.

"What's the status?" Meyer demanded, his voice faltering slightly.

Ruth ignored him, her attention fixed entirely on the sky. The storm's rotation had reversed, spinning with impossible speed in the wrong direction. She had to direct it now, had to send it across the ocean to where it ought to go. But just as she was about to force the front in a westerly direction, the connection snapped, sending the witches reeling backward as if struck by an invisible wave, bodies tumbling like scattered pins, some falling to their knees, others staggering to maintain balance, their linked hands torn apart with such force that several cried out in pain. Lightning no longer flashed between clouds but arced continuously in a circle, forming a wheel of light that mirrored the witches' circle below.

"Was machen Sie denn?" *What are you doing?* "Reverse this immediately!" Meyer ordered.

"I can't," Ruth said, a strange calm settling over her. "None of us can anymore. This is what happens when you take from nature without giving back."

The first witch to die simply... disappeared. One moment Margot stood at her position, hands raised; the next, her body collapsed into itself, leaving nothing but a dark stain on the sand. The others followed in rapid succession, their life energy consumed by the ravenous imbalance they had created.

Guards ran, their orders forgotten. Meyer shouted commands that no one heeded. The storm descended, a roaring vortex of wind and Anima that had transcended its creators' intentions.

Ruth remained still – *stunned* – watching the destruction unfold. Too late she understood what she had refused to see before: magic was not a tool to be used, but a force to be respected. By pushing too deep into the darkness, she had violated nature itself.

As the maelstrom expanded outward, consuming the beach, the tents, and everything within its reach, Ruth remained at the centre, the eye of the storm forming directly above her. The last thing she saw before the vortex closed in around her was the moon, serene and untouched above the chaos below. Half in light, half in shadow – perfectly balanced, as all things should be.

Part One

Chapter One

Eighty years later

The kettle sputters like it's about to spill a secret.

I move towards the tiny potbelly stove by the window, palms gliding over the oak wood counter, weathered smooth like river stones. Energy thrums through the grain into my fingers, a steady pulse that echoes in the roots of every plant in the room. It's a witch thing, this ability to feel the very heartbeat of the earth, a dormant ember of my magic that stubbornly smoulders beneath the skin. Some days, I try to silence it. Most days, I'm grateful for its crackle. Because it reminds me that it was all real.

Dawn prowls across the shelves stocked with jars and vials, coaxing life from every shadowed corner of my apothecary. The light catches my phone, a sleek black rectangle sitting on the worn wood of the windowsill, as incongruous as a neon sign in an old growth forest.

The temptation to check my messages again is almost overwhelming. Did she even see my text?

A breeze tumbles through the open window, and I take a deep breath, inhaling the familiar late summer scent of pine and the wildflowers now blooming in the valleys. Summer is slow to arrive in the Harz Mountains of northern Germany, but once it's here, I notice every smell. Bundles of lavender and chamomile sway from rough-hewn rafters, their rustles a whisper against the kettle's hiss.

My fingers hover over the phone, but I pivot away from the windowsill, leaving my unanswered message to simmer. These devices beep when they've got news to share, after all. I wrap my hands around the teapot – a chunky, misshapen thing I made myself, lumps and bumpy edges everywhere, just how I like it – and pour the steaming water over a blend of chamomile, lemon balm, and a pinch of angelica root. The herbs dance and unfurl in the heat, releasing a cloud of fragrance that gently tugs at my memories, pulling me back to a time when a good cup of tea held more magic than just its scents.

I reach for a cup, grazing the smooth porcelain, and try to centre myself in the simple sounds of morning. Saucer scraping softly against the counter as I pull it closer, metal clinking as I fish out a spoon from the drawer, water droplets plinking softly as they hit the sink. I've always believed that sound is to the present what scent is to the past: smells take you back in time, evoking long-lost memories, but sounds ground you in the moment, helping you appreciate what's going on around you.

Today, however, they barely register, reduced to mere background noise.

I let the tea steep, adding yet another item to my list of things to wait for. Finally, I pour a cup. Just as I bring the steaming liquid to my lips, my phone erupts with a ping. I jerk in surprise, sloshing scalding tea over my hand. So much for sounds grounding you in the present...

I reach for the phone with my unburned hand and open the Instagram app. My account, *Alvas_Naturshop*, boasts a decent following of just over fifteen thousand users. I'm a self-taught herbalist, handcrafting teas, soaps, and balms that I sell online. As I navigate through the app to my direct messages, I see some new notifications waiting for me. A couple of customers have sent pictures of the products they recently received, raving about the quality or thanking me for my personalised touch.

Alva Hausmann is a miracle worker! My skin has never been this soft and supple, reads a post I've been tagged in. The ping, it turns out, was from a potential partner, inquiring about a possible collaboration for a new line of eco-friendly cleaning products. But the one account I'm desperate to hear back from still hasn't replied. I linger on the chat window, the timestamp of my last message a painful reminder of the silence that has followed since.

Sofia, bist du das?

Sofia, is that you? I'd asked her three nights ago. Yet, I knew it was her the moment I saw her video pop up in my feed during a late-night scrolling session. I had been tagged in a negative review of my Soothing Sleep Balm, which had left me feeling frustrated. But as I continued to scroll, desperately trying to distract myself from the criticism, there she was, staring me right in the face: my twin, alive and well.

I pull up her latest video for the hundredth time, marvelling at the audacity of her content, noticing how different she looks now. We aren't identical twins but, growing up, you could easily tell we were sisters, with the same green eyes, the same auburn hair which we also shared with our mother. Now, however, she looks not like me but like a post-rehab Amy Winehouse. Her hair is raven black, her skin adorned with intricate tattoos, her lips painted a daring shade of red. Only her eyes are the same, vivid against a dark swipe of kohl lining.

To anyone familiar with the magical world, her videos are glaringly obvious in their display of witchcraft. While I spend every waking minute trying to repress my powers, Sofia casually performs levitation spells labelled as "yoga tricks," brews potions under the guise of "hangover cures," and shows off her familiar – a feisty ginger cat named Janis Joplin – assisting in her "cute pet helper" videos. It's a wonder she hasn't been reprimanded for her brazen disregard for secrecy. But she seems entirely unfazed by the possibility of discovery, as if she's got powerful allies watching her back.

Indeed, the trappings of her newfound wealth are hard to miss. The designer clothing, the luxurious homes, the expensive cars she's being chauffeured around in... That's right, my sister has a chauffeur now. Flicking through snapshots of her glitzy world, I'm torn between jealousy and scepticism. Something's not right here. How can she afford all this? How did she even end up in London?

The Sofia I knew would've eaten this all up, of course – she always loved the spotlight. But she'd never have been so reckless with her magic.

Then again, the Sofia I knew was supposed to be dead.

I toss the phone aside with a huff and gaze out the window. Our little cabin sits at the foot of the Brocken, nestled in a sun-dappled forest clearing. It's a former hunting lodge, lovingly renovated – fresh white plaster now showcases the dark timber frame; the steep, sloping roof sports new, gleaming shingles. Around the house, the garden runs wild. We've let nature reclaim its territory, only carving out small patches for my herbs and vegetables. Wildflowers nod in the breeze, blotches of colour against the deep greens of the pines. Even in these mountains, you'd be hard-pressed to find a place as charming, as perfectly tucked away from the world as ours.

Well, I say 'ours' but that's not entirely true: the cabin is a rental, courtesy of the national park authorities, for my boyfriend Dennis, a forest ranger. My herbs and I moved in two years ago.

I drum my fingers against the countertop, the tapping growing louder until I catch myself. The silence from my phone nags at me. An insect bite I mustn't scratch. Instead of giving in to the urge to check again, I force myself to a hidden corner of the apothecary. If the new Sofia won't respond, I must make do with the old one, or at least my memories of her.

Reaching behind a stack of books on the topmost shelf, I search until I feel a familiar, smooth surface.

Gently, I manoeuvre a small tin box out of its hiding place and ease off the lid. In it: a collection of tokens that always leaves me conflicted. Joy and pain and regret, all fighting for space in my heart. There's the pressed edelweiss flower from my mother's garden, my father's tiny, whittled eagle, a string of the acorn garland Sofia and I made for our first autumn equinox. But it's the obsidian stone that draws my eye, as always. I pick it up, the weight of it cool in my palm, its surface gleaming as if the night sky itself is reflected in it. I can't for the life of me remember how I got it, but I know it's from that night. The night of the accident. The last time we were whole. Mama, Dad, Sofia, and me. I must have pocketed it without thinking, a small piece of 'before' I carried into 'after.' Now it's a reminder of everything I've lost, and why I swore to lock my magic away for good.

As the obsidian warms in my hand, the memories thaw in my mind, and I regret I opened that box. Soon, guilt gnaws at my insides. Shame prickles under my skin. The old ache takes root, spreads through me, stubborn as a weed.

Maybe Sofia's silence is a gift. Maybe some doors are better left closed. But even as I try to convince myself, I know it's a lie. I blink, hard, fighting the tears. I slip the stone into my pocket, keeping it close yet out of sight as I turn my attention instead to what I know best — my craft.

Today's project: soap.

I move around the room, gathering olive and coconut oil, distilled water, and my chosen herbs. Lavender and rosemary for calm and cleansing, along with a handful of calendula for its healing touch. The familiar movements ground me, pulling me back from the brink of darker thoughts. I'll also need some lye, which waits in its sealed container – a necessary evil of the craft.

There are two ways to make soap: hot process and cold process. Today, I'm opting for the hot method. It's faster, and I need the distraction of a quick result.

As I measure and mix everything in the slow cooker, my mind quiets. This is my only purpose now. Simple, mundane work. Indeed, there's a kind of peace in letting my hands do what they were made for: creating, shaping, moulding. Making something useful and beautiful. When the oils melt, I carefully add the lye solution, and it sizzles slightly as it hits the cooker. The immersion blender whirs, and I watch the mixture thicken into a pudding-like consistency we soap-makers call "trace."

Only when the concoction fills the room with that clean, calming scent do I lose my grip on the present. Sofia's silence, I realise with a sinking feeling, is an answer in itself. And probably the worst one possible.

As kids, she was always the wild one, dragging me into her mischief with a grin and a plan. Her words tumbled out faster than her thoughts, and she could talk anyone into anything. But when she was done with you, her silence was deafening. Like the time I broke her favourite pink sunglasses, then tried to fix them with glue and a clumsy spell. For a whole week, it was like I didn't exist in her world anymore.

A bittersweet pang. Some things never change.

Just then, a flicker in the corner of my eye draws my attention to the stove. The flames dance and dim as if an invisible hand has passed through them. I don't think much of it and with a heavy sigh, I pour the soap mixture into moulds, my thoughts as sticky as the concoction. It's better this way, I tell myself, tamping down the hope that had dared to spark. I don't deserve a second chance, not after what I've done.

Setting the batches aside to cure, I brush a stray drop of soap off the edge of one of the moulds. Immediately, my skin tingles with a voltage that has no business in what's supposed to be a calming bar of soap.

I realise my mistake at once.

"Ach, verdammte Scheisse," I curse under my breath. Distracted as I was, I must have accidentally bound the soap with magic, drawing energy from the fire. Though I try to keep a lid on my powers, this happens sometimes when I'm not careful. Magic is nothing but an exchange of energies, or Anima – the essence which permeates everything. Commanding her means weaving into this living web, adjusting the Anima threads that bind everything together. All it takes is a lapse in focus, and I run the risk of meddling with that delicate order.

I stare at the soap moulds, frustration warring inside me. Even when I try to do something simple and good, darkness finds a way to creep in. Just like old times, just like that night.

I decide to test the soap, lathering a small piece between my hands. Almost immediately, I feel a cold, numbing sensation creep up my arms. Instead of the intended soothing effect, the soap leaves a lingering chill and, to my horror, an angry red rash spreads across my skin. The soap has absorbed my spiralling thoughts and sorrows.

"Oh, *come* on." I scrub my hands in the sink, but the rash remains.

There could not have been a worse time for Dennis to walk in.

"Man, those damn hikers never stick to the marked trails," Dennis grumbles. Having just returned from his morning patrol, he's clad in his usual ranger uniform: sturdy green trousers, a matching jacket with numerous pockets, and heavy boots. His blond hair is slightly tousled from the wind; his eyes widen when he sees me.

"What happened?" he asks, rushing to my side. "Are you alright?"

"It's the soap," I say, wincing as I continue to wash my hands. "I wasn't careful, and now it's... it's turned bad somehow."

"That's not like you," he says, gently inspecting the rash now spreading across my skin like wildfire. "This looks really bad. Come on, let's get some ointment on this."

He leads me to a chair and fetches a jar of soothing salve from one of the shelves. "Here, sit down."

He opens the jar. I sink into the chair, frustration churning inside me. "Must have been the lye," I mutter. "Thanks."

Dennis and I first met in the forest near the Bode Gorge. I was collecting mushrooms along the banks of the Warme Bode River. Dennis, twenty-seven years old at the time and the youngest ranger in the area, was out on his patrol with Hermes, his German shepherd. He approached me, ready to lecture about the dangers of foraging wild mushrooms. However, he soon realised that the chanterelles I had gathered were perfectly safe and edible. We struck up a conversation, and it marked the beginning of our relationship.

He applies the salve, his fingers cool against my inflamed skin. His brow furrows with concern as he looks at me. "So, what's really going on?"

But I don't know how to answer that. Now would be the

time to tell him about Sofia, but I quickly push the notion aside. Had she replied, then I might have had to tell him something. But what's the point now? There's so much I haven't told him already, so much I probably never will. What's one more?

"I got tagged in a negative review, that's all," I lie.

"Is that what's bothering you? For which product?"

"The Sleep Balm."

"Did they complain about the missing 'desired effect' again?" A slight chuckle escapes him.

"How do you know about that?"

"Hey, I read your reviews. You're my girl."

"The thing is, I never said anywhere the balm does *that*!"

The desired effect Dennis is referring to is a rise in radiance that seems to attract... well, let's call them 'interested prospects.' Much like the magical mishap with the soap, I'd apparently infused that particular batch of the balm with a radiance spell when I was ovulating.

"Maybe you should. Might help boost your sales," Dennis jokes, but when he sees my annoyed look, he quickly back-tracks. "There, all better." He screws the lid back on the salve and kisses me on the forehead. "Right, I'm off to shower, and then I expect a feast," he adds with a playful clap on my knees.

Dennis doesn't cook. Never has. We've settled into a house-hold routine where he handles the 'bloke' tasks like car mainte-nance and carpentry, and I take on the role of housewife. I never had the heart to tell him that I'm perfectly capable of doing all of his chores myself.

"Oh, before I forget," he says on his way out, "this one arrived for you."

He reaches into one of his pockets and places a letter on the tabletop. "Looks like another invitation from that pagan cosplay group in Treseburg, begging you to be their Elven Queen..."

"I do have the ears for it," I jest, albeit half-heartedly. "I'll come over soon."

As the door clicks shut, I gather the remnants of the spoiled soap, careful not to touch the contaminated mixture again. Using a pair of disposable gloves, I scrape the congealed mess into a waste bin and thoroughly wipe down the countertop with a disinfectant solution. Meticulously, I clean and sterilise all the tools before putting them away. As I remove my gloves and dispose of them, my eyes flicker over to the letter. I reach for it, intending to toss it into the bin without even opening it. However, I do a double take when I notice the striking writing on the envelope. The address is penned in dark blue ink, the lettering elegant, swirling. The sight of it sends a familiar tremble down my back. I have seen this kind of letter before, but it's been years. Many, *many* years. And back then it hadn't been addressed to me, but to my mother.

What are the chances of such a letter arriving the same week I reach out to Sofia – to a *witch*?

I slide a finger under the flap, and the wax seal breaks with a gentle crack. The parchment feels ancient, yet alive. I unfold the letter. Hastily. Hungrily.

Breath catching in my throat, I begin to read.

Chapter Two

Three days earlier

Ember's grip tightens around her phone. Her eyes lock on the message that glows from the screen, each word a haunting echo from a past she has long since buried.

Sofia, is that you?

The name attached to the message stirs a storm of emotions. Memories she'd fought so hard to drown it doesn't seem possible they could return to the surface.

Alva.

Ember taps on the profile, a strange swirl coiling in her stomach as she scrolls through the feed. The account, which belongs to an herbalist, is filled with warm images and videos that showcase the natural beauty of the craft. Dried herbs and spice jars, old scissors and beeswax candles. Skilled hands wielding pestle and mortar, grinding and blending ingredients to use in soaps and balms.

But it's not the artful feed or the glimpses of herb jars that catch Ember's attention. It's the face that stares back at her from one of the posts, a face that she'd never thought she'd see again.

Alva.

She clicks on the image, and the world around her grinds to a halt. Her chest tightens, an invisible vice squeezing air from her lungs.

Alva. Reaching out to her. A message so unexpected, it might as well have come from a ghost.

The face on the screen is older, the features more defined, but there's no mistaking the resemblance. It's her sister, the once-gangly teenager now fully grown. Tears blur Ember's vision, threatening to dissolve the mask she has built. In that moment, she is no longer the confident, glamorous queen of Soho, but a lost thirteen-year-old, confronted with the one truth she never dared to hope for: Alva is alive.

The office door swings open with a screech, causing her to nearly jump out of her seat.

"What *now*? What is it?" she snaps, whirling around. Pippa Watson stands in the doorway with a look of mild confusion, yet she remains entirely unfazed by Ember's tone. At this point, Pippa has weathered every storm imaginable: the good, the bad, and the downright ugly that comes with being Ember Wild's PA. She's not a witch like her boss, but one of the selected few mundanes invited to see behind the veil, drawn to magic like flowers to the sun.

"The delivery person has been waiting outside the club for the past twenty minutes," she says. "Are you going to sign for the package, or should I send him away?"

Ember sighs, scratching her scalp. "Can't you sign on my behalf?"

"If that were an option, don't you think I would have done so already?"

"Right. Fine. I'm coming." Ember pushes herself up from her desk and follows Pippa out the door and into the heart of the club.

It's hers, the club, fittingly named 'MY PINK CAULDRON'. The cool interior bears her signature touch – a daring fusion of dark elegance and raw, unapologetic sex appeal. Neon signs lie dormant, waiting for nightfall to paint the room in their seductive pink glow. As they make their way through, heels sticking slightly to the beer-stained floor, Ember turns to Pippa. "When did Mardequai want to meet, you said?"

"Tonight, for dinner at the townhouse," Pippa replies without missing a beat, her fingers tapping away across her ever-present tablet.

Ember purses her lips. "Reschedule for lunchtime, please?"

Pippa glances up with a look as dry as a martini. "I'm not sure that will be possible on such short notice."

"Just... just *do* it, alright?" Ember snaps. But, catching the slightest expression of annoyance on Pippa's face, she softens her tone, adding, "Please do try, Pippa darling. It is important."

Pippa nods, already plucking her phone from the breast pocket of her blazer.

Mardequai Guise is Ember's foster father, the man who volunteered to take her in after she lost her family at thirteen. He brought her to Dunmorrough Castle, his secluded Scottish estate, where Ember grew up within ancient stone walls, home-schooled in the arcane arts. As one of the immortal druids, Mardequai represents the other half of the magical community besides witches. While Ember and her ilk have one mortal life in which they draw magic from Anima, druids like Mardequai don't have any inherent magic of their own – except for the whole not-dying thing, which, admittedly, is a pretty sweet deal. Eternal life is a different kind of power, but no less potent. Druids rely on centuries of accumulated knowledge and secrets. Indeed, memory is the foundation druid supremacy is built on.

Outside the club, Ember signs for her delivery. In the background, Pippa works her own unique brand of magic, phone pressed against her ear as she strains to hear over the bustle of Soho – honking taxis, chattering pedestrians, and the thuds of construction work. She cups her hand over her other ear, to block out the noise of the delivery truck reversing.

"He can meet you at The Ivy in an hour, but he only has thirty minutes before his luncheon with the prime minister," Pippa reports.

"That will have to be enough, then."

Just as Ember is about to head back inside the club, a woman approaches, calling out a name that sends a jolt through Ember's body.

"Sofia?"

Ember spins around, heart pounding in her chest. This is the second time today that someone has addressed her by her old name.

But the woman standing before her now is not her sister. As their eyes lock, a name tugs at the edges of Ember's mind. It stays out of reach, or maybe she doesn't actually care to retrieve it, but she does recognise the woman as a member of the Scottish Crossbill Coven.

"Hi, Sofia... I... I'm sorry, I mean Ember. Do you remember me? I'm Effie, Effie Bell?"

Ember might forget names, but she never forgets a face – especially not the face of rejection. She takes in the woman before her. Mousy brown hair pulled back in a tight bun, thick-rimmed glasses sliding down her nose. A frumpy cardigan and a skirt that not even her grandmother should wear in public.

"What do you want?" Bored, Ember reaches for a pack of cigarettes. With a snap of her finger, a small flame appears between her thumb and index finger, and she lights the cigarette with casual grace.

Effie shifts uncomfortably, eyes darting toward the club entrance. "Well, I... I am working in the city now, switchboard girl at the Ley Line Confluence beneath St. Paul's Cathedral. It's right on the convergence of three major lines. Anyway, I-I find London to be... not a very welcoming place? Wouldn't you agree?"

Translation: what Effie Bell means to say is that none of the hip London covens will accept her pathetic arse, and she's come crawling to Ember, hoping to sponge off her recent fame.

But good old Effie Bell must have forgotten Ember's own attempts to join the Crossbill Coven at eighteen, when she was longing for companionship beyond Dunmorrough's confines. The stone-cold rejection she'd faced from the staff village witches still stings. She remembers trudging back to the castle that day, eighteen and humiliated, tears streaming down her face as she'd confessed her failure to Mardequai. He'd found her in the library, curled up in the window seat overlooking the loch.

"My dear child," he'd said, settling beside her with that gentle voice he reserved for her lowest moments. "Those women... they work such demanding schedules, you know. Their duties require complete dedication. They barely have time for sleep, let alone socialising."

He'd ordered her tea and listened as she'd sobbed about feeling so alone on the estate. "You mustn't take it personally, Sofia. Their work is all-consuming. They're wonderful women, truly, but their responsibilities leave little room for the kind of company a bright young woman like you deserves. In fact, I'd prefer it if you sought friendship elsewhere", he'd said, stroking her hair. "You have such potential, my dear. Perhaps it's time we looked beyond the estate for your social circle."

How ironic that now one of those very women stands before

her, seeking the acceptance she'd once craved from them. There's a twisted satisfaction, knowing she's the one with the power now.

"Oh, sweetie, I'm touched, truly." A grin spreads across Ember's face as she leans in close to Effie, blowing out the smoke. "That you'd make the effort to come see me after all this time, thinking you'd like to join my little club of misfits."

Ember looks Effie up and down. With a subtle twist of her hand, the wind picks up around them, swirling leaves and debris in a mini vortex, dancing entirely to Ember's whims. Effie takes a step back, stumbling over her own feet as the wind whips at her skirts.

"But you see, Effie dearest, the sad truth is," – Ember's face shifts, a cruel smile playing at the corners of her lips – "I've seen *street rats* with more charm than you. So why don't you run along back to your little switchboard job and leave the real magic to those of us who know how to wield it?"

Effie's face turns a deep shade of pink, eyes brimming with tears as she stammers out her apology. "I... I'm sorry, I didn't mean to—"

"Save it, darling." Ember cuts her off with a dismissive wave of her hand, which sends a gust of wind toward the club door, slamming it shut behind her like a full stop. "I've got a club to run and a coven to lead. I don't have time for sad little witches who can't keep up."

And with that, Ember turns on her heel and struts toward the Range Rover Pippa has parked up front, leaving a humiliated Effie gaping in her wake.

* * *

The Rover glides through the streets of London, Pippa silent behind the wheel, her eyes focused on the road. In the back seat,

Ember scrolls through Alva Hausmann's Instagram account. How is it possible that she is alive? After all these years, after all the pain, the grief and the loneliness, how could her sister have been out there all along, living a life Ember knew nothing about?

The question sends a shiver through Ember. With it comes a flood of memories, long suppressed but never forgotten, her thoughts drifting back to the last time she saw her sister, to the evening that changed everything.

It happened on Walpurgis Night, a sacred time for witches and druids to gather and celebrate the arrival of spring. The family had joined their mother's coven for the festivities, listening to ancient stories under the stars, weaving enchanted braids, sharing the excitement of nature awakening. The air was loaded with magic, and Ember felt it coursing through her own veins, warm and nourishing like the bonfire they danced around.

The drive home started peacefully enough, but Ember soon noticed Alva's unease in the backseat. At first, she dismissed it as something Alva might have eaten. But as her sister's distress grew, Ember recognised the telltale signs of one of those scary episodes. She had always seen them as just another quirk of her sister's, never connecting them to anything dark or dangerous. But when Alva's eyes rolled back and her body went rigid, and she began muttering words Ember didn't understand, it became clear that something was terribly wrong. Their father, glancing back at his daughter with concern, didn't see the bend in the road until it was too late. The tyres screeched as he swerved, over-correcting in his panic. And then the world spun violently as the car went off the road, shattering glass and crunching metal filling Ember's ears before darkness took her.

The gentle sway of the Range Rover blurs with her memories, making Ember's stomach lurch. She presses her fingertips against the cool window, grounding herself in the present as cabs and bicycles streak past like ghosts. The memory still has the power to disorient her, to pull her back into that night with frightening clarity.

The next thing she remembers is the aftermath: lying in damp grass by the roadside, smoke filling her nostrils as the old VW Kombi went up in flames. Mardequai was there, his arms like iron around her, holding her back as she fought desperately to reach the car, to save those she knew, deep down, were already lost.

"We're almost there," Pippa says, glancing at Ember in the rearview mirror. "Are you alright? You've gone terribly pale."

"I'm fine," Ember murmurs, trying to steady her breathing.

And then, a darker thought creeps in. Why did Mardequai not tell her? Because it seems hard to believe that he didn't know. The man has eyes and ears in every corner of the world.

Ember tap-tap-taps her phone against her thigh before she finally puts it away. As the car pulls up to the entrance of the Ivy, she reapplies her lipstick. Composing herself with a deep breath, she steps out of the car, her head held high, her eyes blazing with a determination that borders on obsession.

Stiletto heels clicking against the pavement, she makes her way towards the entrance. The London restaurant is a hub of activity, well-dressed patrons streaming in and out, their chatter mingling with the city noise. As she pushes through the heavy wooden doors, the maître d' greets her with a polite nod, his eyes widening slightly as he recognises the infamous Ember Wild. She's quickly escorted to her table, weaving through the crowded dining room with an air of confidence she's not sure she's feeling right now.

In one booth sits none other than Mick Jagger; in another – the prime minister, Nigel Hall, with a group of his advisors, soon to be joined by Mardequai. A Tory and staunch right-wing conservative, he looks slightly out of place amidst the glitz and glamour of the Ivy.

Ember settles into her seat, eyes fixed on the entrance. On any other day, she'd have gotten a kick out of breathing the same air as Jagger but today, all she cares to do is wait for Mardequai's arrival. The minutes seem to drag on, each one heightening her anticipation. Finally, after what feels like an eternity, her foster father appears.

As Mardequai enters the restaurant, he walks tall and regal, wearing his favoured charcoal suit, understated and timeless, much like the man himself. His face, though lined with the wisdom of ages, remains striking and austere. Around his neck, he wears a simple silver chain from which hangs a crystal amulet composed of several slender shards – a piece he never leaves the house without, though Ember never dared to ask why.

He makes his way through the restaurant, stopping briefly to exchange pleasantries with the prime minister. As he approaches Ember, the waiter hurries over, greeting him with an actual bow. "Mr Guise, it's a pleasure to see you again. Your usual table is ready for you."

Mardequai nods with something resembling a smile, then he settles into the seat across from Ember, his piercing gaze locking with hers. "Christopher, I'll have a pot of the silver needle white tea, please," he says to the waiter. "But make sure the water temperature is precisely eighty degrees this time. The last pot was a touch too hot, and it compromised the flavour of the leaves."

"Most certainly, Mr Guise." Christopher nods. "And for you, Miss Wild?"

But Ember barely registers the waiter. Instead, she stares at Mardequai, a thousand questions burning on the tip of her tongue, desperate for answers only he can give.

"Just bring a second cup if you please, Christopher," Mardequai says.

As soon as they're alone, he turns to Ember, his voice so

composed she can barely hear him. "I must say, I am not accustomed to alterations in my schedule, especially at such short notice. What could be so pressing that it couldn't wait?" He smiles but his lips twitch with displeasure.

Ember passes her phone across the table, the message from Alva displayed on the screen. Mardequai takes it, and the modern device looks strangely silly in his hands. Indeed, in the thirteen years she has known him, Ember has never once seen him hold a phone.

His preference for traditional communication isn't surprising, of course. He, like most druids, favours the Resonance Network – a system that taps into ley lines and natural energies (and which is, apparently, Effie Bell's current place of employment). It's clever, Ember has to admit, even if it seems a bit outdated to her. That Silicon Valley druid, Elias Klein, did manage to drag the Resonance Network into the twenty-first century when he made it accessible via smartphones. Mardequai, however, still prefers landlines, or better yet, having a disciple transcribe messages for him.

Now, the immortal grasps her phone as if it were a leper's bell he's been forced to hold, his fingers barely making contact. Ember scrutinises his face, searching for any indication that this revelation has caught *him* off guard as well. But his features remain as immovable as an ancient rock face, unperturbed by the relentless march of time or any storms that might pass through.

Ember bounces her leg beneath the table, her impatience building as she waits for him to speak. However confident she might be with anyone else, in Mardequai's presence, she is always the young apprentice, seeking approval from her master.

"Ah, the tea." Mardequai puts the phone aside, all his attention now focused on Christopher, returning with their order.

The waiter sets down a porcelain teapot, wisps of steam escaping from its delicate spout. Beside it, he arranges two intricately painted teacups on saucers, spring blossoms etched in gold. A miniature hourglass is placed next to the cups, to measure the perfect steeping time, and a finely carved wooden box that holds the tea leaves.

All of this is taking so long, Ember almost bursts out of her skin with impatience. Christopher sets down a slender crystal decanter filled with cold spring water, should Mardequai wish to adjust the strength of his brew. With a polite nod and a murmured, "Please enjoy," the waiter discreetly withdraws.

At last, Mardequai speaks.

"When did you receive this message?" he asks, sliding the phone back to Ember across the tabletop.

"Earlier today," she replies.

"And you have not yet engaged with this... person?"

Ember shakes her head, her black beehive hairdo bobbing slightly.

Mardequai reaches for the teapot. He lifts the lid and places a measure of tea leaves inside. He picks up the miniature hourglass and turns it over, watching as the sand begins to flow. Ember watches, too, her anger growing with each grain falling. When the sand finally runs out, Mardequai pours the tea into their cups. He takes a delicate sip, savouring the flavour, then adds a small amount of the spring water from the decanter.

"Very well." He nods and sets the teacup back on the saucer.

And then Ember can no longer contain herself.

"What do you mean, 'very well'?" she hisses. "None of this is very well! You told me my sister was *dead!*"

Heads turn from the neighbouring tables, and Ember feels their stares, but she refuses to back down now, her gaze locked on Mardequai.

The druid takes another sip of his tea, unfazed by the attention they've drawn. He sets the cup down with a clink. "Because that is, of course, what I believed to be true, my troubled child," he says, still infuriatingly calm despite her turmoil.

Ember leans forward as she searches Mardequai's face. "Do you swear it? Do you swear you didn't know?"

Mardequai sits back in his chair. A subtle eyebrow raise, a faint hint of anger.

"I am not in the habit of having my veracity called into question," he says. "But consider this: if I had known of her existence, do you not think I would have summoned her long ago? You yourself spoke of her darkness, her... *visions*, that intriguing connection to a past life. As a druid, do you truly believe I would have permitted such a rarity – such a power so akin to my own – to elude my grasp?"

The clinking of silverware and the murmur of conversation from the other tables suddenly seems too loud as neither of them speaks for a long moment.

Ember's mind races. She never should have told him that, never should have told *anyone* what her sister was capable of.

"I want to go to Germany to see her," she blurts out.

But there is a reason why she hasn't simply boarded a plane already, why she hasn't even dared to reply to the message that has so upended her world: a part of her is conditioned to seek Mardequai's approval, to defer to his wisdom and authority. He has been her guardian, her mentor. The one constant, however aloof, in a life marked by loss and grief. To defy him, to strike out on her own, feels like a betrayal.

"I am afraid I cannot allow that," he replies. "I require your presence here more than ever, now that the Reveal fast approaches."

Ember sucks in air through her teeth, ready to protest, to argue, to fight for the chance to reconnect with the sister she thought lost forever.

Mardequai holds up a hand. "*However*, given that she is

indeed alive, I believe it would be prudent to bring her into the fold, wouldn't you agree? With her rare – shall we call them talents? – she could prove to be an asset to our cause."

"What does that mean?"

Mardequai's smile is a cryptic thing. "It means, my dear, that you need not journey to Germany to see her. I will extend an invitation to her, ensuring that *she* comes to us, here in London."

"What's in it for you?" Ember asks, folding her arms.

"I beg your pardon?"

"Well, I know you're not doing this out of the goodness of your own heart."

A muscle in his cheek twitches, and he looks away for a moment before meeting her gaze again.

"Why, to tell you the honest truth, I might like to use her knowledge of a life past to our advantage."

Ember has always hated that expression, 'to tell you the honest truth'. For what is the truth, if not honest? And why point it out, exactly? Because until now, he'd been lying?

"Use it how?"

"Your sister's memories could prove invaluable. A cautionary tale from centuries past, spoken by one of your own kind, since druid memory alone does not seem to carry the weight it should. Perhaps then, your fellow witches might finally understand the gravity of the path they've chosen."

Mardequai's eyes sweep across the restaurant, lingering on the other patrons with thinly veiled disdain. "Look at them," he murmurs. "Going about their lives in blissful ignorance. They have no idea what's coming."

He takes another sip of his tea before continuing. "When the veil falls, when magic reveals itself, do we truly think they'll respond with wonder? With *acceptance*?" He scoffs softly. "No. First comes fear, then comes hatred. It's written in their history.

Every time humans encounter something they don't understand, they seek to control it or destroy it."

His fingers trace the rim of his teacup. He doesn't seem awfully troubled by that outcome. "Speaking of caution, I feel as your guardian it is my duty to forewarn you," Mardequai says, gently swirling his cup, watching the steam rise and dance in the air. "While I was unaware of her survival, there is a piece of information I did think best to withhold from you, to spare you any more grief and pain."

"What are you saying? What piece?"

"I'm certain she will not keep it a secret herself once she arrives, so I see no harm in divulging it now." He takes another deliberate sip of his tea. "The accident, child..." He pauses for a long moment and sets the cup down. "The accident was her doing."

Chapter Three

A dizzying thrum pulsates in my ears as I slump into the armchair, reading words scratched into parchment. It's the same sensation I felt upon receiving that dreaded tax arrears notice last year – just opening the letter was enough to make my palms sweat.

Yet, the instant my eyes land on the first line, the present fades away, and I find myself slipping effortlessly into memories from thirteen years ago, to a time when magic was still a living, breathing thing for me.

A time when going to high school was made bearable by the fact that homework could be completed with the flick of a finger, leaving ample time for the *real* lessons to commence. A time when my heart was so brimming with joy, I didn't even know what sorrow felt like. A time when I wielded magic with the innocence of a child, not yet aware of the darkness I was capable of.

Truly, when I read that letter for the first time, for a moment there, it feels like coming home:

Gisele Stein

Dear Ms Alva Hausmann,

On behalf of the honoured elders of the Global Assembly of Arcane Guardians (GAAG) I request the privilege of your esteemed presence at the two hundred and fifteenth convening to commune on the matter of magic's role in restoring the earth.

Over the course of seven days, we shall delve into the decision to harness magic to reverse the devastation wrought by human folly upon our realm. During a previous referendum, ICAG-registered witches and druids voted in favour of a magical reveal to guide humanity onto a path of environmental renewal and atonement. This reveal shall be presented to global heads of state during the upcoming Global Summit on Climate Action on September the twentieth. The purpose of this convening is to ensure a judicious preparation for this unprecedented revelation, and I believe your insights on this matter, dear Ms Hausmann, will be of great value to us all.

It has come to my attention that you have not previously partaken in any of our intimate gatherings, nor are you currently an active member of a coven or the magical community at large. Therefore, it would be my utmost pleasure to host you in my humble townhouse for the duration of the Assembly, providing you with a comfortable stay and the opportunity to address any inquiries you may have. The grand opening ceremony shall be held on the fifteenth of September in the Emerald Court at Arcadia House, Westminster.

My staff eagerly await your response at your earliest convenience to make the necessary travel arrangements well in advance. The entire Assembly schedule will be provided to you upon your arrival in London. Kindly note that by virtue of

36

having touched this invitation, a magical contract has been entered into, thus rendering your attendance compulsory.

With warmest regards, Mardequai Guise

When I read it for the second time, however, allowing the words to sink in, the effect is like I've applied that hexed soap all over my body – a numbing, ice cold chill.

The shock washes over me in three distinct waves, each crashing with unrelenting force.

The first wave brings a surge of utter disbelief: magic is on the cusp of revelation! Witches and druids are preparing to emerge from the shadows to heal the wounds of our ailing planet. This is nothing short of extraordinary!

The initial euphoria, however, is swiftly overshadowed by the second, more chilling wave that seeps into my bones like a damp cold: the elders know about me. The secret I've guarded so fiercely, the shame I've carried for years, is now in the hands of a stranger, a man who seems to move in the inner circles of magical governance. What else could this Mr Guise mean by saying my "insights on this matter will be of great value"?

But how? How could he possibly...?

I look up from the parchment, the realisation hitting me like an icy gust through the open window.

Sofia.

Sofia must have told him – whether voluntarily or under duress, I have no way of knowing. Either way, at this point there is not a shred of doubt in my mind that this is no coincidence. Like Sofia, Mr Guise resides in London. Like her, he appears to command vast wealth – judging by his manner of writing, his possession of a London townhouse, and the mention of 'his staff eagerly awaiting my response.'

The third shock is delayed, but when it finally hits, it strikes with the intensity of a bolt of lightning splitting an oak, and it is directly linked to the parchment I hold in my hands: I am now compelled to go. By touching the paper, I have sealed my fate – which would make this a piece of parchment from the legendary Scriptorium of the First Realms in the Kenyan Chyulu Mountains.

Now that I examine the paper more closely, its true age becomes strikingly apparent. I've heard tales of this type of parchment before, but I've never seen any in real life. The number of remaining pieces scattered throughout the world is unknown, and they are highly coveted, typically found only in the possession of the most affluent and influential witches and druids. By magical decree, this piece needs to be returned to its rightful owner, to be used time and time again. The magical society treats these enchanted letters with the utmost caution. No witch or druid would dare touch any correspondence with their bare hands – a lesson ingrained from our earliest training. But I've been removed from that world for so long, the thought didn't even cross my mind.

I press my forehead into my palm, my elbow anchored on the cool surface of my worktable. The scent of dried herbs fills my nostrils, suddenly too strong, almost nauseating. What on earth possessed me to reach out to Sofia so rashly, without a thought for the consequences? Sure, the longing to reconnect was real enough. But it was also a hastily constructed plan with more holes than a colander. Seeing her again – and I only understand this full now – means confronting her with the truth: I am the reason our paths diverged. I am why we no longer have parents. It means facing the mistakes I made, the actions – *my actions* – that shattered our lives.

What's most terrifying, however, is the fact that I was never supposed to step back into that world, to immerse myself once again in the realm of magic, facing the scrutiny that appears to be waiting for me now. Because I'm not allowed to practise magic, whatever spells I do cast are accidental, and I've always been terrified that my lack of control might one day backfire. The fear of what the establishment might do now that they've found me is paralysing. What if they decide I am too dangerous, too unstable to be allowed to roam free? What if they lock me up – or worse?

A searing sensation engulfs my feet, and it's as if flames lick at my skin – a feeling so real, the agony consumes me. The heat, that old familiar blistering pain, is as vivid as if it were happening all over again.

The letter slips from my fingers, fluttering to the ground like a seared leaf. I struggle to breathe as smoke seems to cloud my lungs, choking the air from my ribcage. Panic rises within me, a suffocating force that threatens to overwhelm me entirely, and I burst through the apothecary door, hands grasping at my throat. Leaning against a nearby tree, I focus on the sensation of the rough bark beneath my fingertips, anchoring myself. *Breathe, Alva, breathe.* Slowly, deliberately, I draw in one deep breath, then another and another, until the tightness in my chest begins to ease and the world around me starts to come back into focus. As soon as I feel the ground beneath my feet again, I run, the soft forest earth cushioning each step.

I run, heart pounding in my chest as I delve deeper into the embrace of the woods. I run, trees blurring past me, branches reaching out like grasping hands, urging me onward. I run, legs aching and chest heaving. I keep running – until I'm so far into the woods it feels as though they have swallowed me whole.

* * *

My frantic run comes to an abrupt end when I reach the banks of the Bode River. The rush of water fills my ears, a constant, soothing sound that momentarily drowns out the echoes of screams in my mind. Panting, I collapse onto the rocky shore, my legs trembling from exertion. With shaking hands, I unlace my boots and peel off my socks. The cool air hits my bare feet, grounding me. Desperate for more, I edge closer to the water and slip my feet into the current. But then I whince in agony when not water, but flames seem to touch my feet... *her* feet.

That's right: it's *her*, not me.

And yet, when I feel the rough rope biting into her wrists, her arms wrenched behind her back, it becomes impossible to distinguish her life from mine. The world tilts and spins as I'm shoved forward, bare feet scraping against the splintered wood of the platform.

No, this isn't me, these aren't my memories... But now the visions are too vivid, too immediate to deny. The rough texture of the stake against my back as I'm bound to it. The smell of pitch and oil filling my nostrils as it's poured at my feet. The drumming of a heart as it stutters its final beats.

But it's not the fire that kills me; it's the smoke. The suffocating embrace of heat that steals my breath away before the flames get to ravage my skin, scorch my muscles, char my bones. And I suppose I should be grateful for that little mercy.

This is Ruth's last memory, her final moments. Yet I'm trapped within it, experiencing every excruciating detail as if it were happening to me. The crackle of the first flame igniting. The wave of heat that consumes me, growing more intense until pain settles in. Pain – all-consuming, horrifying pain that tears a scream from her throat. A scream that feels like my own, echoing through my mind until I actually choke it from my own throat.

A fish leaps from the river, its scales flashing silver, and the sudden sound jolts me back to the present. I gasp, my hands clutching at the damp earth as if that could stop me from slipping back into her life.

I know these visions are memories and not mere dreams because, when I was still a child, my parents were able to corroborate the information I gathered, confirming exact dates and locations from the witch's life with historical records.

It's not like I *am* her, though.

Ruth Hausmann was my grandmother, a witch burnt at the stake in 1956 in a deliberate nod to the medieval witch hunts. And the only thing worse than remembering her dying is remembering her living.

The atrocities Ruth and the Schwarzmilan Coven committed during the reign of Nazi Germany were so heinous, so unimaginable, I feel sickened having to bear witness to them over and over again. They claimed to be agents of change, but the depths of their cruelty knew no bounds. When the tides of war turned against the Germans, Ruth swore that she had been acting under duress, that Hitler had blinded her to the truth and that the SS had threatened her into submission. However, for a witch as powerful as Ruth, such claims ring hollow.

And I, the one cursed with the ability to tap into her life like no other, know the truth that lies beneath the surface. Through the fragments of her memories that invade my mind I have witnessed the twisted pleasure she took in the suffering of others, the way she revelled in the darkness that consumed her. The screams that echo through my mind are not just those of Ruth's agonising death at the stake but also the haunting cries of her countless victims.

No, Ruth Hausmann was no mere pawn in the grand scheme of things; she was a willing participant.

It is this intimate knowledge of her true nature that makes bearing her memory so arduous. I'm connected to someone utterly devoid of empathy, consumed only by her own malicious desires.

After Germany's defeat in the Second World War, Ruth fled to Spain, seeking refuge in the remote Pyrenees. There, she lived a life of solitude until she met a man who was unaware of her sinister past. They fell in love, and from their union, my mother was born. However, Ruth's crimes eventually caught up with her when a group of French witches and druids tracked her down, exacting justice for her wartime crimes and taking her daughter to raise under strict surveillance.

For reasons I have never comprehended, I live to tell that tale. Well, *remember* it, anyway. It's not like I'm running around telling everyone that, in another life, I used to be a monster who deserved to die. The only people who knew about the extend of my secret are long dead. Or at least that's what I thought until I read that letter.

* * *

The kitchen is filled with the scent of burnt toast.

I burst in from the garden, shouldering my way through the old stable door that serves as our back entrance. My skin clammy and my breath still coming in short gasps from my sudden escape, I don't notice Dennis until he speaks.

"What happened to you?" His voice breaks through the haze, drawing my attention to where he sits at the table, the charred remains of what appears to be an attempt at grilled cheese congealing in the skillet before him.

"I'm sorry, I... I needed more yarrow, so I went for a quick walk." The lie tumbles from my lips.

"Where is it?"

"Where is what?"

"The yarrow."

"Oh, I... I couldn't find any." I move to clean up the mess he made. "Are you still hungry?"

But Dennis ignores my question.

"So, this is strange," he says.

"What is?" I glance up, only half-interested, until my eyes fall upon the object he has just placed on the tabletop.

It's the letter.

Dread simmers in my chest like a pot left too long on the stove, panic gripping me at the thought that Dennis has read those words. I fight the urge to snatch the letter and burn it on the gas stove. My head is spinning like I'm sitting in the crown of a tree, helplessly swaying in the wind while its trunk is being marked for timber harvest.

The occasional magical mishap is easy enough to explain away, but this? This letter, with its cryptic messages and ominous undertones, is so littered with points to argue that I don't even know where to begin to spin a convincing lie.

If only I hadn't been forced to abandon my magical studies, if only I had been allowed to sign up with ICAG to become a registered practitioner. Then I could simply wipe Dennis's short-term memory and make this entire situation disappear, erasing any trace of the letter. But I can't. I don't know the spell, and even if I did, an attempt without proper training might harm him, and the repercussions would be far worse than a simple soap gone awry.

"You read my mail?" I ask accusingly, hoping to buy some time as I scramble to come up with a plausible explanation. Now I notice the pocket dictionary in his lap. Typical Dennis: he'd rather die than turn to modern technology for translation help.

"It was already open," he counters, folding his arms in front of his chest. "Besides, I saw you from the bathroom window, running off like some maniac. I thought something terrible had happened."

I sink into the chair opposite him, my mind still in overdrive as I try to decide what to say next. It's not like I'm forbidden from telling him what I am; witches have always confided in humans they trusted. However, I suppose others always have an ace up their sleeves. If a relationship falls apart, they can resort to magic to solve the problem and prevent their secret from spreading. So while, on a grand scale, a magical reveal is illegal according to magical law, it is ultimately up to each individual witch's discretion to decide who they allow into that secret world. And traitors are easy enough to contain; after all, who would believe them if they claimed 'magic was real'?

But I don't have that luxury, that safety net. If I tell Dennis the truth and then things go south, I won't be able to simply make it all disappear with the wave of a wand (not that we use those...).

"Are you going to speak at some point, or must I keep guessing? What kind of weird joke is this, seriously?"

"It is... it is not a joke," I say, my fingers lining up breadcrumbs on the table. "It's very serious, actually. That's why I'm struggling to explain it, I suppose."

"It's true, isn't it?"

At last, I lock eyes with him. There is no shock or disbelief. Instead, I find only recognition. He isn't even surprised.

"How long have you known?" I ask, searching his face.

"I don't *know* anything. But I am a biologist, Alva. I study behaviour, patterns in nature. I notice abnormalities. And, well, I *have* noticed certain behaviours of yours that don't..."

"That don't match up with what you've been taught at school," I finish the sentence for him.

He leans over the table, whispering, "Sometimes, when we are out for a walk in the woods, I swear the animals come out to meet us, like they're drawn to you or something. That never happens when I'm alone."

I bite the insides of my lower lip, blinking once and long.

"And I swear, every time we drive to town together, all the traffic lights are green. Every. Single. Time. Not to mention those reviews you get for your products! You know what people call you out there on the internet?"

I nod because, naturally, I'm well aware of the speculation surrounding my craft.

"They are calling you a..." Dennis's mouth forms the word, but no sound comes out. "And now this letter... I mean, what the hell, Alva?"

I take the letter from his hands. My eyes scan the words once again and to my own surprise, calm settles within me, a strength I haven't felt in years. I am a tree who just remembered she's got a heartwood core, strong as steel and grounded through her roots.

I clear my throat. "It might be easiest if you asked me what you want to know."

"Well, first off, who is this guy sending you letters?" Dennis gestures at the parchment.

I can't help but huff out a laugh. Of all the questions, this is the one he asks first. It's quintessentially Dennis, I suppose. He's a Taurus through and through.

"I have never heard of a man named Mardequai Guise, but I suspect he is one of the druids."

"The druids?"

"Immortals. They don't have any magical powers of their own but their influence stems from their ancient wisdom. They're basically like librarians who cannot die."

"But so... *you* are not a druid. You are a ...?"

He still can't say the word, so I do.

"I am what you'd call a witch. Although most of us would prefer to be called other names."

Dennis seems to contemplate for a moment whether he

wants to know about those other names. "There are a lot out there," he notes instead, gesturing at the letter.

"There are about two hundred thousand witches in the world and a couple thousand druids," I confirm. "But those numbers are estimates at best. Like me, not every witch chooses to practise and thus register with the ICAG – that's English for International Council of Arcane Governance."

"So, these people.... they are like... *organised?*"

"Witches and druids have been around for a long time."

"For how long?" He shrugs. "Give or take..."

"*Long*. As long as humanity itself. But they've always been in hiding."

"And now they're coming out?" Dennis takes the letter, scanning it once more.

"It seems that way," I reply.

"And what insights do *you* have on the matter?"

I sigh. As if things weren't complicated enough already. "I don't know. I suppose my sister told them a thing or two. I can't be sure, though."

"Your sister, who is dead?"

I shake my head. "No, she... I found out recently that she is indeed very much alive."

I retrieve my phone and pull up Sofia's Instagram account. Dennis scrolls through her feed, his gaze growing more perplexed with each passing second. Sofia has uploaded a new video since I last checked. A scandalous clip of her pole-dancing in a cage that seems to float above a crowd of dancing heads in a dimly lit nightclub.

"*That* is your sister?"

Dennis continues to scroll through Sofia's feed, an array of provocative images and daring captions. He lingers on a particularly striking photo as he tries to make sense of what he's seeing.

"But... if she was alive this entire time, why didn't she get in touch with you?"

"I guess I will find out once I'm there," I say and take my phone back.

"You are not seriously thinking about going?"

"You read the letter. I have to." I shrug.

"Says *who*?"

"Says the magical paper it was written on."

"So, what, if you don't go, lightning will strike you or something?"

"No, nothing like that. It's more like a self-fulfilling prophecy. I cannot *not* go. I am going to go, no matter how hard I might resist it. At this point, it is written."

"I'm sorry, but that is nonsense." Dennis raises his hands as if to shield himself. "If you decide you don't want to go, you will not go. Mind over matter, simple as that."

"This is Scriptorium parchment," I explain, holding up the paper. "It was soaked in rainwater from the Chyulu mountains in Kenya – the birthplace of magic and the only place in the world where prophecies can be made. Aged in sacred pools for over a thousand years, these pieces of paper absorbed a small amount of those prophetic abilities."

Now Dennis looks at me as if I've just said something in Japanese, my cue that I've taken the conversation beyond what he can fathom.

I backtrack slightly. "Look, just trust me when I say I *must* go to London."

Dennis's eyes search mine, probably trying to make sense of all the impossibilities I've just revealed to him.

Finally, he speaks. "You are actually serious with all this."

"I'm afraid I am."

His shoulders square as he comes to a decision. "Well then, I am coming with you."

"You don't have to do that." I shake my head as if to deter a fly.

"Of course, I do. I won't let you go to London all by yourself to meet some... some thousand-year-old pervert with God knows what other tricks up his sleeve."

A sudden knock at the door interrupts our conversation, causing him to glance at his wristwatch. "Dammit, Frau Fleischer's biology class. I am meant to take them on a walk today." He stands up, running a hand through his hair. "Alright, listen, I have got to go." He leans down, placing a kiss on my forehead before turning towards the door. "Hermes, come on, boy." He whistles, and the dog comes running.

As Dennis slips into his boots, he looks back at me once more. "Listen, we'll talk more later, but I am coming with you and that's final, alright?"

I swivel around in my chair, watching him as he prepares to leave. "You sure?" I ask. "You're not... *freaked out* by all of this?"

A grin spreads across Dennis's face then. "Are you kidding me? This is exciting!" His grin turns into a naughty smirk. "And kind of sexy too, if you know what I mean." He winks at me, and before I can respond, he and Hermes are out the door.

As soon as I am alone, I slump over the kitchen table, holding my forehead as if feeling for a fever. He took that way better than I thought. And yet, the relief I should be feeling won't come. I can't quite say why but I never wanted him to know all that, and now that he does, I cannot take it back. I literally cannot. Because, although I am technically a witch, I am also not one. I am like a moth with broken wings, still colourful but unable to fly.

Sighing heavily, I reach for my phone, Sofia's Instagram account still open on the screen. Her bold images stare back at me, daring me to be brave, too.

With nothing left to lose, I type out another text, my

thoughts spilling onto the screen. *Hello? Are you seeing my messages? I got an invitation to this Assembly thing in London. Are you behind this?* I hit send, and the message joins the others, all unanswered.

Seconds turn into minutes as I stare at the screen, waiting for a response. I'm about to give up hope, but then three small dots appear, dancing below my message.

Someone is typing on the other end.

Chapter Four

"Alright, alright... I got a better one: why was the illiterate witch kicked out of her coven?"

Ember leans against the polished mahogany bar, her pink-painted fingernails tapping an uneven rhythm against her half-empty tumbler of whiskey. The faint smell of beer and chips lingers beneath the stronger scent of cleaning products. Morning light filters weakly through the grimy windows of the Queen's Head, one of Shoreditch's oldest pubs, catching dust motes that dance in the air like subtle spells.

"Em, please. It's ten in the bloody morning..." Saskia Antonov, the youngest member of Ember's eclectic coven, groans and drops her forehead to the bar with a thud, her endless curls spilling across the wood like liquid copper.

"Yeah, not another one," mutters Minnie Allen from Ember's other side. Unlike Saskia's dramatic display of suffering, Minnie, one of the last true psychics, sits ramrod straight on her barstool, nursing a cup of black coffee as if it's the only thing keeping her connected to her ancestors.

"Because she couldn't *spell!*" Ember snorts at her own

punchline, the sound dissolving into a hiccup. She swirls the amber liquid in her glass, ice cubes clinking against crystal, before downing the remainder in a single gulp.

The bartender, a lanky man with stubble and reading glasses perched low on his nose like an afterthought, raises an eyebrow but says nothing. Three young women drinking at this hour isn't the strangest thing he's seen, though he'd never guess the true nature of his customers.

"That's worse than the one about the broomstick and the vacuum cleaner," Saskia mumbles into the bar top.

Ember makes a sound like a disgruntled pony, blowing air through her lips. Her dark hair is mussed from hours of dancing. Glitter still clings to her temples and décolleté. Her pink dress is wrinkled and stained from the night before.

Her phone buzzes in her purse – *again*. She ignores it, just as she's been ignoring it for days now. If only she drinks enough, dances enough, loses herself enough in the pounding music of her club, maybe she can pretend the message doesn't exist. Maybe she can pretend that the name lighting up her screen – Alva – doesn't matter, doesn't mean anything to her.

"Come on, that one was brilliant! You're just sore because no one got your punchline about the mandrakes last night." Ember reaches for the bottle of whiskey next to her glass. But before her fingers can close around it, the bottle slides several inches away, as if of its own accord. The bartender's back is turned, and no one else in the nearly empty pub notices. Minnie doesn't look up from her coffee, but the corner of her mouth twitches ever so slightly.

"Traitor," Ember mutters, but there's no real heat in it. "Careful with that in public. We have an image to maintain, remember?"

"Says the woman who set the DJ booth on fire last night," Minnie replies, her eyes darting to make sure no one is listening.

Ember winces. "Well, *that* was... an accident."

"Like the 'accident' at the Pickle Factory on Friday?" Saskia lifts her head just enough to fix Ember with a knowing look. "You've been off for days, Em, admit it. What's gotten into you lately?"

Ember's jaw tightens, the question hitting too close to home. "Just enjoying life, darling. Isn't that what we're supposed to do?"

The pub door creaks open, letting in a shaft of sunlight that slices through the dim interior. Ember squints toward the entrance, where a figure stands silhouetted against the morning light. Even with her alcohol-blurred vision, she'd recognise that posture anywhere – straight-backed and immaculate in crisp button-down and fitted trousers.

"Pippa Watson, my sun and stars!" Ember calls out, grateful for the distraction. "Come to join the party?"

Pippa approaches, bringing with her the scent of fresh air and subtle perfume – a welcome contrast to the stale pub atmosphere. Her dark hair is pulled back into a neat bun, not a strand out of place. On her face: the old familiar tie between exasperation and fondness. They've been here before.

"Good morning, ladies," she says, but her formality is undercut by her amusement. "I'm afraid I'm going to have to escort Ms Wild here off the premises. I believe she has a lunch date with her accountant."

Ember waves a dismissive hand, nearly knocking over Minnie's coffee in the process. "Accounting? On a Saturday? That's criminally boring, kitten. Tell him I've been kidnapped by pirates. Or better yet, tell him I've eloped with a beautiful mysterious woman." She winks at Pippa, desperate for the faint smile that soon plays around her assistant's cheeks.

"It's Tuesday," Pippa corrects. "And the meeting was rescheduled twice already."

"Tuesday?" Ember blinks, genuinely surprised. She turns to her coven sisters. "When did that happen?"

Saskia finally lifts her head from the bar. "Somewhere between your impromptu fireworks at the club and then dragging us to three different after-hours bars."

Pippa steps closer, now standing directly beside Ember's barstool. "It's time to go," she says. "You really need to sleep this off before your meeting."

"I don't want to go." Ember pouts like a schoolgirl refusing to get on the bus. But then her eyes are drawn to a man in a suit who's just looked up from his newspaper at the far end of the bar, clearly disturbed by her outburst. His gaze locks with hers for a moment, recognition flickering across his face. Something about the look makes her skin prickle.

The man folds his newspaper, leaves it on the bar, and approaches. His suit is expensive but slightly rumpled, like he's been wearing it since yesterday. His face is vaguely familiar... someone she's seen at a party, perhaps.

"Ember Wild," he says, stopping a few feet away. The way he says her name carries a hint of disdain. "Fancy seeing you here."

Ember tilts her head, studying him. "I'm afraid you have the advantage."

"Liam Stonehouse," he says, as though the name should mean something to her. When she doesn't react, he adds, "I'm on the licensing committee for Soho nightlife."

Ah. That explains it. Ember smiles, all teeth and no warmth. "Why, what a small world."

"Indeed, it is." His eyes scan over her dishevelled appearance, then shift to Saskia and Minnie. "Long night?"

"The best kind," Ember replies, turning back to her empty glass. But she can feel his eyes still on her, assessing.

"Actually, while I have you," he says, moving closer, "I've been meaning to talk to you about your establishment."

Saskia and Minnie exchange a subtle glance. Pippa shifts her weight, moving slightly closer to Ember.

"In a professional capacity?" Ember asks, arching an eyebrow. "Because I generally conduct business at my office, not random pubs at nine in the morning."

"Consider this unofficial," Stonehouse says. "A friendly heads-up, nothing more. You see, there's been some concern about your safety protocols at the Sapphire Lounge."

"It's called Pink Cauldron now, love."

"Sure, sure – I'll try to remember that in the report when we inspect the joint."

The threat doesn't worry Ember. Her club is immaculate, both on paper and in reality, thanks largely to Pippa's meticulous attention to detail and refusal to cut corners, even when Ember suggests it might be easier. But the gleam in the man's eyes suggests he's enjoying this way too much, taking pleasure in what he might perceive as having power over her.

"Interesting," Ember says, turning fully to face him now. "And you're telling me this because...?"

"Professional courtesy." He shrugs. "Thought I should warn you, we'll be especially thorough. After what happened with the previous owner, the committee feels the need to ensure everything is above board."

Ah. Now it makes sense. He was probably friendly with David Voss, the one whose reputation Ember had publicly shredded when taking over his club.

"Above board," Ember repeats, unimpressed. "As opposed to how things were run before I took over? The spiked drinks? The security that looked the other way while predators stalked the dancefloor? The electrical wiring that was one spark away from burning the place down?"

Stonehouse's jaw tightens. "That's not—"

"Not what?" Ember cuts him off. "Not what you want to talk about? Not what the committee cared to investigate when Voss was in charge? Curious, isn't it? How those inspections never seemed to find any problems before."

The bartender drifts closer, wiping the same spot on the bar repeatedly, clearly listening.

"Well, the circumstances of your acquisition remain questionable, to say the least," Stonehouse says, lowering his voice. "One day Voss is running the most successful club in Soho, the next he's signing over the deed to you – a complete unknown."

"Not a *complete* unknown, darling, come on. Give me some credit, will you?"

Inwardly, she's still amused at how ridiculously easy it had been – a few doctored security recordings, some creative storytelling about wandering hands and late-night "meetings," and suddenly Voss looked about as credible as Prince Andrew claiming he couldn't sweat. When other women came forward with their own stories, he'd practically thrown the deed to his club at her rather than face the music.

"People don't just walk away from businesses like that," Stonehouse insists. "Not without pressure."

"Are you accusing me of something, Mr Stonehouse?" Ember asks, her voice dropping to something dangerous yet soft. Beneath the bar, her fingers begin to trace a subtle pattern against her thigh, invisible to anyone watching.

"Because that would be a bold move for a man who sits on a committee that repeatedly ignored safety violations until they couldn't anymore."

Stonehouse's cheeks flush with anger. "Watch yourself, Wild. The nightlife scene in this city runs on relationships, and you're making enemies."

"No," Ember says, standing slowly. Though she's shorter

than him even in her heels, something in her posture makes him take a half-step back. "I'm making changes. And if that threatens the comfortable little arrangement you and your friends had, that's not my problem."

She lifts her hand subtly, her fingers continuing their pattern. The air around them suddenly feels different – heavier, warmer.

"Your club might be clean on paper," – Stonehouse tugs at his collar as if it's too tight – "but everyone has secrets. And I'll find yours."

Ember smiles. "Good luck with that. In the meantime, inspect away. My doors are always open. Although you wouldn't be the first to regret accepting my invitation."

Stonehouse opens his mouth to retort but seems to struggle to take a full breath. He tugs more frantically at his collar, which now appears to be shrinking before Ember's eyes – though only she and her coven sisters would notice the subtle magic at work. The fabric of his jacket tightens across his chest, compressing just enough to make breathing uncomfortable.

"Something wrong?" Ember asks innocently. "You're looking a bit constricted."

Stonehouse tries to answer but manages only a wheezing sound. Sweat beads on his forehead as his suit continues to tighten. The effect isn't enough to cause real harm – Ember is too careful for that –but more than enough to cause significant discomfort and confusion.

"I need... air," he gasps, backing toward the door, his face reddening. "This isn't... This isn't over, Wild."

He stumbles out the door, loosening his tie, the glass panes shuddering in their frame behind him.

As soon as he's gone, Ember sways slightly, the burst of adrenaline fading. Pippa is at her side instantly, a steadying hand at her elbow.

"That was oddly arousing," Saskia comments, raising her glass in salute. "But seriously, Em, you need to be more careful. Someone's going to notice."

"The shrinking suit was too obvious," Minnie adds, her tone gentle but concerned.

"He deserved worse," Ember insists, but leans into Pippa's support. "Fine, Watson. Take me home. I concede defeat."

Pippa's lips curve into a small smile. "A historic moment. Should I call the papers?"

"Cheeky," Ember says. "You're lucky you're so pretty, pet."

Pippa begins guiding her toward the door, but then Ember halts once more.

"Wait, wait, wait—" Ember spins around to face Saskia and Minnie, swaying slightly on her heels. "I got another one, I got another one: what do you call a witch who lives in the desert?"

Saskia and Minnie exchange a long-suffering look before responding in perfect, weary unison: "WHAT?"

"A sand-witch!" Ember dissolves into giggles, nearly toppling over as Pippa steadies her.

The bartender snorts softly from behind the bar while Saskia drops her head back to the bar top.

"Well. And that's all we've got for you today, folks," Pippa announces with a mock bow, steering Ember toward the exit as if ushering a reluctant comedian off stage.

Outside, the morning sun is painfully bright, and Ember shields her eyes with a dramatic groan. The hangover is beginning to set in, a pounding at her temples that matches her anxious thoughts. Pippa guides her toward the Range Rover parked at the kerb, her hand never leaving the small of Ember's back.

Once settled in the leather interior, the world spinning around her, Ember pulls out her phone at last and looks at the notification that's been sitting there like a burning coal she can neither cool nor discard. *Hello? Are you seeing my messages?* Alva. A name that makes something sharp twist in her chest after all this time. The feeling she's been trying to outrun – using alcohol and exhaustion, parties and spells – catches up to her at last. A deep breath, a final flicker of resistance, then Ember types out a reply, hits send before she can change her mind.

Come to London, then we'll talk.

Chapter Five

Blood-red swastikas dance in the fireplace, casting ominous shadows across eager faces. "Bravo, Fräulein Hausmann! Bravo! With witches like you at our side, the Third Reich will last a thousand years..."

I jolt upright at the vision, gasping for air, my bare body exposed to the cool night air as the words echo in my mind.

I've always been more comfortable sleeping naked. But Dennis prefers to keep his pyjamas on. In case of an emergency, he says he doesn't want to answer the door to the fire brigade with nothing but his hands covering his acorns. He has always been a bit of an alarmist.

"Another one of those nightmares?" he asks now, holding me.

"Yeah." I free myself from his embrace and sit up, brushing a strand of hair from my clammy forehead.

It wasn't a nightmare though. It never is. It was another memory.

I slide out of bed, the cool of the room a welcome change from the oppressive heat trapped beneath the blanket. Outside the window, the silhouettes of the mountains stand out against the night sky, peaks obscured by inky darkness.

"I'm just going to get a glass of water," I whisper, but Dennis has already rolled to the other side, dozing off again.

As I walk past Hermes lying on his dog bed, his ears perk up. He lifts his head, following my every move, tail wagging, assessing whether my late-night wanderings warrant a bark. With a gentle whine he decides against it and stretches. His nails click against the hardwood as he trots over to me, nuzzling his nose against my hand before he takes my place in the bed.

In the kitchen, the faint scent of smoke lingers from dying embers in the fireplace, the wooden walls bathed in the glow of moonlight. The counter is occupied by our travel documents. Passports, flight tickets, hotel reservation.

It's been two weeks since the letter. Tomorrow morning we'll fly to the UK.

Come to London. Then we'll talk, was Sofia's simple yet loaded reply to my initial messages. I'd considered following up but, in the end, I didn't know which words to choose from the ocean of things I'd need to get off my chest. I still don't.

I reach for a glass from the cupboard, the weathered door squeaking on its hinges. I fill the glass with water from the tap.

Leaning against the counter, I take a few sips as I look down at the passports. I'm not sure if it's a good idea for Dennis to join me. I understand he wants to be a part of this... this new reality I've presented him with, and I suppose that's better than if it were the other way around. But I don't think he has quite grasped the ramifications yet.

For the past fortnight, he's been like a child with a new toy, constantly pleading for a demonstration of my magic, a "little trick", a little "abracadabra". Each time, I've firmly refused. To Dennis, this trip must seem like an exciting adventure into a world of wonder and whimsy, something straight out of a children's book. While for me every moment since Mr Guise's summons has been a battle against my creeping dread.

I trace the edge of Dennis' passport with my finger. Maybe it'll be good to have him tag along after all. It might be the wake-up call he needs to realise that this is far from the fairytale he has in mind.

I set my glass down and, following a hunch, I slip outside the back door into the wild untamed garden. Still naked, my skin is bathed in silvery light from the waxing moon. No wonder the memory chose to surface tonight; they always seem to be at their strongest in the lead-up to a full moon. I open my palms, embracing the nature that surrounds me, seeking calm. The night sky stretches out above me, vast and uninterrupted, except for the occasional passing satellite. This wild pocket of Germany is one of the few places where you can still see the stars in all their glory – and walk around naked in your garden, for that matter.

However, the views here shouldn't be this far-reaching. In years past, vast expanses of coniferous trees dominated the land-scape. But now, swaths of cleared land and fallen lifeless trees scar the once-lush slopes. Prolonged droughts and violent storms have taken their toll, and the notorious bark beetle has ravaged the spruce forests, leaving destruction in its wake.

Dennis and his rangers dedicate themselves to the reforesta-tion efforts, working tirelessly to restore what has been lost. But it's an uphill battle. The forests of the Harz Mountains are disappearing before our eyes.

In the midst of this ever-changing world, I have carved out a sanctuary where at least on a small scale I feel like what I'm doing makes a difference: the garden is a testament to the care I've poured into this little piece of earth.

Early September has begun autumn's transformation in the flower beds. The summer blooms are fading now, giving way to late-season asters and the last defiant roses clinging to their stems. The lavender stalks stand tall but spent, their purple already harvested and dried. My chamomile patch has gone to seed, the flowers now papery and brown, ready to scatter their promise of next year's tea. And among the herbs, the last of the summer vegetables make their final stand – tomato vines heavy with green fruit that won't have time to ripen, and overgrown zucchini plants sprawling across soil that's just beginning to cool with the changing season.

I lower myself to the ground, and the earth beneath my bare skin connects me to the land. I breathe deeply, inhaling the scents of the garden, exhaling my tensions. A sense of calm begins to settle over my racing thoughts and just for a moment the world seems to absorb my sorrows.

Eventually, I feel a presence nearby, a prickling sensation that never fails to excite me. Amidst the shadows from the surrounding woods, a pair of eyes find mine in the darkness. The creature sits perfectly still, but as my eyes adjust, I begin to make out its distinct form, much larger than a house cat, with a muscular body and a short, bobbed tail.

Slowly, the animal steps into the moonlight. Fluid, graceful – allowing me to marvel at its tawny coat, dotted with dark spots. The pointed ears, tipped with tufts of black, twitch slightly in my direction. Before me stands one of the last free-roaming lynxes of the area, a species whose population has dwindled to fewer than one hundred individuals around these parts.

The lynx watches me intently, her amber eyes cautious, but curious. She moves closer now, soundless against the grass. She settles down next to me, and her warmth radiates through her thick fur. Dennis was right: the creatures of the forest usually answer to my call, one of the few remnants of my magic I can't seem to shake off. Or maybe I don't want to.

There's something profoundly humbling about the way this

wild lynx has chosen to place her trust in me, leaning into my touch as if I'm not the only one seeking comfort in the contact. She reminds me that there is a part of me deeply connected to the natural world, a part that finds solace in the company of the untamed. A part that *is* still very much untamed.

The lynx purrs, the vibration humming through her bones, reaching me. Gently, I caress her coat. But as my fingers run through her fur, my mind wanders back to the memory that startled me from sleep earlier.

Fragments of the past flash before my eyes. The terror so alive in my veins makes me constrict, and the lynx looks up at me, clearly feeling my worry.

But now I'm back with Ruth, standing in an elegant Bavarian salon – the Platterhof, as my parents would later confirm thanks to the details I provided, a guesthouse in the Obersalzberg area frequently used for Nazi party meetings. It's 1935, and the air is loaded with the scent of strong coffee, with rage and dangerous ambition. Ruth faces a group of influential-looking men in crisp brown uniforms. She demonstrates her magic, causing the flames in the fireplace to dance and form shapes at her will. The men's expressions shift from polite interest to undisguised awe, then to a calculating hunger that should send her running but doesn't.

Instead, I feel Ruth's misplaced confidence, her belief that she's found a path to legitimacy for our kind, at last. There's a thrill coursing through her veins – finally, after years of hiding and persecution, here are men who see her gifts as strength rather than heresy. Their talks of ancient Germanic traditions and mystical bloodlines strike a chord, promising a world where all witches can practise openly, revered instead of reviled. With each word from the officials, Ruth's resolve deepens; she's certain she has secured a place of honour for her coven amid the highest Nazi ranks.

With a jerk of my head, I cast off the scene before it can play out the dire history that followed.

The lynx perks up her ears now, focussing on something beyond the edge of the garden, beyond my own senses. She gets up, stretches, and with one last nudge against my arm, she wanders off into the woods. I rise as well, picking a strand of lavender which I crush between my hands, to breathe in the calming scent of the herb.

I suppose, in some way, it makes sense that they would summon me to London. After all, I'm probably the only witch alive today with first-hand memories of the last time a magical reveal – however misguided – was attempted. But why would Sofia tell them that? Does she hate me now, is that it? Does she think this will somehow make things right?

My eyes drift up to the moon, an almost perfect circle, save for a thin shadow along one edge.

Try as I might to hide in that dark sliver, come sunrise, it will be made whole.

Chapter Six

Our hotel room is a shoebox with a bed.

Two steps from the door and I'm already at the window, my fingers grazing the weathered sill. I grasp the old sash window, lifting it with a grunt. It slides up reluctantly, wood scraping against wood. The sounds of London rush in – double-decker buses rumbling by, pigeons cooing on the nearby ledge, the constant murmur of pedestrians on the pavement below. A soft thrill runs through me. I've never been anywhere, never set foot outside of Germany since becoming an adult. My father was American, a soldier stationed in Germany – that's how my parents met. When Sofia and I were nine, we travelled as a family to Massachusetts, to see where Dad grew up. But all I remember from that trip is the taste of marshmallows and the excitement of sleeping in a hotel room for the first time.

"Was für eine Absteige." *What a shit hole*, Dennis grumbles, wrestling our luggage through the narrow doorway. "How much did we shell out for this closet, you said?"

"Too much?" I offer a wry smile, watching him try to fit our luggage in the space beside the bed without knocking over the bedside lamp.

I politely but firmly refused Mr Guise's invitation to stay in his townhouse. His magical parchment may have forced me to London, moving me across the English Channel like a pawn, but I won't play by his rules now that I'm here. This shabby hotel room is my act of defiance. He might have set up the game, but he doesn't control all the pieces.

Dennis finally frees himself from the luggage tangle. "Let's get some breakfast. I'm starving," he says.

"Sure, I suppose there's time for that." I reach into my pocket, finding the obsidian rock, which I've brought with me from home. Usually, its cool, solid surface makes me feel calm, but it seems to be producing the opposite effect right now. A faint discomfort ripples through me that only seems to spike my anxiety. Unsettled, I withdraw my hand and make for the door.

"Do you think you'll get by today, all by yourself?" I ask Dennis as the latch clicks shut behind us. Because of my dad, I was raised bilingually and so I speak English rather well. Dennis's foreign language skills, on the other hand, are practically non-existent.

"Am I not coming with you?" he asks as we start down the stairs, each step accompanied by a creak.

"That won't be possible, I'm afraid. The assembly is only for ICAG-members. I don't even know how he's planning on getting *me* in there, to be honest." My stomach tightens at the thought. As much as I try to convince myself that I came here for Sofia, for a chance to reunite with the sister I've lost, I know it's more than that.

Ever since that letter arrived at the cabin, I've been feeling it again. That familiar tingle under my skin, the warmth spreading through my blood like liquid sunbeams. The Anima, now demanding to be felt once more. I've been feeling *magic,* coursing through me with a normalcy I'd almost forgotten. That rush of power, that potential, humming at the fingertips, waiting to be used. My senses seem sharper, too, my surroundings more vivid, the sounds somewhat crisper, as if I've taken off a pair of noise-cancelling headphones. I'm almost bursting to wield again, hoping against hope that there might just be a way for me to be part of this world once more.

"Well, I guess I'll just wait for you here all day," Dennis sighs, pulling my mind back to him. As we descend the stairs, the musty smell of old carpet mingles with a faint whiff of rose air freshener, a futile attempt to mask the building's mould.

"Hyde Park is less than five minutes away if you're feeling claustrophobic."

We reach the ground floor, where the din of London traffic grows louder. The door groans with age as I push it and walk through.

"I saw a deli just around the corner," I say but stop short when someone calls my name.

A man with salt-and-pepper hair leans out the rear window of a black Range Rover idling at the pavement, his keen eyes fixing on me. The driver, a tall blonde woman in an elegant costume, steps out smoothly and opens the back door, which reveals the distinguished gentleman as he emerges.

"So froh, dass ich Sie erwischt habe." *So very glad I caught you*, he says in perfect German. "Mardequai Guise, zu Ihren Diensten. It would be my utmost pleasure to offer you a ride to Arcadia House."

Mardequai Guise effortlessly commands attention in his charcoal suit, understated but impeccably tailored. His face is lined with wrinkles, yet still undeniably handsome: sharp cheekbones, a strong jaw, and cunning grey eyes. There's an aura of timelessness about him – and I'm pretty sure I'd say that even if I didn't know he was immortal.

"How did you know where we are staying?" Dennis cuts in.

"Ah, and this must be the significant other you mentioned you'd be travelling with," Mr Guise says, completely ignoring Dennis's question and reaching out a hand. "Delighted to meet you. I took the liberty to organise a little city tour for you today. Eloise here speaks immaculate German. She would be delighted to show you around town while Alva and I must sit cooped up indoors all day to endure a tiresome procession of debates and lectures. Am I right, Eloise?"

"It would be my pleasure," Eloise responds, her smile just a touch too fake.

"Well, that's... that's actually really helpful. Thank you," Dennis says, his resistance crumbling like the cracked facade of our hotel. Traitor.

"Please, don't mention it." Mr Guise waves off the gratitude with a smooth gesture. "You're my guests in this sprawling metropolis, and here at my invitation after all. Shall we?" He motions towards the open car door, leaving no room for refusal.

Still, I hesitate, caught between the desire to maintain some sense of autonomy and the realisation that I'm already ensnared in Mr Guise's web.

But Dennis has slid into the front seat, and so, with a resigned sigh, I move towards the car as well. As I enter the back, my eyes sweep across the interior, hoping against hope to find Sofia there. But the back seat is empty.

Mr Guise slides in next to me, filling the space with an almost palpable aura. Eloise pulls away from the kerb and merges into the flow of London traffic. A sudden downpour batters against the windshield, forcing her to switch the wipers to their highest setting. The sky has darkened considerably in the last few minutes.

Mr Guise glances up at the rain-lashed windows with a raised eyebrow. "How peculiar. There wasn't a cloud in the forecast today." He turns to me with a smile. "I do hope you haven't been experimenting with weather manipulation, Fräulein. Some might say the Hausmann family hasn't quite learned its lesson about the dangers of such practices."

"*What?*"

"Forgive me," he says, though his tone carries no apology. "I'm getting ahead of myself. You see, I came across a fascinating piece of writing once that chronicled your... *intimate* knowledge of the Sylt Massacre."

My heart stutters. The Sylt Massacre. I've never heard anyone call it that before, but I know exactly what he means. I've had flashes of that day my entire life: Ruth standing on the windswept beach, face tilted skyward as the clouds churn unnaturally overhead. The circle of witches behind her, their faces masks of exhaustion and terror as the storm collapses inward...

"You've seen my file," I say, reeling on the inside. Those childhood evaluations were supposed to be sealed. "So, why did you want me to attend the Assembly, anyway?" I ask, eager to change the subject.

He regards me with those ancient eyes, his hands, a ring on every finger, folding in his lap. "We stand at a precipice, Fräulein Hausmann. The decision has been made: we are to reveal ourselves to the common folk out there," he says dismissively. At the phrase "common folk" (Mr Guise, possibly with calculated intent, used the German equivalent, "Gesindel"), Dennis clears his throat loudly from the front seat. The druid continues, unperturbed, "But not everybody understands the consequences that await us now."

"And what makes you think I have anything to offer that you and your cohort don't already know?" I press.

Mr Guise's lips quirk into something resembling a smile. "Have you ever watched a flock of starlings, Fräulein Hausmann? A thousand birds moving as one, yet it takes but a single creature to change their course. You see, sometimes, the voice that turns the tide must come from within. It is our duty, yours and mine, to forewarn the flock."

"So, what? You... you want me to *address* the Assembly?"

Mr Guise gives a vague nod.

Despite myself, I feel a flutter of relief. I'm not exactly keen on a public speaking gig, but thanks to old Ruth on my mind, I'd been bracing for worse. Tar and feathers, perhaps. The ducking stool...the *pyre.* Then again, who's to say that's not still on the table. I'd sooner bet my life on a coin toss than on this man's assurances.

"And why would I do that, may I ask? I don't exactly have a speech prepared."

"Fear not, a formal address won't be required. I merely have a few... *inquiries*, the answers to which I'm certain will captivate our esteemed Assembly. Your perspective, after all, is unique." His eyes glint as he says this, then he turns to look out the window, tracking the blur of houses as they fly by.

I inhale sharply, ready to object. He may have lured me here, but he can't compel me to speak against my will. The refusal already prickles on the tip of my tongue but then I hesitate. As terrifying as it seems, I can't deny that addressing the Assembly might just be an opportunity, a chance to reclaim my place, to have it all out in the open once and for all and then move past it. Could I be done hiding?

The fear still pulses through me, but now a spark of determination smoulders at its edges.

"And what about Sofia?" I ask.

Mr Guise shifts in his seat. "Ah yes, that is the question, isn't it? What about Sofia? I wondered if you might remember, but perhaps it was too long ago. The truth is, my dear, you and I are acquainted as well. I've always had a fondness for the Germanic lands, you see. I lived in Trier for a time... when was that? *Guter*

Gott, it feels like centuries ago." He says this casually, but it's probably the literal truth. "And I was there, you see, on that fateful solstice thirteen years ago, at the invitation of Markus Steingruber, an old druid acquaintance. You beat me to the last Pfannkuchen, if I'm not mistaken."

His words stir memories I've long tried to bury. That night – the last time I saw my family whole, the last time I felt part of the magical world – resurfaces with a dull ache spreading through my chest. My mind spins, flicking through faces, fragments, fissures of memory from the last solstice I ever celebrated (openly anyway). But no matter how hard I try to remember Mr Guise, I draw only blanks.

From the front seat, Eloise's voice pierces through my thoughts. "Und hier links ist der Buckingham Palace," she explains to Dennis, pointing out the building. As she steers the Range Rover through London's congested streets, Mr Guise leans in.

"In fact," he says, "I was only a few minutes behind when the accident occurred. I must have been the first to arrive on that terrible scene."

A rubbish truck rumbles past, momentarily obscuring my view of the city. I turn to face him. "I don't remember you being there."

Mr Guise's eyebrows rise. "It is a curious thing you should say this. As a matter of fact, I don't remember *you* being there, either."

"What do you mean?"

His gaze remains fixed on me as he speaks. "I arrived at the accident site and found your sister in the grass by the roadside. I assumed you and your parents were beyond saving... dreadful, dreadful thing. But as it turns out," – he still, his eyes hardening – "you were not in that car anymore when I arrived at the scene, now were you?"

Evidently, I'm tempted to snap but I bite back the word.

Mr Guise's stare bores into me as if he's trying to unearth a long-buried secret. "Tell me, Fräulein Hausmann, do you still feel guilty for it?" he asks, and the question burns like ice water. From the front, Eloise points out another landmark, but her words barely register. Instead, my mind races back to that hospital room where I woke up after the accident, with no memory of how I'd even gotten there. Ingrid Brauer, the magistrate of the Elster Coven my mother belonged to, loomed over my hospital bed. Her white-streaked hair was pulled back in a messy bun; the scent of pine and wood smoke still clung to her wool cardigan, at odds with the hospital air.

"Alva, there's no easy way to say this," she said, her voice as sharp as a scalpel. "But your family is gone."

I stared at the starched sheets, unable to meet her steely eyes. But only now, as I replay the memory, do I realise the possibility of those words: *your family is gone.* I'd always assumed 'gone' meant 'dead'. But Frau Brauer hadn't explicitly said that, had she?

Now the thought ripples through my world like a stone falling into still water. Everyone knew my parents didn't make it, but was the magistrate aware *Sofia* had survived?

"You'll be placed in a foster home," she had said, each word a nail in the coffin of my old life. "And you are forbidden from practicing magic. Ever again."

And she never said it outright, but I could feel it – the unspoken accusation, the belief that I, or some malevolent thing within me, was responsible for what had happened.

Eloise, behind the steering wheel, lurches forward with the green light, and I'm yanked back to the present. But the memory lingers, bitter as a pill on my tongue.

"Verstanden?"

"Ja, Frau Brauer," I'd whispered.

I didn't even protest her decree, because I, too, believed the magic that once sang in my veins had become a venomous thing. A *dangerous* thing. Deep down, a part of me agreed with her judgment: I didn't deserve to be a witch anymore.

"Schatz, are you alright?" Dennis's voice pulls me back inside the car. He's twisted around in the passenger seat, his hand gentle on my knee.

"Sorry, what?"

"You look a bit pale. Everything okay back there?"

"We're nearly there," Eloise chimes in, her eyes meeting mine in the rearview mirror. "The backseat always makes me a bit queasy too."

"I'm fine," I reply, aiming for a tone I hope to be both reassuring and firm.

I turn to Mr Guise, finding him seemingly engrossed in the pendant dangling from his neck, a slender crystal amulet of interconnected shards.

"What happened?" I ask him. "That night?"

"Fate," Mr Guise replies, his eyes distant with memory. "Fate is what happened. I pulled Sofia away from the burning vehicle. She was distraught, frantic. The chaos around her only seemed to fuel her panic. I was the only one she listened to. Indeed, I found myself uniquely capable of anchoring her in that storm of fear and confusion." His fingers absently trace the crystal shards. "You see, in all my years I never had any children of my own. A rather unusual choice for a druid. Most of us have fathered at least one, during the passage of the Solantha Comet – the only chance, every one hundred and eight years, to beget a new immortal. Are you familiar with how a druid is sired, Fräulein Hausmann?"

In the front seat, Dennis is practically craning his neck; he'd be dying to hear all about it, I'm sure. But I have no time to indulge his curiosity right now. I nod, rather impatiently, willing Mr Guise to continue with more important matters.

"Well, in any case. I suppose, the allure of creating immortal live is too big a temptation for many of my brothers to pass up. The comet's approach next year will be... *interesting,* to say the least."

"You were never tempted?"

"The last time temptation of any sort took a hold of me, the town crier was still the primary source of news." Mr Guise's lip twitches and he adjusts his cufflinks. "But I digress. That night your sister came into my world, I knew we were destined to do great things together. What a delightfully lively creature she is, wouldn't you agree?"

"Well, until recently I actually thought her dead. So, no. Can't say I quite agree."

At that, Mr Guise throws his head back and lets out a laugh so shrill it seems to fill the entire car – manic mirth, yet with something darker behind it. Even Eloise startles behind the steering wheel, the car swerving slightly before she regains control. "And we, in turn, believed you dead as well," he cackles, then lets out a heavy sigh. "The universe does love its jests, doesn't it?"

I clench my jaw, my irritation flaring. "But what do you mean, *destined?*"

As abruptly as it began, the laughter stops, and Mr Guise fixes me with those gleaming eyes. His chest still heaving slightly from his outburst, he composes himself, his face settling into pensive mode instead. "It was destiny; indeed, it was. From the moment I took your sister under my wing, it was as if she were a long-lost melody finally finding its way back to the instrument." His fingers reach for his pendant once again.

Outside, the iconic silhouette of Big Ben comes into view, but now is not the time for sightseeing.

"So, you just... *took* her." I struggle to control my voice, but my hands betray me, curling into fists in my lap.

Mr Guise's voice is now smooth as polished silver. "The coven made a decision. I was to be her guardian, seeing as she would not leave my side. Your mother, after all, had no siblings, and her own mother, well..." His eyes flick to mine for the briefest of moments. "Ruth's fate was rather... *inflammatory*, was it not?"

The word choice isn't lost on me. My feet tingle with a strange heat, as if the mere mention of my grandmother's name has summoned the flames that claimed her. Mr Guise's slight smile suggests he's well aware of the effect his words have on me.

"So, once all the official procedures were handled, I took Sofia under my wing, to raise her at Dunmorrough, my humble Scottish estate. A place far removed from her grief and pain. To guide her through what proved to be a rather challenging transition into adulthood."

An unbidden image forms in my mind: Sofia, all alone, her hair whipping in the wind as she stands on the misty shore of some remote loch, the Scottish moors stretching endlessly behind her, as vast and sombre as her loss must have felt.

I shake the vision away. "My father had family in the States. My aunt, and my grandfather. They should have been told. *They* should have taken her in, not you."

"Ah, *yes*." The word slithers from his lips. "Is that where you scurried off to before I could snatch you, too?" With that, his fingers pinch the skin of my forearm ever so slightly, a gesture that walks the line between jest and threat.

"Welcome to Arcadia House," Eloise announces from the front not a moment too soon, and I exit the vehicle with barely concealed haste.

Mr Guise, I'm certain, has spent centuries honing the art of verbal chess, each word calculated, never revealing more than he intends. And yet, there's an undercurrent of eagerness he can't quite conceal – a hunger to decipher me, to unravel the enigma I present to him. He already knows of my visions, that much is obvious. Knows that he and his lot are not the only ones anymore with a mirror to the past. But until I know just how much – or how little – he truly knows, I best stay hidden in the dark. Because only in the dark does a mirror keep its secrets.

Dennis rounds the car swiftly, grasping my arm with an urgency that surprises me. His grip is firm, as if he's escorting a flight risk rather than his partner. "Any other long-lost relatives you've neglected to mention?" he whispers. "Now would be the time to tell."

"Actually, now is not the time. Not at all." I wrench myself free, my eyes drawn past him to the sight beyond.

Arcadia House rises before us, a magnificent building nestled right among Westminster's famous landmarks. Its stone facade gleams in a sliver of autumn sunlight, impressive columns framing the entrance, the bridge between the arcane and the mundane, hidden in plain sight amid the bustle of central London.

A diverse crowd flows in and out of those doors – mostly women, from every corner of the globe. Their outfits range from business suits to colourful traditional attire, and they converse in a mix of languages, some clutching briefcases or smartphones, others ancient-looking books or curious artefacts.

To the casual observer, this might appear to be just another international conference of sorts – which, of course, it is. But only the keen eye might notice the subtle oddities – a glimpse of magic here, a whispered spell there.

To me, the scene is as exhilarating as it is intimidating.

"Sorry," Dennis says, brushing his thumb across the bridge of his nose, a gesture of hurt feelings I've come to recognise.

Behind us, Mr Guise emerges from the car, immediately

greeted by a woman in a tailored suit who seems to materialise from the crowd. They exchange hushed words, and I'm glad to get a break from his intense focus on me.

"No, *I'm* sorry," I sigh, turning my attention back to Dennis. "I didn't mean to snap. I'll tell you everything tonight, alright?" I lean into him, wrapping my arms around his waist. "*Including all the juicy details of how druids procreate,*" I whisper, earning a slight chuckle from him. "It's just, right now I need to make sure I don't accidentally set off any magical alarms or offend an elder." I pull back slightly, meeting his eyes. "This world – it's as dangerous as it is magical. One misstep and I could find myself turned into a lizard or something."

"*Really?*"

"No, not really. But I do need to have my wits about me today."

We share a brief embrace before Dennis climbs back into the car. Mr Guise leans in through the open window. "Eloise, why don't you show him that little place in Covent Garden? The one with the excellent pasties."

As the Range Rover pulls away, my unspoken truths linger in its wake. The fact is, I never once told a soul I have family in the States – not Ingrid Brauer, not Dennis, not anyone. I can't quite pinpoint why. Perhaps it was because I barely knew them; I'd only met my aunt once, and Dad's relationship with his father was strained at best. But even if I had known them better, I doubt I would have gotten in touch. My time at the foster home I grew up in was a penance, my guilt feeding on the isolation like a parasite.

I sidle up to Mr Guise and together, we begin the walk towards Arcadia House.

"Before I forget," Mr Guise says as we approach the building, "are you still in possession of the letter I sent you?"

"Yes."

"I'd be grateful if you could return it. You might recall, it's an offence not to return Chyulu parchment to its rightful owner."

"I mean, I don't have it, like, *on* me." I pat the sides of my jeans.

"When we drop you off at the hotel then," he says smoothly.

A beat of silence passes between us.

"Actually, I think I might have left that in Germany," I lie, although I don't even know why I bother. All I know is that, after just thirty minutes in the car with Mr Guise, I've developed an instinct to guard anything he shows even the remotest interest in.

"Pity," he responds, but I can sense it bugs him. Good.

We walk a few more steps in loaded silence before the shadow of Arcadia House falls over us.

"Is she... is she in there?" I ask, unable to keep the hint of hope from my voice.

"Well, no. Sofia has a... rather difficult relationship with the authorities, I'm afraid. Besides, the Assembly is only for members of our community who have been explicitly invited by one of the elders."

I nod, hiding my disappointment.

As we approach the entrance, I notice two women flanking the doors. They're dressed in understated, all-silver bodysuits, and I remember occasionally seeing similarly dressed women when I was growing up, in a picture or during an official gathering Mama would take us to. These witches are magical law enforcement officers, a witchy police force tasked with maintaining order in the magical world.

The line of attendees moves steadily as each person reaches the door. The women greet them with practiced smiles, then extend one hand, palm up. The visitors place their own hands atop, and for a brief moment, the silver witches close their eyes, feeling for something.

I realise this must be how they're verifying ICAG registration. These witches likely have some form of sensory ability, attuned to feel the unique magical signature of registered witches and druids. It's elegant in its simplicity – no wands, no incantations, just a subtle, almost imperceptible check that would look like nothing more than a handshake to unknowing observers.

Nostalgia settles over me, and suddenly I'm thirteen again, watching my mother trace sigils in the air with her fingertips, casting protection spells around our house. It's both comforting and weird, this sudden re-immersion in a world I thought had cast me out.

Most of the people in line are allowed to pass without fuss. However, occasionally, one of the silver-clad women furrows her brow slightly, discreetly directing a visitor to a side entrance. I assume these are either unregistered members or those requiring additional verification. Guess I know where I'll be going in a minute...

And now my heart rate quickens with each step.

The younger of the two witches greets me. She's in her early thirties, with light brown hair in a sleek ponytail and keen blue eyes that move like they're cataloguing everything.

"Welcome to the Assembly," she says, extending her hand towards me. "May I?"

My palm is embarrassingly clammy as I place it in hers. For a moment, nothing happens but then, as expected, that brow of hers furrows.

"I'm sorry, but I'll need you to step this way," she says quietly, gesturing towards that side door.

My stomach drops as Mr Guise follows closely behind, and we're led into a small room not much bigger than a broom closet. Cramped behind a desk sits an older witch, who, up until the moment we enter, looks terribly bored. Her eyes, however, brighten with recognition as we enter. "Mardequai, what a treat," she says, her tone overly friendly, an Irish lilt colouring her words. "It's been far too long."

Mr Guise inclines his head slightly. "Indeed, it has, Siobhan."

"What mischief have you hatched that they send you back here to me?"

"Well, Siobhan, this young witch has come all the way from Germany, and she is here at my personal invitation; however, she's not currently registered as a practicing witch under the ICAG."

Siobhan's gaze shifts to me, her left eyebrow curving sceptically. "People have come from way farther than Germany, Mardequai. If she's not registered, she's not to enter. You know the rules."

"Come now, old friend," Mr Guise says. "Surely, we can make an exception. After all, the Dunnock Coven owes me a debt or two, does it not?"

"A *debt*?"

"Why, have you forgotten the Galway incident? I certainly have not. I so rarely forget a thing."

Siobhan's face pales slightly, her composure cracking. Mr Guise says, now barely above a whisper, "It would be a shame if certain... *details* were to resurface. Especially now, with the Druid Council already scrutinising your every move."

Siobhan's eyes narrow, a silent exchange passing between her and the druid. The tension in the room intensifies, and I'm caught in the middle of what feels like an age-old power struggle between Witch and Druid.

Finally, Siobhan sighs, considering me over the rim of her glasses. "Are you even gifted, lass?"

"I mean... I haven't... It's... it's been a while since I—"

"Go on, then, wield some Anima for me. We don't have all day."

Uncertainty flickers through me as I survey the room. It's been years since I wielded magic intentionally, but I feel the knowledge is still within me, buried deep. I reach out with all my senses, feeling for the Anima around me. The room is alive with the steady hum of the building's electricity, the faint power of sunlight through the tiny window, even the subtle energy of the potted plant in the corner.

My eyes land on a crack in the wooden desk, a jagged line marring its surface. Slowly, carefully, I begin to draw on the Anima sources around me. It's like trying to remember how to ride a bicycle, clumsy at first, but then muscle memory kicks in.

I focus on the crack, channelling the gathered Anima. Gradually, the crack begins to close, fibres weaving back together like patchwork. As I do this, the plant's leaves droop ever so slightly, and the overhead light dims – it's working.

It feels like using an untrained muscle after an injury, my body craving for what it was always meant to do. But as my desk repair nears completion, I feel something shifting inside me, and that alarms me. My powers surge, threatening to overwhelm my work as a wanting rises within me. A wanting for... *more*. Yes, more. I want to keep drawing energy, and not to fix, but to *destroy*. To splinter the desk, reduce it to kindling.

And then my breath catches when for a moment there, I'm not sure I can stop. It takes every ounce of willpower to sever the connection between Anima and me. Alas, the desk is repaired, but my hands are trembling from the near-slip of control.

"Very well then," Siobhan says, not unkindly. She seems satisfied with my demonstration – and, thankfully, oblivious to my internal struggle. She retrieves a thick book, its cover embossed with ancient runes.

Mr Guise, however, has noticed what happened. His eyes are fixed on me and there's a slight upturn to his lips – he has seen something in me that he's delighted to have found, and now

I can't shake the feeling that I've just revealed more than I wanted, after all.

"If she's to participate at the Assembly, she needs to register right now," says the witch. "Normally, you're supposed to do that with your local coven, have a proper initiation and all. But I suppose you can join a London coven for now... Let's see..."

As she opens the book, I notice that the pages, undeniably, are made of Chyulu parchment, more than I ever thought existed in the world. The use of the material makes perfect sense, seeing as Chyulu parchment is inherently binding. Once your name is inscribed on its surface, you've entered into a magical contract.

"Most established covens in London are closed to new members, but there's a new one still accepting..." Siobhan glances at me, her lips twisting. "Beggars can't be choosers, I suppose. The Venus in Furs Coven it is." Her nose wrinkles at the name. "I'll need to contact the magistrate to see if she'd be happy to take you on. This might take a while."

I nod, still buzzing from the rush of wielding Anima again.

"That won't be necessary," Mr Guise says.

"Why is that?" Siobhan and I ask simultaneously.

"I happen to be acquainted with the young witch who founded this particular coven."

Siobhan scrutinises him. "I know you are, but still..."

My mouth forms a small O as I'm about to ask the obvious question, but then my eyes land on the top of the page. The answer is right there in bold handwriting: Ember Wild. A jolt of excitement runs through my body. In just an instant, the distance between Sofia and me has shrunken dramatically.

"Your diligence is commendable, Siobhan. But the wheels of time are turning, and we must not impede their progress any further. Consider it done and let this be the end of it."

Siobhan's lips twitch once more. "Sign here, please," she says, handing me a quill, her eyes still on Mardequai.

And suddenly, it's that easy. Just like that, I'll be a witch again, officially, legally, and for real. Ingrid Brauer's words echo in my head. *You must never practise magic. Ever again.*

I realise I have a choice now. If I don't register, I can't go inside. If I can't go inside, I've thwarted Mr Guise's plan – whatever that might entail once we're past the threshold. But what's he to do now if I refuse? I could just walk out of here, seek out that Cauldron club myself. I don't need him for that. I don't *need* to become part of this world again, do I?

My hand hovers over the parchment. Beyond the stone walls, I can feel the pulse of magic, a siren song calling me home. It thrums through my body, making my skin crawl and my heart rate pick up. The longing rises in me, too, a dangerous current threatening to sweep away years of restraint.

And then, for just a moment, I hear Ruth's voice, a whisper in the back of my mind. *Go ahead,* she murmurs. *You know you want to.* The very fact that I can hear her, and that her words excite me, should be enough to make me turn and run.

"What's it going to be, lass?" asks Siobhan.

I meet her eyes, then Mr Guise's, and finally look down at the parchment before me. My hand trembles slightly as I grip the quill. With a flourish that feels significant, I write my name on the paper.

And the ink glimmers as it dries.

Chapter Seven

The Mandrake penthouse is a showcase in luxury, the midday sun streaming through the floor-to-ceiling windows exposing every detail. At the heart of the room lies a king-sized bed, its frame encased in sleek white Veronese marble, vintage chandeliers dangling from the high ceilings above. Beneath the sumptuous Italian sheets, Ember lies intertwined with last night's conquest – a striking redhead with milky skin and a smattering of freckles in exactly the right places.

Ember was offered a residency at the one-of-a-kind suite on the condition that she tagged the hotel in her posts and allowed them to advertise her stay. She jumped at the opportunity, feeling it was high time she established her own space in London away from Mardequai's Belgravia mansion. She had expected some resistance from him, a token protest at the very least. Yet Mardequai had acquiesced with a mere nod, his easy compliance catching her off guard. It was rare for a man who relished exerting his dominion over others to surrender even an iota of control, and the lenience left Ember wondering.

Once released into the wild, she couldn't resist putting her own signature touches on the suite, insisting on "up-embering" it to her needs. The once muted colour palette has been replaced with bold splashes of hot pink and fun gold accents. Plush velvet furnishings in rich tones invite languid lounging, while exotic plants add a touch of wildness – and a convenient source of Anima, should Ember ever run dry. She only left untouched the sprawling marble bathroom, a sanctuary unto itself with double vanities, a steam room, and a six-person Jacuzzi bath including a retractable roof (and the scene of last nights' champagne-fuelled tryst).

The electronic beep of the door signals someone entering with a key card, and Ember stretches like a sated cat at the sound. Moments later, Pippa strides into the suite, a garment bag draped over one arm while the other balances a cardboard tray laden with two coffee drinks. A ginger cat opens one eye from its perch on the windowsill, observing the commotion with lazy indifference.

"Rise and shine, Sofia. Today is a big day, and when I say that I mean that it's a big day for me, not you." Pippa glides across the room, hanging the bag on the bathroom door before depositing the coffee tray on the nightstand. Her insistence on using Ember's given name is a small act of defiance, one that irks her charge to no end. Yet she's the only person who can get away with it without facing Ember's wrath. "I've got a laundry list of errands to run before tonight," says Pippa, "so let's make this painless for both of us, shall we? Out of bed – now. You've got a facial at two, Milo's due for hair and makeup right after, to render you presentable, early dinner with the coven at six, then it's off to the club."

Ember's tousled head emerges from beneath the bedsheets, a mischievous glint in her eye. "Only presentable? How about utterly ravishing?"

"Let's not set ourselves up for disappointment, shall we?" Pippa says, proffering one of the coffees. "Up you get. I'm not even supposed to be here right now but you're already running behind schedule, so chop-chop!"

Ember's spindly legs, adorned with intricate tattoos that wind like vines up her thighs, swing out from under the sheets. She reaches for a silk kimono, embroidered with golden wings on the back that seem to spread as she moves. She leaves it deliberately loose and open at the chest, the fabric whispering against her skin. Not that Pippa seems to notice; she's already busy arranging the chaos that is Ember's life on her tablet.

Ember's raven hair, a wild tangle this morning, frames her face in an artful chaos as she pads over to the dining table, nearly tripping over Janis Joplin, weaving between her legs with a demanding meow. The table is littered with the remains of last night's escapades – champagne bottles, a scatter of tarot cards, and bizarrely, a taxidermied fox wearing a cute top hat. Ember perches on the edge of the table, crossing her legs as she sips her coffee.

As the caffeine kicks in, so do the intrusive thoughts she's been desperately trying to drown in alcohol for days.

"I've got a different idea: how about we scrap all those tedious plans you've made and jet off somewhere instead?" she suggests. Janis Joplin hops onto the table, delicately avoiding the tarot cards as she snarls at the taxidermied fox, then pushes the creature until it drops to the floor. Ember picks up the cat, consulting her for travel advice. "Cappadocia, perhaps? Hm, what do you think, Janis? Or Tokyo! I hear the autumn foliage in Rikugien Garden is particularly stunning. My treat, of course."

Pippa studies Ember over the rim of her coffee cup. "What's going on with you? You've been especially unhinged lately. Is this about the GAAG?"

"You mean the *Gaaaaag!*," Ember corrects with a face that suggests she's about to hurl.

The upcoming Global Assembly of Arcane Guardians has become a sore point for many young witches, Ember included. The old guard barely acknowledges the perspectives and concerns of the younger generation, and with minimal representation at the GAAG, their voices are effectively silenced. Hence the reason Ember decided to throw a *Gaaaaag!* party at the Cauldron, an anti-assembly bash on the opening night of the great gathering. It's to be a raucous celebration of youth and rebellion, a clear message to the establishment that they won't be ignored. The buzz around the event is already electric, promising to draw young witches from across the globe. And yet, at this point that's nothing if not everyday life for Ember. Last week, she partied in Saint-Tropez, and just yesterday, she was spotted shopping on Bond Street with Celeste Devereaux, the social media savvy witch known for her viral spell-casting tutorials. No, the true source of Ember's recent unrest lies not in her burgeoning fame, but in a closely guarded secret she's yet to share with anyone – including Pippa.

"Do you have siblings?" Ember says suddenly, deceptively casual.

"I have two brothers. Mike and Edward."

"Younger or older?"

"Older. They run a pub together, back in Surrey."

"I'd like to meet them some day."

"No, you wouldn't."

"Why?"

"Because they'd probably — Oh, goodness gracious, I thought you were alone." Pippa's fingers instinctively flutter up to her brow and she spins to face the window when Ember's flame-haired companion emerges from the tangled sheets, unabashedly nude.

"Where am I?" the redhead mumbles.

"Why, you're in heaven, darling," Ember replies, spreading her arms. "Allow me to introduce you to Pippa, the Angel of Schedules and Caffeine Delivery. And I, of course, am – *God*, here to absolve your sins and turn them into art."

Pippa's eyes roll so hard they almost turn white. "That's quite enough blasphemy for one morning," she says. Turning to the bewildered redhead, she continues in a more professional voice, "You're at the Mandrake in Fitzrovia, dear. Would you like me to call you a taxi?"

"Nah, I'll take the Tube," the redhead replies, glancing around for her clothing.

"The nearest station is Tottenham Court Road," Pippa offers helpfully.

The redhead nods, gathering her things. She shimmies into her dress, runs a hand through her tousled curls, and stuffs her shoes into her oversized handbag. With an awkward wave and a mumbled "thanks for...," she shuffles out of the room.

Pippa takes a long swig of her latte as if to hide what she's thinking. But, naturally, she can't stop herself. "You know, you witches are absolute rubbish at relationships."

"Is that so? Do enlighten me, O Wise One."

"Come off it. As if you didn't use a forgetting spell on her to avoid the morning-after awkwardness."

Ember saunters towards the bathroom, coffee sloshing dangerously. "How many witches have you met besides me?"

"I've met, you know, a few..." Pippa's voice rises as Ember disappears from view. "And that is why I can say with absolute confidence that I have no desire to ever hook up with one."

A laugh echoes from the bathroom. "Bold of you to assume you haven't already."

Pippa darts after Ember. "You wouldn't *dare*," she warns, even pointing a finger for emphasis.

Ember grabs her by the shoulders. "No, I wouldn't. Not with you anyway," she lies. Letting go of Pippa, she allows her robe to drop to the floor, as her assistant studiously looks the other way. "But don't knock it till you try it, that's all I'm saying. Can't you picture it, Pippa darling?" Ember pulls open the steam room door, releasing a billowing cloud of vapour. She steps inside, her silhouette blurring as the mist envelops her. "You, me, a stone cottage in the Surrey Hills. A couple of chickens, a couple of sheep? Mike and Eddy coming over for a picnic and some Pimm's?"

Pippa snorts, leaning against the doorframe. "Don't call him that to his face – not that you'd ever meet him, mind you."

"Why is that?" Ember's voice is now muffled by the glass.

"My family doesn't know I work for you." Pippa shrugs. "They think I'm in finance."

Ember's head pops out, wreathed in steam. "My, my, Miss Watson. You've been holding out on me. I do love a woman with secrets."

Pippa blinks twice, then: "You want that facial at the salon or up here?"

"I want it right here, angel. Why come down from heaven when it's so nice and steamy?" Ember winks suggestively.

Pippa turns on her heel. "Salon it is. I'll be back in half an hour to collect you," she calls over her shoulder as she exits the room.

Ember chuckles and retreats into the steam room, the door closing with a soft thud.

She leans back against the tiled wall, letting the warmth envelop her. For a moment, she revels in the silence, her muscles relaxing as her skin absorbs the steam. Outside, Janis Joplin paws at the door, letting out a disgruntled yowl at being left behind.

But as the minutes tick by, a subtle shift occurs. The warmth that was so inviting now feels a touch too hot. It's almost oppressively hot in here now, as if the small space might soon explode around her. And in her sudden panic at the sensation, her mind wanders to those places she's tried to avoid for days.

Alva must have arrived in London by now.

At the Ivy, Ember had asked Mardequai what he meant, suggesting the accident was Alva's fault. In her mind it had always been a tragic combination of events – her father's distraction coinciding with that dangerous bend in the road. She'd never so much as entertained the notion of blaming her sister.

But Mardequai's response sent a chill through her. "You yourself have spoken of the darkness within her, child," he said, his eyes grave. "Those memories of your grandmother's dark deeds – they've cast longer shadows over her than your youthful eyes could have perceived." And then, a warning: "Exercise caution when you reunite with her. Remember what I've taught you, the most treacherous waters are those that appear calm on the surface."

And that's how it happened: with those words, Mardequai had planted a seed of doubt in Ember's mind, one that refuses to be uprooted no matter how much she yearns to see her sister again. And it isn't just his cryptic warning; if she's being honest there has always been an undeniable undercurrent of anger simmering beneath Ember's skin, a rage she only now admits she has buried deep, pushed down because it had nowhere to go, no one to direct it towards.

But faced with Alva's survival, Ember finds herself grappling with an uncomfortable question: has she only absolved Alva of blame because she believed her sister dead? And does her reappearance change the story Ember has told herself for years?

Emerging from the steam room, she shakes her head as if to rid herself of the worry, then steps into the adjoining shower for a quick rinse. Refreshed, she slips into a pair of high-waisted black leather pants and an emerald-green blouse. As she zips up her ankle boots, her fingers tremble slightly, though probably more from the booze than the distress. Ready or not, she's about to dive headfirst into the stormy waters she's been avoiding. Alva's arrival in London means there's no more avoiding the past, however bitter it might taste.

Ember gives herself a final once-over in the mirror, when Pippa's voice pulls her back.

"Oi, Cinderella! Your carriage has arrived. Though if you don't hurry, it might turn back into a pumpkin... or I might just leave you here."

Chapter Eight

Few places exist in the world where Anima courses as freely as breath – Arcadia House is one of them.

The grand entry hall expands before me, an impressive space representing both magical heritage and modern politics. Unlike the fantastic scenes from children's books, the magic here is subtle, almost invisible. The building has the grandeur of the UN General Assembly, but with an undercurrent of raw Anima that sets my skin tingling.

Large windows line the walls, allowing sunlight to stream in, which nourishes the abundance of plants strategically placed throughout the room. Philodendron moonlight cascades from hanging baskets, its leaves stretching down like long fingers. English ivy creeps along trellises, forming living partitions between seating areas. Snake plants stand tall in corners, their sword-like leaves strong and imposing despite the little water they require.

These types of plants, known for their ability to generate Anima with minimal draw on their surroundings, create a perfectly self-sustaining magical ecosystem.

For me, the temptation is almost overwhelming. My fingers crackle with magic, wanting nothing more than to reach out and grasp some of that energy swirling all around me, to wield it simply because I now can. I glance at Mardequai, who has been keeping a watchful eye on me the entire time. But suddenly, a commotion erupts back at the entrance – a group of druids and witches engaged in a heated debate – and Mardequai's attention is drawn away as he turns to assess the situation.

Seizing the moment, I act. Attempting a small spell from my childhood, I use a simple air-fetch charm to make a brochure from a nearby pile soar through the air into my hand.

As I draw on the Anima, it rushes into me, wild and oh so intoxicating. But no sooner does the brochure lift from its pile, than I realise I've underestimated my powers. It's like trying to hold a glass sculpture with soapy hands. The brochure, instead of gently floating, shoots upward, spinning out of control, threatening to tear itself apart.

With effort, I force myself to release my grasp on the Anima. For a heart-stopping moment, it seems to resist, clinging to me like static. Then, all at once, it snaps back like a rubber band, leaving me slightly shaken. The brochure falls to the ground, its edges crumpled and slightly singed. I hope no one saw that.

But just as I'm about to reach for the brochure, Mardequai turns back. He bends down, picking it up with a fluidity that belies his age. As he hands it to me, a smile plays at the corners of his mouth.

"Eager to flex those magical muscles, are we?" he asks.

"That wasn't me," I lie, taking the brochure from his hands, then stuffing it into the back pocket of my jeans.

With a gesture, Mardequai leads the way, and I sidle up next to him. We're like two leaves carried by the same stream, flowing in the same direction – close enough for our edges to brush occasionally, yet separate at the same time.

Around us, witches from across the globe fill the space, their lively chatter the dominating sound beneath the rustle of leaves. Some pause near the plants, their hands hovering, casually drawing on the Anima with subtle gestures as they keep up with their conversations. Others engage in quiet demonstrations of their craft, manipulating small objects or magically refilling near-empty water bottles. Every once in a while, one of the silver-clad witches weaves through the crowd, ensuring law and order at such a large gathering.

Druids are present too, but they're vastly outnumbered, perhaps one for every ten witches. Indeed, the druids pass through the Assembly Hall like great sharks gliding through a sea of darting, colourful fish.

As I step into this spectacle, I can't help but feel a pang of regret for a choice I had no part in making. The Reveal will mean the end of what I've always cherished most about magic: the comfort of knowing there's this hidden world no one else knows about. Magic has been my sanctuary in a world that often feels devoid of any wonders, a reminder that there's more than meets the eye, a private joy that made my days bearable, whether I actively wielded Anima or not. And now, that sanctuary is about to be thrown open to the masses, its mysteries laid bare for all to see.

Had I been able to vote, what would my choice have been? Initially, my gut gravitated towards a strong yes, but I cannot deny my worry to share all this with the world.

I cast a side glance at the man next to me, my steps involuntarily syncing with his. Mardequai's gait is unhurried, his demeanour relaxed. Yet there's also tension in his body, a subtle alertness in the way his eyes flick from face to face as people pass.

Why *would* he have me speak today? I know *my* reasons, but I can't for the life of me figure out what his game is. Does he think I'll warn everyone against the madness of a reveal? I suppose I could understand the sentiment. After all, druids have lived through centuries of witch hunts, persecutions, and at least one misguided attempt to merge the magical with the mundane. They have seen firsthand how fear and greed can corrupt even the noblest intentions. But even if I were to paint a vivid picture of the dangers that might await us, does he really believe that *I* could sway the entire magical community at the last minute? Besides, I have no intention of doing that. The more I highlight Ruth's darkness, the more shadows I cast on myself.

Dread fills me at the thought of standing before all these people. Will they see me as a valuable resource, an oracle who can guide them around potential pitfalls — or as a threat to be neutralised, a reincarnation in the flesh of the most notorious witch in history?

I break away from my imposed companion, drifting towards a large table where two people are engrossed in conversation over a miniature version of downtown London. As I approach, I overhear two witches standing nearby.

"Who's that?" one asks, nodding towards the man at the table.

The other witch looks shocked. "You don't know? That's Elias Klein, the famous Silicon Valley druid. Word has it he's got more riches than Elon Musk and Jeff Bezos combined."

I turn my attention back to the table, studying Klein. He looks more like a hip college professor from the sixties, with his brown corduroy pants, sky-blue button-down shirt, and waxed canvas messenger bag hanging off his shoulder.

As I draw closer, I overhear the discussion he's engaged in.

"Look here," says Klein, his finger hovering over the painted river running through the mini city. "The Anima flow along the Thames has weakened considerably in the past ten years. If this continues, we'll see the Resonance Network operating at critically low levels."

The witch beside him, her long hair hanging over the table, nods gravely. "It never used to be like that. I remember when I was young, the river was so charged that we'd bottle Thames water for our workings. Back in '82, I used a single vial to keep the Tube running for ten hours straight during that massive power outage. Trains moved smoothly, signals stayed green, and not a single commuter suspected a thing." She shakes her head, a hint of nostalgia in her eyes. "Now, you'd be lucky to keep a single station operational for a minute with the same amount."

As I watch, she manipulates the model with subtle hand movements. Glowing lines begin to pulse through the tiny city, some bright and strong, others barely flickering.

Klein's voice grows serious. "This is why I strongly recommend working with modern technology as soon as the magical reveal is underway. We need to integrate AI into the Resonance Network. Without this fusion of magic and tech, we're looking at catastrophic failures within a year. Maybe less. The time to shift is *now*."

The elderly witch looks sceptical, but Klein continues with conviction.

It's then that the enormity of the situation begins to sink in for me. My personal concerns, which seemed so all-consuming just moments ago, feel trivial in comparison to the giant shift about to take place. This is *world-altering*. How are we – and I suppose it *is* "we", as of ten minutes ago – supposed to manage a global transition of this magnitude? It's like introducing an apex predator into an ecosystem that's never seen one before. The balance could shift dramatically, but whether towards harmony or chaos I could never dare to predict.

My eyes drift across the room, landing on Mardequai. He's engaged in an intense conversation with a group of druids. Even from this distance, I can sense the gravity of their discussion. Suddenly, he looks up, catching my gaze. With a nod at his companions, he makes his way towards me.

"It is time to take our seats," he announces. "The welcome ceremony is about to commence."

As we enter the main hall, I'm immediately struck by its breathtaking openness. There's no roof; instead, a canopy of ivy vines stretches overhead, filtering the sunlight into a dappled pattern on the floor. I've seen images of this space before, but being here in person is entirely different.

Passing through the grand oak doors is like stepping into an amphitheatre nestled in the heart of a forest despite being in the centre of London. The circular room descends in tiers, each level a harmonious blend of stone and nature. Moss-covered steps lead down to a central dais, while ferns and small flowering plants sprout from crevices in the walls. The air is noticeably fresher here, tinged with the scents of earth and growing, living things. Small streams trickle down the walls, feeding the plant life and creating a soothing background murmur that drowns out any traffic noise from outside.

This is the Emerald Court.

Mardequai motions me across the moss-covered floor towards the stairs on our right. As we ascend, I notice how the stone seems to give slightly underfoot, as if the entire structure were alive and breathing. We approach a section that looks like a gloomy gathering of storm clouds. The druids, all seated together in their grey suits, create a stark contrast to the greenery surrounding them, as if winter has frozen over this corner of the Emerald Court. As I study their faces, I can't help but wonder about their true ages. Some appear middle-aged, others elderly, but their eyes tell a different story – one of centuries, perhaps millennia of experience. I recall the whispered tales I've heard about the fate of druids who tire of their endless existence.

They say that when immortality becomes too much to bear, these ancient men retreat to secluded monasteries high in remote mountain ranges. There, they enter into profound meditative states, their consciousness practically merging with the very stone of the earth. Over time, they become indistinguishable from the mountains themselves – alive, yet as still and patient as the rocks.

Looking at the assembled druids, I wonder how many of them are approaching that final retreat.

We reach Mardequai's seat, marked with his name on a plaque integrated seamlessly into the armrest.

"Ambrose, old friend," he greets the man seated next to him, whose nameplate reads A. HUDSPETH.

"Ah, Mardequai. I wondered when you might be arriving." The man's eyes land on me. "And who is this? A new protégé?"

"No," Mardequai replies with a hint of amusement. "This... is Alva Hausmann, and she has thus far proven impervious to any of my persuasions."

Ambrose's eyes lock onto me at the mention of my name, and I feel a familiar dread settle in my stomach. It's been years since I've faced this reaction, but bearing my grandmother's name has always been a burden. My mother, with her gentle nature and her tireless dedication to using her magic for good, had begun to unravel the harsh legacy she was left with. She must have been tempted to adopt Dad's surname after their wedding, but witches aren't permitted to change their names; it's a way of magical bloodline tracking, similar to how some indigenous cultures maintain specific naming systems to preserve family or clan identities. And so, the scrutiny never truly faded, following us like a persistent shadow. Naturally, when word spread of my ability, cursing me with perfect recall of Ruth's life as if it were my own, things once again became... complicated.

Now Hudspeth takes my hand in greeting, and I brace

myself for those usual reactions: fear, suspicion, judgment. But what I see in his face is something else. It's not scrutiny or condemnation that widens his eyes – it's utter shock.

He lets go of my hand without so much as a 'How do you do?', then settles back into his seat.

"I suppose we'll have words later?" Hudspeth mumbles, eyes fixed ahead, words barely emerging from the corner of his mouth, but rather disappearing in his own cheek pouch.

"Indeed, my friend. Indeed." Mardequai settles into his seat. I clear my throat, arching an eyebrow to highlight my own lack of seating.

He glances up at me. "Ah, yes. May I ask that you sit with your kind, please, Fräulein?" He gestures towards the neighbouring tier. "We are all united under the same roof, of course. However, druids and witches are like oil and water in a single vessel. While we coexist, we do not mix well, I'm afraid."

I nod and make my way over to the witch section, suddenly aware of the sea of strangers. Hesitating, I scan the rows for an empty seat, unsure where to place myself among them.

"Would you like to sit here, love?"

I turn to find a witch a few rows up, her ginger hair braided around her head like a crown. She pats the empty seat beside her, a smile activating the wrinkles around her mouth. "My cousin couldn't make it, so this one's free."

"I'd love to, thank you," I reply with relief and settle into the seat.

The witch who offered it extends her hand. "I'm Maeve, by the way, of the Waxwing Coven, Newport."

"Alva," I respond, grateful Maeve went for first names and covens only. Still, I feel a flush of embarrassment when I add, "of the... um... Venus in Furs Coven?" I say the last part quickly.

Maeve snorts. "You kids today," she mumbles, then she reaches for a brochure and starts leafing through it.

I gaze around the amphitheatre, taking in the diversity of faces and languages. I spot Māori tattoos, African head-wraps, and the red dots of the bindi. To my right, a group chats in Mandarin, while somewhere behind me, smooth French tones blend with the old familiar guttural sounds of German. Only when I hear my mother tongue does the thought strike me that I might recognise someone – or someone might know *me*. I carefully look over my shoulder, scanning the witchy section to my right. I certainly wouldn't want to run into Ingrid Brauer right about now. Then again, I doubt she'd be here. My mother's coven was a rather small one, and Frau Brauer, if I remember Mama's stories correctly, had never travelled farther than the Dutch border to restock on cannabis, which she was rather fond of smoking.

Relieved as I remember this, I give the section a good scan, but nobody looks familiar. I notice, however, that many attendees have kicked off their shoes. Another memory flashes, of my mother, laughing as she pulled me barefoot through the garden, teaching me to feel the earth's heartbeat, something I have since fiercely maintained. Dennis worries about me whenever we go for walks back home in the woods, scared I might catch a splinter or, I don't know, step in some deer poo. Merely to appease him, I'd told him I'm into this whole 'earthing thing'.

"You're so woke," he'd teased me. "Earthing yourself like some Berlin hipster."

I suppose he had a point. Earthing, after all, is just a fancy word for walking the way we're supposed to walk – barefoot, connected to the ground. It's the same with everything these days. We "forage" instead of... *finding food*. We don't just sit in the shade of trees – no, now it's "forest bathing". Even "Nature" gets capital letters now, treated like some separate entity. It's as if we're trying to rediscover what we never should have forgotten in the first place.

Not hesitating, I slip off my own shoes like the rest of the witches, toes curling into the moss-covered floor.

There is, of course, a glimmer of hope in this fumbling human attempt to reconnect, and it's happening not a moment too soon. Perhaps it's even this very shift that pushed the magical community to finally take the plunge and reveal themselves.

As I look around the court, lost in contemplation, I suddenly lock eyes with a man – a druid, I can only assume – staring intently at me from across the space. A serious face, his lean frame accentuated by a well-tailored suit. He stands rigidly beside one of the moss-covered pillars, his posture taut as if he's suppressing a scream. Although it's practically impossible to tell a druid's true age, in human terms he appears to be in his early thirties, thirty-three, thirty-four tops.

There's something unsettling about the way he looks at me, as if he's peering straight through my skin. His stare is unwavering, and I find myself fighting the urge to fidget or look away.

His intense scrutiny makes me acutely aware of my desire to blend in, to be just another attending witch. But under his gaze, I feel exposed, as if every secret I've ever kept is written plainly across my forehead. I resist the urge to shrink back, to make myself smaller. Instead, I meet his eyes with what I hope is a look of cool indifference, but my heart betrays me, racing ahead, while my palms grow damp.

A deep gong reverberates through the chamber, and I break eye contact with the stranger, drawn instead to the grand oak doors, which begin to close of their own accord, like the petals of a giant flower folding in at sunset.

Inspired by Maeve, I remember my own brochure I'd snatched earlier. Drawing it from the back pocket of my jeans, I unfold the glossy paper and scan its contents. The Assembly stretches over the course of a week, including field trips to the countryside, workshops around human–magic interactions, and panel discussions on PR efforts and risk factors. The big reveal is scheduled to happen at a climate summit on Wednesday. My eyes linger on the "Historical Context of Magical Intervention in Human Affairs" panel, a knot forming in my throat. This, no doubt, will contain a deep dive into my family's history.

I lower the brochure, the scope of this entire endeavour becoming more and more apparent to me as the Assembly begins to hush around me. I can't resist the urge to let my gaze drift back to where the stranger had been standing. But the corner is empty now. I blink, wondering if I imagined him, when a witch in a cerulean blue robe, her dark skin adorned with shimmering gold armlets and her stride exuding quiet authority, takes to the podium. A low hum begins to build, and I look around at the sound, watching as witch after witch joins the growing chorus. Their voices blend into a resonant drone that vibrates through my bones, grounding yet electrifying. But as my gaze sweeps across the room, drinking in this display of unity, it suddenly snags on that intense stare again. Two rows up, in the (non-humming) druid section over my left shoulder, sits the brooding stranger, eyes once again burning into me with unwavering focus, almost as if in pain. The hair on the back of my neck stands on end, a chill racing down my spine despite the warmth of the collective energy in the room. Those scant few feet between us shrink to nothing under his gaze, and I feel laid bare, stripped of my cover like a diary ripped open to its most private page.

Chapter Nine

Silence falls like a curtain as the woman on stage raises her hands. With her arms outstretched, she draws every soul in the amphitheatre toward her like a conductor calling her orchestra to attention.

Maeve leans over and whispers excitedly in my ear, "I've always wanted to hear Gathoni Nyong'o speak in person!"

I glance down at the brochure in my hand, confirming that yes, this is indeed the head elder presiding over today's welcome ceremony.

"Sisters, brothers, esteemed colleagues, and dear friends," Gathoni Nyong'o begins, her voice resonating like the deep notes of a cello. "Today, we stand at the precipice of a new era. Some of us have voted in favour of the Reveal, others against it. But it fills my heart with joy to see that witches and druids unite in its execution despite any personal preferences."

I feel a ripple of excitement course through the audience as Gathoni speaks of collaboration with humanity. Her words carry the distinct cadence of her East African heritage as she explains how interconnectedness is the foundation of Anima herself.

"Collaboration, my friends, is the song of this earth. Look at the forests, the coral reefs, the savannahs – every ecosystem thrives on symbiosis. Each creature, each plant, each organism plays its part in the dance of life."

"But humans," she says, "humans have long strayed from this path. They've chosen competition over cooperation, domination over harmony."

As she points toward the concrete jungles and polluting industries of humanity, I find myself nodding along, captivated by her vision. She speaks of humans having lost their connection to nature, her voice softening with motherly concern.

"This is why we must reveal ourselves. Not to rule over them, not to save them – but to *remind* them. To show them that there is another way. To reawaken their sense of wonder, their connection to Anima and Mother Earth."

The head elder inhales deeply before elaborating on how witches can teach humans to reconnect with nature. Her words stir something deep within me, and as the room erupts in humming affirmation, I join in. Maeve next to me squeezes my hand, and I realise I've been holding my breath. Sitting here, amongst witches, I'm overcome by a sense of home I thought I'd lost for good. This is where I belong, where I have always belonged. And I want to be a part of this; I want to *do my part*.

Gathoni continues, walking around the stage and emphasising cultural sensitivity in our approach. She speaks passionately about the integration of magical practices with traditional knowledge, particularly in regions like her Kenyan home, where beliefs in witchcraft often inspire fear.

As I listen, the magnitude of this endeavour truly sinks in. Over two hundred thousand witches worldwide, plus about a tenth of that number of druids. All consulted, all given a voice. My mind spins trying to comprehend the years of planning this must have taken.

Curious, I flip through the brochure, searching for answers about how united we truly are, wondering if the vote was a landslide or a close call. But Gathoni's next words snag me out of my distraction, making my stomach twist with shame and guilt.

"...but I cannot stand here before you and speak only of the promise our Reveal holds without addressing its perils, too." Gathoni's hands grip the sides of the podium as if drawing strength from it. "We owe our gratitude to the Druid Council for reminding those of us without eternal memory of a chapter so dark, it stains not just human history, but the annals of witchcraft herself." Her voice lowers. "I speak of Nazi Germany, and the fateful decision of the Schwarzmilan Coven. In their arrogance, they broke our most sacred laws. They revealed themselves to the Gestapo out of a twisted ambition. These witches believed they could manipulate the Nazi regime. They believed they could use Hitler's obsession with the occult to gain power and influence. They offered their magical abilities to enhance the regime's eugenics program, thinking they could create a new order where witches would rule from the shadows."

A collective discomfort takes hold of the audience, and my own chest tightens like Gathoni's grip on the podium.

"They believed they could outsmart evil, that they could ride the lion without being devoured. Instead, their actions unleashed untold suffering and pushed our entire community to the brink of exposure under a regime hellbent on exploiting our abilities for their gain."

"Begs the question of what's so different this time around," mumbles a witch somewhere behind me, and a few heads close by nod in agreement.

A sickening feeling climbs up my throat then, and I struggle to keep Ruth's memories at bay. Sweat beading on my forehead, I catch Mardequai's attention fixed on me. There's a tiny sliver of something in his eyes – reassurance, perhaps – that, despite myself, I find comforting.

But Hudspeth's stare practically flays me, and he isn't the only one bristling. Two rows up, the intense-looking druid's fingers are balled into fists, his jaw clenched tight. He's deliberately not looking at me, I can tell, staring straight ahead with such force that I can almost feel the effort it's taking him not to turn and... what? Lash out? Accuse me? He, too, knows something about me, that much couldn't be more obvious. But what, and how? Who *is* this man?

Just as I think this, his head shoots back in my direction, and I turn away, sinking lower in my seat, wishing I could disappear.

"...but while those crimes committed must never be forgotten, we must also remember two crucial points: one, Schwarzmilan was an isolated incident, born from a misguided sense of superiority, sprouted from a hotbed of frustration and resentment. Never before in the history of witchcraft has a coven disregarded this community; never before has a branch broken off from the mother tree, nor will one ever dare to do so again. We have learnt a hard lesson, and we have put laws and systems in place to prevent this from ever happening again."

Gathoni pauses, her silence heavy with history.

"And two: Those who committed that terrible treason are long gone, punished accordingly for their crimes."

As if summoned by those words, a searing phantom pain crawls up my legs, so intense and unexpected that I have to bite my lip to keep from crying out. I grip the edges of my seat. Panic claws at my throat, threatening to suffocate me as the reason for my presence here today crashes into me with the force of a train – to speak my truth before the Assembly. A truth that could unravel everything Gathoni has just said.

"It was witches," she says with deep regret, "who strayed from the right path. Some argue it's precisely for this reason that we weren't granted the eternal life our wise brothers were given. For no being as powerful as a witch should live forever. To wield Anima as we do requires checks and balances – limitations, yes, but also advice from those who've witnessed centuries unfold, who observe the natural cycles of those who come and go."

She turns toward the druid section as she speaks, her gesture encompassing most of the Emerald Court. A low hum of acknowledgment comes from the witch contingent. But as I observe the druids, I notice a subtle tension in their postures, a tightening around eyes and mouths. They don't seem entirely... *pleased* with this recognition, likely viewing their role as far more significant than mere 'advisers' to the witches. The relationship between our two factions suddenly seems a lot more complex, and maybe more fraught with conflict than I'd previously realised.

"We'd be wise to heed that advice and listen to their cautionary tales. Which is why it is my utmost honour to give the podium to our next speaker. Please welcome to the Assembly, GAAG Elder, Druid Council leader, and my old acquaintance, Mardequai Guise."

As Gathoni finishes her introduction, Mardequai rises with a dignified grace that befits his station. He makes his way towards the podium, and my heart rate quickens with every step he takes. If he's speaking now, could my turn be next? The thought sends anxiety through my body, and I shift in my seat. My foot accidentally lands on Maeve's bare toes, and I whisper a hasty apology.

Mardequai takes his place at the podium. "Cautionary tales. It is an interesting notion, is it not?" His gaze sweeps across the court as if he were standing in the hallowed halls of an ancient cathedral.

"A tale is a fable – a story, a fiction. Tales arc mere words we speak, and the more they are shared, the more they change. The more time passes, the easier it is to forget what must never be forgotten, especially when the voices that first spoke the tale have long fallen silent. This is why Auschwitz still stands, why Mandela's prison cell on Robben Island was not erased but transformed into a memorial. Their presence endures as a testament to human error, silent yet powerful reminders of the darkness we must never allow to resurface.

"But *our* reminder, I'm proud to say, is not a silent one. The Druid is our memorial. The Druid is a living community, here to stand guard as time presses on, like the steady pulse of the earth itself, constant through eons of change." He gestures towards the druid section, his arm outstretched like a prophet's.

"The atrocities the Druid had to witness are etched into His very being. And while some immortals may see promise in an open world, most have urged caution against this Reveal. For the Druid knows. The Druid... *remembers*. We remember everything. We've seen time and time again how humans recoil from the unknown, how easily their fear twists into hatred, and hatred into violence. It was the druids who sheltered witches during the darkest times of the Inquisition. We offered sanctuary in our hidden groves, married witches to provide them cover and protection, and established covert convents where magical knowledge could be preserved and passed on in secret. When the flames of ignorance threatened to consume all that was mystical and sacred, it was the druids who stood as silent guardians, ensuring the survival of our shared magical heritage. We've watched civilisations tear themselves apart over differences far smaller than magic. The human spirit, we've learned, is as capable of great wonder as it is of terrible fear."

Mardequai lets that sink in, and I don't know about everyone else, but I'm surprised by the critical tenor his speech is taking. "Like the lion in the savannah, outnumbered by the many, the druid could not overcome the witches during this referendum, and so, as always, we remain somewhat... removed from yet another fateful decision. We have seen empires rise and crumble to dust, witnessed the birth and death of entire belief systems, and we have outlived them all. And we will watch, and we will witness, as we always have."

The pause that follows is a long one, and I'm already expecting him to finish when Mardequai raises his voice again, now with a distinctive hard edge. "But as I stand before you today, I make no secret of this: should the Druid ever conclude that this community has erred, and should a different path present itself," – a breath, a sweeping look across the assembly – "He will not hesitate to take it, and He will welcome anyone who aligns with His vision of a safer, more prudent future."

At that, the court explodes with chatter. This may be my first Assembly, but even I can tell what Mardequai just said was more than controversial – it was *egregious*. My eyes find Gathoni, seated at the foot of the stage. Her face is almost perfectly controlled, neutral even. But underneath, I catch a glimpse of something else. Discontent, disappointment... *disapproval*, all simmering just below the surface.

And then I finally understand: Mardequai is well aware he cannot undo the vote or sway the entire magical community. But he *can* fracture it, leading as many as will follow away from the fold. And he intends to use my testimony to bolster his argument, to pull the undecided to his side and offer those who voted 'No' an alternative path. *That's* the whole reason he wants me to speak: to divide the Assembly.

I must not let that happen. I won't be his pawn.

My legs seem to move of their own accord, and I rise abruptly. Maeve shoots me a curious glance, but I avoid her eyes. As casually as I can manage, I begin to make my way up the tiered steps, aiming for a discreet exit at the back. My heart pounds in my ears, drowning out the murmurs around me as I'm taking the steps two at a time.

But then Mardequai's next words echo through the court. "You need not take the druid's word for it any longer. It is my duty to bring to this Assembly all the facts, no matter how close to the Reveal we might be…"

I stumble, my foot catching on the edge of a step. I lurch forward, arms flailing – directly towards the intense druid who's been staring at me all this time. In a blur of motion, he leaps from his seat, strong hands grasping my arms. And then our eyes meet up close. His are a striking blue-grey, showing a mess of different emotions, changing so rapidly I can't read any of them. For a second, we're both still, caught in that strange silence. It feels like there's a whole world of unsaid things between us, but how could there be? We've never met before.

Then Mardequai's words slice through our frozen hold, sharp as winter wind. "My dear friends, this might come as a shock to you, but today I present to you… Ruth Hausmann of the Schwarzmilan Coven."

My grandmother's name hits the court like a thunderclap, and the strange druid's grip on my arm vanishes as if I've suddenly burst into flames. As he lets go of me, I collapse to the floor, discarded like a poisonous weed he has mistakenly picked up.

I feel a thousand eyes turn towards me when, slowly, I face the court. It's the most unnatural sensation I've ever experienced – being stared at by so many people, seen not for who I am, but for who they *think* I am.

"Come, witch, come," Mardequai calls, waving me over.

As if sleepwalking, I descend the stairs towards the centre of the room, nervously rubbing the rock in my pocket for comfort. I catch a glimpse of Maeve, her mouth literally hanging open. But then something strikes me as I move: the energy from the room, as of yet, feels more like confusion, like a swirling mist of bewilderment. And it should be. I'm not *her*. How could I be? I'm only twenty-six. I've never so much as killed a spider. How could anyone think I'm her? But, just as this thought forms, I feel Ruth within me, a dormant fire suddenly sparked. Her presence flickers at the edges of my mind, my heart, my soul. I even hear that chilling murmur in the back of my head again. *Oh, but you are me, child. More than you know...*

I reach the podium, and suddenly, unbidden, another memory that isn't mine flashes before my eyes. Standing motionless in the eye of a supernatural tempest, lightning crackling in endless circles overhead, bodies crumpling around me as the storm devours everything in its path. Guards fleeing, witches dying, screams swallowed by howling wind, and through it all, that intoxicating sense of having transcended every boundary, every limit. For a heartbeat, I'm there — I'm *her* — the terrible calm at the centre of absolute destruction.

But just as quickly, I'm back in the present, where Mardequai now steps aside, gesturing for me to take his place at the podium. I turn to face him, our eyes meeting. But now his expression is unreadable.

Whatever it is he wants to extract from me, I must give him anything but.

I must keep it together now.

Chapter Ten

"Would you mind explaining to the Assembly why I have summoned you today, Fräulein Hausmann?" Mardequai asks, his voice carrying across the hall.

I stand behind the podium, my hands gripping its edges to centre myself as a thousand eyes bear down on me. I swallow, trying to moisten my irritatingly dry throat. This moment, standing before the Assembly, is my one chance to reclaim my place in the magical community. After thirteen years of exile, I need them to see me as Alva, not as the shadow of my grandmother. The irony isn't lost on me that I must speak of her to free myself from her.

"Well, first of all, I would like to point out that I am not who you said I am." My small voice betrays my nerves, and for a fleeting moment, I wish I could sound braver and more sure of myself. But then I realise – that kind of tough, take-charge attitude is pure Ruth. Right now, distancing myself from her image is probably the smartest play I could make.

Mardequai's eyebrows rise in mock surprise. He faces the

court. "Why, now you have me confused. You say, your name is not Hausmann?"

"No, I mean... yes, my last name is Hausmann. But my first name is not Ruth, it's Alva."

"How curious. Do please enlighten us, then: who is Ruth Hausmann?"

The bane of my existence, I think bitterly.

"She was my... my grandmother."

A collective gasp comes from the spectators, and I can feel the shift in the room. My relation to the Schwarzmilan magistrate is already enough to condemn me, I realise with a sinking feeling.

"So... why would I have referred to you as Ruth?" Mardequai asks loudly.

"You tell me," I reply, sounding steadier than I feel.

"And so I shall," Mardequai says, and I chide myself when I realise, I probably played directly into his hands. He reaches into his jacket and draws out a folded parchment. As he faces the court, he does so with a note of grave importance.

"I have here a report from the German Magical Ability Assessment Board, dated June 11, 2003. It details the examination of two five-year-old witches: the sisters Alva and Sofia Hausmann."

My stomach churns as I hear this, panic rising like bile in my throat. I didn't think he'd have gotten his hands on an actual copy of my file.

"The report states, and I quote: 'Both subjects exhibit an uncommon ability to access and recall memories from past lives. This manifestation is thus far unheard of among witches and warrants close observation. Sofia Hausmann's ability is classified as Level One, Minor. Her visions are infrequent and lack detail. Current assessment: Unharmful. Alva Hausmann's ability is classified as Level Four, Of Concern. Her visions of Ruth Hausmann's life are vivid, frequent, and show an unusual level of historical accuracy. The board mandates re-examination of Alva Hausmann at two-year intervals until maturity. Close monitoring is advised due to the refined nature and potential implications of her ability. The report concludes with a note: Should Alva Hausmann's ability continue to develop at its current rate, reclassification to Level Five, Dangerous, may be necessary in future assessments."

Mardequai looks up from the report, his eyes locking onto mine. "Is this an accurate account of your assessment, Fräulein Hausmann?"

I feel a surge of defiance rising within me. "Yes, but like the report states, they are just that – visions, nothing else."

Mardequai pivots away from me, his arms folded behind him. "What happened on the third of August 1944, Fräulein Hausmann?"

I feel the blood drain from my face. My throat constricts, and I force a swallow, trying to get rid of my panic. I can't believe he's trying to make me go there.

"Fräulein Hausmann?" Mardequai turns toward me expectantly.

"I... I believe that was the day of the Sylt Massacre."

The moment that last word leaves my lips I want to snatch it back. Damn him for planting it in my head earlier. I could have, should have, phrased that more carefully. But it's too late; here comes yet another collective gasp.

Thankfully, now Gathoni rises from her seat. "Mardequai, this is hardly the time nor the place—"

"But isn't it?" Mardequai interrupts her, smooth as the fine wool of his suit. He turns to speak to the Assembly. "Nobody present on that dreadful day survived. Well, save for the Hausmann witch, but after her capture she refused to speak of what transpired. For decades, we've had to piece together what happened from fragments. Scattered reports, weather anomalies, and the charred remnants left behind. Until now, the full truth has remained hidden in shadow. But don't we all wish to hear it? To understand the full scope of our history, so that we can make informed decisions about the Reveal? Isn't that, after all, what this Assembly is for?"

A low hum of assent rises from the gathered witches and, from the druid section, a rhythmic knocking begins as they collectively bang what appear to be signet rings against the benches in front of them.

Gathoni's lips press into a thin line. She looks around the room, then makes a resigned gesture with her hand. No other choice but to allow this nightmare to continue.

Mardequai turns back to me, a glint of triumph in his eyes. "Please, Fräulein Hausmann, walk us through it. What happened on that day?"

I fight against the visions now threatening to overwhelm me, trying to state everything matter-of-factly. I close my eyes, and her memories flood my mind. "There... there was a weather facility on the island of Sylt."

"What was its purpose?" Mardequai asks.

"To create storm fronts," I reply, angling my face away, focussing on a nondescript spot to my left. "The Nazis... well, they wanted to disrupt Allied bombing raids on northern Germany."

"Go on," he urges.

"Ruth was... she was directing a circle of witches," I struggle to continue. "To manipulate the weather."

"And were all the witches willing participants?" Mardequai asks, leaning forward.

I shift uncomfortably, my silence stretching too long.

"Fräulein Hausmann?" he presses.

"Some were," I say finally.

"Some," he repeats. "And the others?"

I look away. "The others... they didn't have a choice."

"How so?" Mardequai is relentless.

I grip the podium tighter, my knuckles white. "Their families...," I gulp. "Their children were being held."

"Held where?"

"In the camp. Under guard." The words feel like shards of glass in my throat.

"And what would happen to these children if the mothers refused to cooperate?"

I remain silent, my jaw clenched.

"Fräulein Hausmann? Are you still with us?"

"They would be killed," I whisper, the admission tearing something inside me. "In front of their mothers."

A horrified silence falls over the Assembly. Even those who had been whispering among themselves grow still.

"What happened next?" Mardequai prompts.

I manage an irritated look in his direction. "I think we've established enough about what happened that day. The rest is irrelevant to why I'm here."

Mardequai turns to face the Assembly. "Irrelevant? I think not. We stand at a crossroads in our history, and your testimony speaks directly to the danger of human interference with magical forces."

I look desperately toward Gathoni, hoping for an ally. Her eyes meet mine, and I see a flicker of sympathy there, but it's quickly replaced by resignation. "The Assembly requires a complete accounting. You must continue," she says.

I feel trapped, cornered. But I see no path of escape. With a deep breath, I do as she says. "The Nazis ordered them to create a storm larger than ever before," I say. "But they wouldn't allow the proper balancing rituals afterward. Ruth tried to explain the danger, but they wouldn't listen." I press my eyes shut as the memory intensifies. "I can see her at the centre of the circle, directing the others. The storm above growing too powerful, too quickly." I stop, my hands trembling. The memory continues to play vividly behind my eyes, but I cannot – will not – speak it aloud.

"And then?" Mardequai asks with that infuriating persistence, like a teacher coaxing a reluctant student.

I shake my head firmly. "I've said enough."

"The circle collapsed, didn't it?" Mardequai states coldly. "The unbalanced magic rebounded. The storm turned inward with catastrophic force. Every witch in that circle died, all except Ruth Hausmann, the puppet master behind it all." He gestures toward me. "And the children being held hostage? They perished as well. Thirty-one magical children, gone in an instant – all because humans interfered with powers they could not understand."

Murmurs of horror spread through the hall. Some witches look away, unable to bear the weight of this revelation.

"I dare ask, Fräulein Hausmann, what was the true cause of this catastrophe?"

I recoil, all too aware of where he's trying to lead me. "I'm not here to interpret history."

Mardequai's reassesses me, just slightly. "Let me rephrase my question: would this catastrophe have happened if you hadn't conspired with the Nazis – with humans?"

"It wasn't *me*, that's what I keep trying to tell you," I say, desperate to reclaim control of this horrid conversation. "I came here hoping to clear my name, not to speculate about alternative histories or be used as a prop in someone else's argument."

The Assembly stirs restlessly at my unexpected defiance.

But Mardequai recovers quickly. "No need to speculate, because the answer is clear to everyone here. The Sylt Massacre was a warning – and one we seem determined to ignore. What the witch sisterhood has repeatedly failed to anticipate is just how relentless humans are in their pursuit of power. They do not merely use what they discover. No, they exploit it to its breaking point, heedless of consequences that echo for generations."

He paces before the assembly, growing more passionate. "And now, we propose to reveal ourselves to a world whose technology and ambition far exceed what existed in 1944? To humans who have already pushed natural systems to breaking point without magic? What do you suppose will happen when corporations and governments learn they can accelerate their exploitation of nature through magical means?"

His eyes, cold and piercing, find mine. "The disaster at Sylt was contained. But a global reveal in today's world? There will be no containing the consequences when humans inevitably push magic beyond its limits, as they have done with every other power they've discovered."

Suddenly, without warning, I feel something stir within me – not Ruth's memories, but Ruth herself. A presence I've only felt in nightmares, pushing against my consciousness with terrifying strength.

"And was this not precisely why you aligned with the Nazis in the first place?" Mardequai asks. "A misguided attempt to control how magic was used in the world? How did that experiment end, Fräulein Hausmann?"

Something dark and vicious surges within me then, breaking through barriers I didn't know could fail. My mouth opens, but the voice that emerges isn't mine.

"*You* dare question me about control, druid?" The words tear from my throat in a hissing voice I've never used before – harsh and dripping with contempt. "Your kind has choked witches' power for centuries! All I wanted was to pry away the boot you placed on our necks!"

Magic erupts from my fingers then – the kind of magic I haven't used in thirteen years, or maybe ever. The podium splits with a deafening crack, a jagged fissure racing down its middle. I stare at my hands, watching as they move with someone else's purpose.

Even Mardequai's eyes widen in genuine shock – this clearly isn't the response he anticipated. For a moment, his facade slips, revealing something... something almost like fear.

"Enough!"

Not a moment too soon, Gathoni Nyong'o's voice resounds as she joins us on stage. "We are not here to relive the horrors of the past or to place blame on those who were not even born when these atrocities occurred." She lets that settle, making eye contact with a few people in the crowd. "Now, if the Assembly doesn't mind further delay, I must make a few inquiries of my own."

A low hum of assent is the reply, the familiar sound of collective agreement. Next, Gathoni approaches the podium, leaning in close to me, her voice dropping to a murmur only I can hear. "Alva, we must turn this around now, do you hear me? We cannot risk a fracture in our community."

I nod, a flicker of relief sparking at her use of 'we'. For the first time since this ordeal began, I don't feel entirely alone.

"First of all, Alva, I would like you to understand that you are not required to answer any questions if you don't wish to do so. This is not a court hearing. This isn't even in our already tight schedule," she adds with a sharp look at Mardequai, who has stepped off the stage.

"I understand, but I... I want to," I reply.

Gathoni nods, her chest rising as she fills her lungs before she begins her questioning. "When were you born, Alva?"

"On the twenty-eighth of January 1998."

"Tell me about your mother."

I inhale deeply, knowing this is my chance to set the record straight. "Well, after my grandmother Ruth was found and... burned at the stake, the Elster Coven took my mother in. They kept a close eye on her, given who *her* mother was, but as it turned out, my mother, Annemarie Hausmann, was the kindest, most selfless witch you'd ever meet." I feel a small smile tugging at my lips. "She used Anima to heal injured animals in the forest. Once, when I was ten, she spent three months nurturing a fallen owlet back to health. Another time, she used her magic to help local farmers after a terrible flood of the Elbe River, coaxing life back into their dead crops."

Gathoni nods encouragingly. "What did she teach you about Anima's relationship with nature?"

I clear my throat, memories of my mother's garden coming back to me. "That everything must be in balance. That for every taking, there must be giving."

"And in your own experience with these memories of the Sylt Catastrophe, what lesson do you personally take from them?"

I consider my words carefully. "That the catastrophe wasn't caused by Anima itself, but by the disregard for its laws. The Nazis saw balance as inefficiency. They wanted power without responsibility, taking without giving back."

"And do you believe this is unique to that time and place?"

"No," I say. "But neither is the capacity to learn and change. Humans have repeatedly made mistakes, yes – but they've also shown remarkable ability to adapt when confronted with the consequences of their actions."

Gathoni nods. "Would you say, then, that the lesson of Sylt is not that magic should remain hidden, but that the principles of balance that govern magic are precisely what our world needs most urgently right now?"

"Yes," I reply, understanding where she's guiding me. "Sylt

happened because natural laws were ignored. But those same laws – the ones witches have honoured since the dawn of time – are exactly what can save our planet now. Balance, reciprocity with nature, taking only what can be regenerated – those are the things the world needs now."

A different kind of murmur spreads through the Assembly – thoughtful, considering.

"And in your twenty-six years on this earth, Alva, have you ever used your own magic to harm anyone, witch or human?"

I hesitate, wishing she hadn't asked me that. We were just about to turn things around.

"Once..." I reply, the word so small it seems to dissolve like mist.

And now we both wish she hadn't asked me that.

"What did you do?" Gathoni asks, and I can hear the annoyance flaring in her voice. She needs to win this, maybe even more than me.

"There... there was an accident when I was thirteen. It was my fault. Afterwards, I was barred from practicing magic, and I've never used it again – until Mr Guise forced me to register so that I could attend the Assembly today."

Somewhere, at the back of my mind, there is a slight satisfaction when I hear the Assembly murmur at least some disapproval. I thought Mardequai overstepped in that little room with Siobhan, and the anger on his face confirms it now.

"An accident?" inquires Gathoni.

"A car accident." I nod. "I lost control of my powers for a split second and they... they died."

And now I struggle to make myself smaller, practically hiding behind the cracked podium. My gaze drops to my hands, then to the fissure running through the wood beneath them, and I wish I could vanish into that crack, away from the hundreds of eyes judging me.

"Who died, girl?" I hear Gathoni right next to me, soft and quiet and tender.

I look up at her, and somehow, she knows, and I don't need to say it out loud.

She nods, a motherly warmth softening the lines on her face as she squeezes my hand, then turns her attention back to the Assembly.

"I wonder, Alva, if you look at our world today – the climate crisis, the extinction of species, and the resulting weakening of Anima – what do you see as the greater risk: revealing ourselves and our understanding of natural balance, or remaining hidden while the world continues on its current path?"

I take a deep breath, feeling something shift inside me – not Ruth this time, but my own conviction growing stronger. "The greatest risk would be to do nothing. To watch from the shadows as the same imbalance that destroyed Sylt spreads across our entire planet."

Gathoni turns to face the Assembly fully now. "We have heard warnings of what happened when magic was revealed to the worst of humanity. But perhaps the true lesson is not that magic should stay hidden – it's that the principles that govern magic are precisely what humanity needs to learn now, before it's too late."

She gestures toward me. "Standing before you is not Ruth Hausmann, nor her legacy of destruction. Standing before you is a young witch who has carried the burden of these memories precisely so that we might learn from them. Not to hide in fear, but to step forward with wisdom."

The hum that rises from the Assembly is different now – not unified in agreement or disagreement, but a complex orchestra of both. Gathoni has accomplished what she needed: not unanimous support, but a community engaged in genuine debate rather than fractured by fear.

She raises her voice for all to hear. "I must ask you one more question, Alva, and then we shall be done with this ridiculous interrogation."

I straighten my shoulders, my fingers brushing against the splintered wood as I compose myself.

"Given everything you know about the risks, had you been a registered witch at the time of the referendum, would you have voted in favour or against the Reveal?"

I do not hesitate to reply. "In favour. Strongly in favour."

Whispers travel through the court like wind through dry summer grass. I catch fragments of surprised exclamations, sceptical murmurs, and a couple of hums.

"And may I ask why?" Gathoni asks and turns around to face me, her hands clasped behind her back.

"Because I believe in the goodness of people. Witches, druids, humans – we all have the capacity for kindness, for compassion, for growth. That's how my mother raised me, and it's how I honour her memory." I dare to look up at the tiers, to address my fellow witches for the first time. "I may carry the burden of my grandmother's atrocities in my mind, and that's something I've had to live with since childhood, but it's my mother's love and goodness that guide my heart, and my choices. And whatever darkness I might harbour, I promise you, I will always – *always* – choose the light."

But what if you're not the one who's choosing...? I panic when Ruth stirs within me once more, trying to push to the front of my mind. But I can also sense the shifting energy in the room, and I know now is the time to bring it home.

"And as long as that's the beacon we follow as a community," I say, casting Ruth off, "as long as we all stand united, I know that this Reveal will illuminate the best in all of us, magical and non-magical alike."

Gathoni looks at me, a glimmer of satisfaction in her eyes

that sends a shiver through me. "Thank you, Alva," she says. "You may return to your seat."

I step away from the podium, my feet feeling oddly disconnected from the rest of my body. The room seems to sway slightly as I make my way back up the stairs, the Emerald Court blurring into an indistinct canvas. I suppose I've done as well as I could have, given the circumstances. And yet, even if I stand by every word I've said, there's a nagging doubt in the back of my mind. While I truly believe in the goodness of others, as of this moment, there are two people I'm no longer convinced about:

Mardequai and myself.

Chapter Eleven

"**Y**ou did *not!*"

"I'm telling you, by the end of the play they were eating out of my hands – *literally*." Zara Thorndike leans back in her chair and sips on her negroni. The flickering candlelight dances across her smug features, casting a warm glow over the intimate back room. Velvet panels the colour of green jade line the walls, complementing the brass sconces and the white-clothed table beneath baroque chandeliers.

"But weren't you scared the ICAG might get a whiff of this?" asks Saskia, the youngest at the table.

"Witch, *please*," replies Zara. "The ICAG has got their hands full enough as it is. They've got no time to pay any attention to what I cook up in some dark, dingy theatre."

An actor with the Royal Shakespeare Company, Zara is the newest addition to Ember's coven. Apparently, during her latest performance, she had infused her fake blood, to be spilled for her beheading, with hexed horny goat weed, which resulted in the first three rows tackling her on stage like a football team, hungrily licking the fake blood off her bare skin.

"So, you're not as important as you had me believe after all, then," Ember says now, picking at her food. She sits at the head of the table, plate barely touched, mind clearly elsewhere. Her thoughts keep drifting to Arcadia House, to be exact, to the Assembly where Mardequai and her sister are both present. He insisted he welcome Alva in the city without Ember, and although she didn't like it, she let it happen. After all, Mardequai has a way of getting what he wants. Still, the fact that she's *here* instead of *there* gnaws at her, leaving her on edge and itching for trouble.

"Don't worry, babe," Zara murmurs, "I'm just getting started. Give me a week, and I'll have the whole West End under my spell."

Waiters glide into the room now, each bearing Pavlova, the towering confection of spun sugar and cloud-like meringue piled high on gleaming silver platters. They move with an eerie grace, their eyes slightly unfocused – a telltale sign of fresh Whisper-locks, the magical equivalent of an NDA, binding them to secrecy regarding anything that happens back here.

While the front of Alfie's, the legendary restaurant on Denmark Street, is open to the public, this private dining room, known as the Studio, is reserved for magical gatherings. The choice for tonight's coven dinner is no coincident. Denmark Street, a narrow, unassuming Soho lane was once the epicentre of the British music scene, thus a mecca for fanatics like Ember. Once upon a time, recording studios and music publishers crammed into historic buildings, and guitar shops lined the street, where legends like Bob Marley and Jimmy Page bought their instruments.

Though Ember despises how much it has changed in recent years (there is a Primark on the corner now, for fuck's sake!), she keeps coming back for the nostalgia. Alfie's, owned by Miles Burton, has been a fixture here since the 1950s. A druid with a passion for the musical arts, rumour has it, Burton's deep pockets were behind some of Britain's greatest musical talents, allegedly launching The Who and Pink Floyd, even whispering in Amy Winehouse's ear.

Ember was quick to zero in on Burton and his fabled head chef Inaaya Bajwa – the youngest chef in history to earn three Michelin stars, an accolade that left the culinary world baffled. Naturally, the secret ingredient to Inaaya's dishes is her discreet use of magic, enhancing her truffle pasta with flavours that transport diners straight to Umbria, and her fruit tart with an eternal freshness that keeps even the most discerning critics mystified.

The waiters leave, and Ember plucks a toothpick from the table. She places it between her lips. "If you know what's good for you, you will hold out on any more magical displays – *babe*. Make no mistake, ladies," she addresses the entire table now. "The ICAG has heightened both their international surveillance and their punishments in the lead-up to the Reveal. They are well aware we can hardly conceal our excitement, that we're all itching to come out of the closet. So, unless you'd like to celebrate the next Imbolc at Saltholm, I suggest you lie low. It is only for another week, for crying out loud."

The mention of Saltholm sends a shiver through the room. A salt island located deep in the Atlantic, Saltholm is the world's only magical prison – but given the fairly low numbers of witches and druids (compared to the human population), one is all that's needed, especially one as dark and depressing as 'the Holm'. The very essence of the place – salt – numbs witch powers, and prolonged exposure can drive even the strongest to ruin. Some witches emerge with a permanent dampening of their magic, finding themselves unable to perform even the simplest spells. Others suffer from long-term damage to their craft, so that casting one type of spell involuntarily triggers others, making their powers dangerously unstable.

However, salt doesn't affect druids, which is why their sentences are dealt in millennia. Indeed, since Saltholm's establishment in the fifteenth century, none of those druids convicted have yet completed their terms. The concept of a 'life sentence' truly takes on an entirely new meaning when applied to beings who do not age or die.

"And when did *you* become such a bore?" Zara challenges, her eyes glittering dangerously.

Instantly, everyone falls silent, tension crackling in the room as Ember's gaze locks onto Zara. The toothpick glides into the corner of her mouth with a sly smile. In slow motion, Ember steps first onto her chair, then onto the table, her stilettos sinking into Saskia's dessert, then crushing a plate of uneaten seared scallops.

The other witches' reactions cascade in sequence as Ember stalks across the tabletop: Minnie's fingers fly to her temples, visibly straining against the onslaught of emotions. Ember's heel catches the edge of Eun-Ji Jeo's glass next, sending her wine spilling across the tablecloth. It seeps towards Adanna McClendon, who pushes back her chair with a screech, bangles jangling as she narrowly evades the spreading stain.

Reaching Zara, Ember sinks to her knees, face inches from hers. The pink fabric of her cocktail dress shimmers daringly, its hem pooling around her like the spilled rosé. Zara's fingers twitch as she attempts to draw Anima, but before she can even complete the gesture, Ember flicks her wrist dismissively, dispelling Zara's nascent magic and instantly channelling her own. Candles flicker and dim, the chandelier above them going dark as Ember gathers Anima in her orbit, toothpick still pinched between her teeth. The witches at the table hold their breath, wide-eyed and frozen in place. Without touching Zara, Ember constricts her throat, lifting her slightly off the chair. Zara's feet dangle, her face turning an alarming shade of purple. Minnie, especially, can't seem to stand the tension, her finely attuned senses on overdrive at Ember's power display.

"Are we still bored now?" Ember sounds almost childlike. But it takes no clairvoyant to hear the threat simmering underneath. "Or are we perhaps realising that we must not call our magistrate silly names or question her authority?"

At that moment, a woman bursts into the room, her dark hair escaping a once-neat bun, streaks of flour dusting her bronze skin. "I'm *done*, witches," she declares, tossing her apron in the corner and revealing a golden dress with a plunging neckline. "I have human-ed enough for one night! Let's have some shots before we hit the Cauldron. I'm dying to — *Oh...*" Inaaya, the chef, startles when she spots Zara floating in the air like a puppet on invisible strings. "What did I miss?"

Like a mic drop, Ember releases Zara, who collapses back into her chair, gasping for air.

"Nothing of note, Inaaya darling," Ember replies. She rises, smoothing her dress. "Zara here had choked on a silly little comment, and I was kind enough to perform a Heimlich to save her. Ain't that right, babe?"

Zara inclines her head, a cocktail of humiliation and oxygen deprivation painting her cheeks pink.

"Now, shall we get back to our lovely dessert? It looks like Inaaya has prepared a divine Pavlova."

The room collectively exhales, the tension breaking like a fever. Saskia looks down at her plate, disappointment evident as her fork slices into her own dessert, all squished and bearing a distinct hole where Ember's heel had stepped.

Chapter Twelve

Most of life rushes by in a stream of memories, blurred into one murky torrent. But every so often, a moment seems to freeze in time, razor-sharp like a shard of ice, standing out with startling clarity that redefines your life. This, I know, will be one of them.

I'm seated on a chair in the corner, back in the small room where Siobhan had registered my name hours before. Late afternoon sun slants through the window, casting long shadows, while I await what I can only guess will be my verdict. At least the potted plant that had wilted under my hand earlier has made a surprising recovery. Not only has it bounced back, but it's now sporting a few fresh leaves and a bud on the verge of blooming.

After my public interrogation, I had to endure another three hours of talks and speeches. Among them was an elderly witch from France, who spoke with passionate intensity as she reminded us of the historical persecution of witches, citing the Malleus Maleficarum and the witch hunts as grim warnings from the past. Her words emphasised the need for protective measures: magical wards, legal safeguards, and safe havens for witches who might face hostility. But it wasn't all defensive strategies. She also stressed the importance of a proactive approach, introducing a coordinated PR campaign to educate the public and dispel myths about witchcraft. What resonated most, however, was her call for solidarity among *all* women, magical and non-magical alike. She envisioned a united front to heal the planet, promote the divine feminine, and take leadership roles in the environmental movement. Needless to say, the druids didn't look too excited at the prospect.

Next was Elias Klein, whose lecture on technological and scientific integration would have fascinated me under different circumstances. But with my fate hanging in the balance, I struggled to focus. Unlike Mardequai, Klein seemed excited about the Reveal's potential. He spoke of collaborating with scientists, combining magical and scientific knowledge to tackle environmental challenges. His visions of a fusion of the Resonance Network and Artificial Intelligence to produce magic-enhanced renewable energy painted an optimistic future that he seemed almost desperate for.

As the official part concluded, the gathering moved to a sprawling courtyard. Stone pathways wove between lush gardens and tinkling fountains, the space alive with the hum of conversation and clinking glasses. The aroma of a lavish dinner wafted through the air, making my stomach growl with hunger. But instead of joining the mingling crowd, I was escorted here, to the small back room, by a witch with curly grey hair and an expression that made it clear I was not to argue. Her gentle but firm grip on my arm left no doubt that I wasn't to join the festivities just yet.

The door bursts open and Gathoni Nyong'o rushes inside, followed by three other women. One of them is the witch who escorted me here. The second one is tall and willowy, with piercing eyes; the third witch is small and stout, reminding me of a tea kettle.

Gathoni's voice hits the room, and it is sharp with urgency. "Now, will someone please explain to me what on *earth* transpired within the Elster Coven that led to Alva's disastrous performance today?"

Her words hit me like a slap. I thought we'd done rather well together. My mouth opens to argue, but the tall witch beats me to it. Clearing her throat, she begins to speak with a heavy German accent, "Well, I wasn't the German head magistrate thirteen years ago, but I am of course familiar with the Hausmann case... I mean, to the extent every German witch would be, I suppose. I'm not an expert on the subject by any stretch—"

"Now is not the time to clear your name, Katharina. Just tell it as it happened. Who had the *brilliant* idea to bar Alva from practicing magic?" Gathoni's impatience is evident.

"I'm not... I'm not entirely sure..." stammers Katharina. "But I suppose the decision would have been made by the magistrate of the Elster Coven back then."

"Let's confirm that, please?" Gathoni addresses the stout witch, who nods obediently.

Meanwhile, my mind is working overtime. Gathoni is not asking what I expected her to ask, about Ruth, about her memories.

I work up my courage to speak. "I'm sorry but... why does that matter now?"

Gathoni lowers herself into the chair behind the desk. "Because no witch can be forbidden from using her magic, Alva," she says, and her eyes fix on mine. "We can be prosecuted and sent to Saltholm, or in the case of your grandmother – executed. But to forbid a witch from wielding Anima is like forbidding her to breathe – it's impossible."

My fingers twitch involuntarily, a spark of Anima dancing between them. "I'm not sure I understand."

"Whoever told you never to practise magic again," explains Gathoni, "made you believe you would commit a crime if you did wield Anima. And I wouldn't be surprised to hear that you probably spent the last thirteen years in agony, beating yourself up for every slip, every lapse of control whenever your magic erupted."

A long-held breath escapes my mouth. "You have no idea."

"The question is why," says the stout witch. "Why lie to her?"

"Exactly," agrees Gathoni. "Can you tell us what happened to you after the accident, Alva?"

I nod, eager to tell my side of the story. "I was sent to live at Haus der Hoffnung, a foster home in the next town over, and the Elster Coven magistrate came to test me regularly – not every two years, but every six months, to check if my visions had gotten worse."

"And had they?"

"No, they had not."

"And why would you say that was?"

I think for a beat, afraid of what the truth about my past might mean for my future. But now is not the time to mince words; Gathoni demands straight answers, and I suppose I owe her that much.

"I think it was because I wasn't allowed to practise," I confess. "She... Ruth... she seems to feed off of my powers. It might... it might make her stronger." I look around to gauge the reaction in the room, and when I find it shifting against me, I quickly add, "But my magic makes *me* stronger, too. I've been feeling that... well, lately."

"So, it is as I suspected," concludes Gathoni. "We have ourselves an active volcano here that's been capped for over a decade. I must say, I am appalled to hear the German congregation kept this under locks all this time. A witch with a druid's ability to remember the past – and not just any past, but one of the most *crucial* times in history – the only other time a reveal was attempted. The one incident that forever overshadows what we're trying to do here." She faces Katharina, who seems suddenly very busy with a loose thread in her cardigan sleeve. "That you thought it not important to mention Alva as we prepare for this Reveal, I struggle to reconcile."

"Well... we," Katharina stammers, "I suppose we would have mentioned her, but everyone thought she'd died in that accident. Everyone except the coven magistrate, as we now know. Under her watch, Alva must have sort of... disappeared."

"N-not on purpose, I swear!" I call out defensively. "I just lived at Haus der Hoffnung, and then, the day I turned eighteen – I left. But I didn't know what to do with myself. I had no money, no qualifications, and no magic. So, I... I went to live in the woods."

I take a breath, embarrassed as the memories of my homeless chapter flood back for all to hear. "I lived off the land, studying the plants and herbs, learning their properties to survive," I explain, leaving out the grimmest of it – how sometimes I would scavenge through restaurant dumpsters for half-eaten meals, how I sought shelter in abandoned buildings or under highway overpasses when the weather turned harsh, how I learnt to practically turn invisible, hiding from any shady people who crossed my path...

"How long did you live like this?" asks Gathoni.

"Just under three years," I reply, biting the insides of my cheeks, my eyes landing on hers. "But eventually, I started making my own herbal remedies. Salves and soaps and such. I'd sell them in the streets and sometimes at farmer's markets. I did so well," – proud tears brim in my eyes – "that I could afford to move into a small apartment and register a proper business. And that's what I've been doing these past eight years."

"I never meant to disappear. I just... I didn't think I belonged anymore. So, I made my own little corner where I could at least feel useful."

Gathoni leans forward, resting her elbows on the desk. She brings her hands together, her fingers interlaced as she presses them against her chin. "I don't yet know what to make of you, Alva Hausmann," she says. "But this much I know for certain: our sisterhood has failed you in more ways than you might have realised until this point. And for that I am deeply, *deeply* sorry." There is a softening in her features, but unlike on stage earlier, she seems more careful not to let it show now.

"And what of the sister?" She addresses the entire room again, but it's me who replies.

"Mardequai took her the night of the accident! I thought she was dead until a month ago."

"What was *he* doing there?" Gathoni turns to Katharina, but she just shrugs in reply.

Gathoni sighs, holding her head with both hands at the temples, but whatever thoughts she might harbour about the druid leader, she keeps them to herself.

"I believe Cor Kettering might have some insights," murmurs the elderly witch in Gathoni's ear. I'd almost forgotten she was there until now.

"Fetch him, please?" orders Gathoni. "But discreetly."

The witch nods and quietly slips out of the room.

There's a pause, and I decide to fill it. "May I ask, what's going to happen now, with the Reveal and all?"

"Well," sighs Gathoni, "we anticipated some form of resistance, of course. The vote was a tight race, after all. But I suppose we didn't expect a strong opponent such as Mardequai. It does complicate things, to say the least."

"I would like to help, if I can."

"And I expect you to," replies Gathoni, not missing a beat. "Make no mistake, Alva: your testimony today has made you one of the key figures of this Reveal. Your name is now tied to this event just as much as mine. Historians will write about you. I expect you to stand with us over the weeks to come. But let there be no confusion," says the head elder, and then I understand her sudden reserve compared to earlier. "This does not mean that I trust you. On the contrary: your display today, your *outburst*, it has me deeply concerned. Deeply concerned as to who truly resides in there." She points at my chest where the heart is. "You have yet to prove to us that your passionate conclusion – however well delivered it may have been – is backed by your actions. We will watch you very closely. Very, *very* closely as the Assembly unfolds over the coming days. Everyone will," she says, her eyes piercing through me. "But for now, I suppose you may all go."

Gathoni shows us the door, and Katharina is out of the room so fast you'd think she left the stove on at home.

I, however, linger, one more question slipping off my tongue as soon as the head elder and I are alone.

"And what of my magic? Do I have your permission to wield it again?"

"You never needed my permission, nor anyone else's."

"Thank you," I sigh, suppressing the relief from showing on my face as I rise and turn to leave.

"Alva?" calls Gathoni, and I stop to face her once more. "Make no mistake, you've made a powerful enemy today, and we don't yet know the lengths to which he will go to assert himself, or what he will do next. Do be careful over the coming days."

I nod, a flash of heat surging through me, followed by an immediate chill. Reaching the door, I cast another glance at the potted plant. A delicate, small flower has bloomed, its petals yellow like hope.

Stepping into the hall, I nearly collide with the angry druid again. But he passes without acknowledging me, his eyes pinned straight ahead. I do notice the tension in his jaw, the slight twitch of his fingers at his side.

"Ah, Cornelis," Gathoni greets him as he enters. "Thank you for seeing me. I hear you might be able to shed some much-needed light on our situation."

Out in the hall, I strain to catch another word from within the room, but the door clicks shut, leaving me adrift in silence. The hairs on the back of my neck prickle when I realise my suspicion was justified; the young druid knows something. Something about me, something about my past.

I drift toward the exit, and a ray of sun streams through the window, bathing the corridor in golden light. Dust motes dance in the beam, swirling bright like tiny stars. The light seems to sharpen every detail around me – the edges of the wooden panelling, the intricate patterns in the carpet, the gleam of the brass doorknobs.

And yet, I know it reveals only the barest hint of all there is to see.

Chapter Thirteen

"Will you slow down, for crying out loud?"

Dennis hurries after me through the busy London street. Evening commuters rush past us on the pavement, their briefcases and shopping bags swinging, occasionally grazing one of us.

"Hey – I'm talking to you!"

I scan the intersections, searching for anything that might look familiar. Finally, exhausted, his words get through to me, and I slump onto a park bench.

"What's gotten into you? You're acting like a madwoman." Dennis pants as he catches up, collapsing next to me. "And why are we even walking? I'm exhausted! Why couldn't we just catch another ride with Eloise?"

I hunch forward, elbows on my knees, and run my fingers through my hair. "Because it didn't go so well, okay?"

"What happened?"

A chilly autumn breeze nips at my skin, and I pull my jacket tighter around myself. My eyes remain fixed on the ground. "Let's just say, Mr Guise isn't as nice as you thought he was."

"I never said he was nice," replies Dennis as he ties his shoelace. "But I will say this: his driver sure knows how to beat the traffic like a Formula One racer."

Apparently, Eloise had taken Dennis on a whirlwind tour of London's landmarks, from Big Ben to the Tower of London, before dropping him at Arcadia House to find parking. But the moment I emerged, I'd yanked him away, leading us into this maze of unfamiliar streets. I wouldn't have accepted as much as a bottle of water from the druid anymore. Then again, I doubt he would have extended any such courtesy after what transpired today.

"You've got to give me some answers here, seriously," Dennis demands.

I clench my fists, nails digging into my palms, and take a deep breath before meeting his gaze. This is exactly why I shouldn't have let him come. I'm barely treading water myself, let alone explain the depths to someone else.

"He manipulated me, okay? Used me to sow discord in the Assembly over the Reveal. I stood up to him, but now... now I think I might have made an enemy of him."

And probably not just him, I think grimly.

"Nah, come on. I'm sure he'll come around. Eloise says he's like this model boss. Always fair, pays generous bonuses and all that..."

"You don't understand. When he was still unsure of my stance, he was all charm. But now that he knows I oppose him – I don't know what he might do. I think he might be... I think he might be dangerous, Dennis."

"*Dangerous?* Dangerous, how?"

I study his face for a long moment, weighing whether to voice the suspicion that's been gnawing at me ever since I learnt Mardequai was present that fateful Solstice night.

"Look, I can't prove it or anything, but I think he might have had something to do with the car accident back then."

"What makes you say that?"

"It's to do with what he said on the way to Arcadia House this morning. Something doesn't add up. I don't know. It's... it's just a feeling."

And normally, the mention of my gut feelings, my reasoning that something 'just feels off', would set his teeth on edge. Like the time I insisted we take a different trail because I sensed our usual path would be obstructed (later, we discovered a massive tree had fallen and barred the way), or when I urged him to postpone our camping trip due to an inexplicable sense of unease (a severe storm hit the area that weekend). He'd always brush off these intuitions, attributing them to coincidence or my overactive imagination. But not today. Today, he nods with sudden resolve, then says, "That's it. We're flying home tonight." He grabs my hand, attempting to pull me up from the bench.

But I won't budge. "Don't be silly, Dennis."

"I'm actually dead serious right now. I've had about enough of this circus. If my girlfriend is in danger, I reserve the right to do whatever I can to keep her safe."

His hero complex would be touching if it wasn't so misguided right about now.

"It's not that simple. I can't just pack up and leave."

"Why *not*?" He throws his hands in the air.

"I'm kind of needed here."

"Needed for what?"

I take a few steps towards him, and a breath to calm my voice for this next thing I'm about to say.

"Look, I know this is hard to grasp, but our world – the *entire* world – is about to be turned upside down, okay? This magical reveal will change everything, do you understand? Everything everyone everywhere thought they knew about how the world works. It's like... it's like introducing the internet, only a million times more intense because it will soon come to light that magic has been there all along. Don't you see? There is no turning back from that. And it is going to affect us whether we hide from it at our little cabin in the woods or not."

Dennis opens his mouth as if to argue but then closes it again. "But wouldn't you feel better facing all this from the safety of your own home, surrounded by the people you know – your friends, your family?" he asks eventually.

I don't answer, my gaze drifting across the street to a restaurant window. Inside, a group of thirty-somethings laugh as they dip bread into a pot of fondue. As much as I cherish the cabin and the forest, my apothecary, the hard truth is that it's not *my* home, not really. And those people aren't my friends or my family – they're his. Over the past few years I've been playing house, convincing myself I belonged there because I didn't belong elsewhere.

Until now.

"I can be useful here," I say with a voice that's both small and determined at once. "I know this is a lot for you but try to understand: for years I've felt like I've been living someone else's life. This is my chance to reconnect with who I really am. I can't walk away from that, not now."

"Even if your life might be in danger here?"

I bite back the urge to tell him my life will probably be in danger *everywhere*. Instead, I reply, "Even then," and gently tap his knee. "Now, let's get you back to the hotel, shall we?"

"*Me?* What about you?"

I squint slightly. "There's something else I need to do tonight."

"Your sister." Dennis nods, glancing across the street. "Well, I'm not leaving you alone in this city, especially if someone might be after you, and that's final."

"I thought you were tired."

"I'll *manage*," he snaps, puffing up his chest. "But we're taking a taxi, no more walking." He steps between two parked cars, looking to hail a cab. "Where does this sister of yours live, anyway?"

I sigh and follow him. "Dennis, I... I don't want you to come."

He freezes, his hand still raised to flag down a taxi. Shoulders tense, he turns to face me, his eyebrows pushed together in irritation. He's not used to me asserting myself like this. Back home, I usually defer to his lead or carefully phrase things to make them sound like his idea. "What has gotten into you these days? We always do everything together."

"This is one thing I must do alone."

Dennis shakes his head, paces a few steps, then whirls back to face me. "I don't even know who you are anymore."

That's because I never told you. Another thought I keep to myself.

"Come on, let's get you a taxi," I say gently.

"Let's get *you* one," he says.

"I think I'd rather walk."

Dennis's face hardens. He turns away, only to spin back around. *"By yourself?"* His voice rises, arms clapping on the sides of his jeans. "You're going to walk around all by yourself, at night, in London?"

"I'll be *fine*," I reassure him. "Witch, remember?" I point at myself with both thumbs.

Dennis pinches the bridge of his nose, and then a long silence follows. "Here, take my jacket at least. Yours is way too thin for this weather." He takes off his jacket, a rugged waxed cotton affair that screams 'outdoorsman,' and holds it out to me.

"Thanks, but I'll be f—"

"If you say 'fine' one more time, I swear to God I'm going to lose it! Now will you please just take the *fucking* jacket?"

I wet my lips and nod. I take off my own coat and hand it to him, then slip into his, the smell of wax engulfing me.

Dennis flags down a taxi and climbs in without another word. I lean into the open window, giving the driver directions to our hotel. Only when the cab merges with the traffic and vanishes around a corner, do I heave a sigh.

I turn on my heel and set off in the opposite direction.

Now that I'm alone, the London night pulses with energy around me, and I breathe it all in. The heavenly scents spilling from restaurants, the crowds gathering outside the many pubs, the car horns and distant sirens. And amid all this life, a surprising lightness settles within me despite the heavy day I've had.

It's been so long since I've been a stranger like this.

Sure as hell, it was tough being homeless, a fate I wouldn't wish on anyone. But there was also an undeniable sense of freedom. I would never choose to go back, of course, but I suppose it's only natural to find silver linings even in the darkest skies. And joy is a stubborn feeling; it demands to be felt every once in a while, no matter how grim life gets.

I still remember how I felt so grateful when I found that secluded forest cave to sleep one summer, its entrance perfectly hidden behind a curtain of ivy, or the day a stray dog decided to follow my every step, becoming my only friend in a world that seemed to have forgotten me.

It's amazing how little you actually need, how invincible you can feel when you have nowhere to go, nowhere to be. I was like a wolf back then, roaming through the woods. Wild and free, answering to no one but the nature that surrounded me. Every new day was a challenge, every meal a triumph. I didn't have a home – so *everywhere* became my home, and no matter where I went, I always found unexpected beauty, catching me off guard with its simplicity. A stunning sunset, a perfect wild strawberry, the rustle of leaves in the wind that seemed to whisper secrets just for me.

That wildness, that connection to something primal and true, still lives within me. And here, on this bustling city night, I feel it stirring once again.

I meander through the streets, losing track of time, embracing the unfamiliar. I pass Trafalgar Square, its majestic lions standing guard, and I catch all the subtleties of the city: a street musician's melancholic violin echoing off ancient cobblestones, a group of pigeons strutting boldly across the street in a perfect line, the scent of freshly baked pastries wafting from a tiny corner bakery.

And underneath it all, I feel the pulsing energy of Anima rising and falling within and around me like flames in an eternal fire.

Cautiously, I begin to wield my magic again, trying a few small spells: warming my hands without touching them together, making my footsteps silent on the pavement, causing a snow globe in a shop window to swirl its flakes. They're simple enchantments, nothing that would affect anyone around me, just little joys for myself. Indeed, these are child's play, really, but they're all I dare attempt for now. I'm too wary that Ruth might awaken, might stir within me as I access my powers.

But tonight, she remains dormant, and I feel a happiness I haven't known in years, like a bird testing out a pair of mended wings.

However, somewhere at the back of my mind, there's also a sting of betrayal, a pang for the path not taken, the life not lived. Where would I be today, had I known I was allowed to do this all along? What life would I have made for myself, had Brauer not forbidden me to use my magic?

But I suppose it's no use, dwelling on those might-have-beens. And perhaps it's them that makes this moment truly shine. My magic, long dormant, now reawakens within me, and each remembered spell becomes a new discovery, each flicker of my powers an adventure.

Slowly, I wind my way towards the Soho district, using the maps at bus stops to navigate. Piccadilly Circus greets me with its dazzling billboards. I pause here, taking in the spectacle I've only ever seen on TV. The bustling crowds of Leicester Square sweep me along next, where the air is rich with the smell of street food and the excited chatter of theatregoers.

Finally, I find myself beneath the iconic Soho sign, its letters illuminated and drawing many a tourist for a selfie. The street buzzes with life here – people spilling in and out of bars, the faint thump of music from underground clubs, the street artists performing their clever tricks. Only Sofia's club eludes me. My phone proves useless, too: My Pink Cauldron's address yields no results across social media or search engines.

I'm about to give up, but then I remember, I am a witch; I have resources at my disposal beyond human technology. It will take some getting used to, to turn to Anima for answers again, but now Mama's words echo in my mind, clear as if she were standing right next to me. "Every answer you seek is out there, but you won't find it if you do not think to ask for it," she'd often tell us growing up.

And so, I close my eyes to centre myself, focussing inward to let the sensory overload of Soho fade to a distant hum. And in this tiny pocket of calm within, I pose my question to that force I know is always listening:

Where is she? Show me the way.

I resume my walk, seemingly aimless once more, but to my delight, it has worked, and now I feel that unseen force guiding my steps. I know this only happens when you truly surrender, when you don't try to force a direction or impose your own expectations. Otherwise, it's your mind leading you, not Anima. I'm a little proud of myself that I managed to pull it off.

As I let go, the city becomes a living labyrinth, which I pass with ease. I'm swept along by a sudden surge in the crowd, carried down a street I hadn't intended to take. A traffic light turns red just as I approach, halting me at an intersection I might have passed. A double-decker bus blocks my path, forcing me to detour down a narrow alley, where a street performer's circle of onlookers parts just as I arrive, revealing a path I hadn't noticed otherwise.

I'm a leaf caught in a breeze, a twig carried by a stream's current. I don't fight it, I don't question. I simply flow, trusting that I'll end up exactly where I need to be.

Eventually, I find myself in a quiet cul-de-sac, and my heart quickens as I spot a neon sign above an unassuming building. It's not yet lit, but I recognise it instantly from Sofia's Instagram posts: My Pink Cauldron. The club's doors, however, remain firmly shut; it's still too early for the party to begin.

Nervousness spreads through me as I stand before this physical manifestation of my sister's new existence. I've found her, or at least, I've found where she might be. Now comes the hard part: the waiting.

I scan the surroundings, finding a small kebab place across the street. Its faded awning and flickering OPEN sign give it a worn but welcoming look, and the aroma of spices and frying fat make my mouth water, reminding me I haven't eaten in forever.

I push open the door, a small bell jingling above me. I order a falafel wrap and find a seat by the window, my view perfectly framed to watch Sofia's club come to life.

But as I unwrap my meal, a knot of nervous anticipation in my stomach makes it hard to eat. The chance of seeing her again tonight, of actually *speaking* after all these years, suddenly feels overwhelming. What will I say? How will she react? I force myself to eat, staring out the window.

The night presses on and people begin to gather outside the club. One by one, they arrive – some in groups, others alone. And somewhere inside is my sister, oblivious to the fact that her past is sitting just across the street, eating falafel.

At last, I crumple up the remains of my meal, tossing the wrapper into the bin. I slip back into Dennis's jacket and with another jingle of the bell, I exit the tiny eatery.

The neon sign has just flickered to life, a pink glow that beckons me across the cobblestones.

Part Two

Chapter Fourteen

No thunderstorm matches the electric atmosphere of a Soho club on a Friday night, packed to the rafters with witches.

Tonight, My Pink Cauldron pulses with female energy, a madhouse where witches can be their true selves. Anima erupts from fingertips as drinks are summoned across the bar, while on the dance floor, witches dance and sway to gritty beats, feeding off each other's ecstasy, which raises the energy in the entire room to an intoxicating high.

Ember surveys everything from her vantage point above the crowd, keeping an eye on the giant clock on stage as it ticks closer to midnight. The club's magnificent domed ceiling arches high overhead, its golden designs interrupted by pink neon signs. Below, the circular dance floor is ringed by arches and columns, providing intimate alcoves for those who've found their match for the night.

Tonight's open display of witchcraft, however, is an exception. Usually, the Cauldron welcomes a mix of magical and mortal partygoers alike. However, Ember Wild is known for her tough and unpredictable door policy. The selection criteria are purposefully random – one night, a dishevelled street artist might be ushered in with a wink, while the next, a Hollywood A-lister finds themselves turned away.

On witch-only nights, the famous 'black box' makes an appearance. This mysterious photo booth–like structure demands each patron enter alone, waiting in the dark space for Mother knows what to happen. For witches, it serves as a covert way to demonstrate their magic, a discreet display of Anima securing them entry. Humans, however, exit the box bewildered, spending the night speculating wildly. Some believe it's an AI body scanner, others swear it's a lie detector, while a few insist it's a portal to another universe.

But the club's mystery extends far beyond the near-impene-trable door. A stringent no-photo rule was put in place by Ember, with cameras and smartphones tucked away in lockboxes by the entrance. Naturally, the secrecy only adds to the allure, and people from around the world are flocking to the Cauldron, hoping to make it inside.

As the clock on stage ticks down its final ten seconds, the voices from the dance floor below rise in a countdown. "Five, four, three..." High above, Ember steps into an ornate birdcage suspended from the domed ceiling. The stroke of midnight unleashes a frenzy of applause, screams, and whistles as the Queen of Soho descends gracefully from the ceiling, Nina Simone's velvety voice enveloping the space, singing of a new dawn and a new day. Ember makes the cage sway seductively, while below, the sea of dancers pulses. Her outfit has changed since the coven dinner. Now she is a dazzling display of glitter in her form-fitting jumpsuit that catches and reflects the pulsing lights.

As Nina Simone's voice melds into the Austin Millz remix, the iconic chorus of 'Feeling Good' erupts into a thumping beat, and Ember's cage soars above the heads. She hangs daringly off the side, her fingers trailing hats and hair, leaving glittering traces of stardust.

Yet, suddenly, amidst all the ecstasy, an unsettling feeling tugs at Ember. Something feels off here tonight, something she can't quite grasp or explain, but her focus is repeatedly drawn to the back of the club – a pull she can't resist, intensifying the more she tries to ignore it.

As the song finishes, her cage descends onto the stage, and Ember climbs out, bowing before her cheering audience. She's still trying to catch a glimpse of the back, but now the stage lights are blinding her. Composing herself, she silences her witches with a single gesture. Pippa discreetly appears at her side, passing her a microphone, and Ember's voice carries across the hushed crowd.

"Welcome to *Gaaaaag!*" she calls out, the word stretched like chewing gum and followed by a mock retching that elicits laughter from the crowd.

"Tonight, my fellow sisters, the high and mighty are gathered over in Westminster at Arcadia House, discussing *our* future. But were we invited?"

She holds out the mic.

"NO!" the crowd roars.

"Were we consulted?"

Another pause for the resounding "NO!"

In the front row, Eun-Ji, Saskia, and Inaaya beam up at Ember, basking proudly in the glory of their coven magistrate.

"They gave us the right to vote, but I'm asking you, witches: what good is a vote if the choices are made *for* us, anyway? What good is a vote if we do not get to decide what will happen after we went to the ballot box?"

The crowd cheers, and Ember revels in the attention. But

even as she speaks, that peculiar tug pulls her again, drawing her focus beyond the stage lights.

Shaking it off, she continues, "They think they can contain us, but our magic is too wild to ever be controlled. It fills my heart with pride, knowing that witches from every fucking corner of this globe are here tonight. And let me tell you, once our magic is freed, none of us will be silenced any longer! We will shape this new reality. We will show them what we are capable of! Because once we roam wild – we will be fucking *invincible!*"

More cheers erupt.

"So tonight, let's celebrate our magic, our sisterhood, our freedom to be who we truly are. Let them have their boring meetings and their outdated traditions. We have each other and we have tonight and together, we will own TOMORROW!"

And then the crowd goes wild. But Ember can't shake that nagging feeling any longer. She steps off the stage, pushing past her coven sisters, eager to get to the back of the club, searching for that something – or someone – reaching out to her.

Ember mingles briefly, exchanging quick hugs and welcomes, her progress through the crowd painfully slow as eager witches vie for her attention. Finally, the crowd parts, and it reveals a solitary figure. There, pressed against the back wall, stands – Alva. Hands tucked into the pockets of an oversized jacket; hair scraped into a messy ponytail. She lifts one hand to wave, her lips forming a 'hi' that's swallowed by the music's beat.

Ember approaches, stopping just close enough so they can hear each other over the music.

"Is it really you?" she asks. In reply, Alva's arms open for an embrace, but Ember remains rooted to the spot. Within, her heart thrums louder than the bass, but without, her entire body has gone into shock.

She'd anticipated this all day, of course, knowing Alva would materialise eventually. Yet now that it has happened, Ember feels strangely hollowed out, empty, as if all her prepared reactions have eluded her.

The Alva before her still looks like the sister she remembers, but also not. She looks older, naturally. But also, tougher somehow. When they were young, Alva was always the gentle one, the graceful one. Now she stands battle-worn, eyes sharp, posture guarded. The past has carved its mark into her; the innocence of a child now transformed into a rough outline of lived experiences.

Alva is about to say something when from behind, an overeager witch collides with Ember. Her hair a chaos of glitter and pink streaks, she says breathlessly, "Ember Wild! Holy shit, I can't believe I get to meet you! This party is fucking mad! And your speech? Goosebumps – am I right? Hey, I was wondering if you—"

"Appreciate it." Ember brushes off the witch with a smile that doesn't reach her eyes. Turning back to her sister, she leans in close, speaking into Alva's ear. "Let's go somewhere quiet, yeah?"

Ember spins on her heel, cutting through the crowd like a hot knife through ice. She can sense Alva behind her, that magnetic pull towards her sister that both warms and chills her now.

The club's office is a reflection of Ember's tastes – rose-coloured walls adorned with vintage rock posters, shelves lined with funky accessories for her performances, as always a giant vase of pink roses, and a large window overlooking the writhing dance floor below. Up here, the club's beat is reduced to a distant throb.

"Please, have a seat," Ember gestures towards a velvet chaise lounge, its black colour a gritty contrast to the room's pink overload.

"Thank you." Alva shrugs off her jacket and perches on the edge, hands clasped between her knees.

Ember fidgets despite herself. "Can I get you anything? Water? Something stronger, maybe?" Her fingers twitch, itching for a drink to calm them.

"No, I'm alright."

"Suit yourself," Ember murmurs, gravitating towards an art déco bar cart beside her desk.

"Es tut gut, dich zu sehen." *It's good to see you,* Alva says, the simple sentence enough to break Ember's wall like a wrecking ball. She busies herself with making a dry martini.

"How was your flight?" she asks for lack of knowing what else to say.

"Good. You know, whatever."

"And the Assembly? I assume it's been a while since you were at a magical gathering like that."

"It was... overwhelming, to say the least," Alva admits. "Oh, and I should probably mention... I'm not sure if you were officially notified or anything, but they made me a member of your coven. It was the only way they'd grant me access to Arcadia House."

Ember's eyebrows shoot up in surprise. "They did?"

New admissions typically require a coven-wide vote. There's only one person she can think of to bypass that process. "Right, yes. Of course, I was informed," she lies smoothly. "It's not an issue. It's not like you'll actually be participating in coven affairs or anything."

She catches the flash of hurt crossing Alva's features; that probably came out harsher than necessary. Searching for a way to change the subject, Ember blurts out next, "So, word on the street is you caused quite the stir at the Assembly."

Alva's lips form a humourless smile. "Well, let's just say your foster father won't offer me a ride in his fancy car again any time soon." She scratches her temple, a gesture so achingly familiar it makes Ember's chest constrict.

A short laugh, then she seeks refuge in a long sip of martini.

"Is he good to you?" asks Alva. "Are you... you know... *safe?*"

The question catches Ember entirely off-guard. "*Am I safe?* What kind of question is that? Of course I'm safe." And then irritation flares in her chest. "What is this? Y-y-you show up here at *our* invitation, you come waltzing back into my life instead of waiting for me to contact *you*, and immediately you start throwing accusations at the man who raised me? The man who took me in after *you*—"

She bites back the words, but it's too late. The accusation hangs between them now, a pendulum blade swinging dangerously close to that raw wound she has built her entire identity around.

"You blame me for it," Alva states, her eyes fixed on the table's edge, tracing it with her thumb. "You have every right to."

Ember sinks into her office chair. She lights a cigarette, hunching forward with her elbows on the desk. One hand cradles her forehead while the other brings the cigarette to her lips.

"I don't know." She takes a long drag, exhaling smoke. "I don't know how I feel, to be honest. I – I don't know *you*, not anymore."

"You know me better than anyone." And the sad smile now showing on Alva's face speaks volumes about *her* past thirteen years. Ever since discovering that her sister was still out there, Ember has been wondering, has been trying to picture it – the life Alva has built for herself. She could have kids, for crying out loud, she could be married. But there's no ring on her finger, nor is that the vibe she gets from Alva.

Ember considers her sister for a while, landing on her over-sized jacket.

"What about him, then?" Ember asks, nodding towards it.

"Him? Who?"

"Your jacket donor."

Alva looks down into her lap, as if just remembering what she's wearing. "Oh – *Dennis*. He's back at the hotel. Yeah, he's alright. But he's not, you know, family."

That last word burns through Ember like acid. She gets up and strides to the window overlooking the dance floor. She plants her forearm on the glass and leans her head against it.

"So, it *was* you, then. Who caused the crash?"

"It was an accident."

Just as Mardequai predicted, Alva doesn't even deny it.

"Was it?" Ember's reply comes quick, unfiltered.

"How can you even ask me that?"

Ember sighs, fogging up the glass. "I don't mean to say you did it on purpose but... come on, Alva." She turns back around now. "We both know you weren't always the one calling the shots of your own life. And from what I hear of the Assembly today, that much hasn't changed."

"She... I..." stammers Alva. "*No one* intended for that car to crash, if that's what you're suggesting. Whoever... *whatever* it is that causes these episodes, it was in the car with us, too. It would have died, too, that night." She rises, moving to stand beside Ember at the window. "It was a loss of control. It *was* – an accident."

The silence lingers between them, thick with questions, the flashing lights from the dance floor casting shadows across their faces.

When she finally speaks, Ember's voice simmers with suppressed rage. "And how do I know such an 'accident' won't happen again? How do I know you won't rip away everyone I love, just like you did then?"

The words have a sting to them, and Ember regrets them

instantly. It was a deliberate attempt to wound, to place the blame squarely on Alva's shoulders. A low blow, and they both know it.

But the truth is: that is not even Ember's concern. Not really, anyway. It's not like *she's* got anyone in her life she holds dear, either. If anything, suffering such a loss at an early age has taught her not to let people come too close. Because if you don't let anyone in, you can't lose them, either. Sure, there's Pippa, but even that relationship is transactional at best. Pippa is an employee, who, however close, would dust herself off and move on if Ember were to vanish tomorrow.

No, her hesitation has little to do with fear of her sister's darkness. It's rooted in what she herself has become, the person grief and loss have made of her. Every decision she's made since that fateful night has led her down a path far from childhood innocence. Indeed, under Mardequai's guidance, her life has become a chess game of morally grey moves and cunning schemes. She's made a life for herself where vulnerability is a weakness she can't afford. 'Sofia Hausmann' is long gone, buried along with anything their mother might have taught them.

But Ember Wild thrives on intrigue, on manipulation. To embrace Alva would mean confronting the Sofia she left behind, and Ember's not sure she's ready for that, or if she even wants to.

"You're right," Alva concedes, and for a moment, Ember struggles to recall what she even asked. "You can't know it won't happen again. I'm sorry, I... I shouldn't have come."

Alva turns away, reaching for her jacket. But her steps, Ember can tell, are deliberately slow, each pause full of hope — hope that Ember might have more to say, might ask her not to go.

"I still get them too, you know," Ember finds herself admitting. "The visions. I still dream of her."

Her fingers unconsciously trace the tattoo on her collarbone as her thoughts drift to the visions that have stayed with her over all these years. Unlike Alva's intense, dangerous experiences, Ember's connection to the past has always been more elusive. Fleeting glimpses and hazy snapshots of another time. But as children, they often found pockets of joy in Ember's visions, playfully reenacting the old hag's garden antics – which must have been such a welcome break for Alva, who struggled with her darker version.

"Remember, remember, the dreams that you hold..." Alva sings quietly now, her back still to Ember, unaware that her sister's hand is hovering over the very lyrics inked into her skin.

Alva turns back. "Have yours gotten stronger lately? The visions, I mean."

"Not really," Ember replies. "Still just some old hag, bustling about in her garden, singing a lullaby." There's still a wall there, a reluctance to fully open up. "Why, are yours? Getting stronger?"

"Maybe. I'm not sure."

Their eyes meet, and suddenly, the distance between them melts away, and they're thirteen again, sprawled on the grass beneath the stars in their childhood garden. From inside the house, their parents' voices drift over to them as they clean up after dinner. Gazing at the stars, the twins spin theories about the why. Why, of all the magical siblings in the world, they were the ones getting these glimpses into the past, giggling over the possibility that they're ancient fairies from a distant land, or that they're picking up radio signals from parallel universes with their hair. And together, they're singing the lullaby from Ember's vision:

Remember, remember, the stories of old,
The memories that slipped through your fingers like gold.
Let magic uncover what time tried to hide,
As the lost becomes found, with you by my side.

Remember, remember, the dreams that you hold,
The wonders inside you, waiting to unfold.
With each passing moment, each wish and each star,
Your song holds the key to where memories are.

"I've missed you," Alva says, placing her hand over Ember's on the tabletop. Just then, Pippa Watson bursts into the room.

"Oh! I'm so sorry, I didn't realise you had company." She dramatically covers her eyes, nearly colliding with the doorframe as she spins to leave.

"It's fine, Pippa," Ember calls out. "This isn't one of our 'morning after' scenarios. This... this is my sister."

Pippa snorts. "Right, and I'm Beyoncé Knowles."

"No, really, darling. This is my sister, Alva Hausmann from Germany."

Alva extends her hand. "Nice to meet you."

"Oh... Oh, *hi*. Wow." Pippa shakes Alva's hand, gobsmacked. "It's a pleasure. I've heard... well, I've heard so much about you. Just not exactly in a..."

"Not exactly in an *alive* kind of way?" Alva finishes.

"Yes – right, I... I had no idea."

Ember interjects, "What's the news, Pip-squeak?"

"Well, yes, I'm terribly sorry to interrupt but I'm afraid Daphne Kirk has arrived."

"*Daphne Kirk?*" Alva echoes with a hint of awe. But her smile is too bright now, too casual, as if everything is suddenly back to normal. It feels unearned, and Ember's defences snap right back up.

"Of course, how could I forget?" Ember strides to Pippa, who's holding out an oversized suit jacket and a pink top hat. As she dons the items, Ember turns to Alva. "Terribly sorry, but duty calls. You should probably head out now. Or... stay if you like, enjoy the party. But I'll be tied up with Daphne all night. You know how these celebrity types are..."

Ember makes for the door without another word.

"Come on, Sofia, I... I just got you back," Alva pleads.

Ember's hand rests on the doorknob, her body half-turned to leave. She stands there for a long moment, the silence broken only by the muffled bass from the club below. Pippa shifts from one foot to the other, her eyes darting between the sisters before she gently touches Ember's elbow. Ember's jaw clenches, then relaxes. Turning back to face the room, she asks, "Where are you staying?"

"At the Bowery Arms Hotel, near Hyde Park," Alva replies.

Ember's head dips in a single, terse nod. She slips out of the room, her fingers trailing off the doorknob, leaving the door slightly ajar.

Chapter Fifteen

If I had to choose one word to describe my sister Sofia growing up, it would have to be 'iconic.' Though, as usual, she'd already chosen the word herself: whenever someone asked what she wanted to be when she grew up, she'd reply, "I'm going to be an icon one day". It was the word itself that seemed to set her apart, a glimpse of the future she was creating for herself.

Hitting puberty, my sister, the eternal music freak, developed an almost obsessive fascination with the '27 Club' – Kurt Cobain, Janis Joplin, Jimi Hendrix, Jim Morrison, Amy Winehouse – all those legends passing in their prime, at the too-young age of twenty-seven.

But Sofia didn't want to be *famous*, exactly. She didn't want to become a celebrity, an actress or a musician or the like. No, she simply knew deep down that one day, she was going to be *known* – that one day, she was going to stand out somehow. Once, I'd asked her how she knew this, how she could be so sure that it was going to happen.

"It's just something you know," she'd reply with a shrug.

I always marvelled at this about Sofia: she had absolute faith in her own destiny, and she was blessed with a confidence I could never muster.

Which is why, when I thought I'd lost her at age thirteen, not only was I stricken with guilt and grief – I also lost faith in this world. Because the one thing I'd thought to be unshakable – Sofia's future – had seemingly been snuffed out. Nothing made sense anymore after that.

Indeed, at Haus der Hoffnung, I often caught myself imagining Sofia walking through the door. I chalked it up to the lack of closure, never having a body to bury. But now I believe there was more to it. Maybe it was a twin thing but some part of me always knew she must still be alive.

As I stand in her office, watching through the glass as she takes the stage of her own club with none other than Daphne Kirk, I'm overwhelmed by a feeling so big it brings tears to my eyes. It's more than gratitude – it's a profound sense of awe. Despite all of life's mysteries and tragedies – despite everything fate has thrown my way – in this moment, my faith in a greater plan is restored. Because Sofia is alive – and she has become, quite frankly, *iconic*.

My chest swells with pride as I watch her and former eighties-it-girl Kirk on stage, recreating the legendary White Stripes pole dance video to 'I Just Don't Know What to Do with Myself', first performed by top model Kate Moss.

I turn away from the glass, grab Dennis's jacket, and quietly exit the office. It's only when the door clicks shut that another thought takes root. Had I expected more? I suppose a part of me had hoped for a more emotional reunion. Tearful hugs, heartfelt declarations. But maybe that would have been asking too much. Maybe I should call myself lucky that she agreed to see me at all.

As I pass through the club, I catch one last glimpse of Sofia, now in a tight embrace with Daphne Kirk as they finish their performance. I can't help but wonder if Kirk is one of us – a witch – or if she's under a Whisperlock. I really, really hope it's the former. There's just something about one of us hiding in the glare of the spotlight that's oddly comforting.

In the cloakroom I locate my locker. As soon as I retrieve my phone, its screen lights up, revealing a flood of messages from Dennis. Quickly, I type out a response:

On my way back to the hotel now.

His reply comes instantly: *Okay, but take a taxi this time. Promise me.*

Promise, I text back.

Pocketing my phone, I push through the club's heavy doors. The thumping music fades, replaced by the soft patter of rain on cobblestones. I step out onto the street, droplets immediately speckling my face and clothes – which makes the promise an easy one to keep.

I take my place at the end of the taxi queue; a line of black cabs stretches ahead like a funeral procession for the night's unfulfilled expectations of those who couldn't get into the club. Dennis's jacket clings to me as I pull it tighter against the relentless rain.

But then a sudden prickle at the nape of my neck makes me stiffen. Something's off. The air feels charged with more than just the rain — *Anima,* and someone appears to be wielding it, aiming it at me.

Witches develop a sixth sense for these kinds of energy shifts, and our defences grow stronger with experience. It's like prey spotting a leopard in the bushes; as soon as the predator is seen, the prey will sound alarm calls, thus thwarting any attempt at an ambush. This is why seasoned witches rarely fall victim to hidden hexes, like forgetting spells.

But who would try their luck here, out in the open, and on me?

I force myself to appear calm, but now my mind races. Under the pretence of checking my phone, I scan the crowd, hoping to find the witch responsible. Panic rises as I recall Gathoni's warning. *You've made a powerful enemy today, and we don't yet know the lengths he will go to...*

I suppose I could muster a defence spell if I really tried. But if I do, I would also reveal that I am aware of the attacker. And Mother knows what might happen then. I'm woefully unprepared for any form of magical confrontation, let alone a witch's duel.

But the stranger's magic keeps swelling around me, an invisible force tugging at me. Feigning nonchalance, I step out of the queue, convincing myself that I'll have better luck hailing a taxi on a busier street around the corner, anyway.

I break away, heading for the main street. As I round the corner, the scent of rain-soaked asphalt and old frying fat from closing restaurants masks the Anima entirely. Damp trash bags line the kerb, ready for morning collection.

I move on, flinching every time tires hiss through puddles. The further I walk, the more the witch's grasp on me wanes, until I exhale a shaky breath of relief. Maybe this is normal, I rationalise. What do I know about the magical world after so long? Perhaps witches like to test each other's defences, kind of a witchy game of tag.

A taxi's headlights cut through the streaks of rain, and I raise my arm hopefully. But it glides past, leaving me in a spray of gutter water. Thanks, I guess. I trudge on, eyes peeled for another one, nerves settling further as I visualise a hot shower and a warm bed.

But just as I've almost convinced myself all is well, it comes for me again – Anima, reaching out like ice-cold hands. This time, the assault feels more potent, and it catches me entirely off guard. Before I know it's happening, my vision blurs, and I fear I might collapse right there on the pavement. Fighting vertigo, I manage to turn my head.

There she is, the witch, standing still amidst the bustling partygoers. I cannot see her face against the headlights; it's more of a feeling that tells me our gazes have locked, and it tells me with chilling certainty that this is no game at all.

No sooner do I realise it than the Anima envelops me like a snake, constricting tighter around me as I try to fight it. It's a freeze spell, created to temporarily immobilise its victim. My panic rising, I attempt to repel the stranger's magic and just about conjure up... well, *something*.

Fresh terror seizes me when I watch her break into a sprint next.

Startled, I begin to run, too, each step sending jolts of adrenalin down my legs. Now the downpour intensifies, blurring my vision as I career around a bend – only to find myself trapped in a dead end, brick walls towering on three sides, too tall to climb.

I whirl around, bracing myself for the witch who's hunting me.

Wildly, I search my mind for a protective spell from my childhood, but nothing will come to me. When a dark figure, haloed against the passing car lights, appears, I almost freeze of my own accord, no spell of hers necessary.

Anima flows towards her as she begins to murmur, her voice rising in an eerie melody that seems to resonate deep within the surrounding bricks. Spells are more powerful when spoken aloud, even more powerful when chanted – and this witch is singing.

Instantly, agony rips through my body, my limbs turning to blocks of ice. If she maintains the spell long enough, I could literally freeze to death. Now immobilised, I struggle to summon my own powers but have no chance to muster any kind of defence as Anima slips through my grasp like water. But then, from the recesses of my mind, Ruth's voice slices through, my dark saviour, summoned by the pain. "Lass mich, Kind. Du weisst nicht, was du tust!" *Let me, child. You don't know what you're doing.*

The other witch's song grows even louder now, drowning out the city in my ears, and I'm faced with an impossible choice – surrender to Ruth or face this threat alone and unprepared.

Ruth surges forward before I can even make the call, her might becoming overwhelming as she uses my body like a vessel she steers to her whims. Through my eyes, she surveys, then acts, I must admit, with the swift precision needed right now. Her hands – *my hands* – move delicately, skilfully extracting Anima from the rain. The magic coalesces into hot threads around me, forming a protective shield.

Now the other witch's spell can't get past Ruth's barrier, though the impact as it crashes against the shield sends tremors through me. But Ruth doesn't falter. Ruth doesn't stop at defence. Instead, she gathers more Anima, now drawing it from the electricity buzzing somewhere in the apartments behind the walls. She moulds the energy into blade-like shards, and for a second, they hover menacingly in the air – an impressive way to use magic I've never seen in my life. With a thrust of my hand, Ruth sends her shards hurtling towards the assailant, whose song falters as she stumbles backward. Another volley of Anima shards, and at last she turns tail, fleeing before Ruth's magic can impale her.

Once I'm safe, Ruth releases her hold on me, and I waste no time in running after the attacker witch. *"Who are you?"* I shout breathlessly as I give chase. "Who sent you?"

But as I round the corner, she's long gone.

I flag down a taxi, heart pounding as I slide into the back seat. The driver remains blissfully oblivious to the danger I expect at every red light. Feverishly, I scan the surrounding cars out of fear my hunter might come back for me.

There is, of course, a chilling precision in the timing of all this: I defy Mardequai, and only hours later, this assault on my life follows? It can't be coincidence. Then a new fear grips me: Mardequai knows where I'm staying. The Bowery Arms looms in my mind, no longer a safe haven but a potential trap.

As we pull up to the hotel, I delay as much as I can, fumbling with my wallet, coins slipping through my fingers as I pay the driver. My eyes dart across the pavement, searching for any sign of danger between parked cars and darkened alleyways. Out of other options, I turn to the driver. "I'm sorry, this might sound terribly silly, but would you mind walking me to the door? I've had a bit of a scary night."

"Of course, love," he replies.

Together, we step out into the night, and the short walk to the entrance feels like my very own gauntlet. At the doorstep, he asks, "Will you be alright from here?"

Every instinct within me wants to scream no, but I also can't push this man's kindness much further.

"Yes, thank you," I force out.

"Have a good night, ma'am," he responds and turns to leave.

I watch him go, the taillights of his taxi disappearing as I slip inside the hotel.

Ascending the stairs, taking two steps at a time, I fumble for my key card. Every creak of the old staircase sets my nerves on edge, and I keep scanning behind me. At last, the card reader beeps, and I practically fall into the room. The solid sound of the lock as I engage it feels comforting, even though I know no door lock will ever stop a witch.

Inside, Dennis's familiar snoring fills the room. On any other night, I'd find it irritating, but now it's a bit of normalcy after a night far out of my comfort zone. I creep to the window, parting the curtains just enough to see the pavement below. It's empty of pedestrians, but every car that passes just a little too slowly has me worried.

At last, tiredness overcomes me, and I change quickly into one of Dennis's T-shirts.

I slide under the covers, pressing close to his warmth. Finally, he stirs, his arm instinctively wrapping around me.

"So, how did it go?" he mumbles, and I burrow deeper into his arms, knowing full well that his protection won't hold against any magical threats, yet clinging to the illusion all the same.

"It went alright, I think," I mumble back, not wanting to worry him about what transpired on my way home.

A sudden snore signals he's drifted off again, but I'm still painfully aware of every creak in the old hotel. My eyes dart to the door at every distant sound, half expecting my attacker to burst in at any moment.

I don't know when I finally fall asleep, but my dreams that night are dark and dire.

Chapter Sixteen

I jolt awake like a startled hare bolting from its burrow.

My hand instinctively reaches for the familiar contours of my bedside table at the cabin, finding nothing. Then I realise I'm not in my own bed; I'm in a London hotel – and what roused me was a knock at the door.

I stumble out of bed, fumbling to pull my coat over the over-sized T-shirt I slept in. At the door, I hold my breath, pressing my ear against it. Another knock makes me jump, my heart racing.

Mentally rehearsing one of my mum's defence spells I finally remembered last night, my whole body tingles with Anima when I crack the door open the tiniest sliver, peering into the hallway. Initial relief washes over me as I recognise male features – not a witch, then. But that relief instantly goes out the window when I realise *who* it is.

In the hallway stands Cornelis Kettering, the druid who wouldn't stop staring at me during the Assembly, his gaze now just as intense as it was then, maybe even more so up close. His piercing blue eyes and sharp cheekbones further accentuate the cold disdain etched across his face. I'm about to say something when he raises his hand, a bit too suddenly – perhaps to knock again or shake my hand. Either way, my frayed nerves misinterpret the gesture entirely. Without hesitating, I unleash the spell I'd been holding at the ready, a burst of Anima erupting from my palms, catching Kettering in the stomach. His eyes widen in surprise as he's thrown backward, tumbling down the flight of stairs with a series of thuds and swear words – in what I believe to be Dutch.

Dennis's voice carries from behind me: "What happened now?"

"You've *got* to be kidding me," the druid curses from below.

I quickly scan the hallway, ensuring he's alone, then I hurry down the creaking stairs, apologies tumbling from my lips. "Oh shit, y-you scared me! I am so sorry! I didn't mean to—"

"I doubt that very much," he interrupts.

I reach out to help him up, but he recoils as if my hand were covered in thorns.

"DON'T! Don't you ever touch me, witch!" His harsh voice makes me flinch.

"Alright, alright, I'm sorry," I say, raising my hands in a placating gesture.

Now Dennis bounds down the stairs, barefoot and in boxers, but apparently ready for trouble. The scent of sleep wafts past me as he positions himself between the druid and me. "Who are you?" Dennis demands.

The druid grimaces as he grips the railing to pull himself up, gingerly probing his back.

"My name is Cornelis Kettering. I am here to escort the Hausmann witch to today's Assembly gathering." His reply is brief, professional, but still laced with disdain. Indeed, he sounds more like a sixteenth-century inquisitor, here to lead 'the Hausmann witch' off to the pyre.

"Escort me? On whose order?" I ask, crossing my arms, feeling exposed in my lumpy old T-shirt.

"Gathoni Nyong'o."

Relief overcomes me at the mention of the head elder's name – not Mardequai's.

The tension in my body eases, but it's short-lived. This isn't a kind gesture, I realise. This is a surveillance measure. The druid isn't here to chaperone – he's here to *watch* me, and probably report on my every move.

I study Kettering with fresh suspicion. "Thank you, but I'll find my way to Arcadia House alone." I'm already turning away from him, when he raises a very valid point.

"Only the Assembly isn't meeting at Arcadia House today, is it?" the druid says, adjusting his coat after the fall.

"It isn't?"

"Today is a field day, Beatrix Kiddo, so no. You're supposed to be at the Wytchwood in Oxfordshire at nine. That's a two-hour drive from London, if you don't account for traffic. Which means you're already late." The druid begins descending the stairs, his whole demeanour as icy as the draft coming up the stairwell. "You might want to put on some pants. I'll be waiting at the car."

The scent of him lingers, a mix of sandalwood and something earthy.

"I won't get into a car with you," I say, hating that my voice wavers.

He turns to glance up at me through the banister. "Suit yourself, witch. I don't care *how* you're planning on getting there; the car would certainly be the quickest. But let's get one thing out of the way right now, shall we?" he says, his stormy eyes locking onto mine. "I don't like it any more than you, but I'm under strict orders not to leave your side. Which means I will be your constant shadow for the next six days. So how about you don't set us off on the wrong foot – at least not more than you already have – and just cooperate?" With that, he disappears behind the staircase.

I turn to Dennis, speechless.

"Auf gar keinen Fall!" *No bloody way,* he declares, eyes flashing with anger, teeth clenching with disapproval. His opposition would likely be less fierce if my escort were a white-bearded druid, jittering from old age, not this – undeniably – handsome grump who could best Dennis in a fight with ease.

"I don't think I have a choice here," I say as gently as I can, then make my way back up the stairs.

"Fine. I am coming with you, then." His tone brooks no argument, but we both know it's futile.

"Come on, Dennis. You know that's not possible."

Back in the room, I slip into a pair of jeans and a fresh long-sleeve shirt, then splash some cold water on my face, the shock helping to clear my head before I reach for my makeup bag.

"What are you doing that for?" Dennis points at my mascara brush.

I consider him through the bathroom mirror while I apply my makeup. "What do you mean? I do this every morning."

"Just wondering why you're primping for a day with Mr-Tall-Dark-and-Handsome down there," he says through gritted teeth.

I almost laugh when I hear this until I realise, he's actually serious.

"I'm not 'primping' for anything, okay? I... listen, can we please just not start the day fighting?"

A car horn blares from the street outside, conveniently cutting through a conversation I'd rather not have right now, anyway.

I push past Dennis and turn to the window. Down below, Kettering leans against a silver Volkswagen, hand pressed firmly on the horn. Even from this distance, I can see the impatience on his face.

"Mother of Nature, could he *be* more annoying?" I mutter, turning back to Dennis while simultaneously reaching for my shoes. "Look, I'm sorry but I've got to go now. Just, you know, just try to enjoy your day. You're on vacation after all."

"Some vacation," Dennis mutters, then steps into the bathroom, closing the door behind him.

I linger, my hand half raised to reopen the door. I know I should say something more, offer some words of comfort, but they elude me entirely. My fingers twitch and curl, thumbs brushing against their tips in a fidgety pattern. Finally, with a sigh, I grab my coat and slip out of the room.

Stepping out onto the rain-slicked pavement, the cold morning air bites at my skin and I round the car. The druid ignores me and slides into the driver's seat. The car's interior smells of new plastic and artificial pine. From the rearview mirror dangles a laminated rental tag.

"I need coffee," I say, my voice rough from too little sleep as I fasten the seatbelt. At the push of a button, the electric engine hums to life.

"There's no time for that." Kettering manoeuvres the car into a constant stream of morning traffic.

"Well, last time I checked, shadows don't get to have a say," I say, my throat tingling with Anima as I think of spells to hex him with. "We're stopping at the next coffee shop, or you're going to experience firsthand how a witch without her morning caffeine will turn this little jaunt to the countryside into your worst nightmare."

* * *

One and a half hours of determined silence later, the druid turns off the highway, and a patchwork of green fields and perfectly aligned hedgerows unfolds before us. Mist still sits in the valleys, barely dissipating in the autumn sun as the narrow country lane leads us through the serene landscape of Oxfordshire.

Out of the corner of my eye, I steal a glance at Kettering, curiosity getting the better of me. How old is he, really? I heard once that druid children age normally until adulthood, making it almost impossible to distinguish them from humans early on. But once the first signs of aging fail to appear – crow's feet around the eyes, subtle lines across the forehead, a grey hair here and there – you've got yourself a genuine druid. If I had to guess, Kettering was probably sired during the last Solantha passing, maybe the one before. That would put him somewhere between 108 and 216 years old. *A real cradle robber*, I think wryly, suppressing a smirk. It's strange to think this man, who looks barely older than thirty, might have witnessed the Battle of Waterloo *and* the birth of the internet.

"So, what's with the staring?" I ask, fidgeting with the empty paper cup in my hands.

"This might come as a shock to you, but keeping your eyes on the road does wonders to avoid crashing," he replies, sounding bored, but his knuckles give him away, whitening as he grips the steering wheel.

"I mean during the Assembly. You know me from somewhere, admit it."

"I don't know you," he says.

"Yes, you do."

"It doesn't matter."

"It matters to *me*."

"That is none of my concern."

He pulls to the verge, braking probably harder than necessary. I turn to look at him, not even trying to hide my irritation. "What are you? A robot?"

"You have arrived at your destination," he intones in a mock robot voice.

"So, you're funny now?"

"I don't do funny," he replies and takes off his seatbelt with a nod out the windscreen. "This is the Wytchwood. This is where the Assembly meets today."

My mouth forms a silent O as my gaze follows his.

Ahead of us, a line of cars is parked along the edge of a small woodland. Beyond the trees, an open field comes into view, dotted with people all moving towards a central point. As I open the door, the murmur of voices carries on the crisp morning air, mingling with birdsong.

I step out of the car, the damp grass wetting my shoes. As I bury my hands in my pockets, seeking warmth, my fingers brush against my smartphone in one pocket and curl around the familiar smooth surface of the obsidian rock in the other, its presence comforting, as always.

Hesitantly, I approach the gathering, hanging back in the last row. The witches and druids have formed a loose circle around a young witch perched atop a tree stump, barely twenty and already carrying herself like a woman who has never once doubted her right to be heard.

"For decades, we've worked in the shadows, using our magic to heal this wounded planet, haven't we? Cleansing rivers, regrowing deforested land, even guiding scientists towards renewable energy breakthroughs. But it's not enough. It's never enough.

"Remember the 'miraculous' wildlife recovery in Chernobyl or the 'rapid' rebound of the Australian coral reefs? Humans patted themselves on the back, thinking the problem was solved. But it only led to complacency. 'Nature can heal itself if we just step back', they keep saying. And that's what happens if we keep acting from the shadows.

"Let's also not forget that those were isolated successes in an ocean of ongoing destruction. For every forest we regrow, ten more are cut down. For every endangered species we bring back, a hundred more face extinction."

The crowd murmurs, some witches exchanging worried glances, some druids nodding grimly.

"You see, we can no longer afford to work in secret. Our efforts, powerful as they might be, remain way too localised, too limited. We need to come forward and share our knowledge openly, so that we can integrate our magic with modern science and technology."

The young witch takes a breath, her eyes sweeping across the gathering before she continues.

"Let's imagine a world where our magic could actually end global hunger, where our rituals could be scaled up to cleanse entire *oceans*. Let's dare to picture our healing spells working in tandem with modern medicine. But more than that, let's dare to inspire. The reveal of our existence, of Anima, pulsing through the earth beneath us, could reconnect humanity to the true wonder of our world. It could spark a real shift, a global reawakening to their own role in this world."

As her words carry across the open space, I feel Kettering looming behind me, the proximity raising the hairs on the back of my neck. Suddenly, my phone blares to life, its ring disturbing the moment of reverent silence. Instantly, all eyes swivel around to me, all accusatory stares. My cheeks burn as I fumble around in my pocket, fingers clumsy as I struggle to get the phone out.

"Sorry, I am so sorry...," I mutter, switching it off at last. Goddammit, Dennis.

And who'd have thought it could get worse? But now annoyance yields to recognition on their faces, as their memory of yesterday's Assembly clearly lingers. Wonderful, now people actually take subtle steps away from me, creating an island of space that singles me out as the outsider.

Not a moment too soon, the young witch's voice pipes up again.

"Today, witches and druids have gathered all around England to restore natural habitats. From the chalk streams of Hampshire to the peat lands of Yorkshire, from the wetlands of Norfolk to the cliffs of Dover. And if we do this right, the news will pick up on this remarkable recovery we're attempting, so we can present our results at the climate summit, showing what we are truly capable of."

Across the crowd, movement catches my eye, and then I spot him – Mardequai. Our eyes meet, a silent exchange, but it's chock-full with tension. The druid stands in earnest discussion with a witch about his age – if we go by his looks alone. Her hair falls in wild waves of red streaked with silver; her face is etched with harsh lines around the eyes and mouth. As she listens to Mardequai, her eyes, too, flick towards me, and I lower my gaze quickly. Clearly, they are talking about me.

"We here at the Wytchwood have an important part to play in this countrywide effort," the instructing witch says. "Covering a hundred and twenty square miles, from the Cotswolds to the floodplains of the Thames, the Wytchwood remains the least developed region in the whole of Oxfordshire. Traces of ancient habitats can still be found here, as well as limestone grasslands and even woodland from a thousand years ago. If nature can regain a real foothold anywhere in the county – it is here."

She jumps off her stump and claps her hands together. "Alright, now let's get started! I suggest we split into three factions. This corner here will create ponds," she says as she herds part of the group like sheep. "You people here will grow new saplings, and you to my left will rejuvenate old trees. As is our tradition, witches will work in partnership with druids on this. Druids give knowledge and advice, witches will execute. So, if all witches could please gather around a druid? Oh, and if the druids could also take a couple of snapshots and videos with their smartphones, please? That would be much appreciated so we can present evidence during the summit."

A collective grumble rises from the half a dozen or so druids, as the witches begin to bustle about, gravitating towards them. I suppose I've already found my partner, if I like it or not. Kettering and I are like rue and basil, planted in the same pot. Minutes pass as everyone else shuffles around, but I'm still the only witch on this druid's team.

"I see you're real popular," Kettering says.

"What makes you think it's me?" I reply, but he just fixes me with a look that could sour honey, eyebrow arched as if to say 'Witch, *please*'.

"Come on, Carrie White, let's make you an influencer then," he says and trudges off into the woods.

But I don't follow him. Instead, I find Mardequai, who leads his group of witches up a nearby hillside, his mean-looking companion still close by his side. I hug the tree line, stumbling over fallen trees and rocks as I move, desperate to get closer and overhear what they might be talking about. The wind carries fragments of their conversation, snippets that only fuel my determination, but I still cannot hear. Hunched low, I inch forward when the breaking of twigs betrays Kettering coming up behind me.

"Where do you think you're going?" he asks, his voice forever tinged with irritation. "We're supposed to go into the woods, not into the fields."

I ignore him, my focus entirely on Mardequai and the witch as I use a fallen tree as cover.

But then, to my frustration, Kettering's voice booms out.

"Good morning, Mr Guise, Mrs Morrigan?" He waves to Mardequai and the witch. Mardequai returns the gesture, but when his eyes land on me, his face darkens.

"What are you doing?" I hiss at Kettering.

"I'm greeting one of my brothers," Kettering replies. The glint in his eye tells me he knows *exactly* what he's done. I'm about to turn on my heel, huffing in annoyance, but then Mardequai yells something, and I stop cold when I hear it.

"I see you drew the unfortunate straw to pair up with the Hausmann-witch today, Cornelis. Quite befitting, I suppose. You two, after all, go way back."

The witch beside him leans in, whispering something, the act alone vexing me. Her eyes dart to me again, and they are filled with spite, but there's also a flicker of shock, as if she's seeing a ghost. Mardequai, too, casts me one last glance, lips curling into a sneer. Then, as if I'm not even worth acknowledging, he turns his back.

I, too, walk away, now turning to Kettering for answers. "What did he mean, you and I go way back?"

But he doesn't answer, only sets his jaw in a hard line as we make our way deeper into the forest.

"Come on, Cornelis." I try again, a little gentler this time. "I know you're hiding something."

He doesn't even glance my way.

"Was it during the war? Did you... did you know my grandmother?" I press, but now with a sense of dark foreboding.

Still nothing.

"Look, I'm sorry if I've done something or said something to offend you, but you can't just ignore me forever."

As if trying to outrun my questions, his pace quickens, which strikes me as incredibly silly. What are we – twelve?

"For heaven's sake, Kettering!" I exclaim, grabbing his arm. "Just – spit it out already."

Finally, the druid snaps. And then I wish he hadn't. As he whirls to face me, his eyes blaze with pain and rage and disgust – all directed at me. "You want to know? Fine! I'll tell you." He takes a step towards me, and I back up against a tree. "You killed my family, *witch*," he spits out.

I feel the blood drain from my face. "What? No, that can't be..."

"Oh, but it is." Kettering's voice drops to a hurt murmur. "They were... they were there... they were on Sylt." He leans in close, his eyes bearing down on mine. "So, forgive me if I'm not in the mood for small talk with the mass murderer responsible for ending my daughter's life."

With that, he lets go of me and stalks away, leaving me stunned from the hot blaze of guilt his words have sparked. I want to say something, my mouth already opening, but what could I possibly say to make *this* right? Regret settles in now – for pushing him, for dredging up his painful past. I want to apologise, maybe make amends somehow, but nothing I say could ever be good enough. *I* will never be good enough.

Now alone, I plunge deeper into the woodland, the air growing thick with the scent of September, each step of mine heavy like I'm wading through a thick bog. All around, witches disperse to go about their tasks of doing good. I watch them and feel more out of place than ever. Some plant seedlings with reverent care, others kneel to pick up the first acorns of the year, cradling them to infuse them with Anima. Close by, I see a witch pressing her palms against an ancient birch until its branches begin to creak and stretch with new growth, fresh green shoots spiralling outward.

I, too, pretend to search for a suitable old tree, but really, I'm still trying to process the horror of what I've just learned. To my surprise, I notice that Kettering still follows me.

"Are you going to do something at some point?" he asks when he realises, I've spotted him.

I turn around, but what I'm about to say sticks in my throat as I meet his gaze, those flinty eyes of his still filled with endless amounts of pain. I'm tempted to just run off, to flee from this entire situation. But I know I can't.

"I... I don't know how to," I admit then, my head slightly nodding toward a nearby tree.

Kettering's jaw clenches, but something about my confession must get through to him because he lets out a sigh, leaning against a tree trunk as if defeated.

"Look, I know it doesn't change anything, but I'm so sorry for what she did. If there was any way I could make it right—"

"You can't," he cuts me off and quickly changes the subject, explaining how to rejuvenate a dying tree. "A witch must first feel for its soul. She must access the flow of life within its core, no matter how faint it may have become. Then, she can channel her energy into the trunk, feeding it, nurturing it back to health."

As he speaks, I can almost see the invisible threads of Anima, coursing through the entire forest.

"The witch must focus on thoughts of growth, of expansion," he says. "Visualise the tree as it once was, and what it could be again. Her magic will be like a catalyst, reminding the tree of its own will to live."

I'm about to give it a go, but then his guidance is tainted by a cold finish: "Of course, given your history, I expect you to be better at destroying something than healing it."

His words land exactly how he wanted them to, burrowing into me like parasites, feeding on my shame. Despite it all, I try my best to push it down. I must try. I must prove to him that I can do something good – anything good.

Determined, I turn to face an ancient, gnarled oak, its weathered bark like dinosaur scales. I try to reach out, hovering my palms gently in front of it before I close my eyes.

As feared, nothing happens. I push my brows together, focussing harder, willing something to occur.

"Having trouble finding the 'on' switch?" Kettering mocks, breaking my concentration. He wants me to fail at this. But I grit my teeth, now more than ever refusing to give up. Taking a breath, I try again, now with much more force stirring within me.

Still nothing.

My frustration mounts as I force my energy onto the tree. But then I remember the druid's words about connecting with the tree's soul. I need to soften my approach, open myself to its presence instead of forcing my will upon the oak. Offering help instead of asserting my power.

And then, to my amazement, the woods fade away, replaced by a tingling pulsing beneath my fingertips – the tree, reaching out ever so gently. Awed by this connection, I ask what it needs, what I can do for it – and to my utter relief, I feel an answer coming. As a result, I allow Anima to flow through my hands and into the tree, a stream of energy surging through withered roots and once-dead branches.

A gasp escapes me when I feel the tree reviving, its might strengthening.

"Turn... turn sideways, goddammit," Kettering instructs. He shifts to position himself right next to me, capturing the moment with his phone. "It needs to be obvious that it's you doing this. Otherwise, what's the point?"

Emboldened, I lean into my task. Confidence swelling, I feel a heady rush of power in my chest. But as my magic grows stronger, so does something else – *someone* else. Ruth stirs somewhere deep within me, apparently awakened by my rising powers. Instantly, she twists the flow of energy, corrupts it somehow so that the oak's branches begin to crack – then blacken as if someone has poured a barrel of tar over them. Leaves wither and fall, raining death and decay all around us.

I whirl towards Kettering, but I know I'm no longer in control. Behind me, the tree continues to die, and something dark within me even revels in the demise. Instead of rejuvenating the tree, now I'm sapping its remaining life, draining it until it flows into my own body, which is terrifyingly intoxicating. Each dying leaf, each cracking branch, sends a thrill through my veins until raw hunger urges me to unleash the overspill of power unto the entire forest.

"RUTH, stop it!" Kettering commands, grabbing me. And in that split second when our eyes lock, I see myself reflected in his gaze. Shock has widened his eyes, mixed with a hatred so hot, it burns.

Seeing his reaction, I just about manage to claw back control over my own body. I stumble backwards, gasping for breath, pushing Ruth back to that dark corner somewhere deep within me. Then I fix Kettering with an exasperated look.

"Don't you ever call me by her name again. *Ever* – do you hear me?" I manage, each word a struggle as I recover from the loss of control. "I am *not* her."

I turn away from the druid, facing the damaged oak, tears swelling as I take in the destruction. Hands shaking, I push past the tree, seeking solitude deep in the woods. Soon, the chatter of the group fades in the distance, replaced by a stillness that seems to press in on me from all sides. Kettering lingers, the perfect shadow – always close by, yet never quite within reach.

Trying to ignore his presence, I spot a delicate wood sorrel nestled between exposed roots, its yellow petals drooping lifelessly. Dropping to my knees, I ignore the chill seeping through my jeans from the damp leaves. Desperate to prove myself, I stretch out my hands again, trying once more to channel some goodness. Once more, I grasp for that elusive thread of Anima, but it slips from my hands like a wet bar of soap.

"Please," I whisper. "Show me how to help you." The plea becomes a quiet song, growing more urgent with each repetition. "Show me how to help you... Show me how to help you..."

Suddenly, the tiny petals twitch, then the faintest glimmer emanates from its stems, making my heart leap in my chest – it's working!

I'm about to make the sorrel bloom again, when out of nowhere, something slams into me, knocking all air from my lungs. Then I feel a pair of strong arms wrap around my waist – Kettering, dragging me onward until I land hard on the forest floor. My panic spiking, everything becomes a blur of greens and browns, twigs and roots tearing at my clothes, scraping my skin. Then a deafening crack splits the air, and for a moment, it's as if time stands still. Just when I'm gazing around to find out what's happening, the ground beneath me shudders as if an earthquake has occurred.

I catch a glimpse of what the druid helped me to evade: a beech tree, tall as a three-storied house, crashing down, its massive trunk splintering exactly where the wood sorrel was. One of its branches just about catches my coat, tearing the fabric.

For a few disorienting moments, I can't even fathom what happened. My head spins, adrenalin shooting into my legs, while Kettering's body presses me into the damp soil, his chest heaving against my back as leaves rain down on us. Despite myself, I'm acutely aware of every point of contact between our bodies, the warmth of his breath, the grip of his hands on both my arms.

As if I were made of burning coals, he rolls off me and scrambles to his feet. His eyes dart wildly around the clearing, and I follow his gaze, my own heart racing as I scan between the trees. *Who did this?*

The air is still charged with the unmistakable residue of wielded magic. It's even visible amid the trees, a faint shimmer like heat waves coming off hot tar. Yet we are alone. No one lurks behind the fallen tree; no rustle betrays the assailant. Just Kettering and me, and the fallen giant, its abrupt collapse telling me that this was not an accident. As of this moment, I'm certain that someone wants me dead.

* * *

Kettering pulls up to the hotel just as night settles over London.

The rest of the day passed in a tense blur. After my near-miss with a falling tree, I'd gone to hide in the car, not in the mood to risk any more magical mishaps. I wanted to flee the scene entirely, but Kettering's rental was hemmed in on both sides, so we were forced to wait until the forest restoration was concluded. Naturally, the druid chose not to join me inside, instead taking up a post leaning against the bonnet, his eyes wandering over the surrounding trees, his head tilting occasionally as if tracking something soaring past. I could have sworn he was birding.

Back at the Bowery Arms, I step out onto the pavement, when, to my irritation, Kettering follows me.

Finally, the tension that's been building all day snaps.

"Look," I say, whirling to face him, "I know you're under strict orders and all that, but I swear, if you won't let me walk to my room alone, I'm going to scream all the way up to the second floor. Go home, I beg of you – or, you know, go to wherever it is you're staying tonight."

"That's precisely what I am doing," Kettering replies, retrieving a key card from his wallet. "I checked into the hotel last night."

"You've *got* to be kidding me."

"By the way, you might want to tell your boyfriend he should try sleeping on his side. I could hear him snoring through the wall. How do you sleep through that? Unless it wasn't him, of course – but you."

Heat rises to my cheeks, and I don't know if it's embarrassment or rage, but I'm tempted to unleash every ounce of my magic either way, his opinion of me be damned.

"Why didn't you just let the tree hit me?" I blurt out instead, whirling back around, my voice drawing curious glances from passersby.

For a moment, I think I can see Kettering's usual indifference cracking, but once again, all I get from him is stony silence.

"Goodnight, Kettering," I mumble. I turn on my heel and stride towards the hotel entrance.

But I know he won't be far behind.

Chapter Seventeen

I hurry up the stairs, determined to escape Kettering, if only for the night. But when I arrive on the second floor, the sight of Dennis stops me cold. He's sitting on the steps, phone in hand, his packed bag beside him.

"What are you doing out here?" I ask, guilt roiling in my stomach. Only now do I realise that he had all day to wallow in the morning's tensions, which still hang unresolved between us. Dennis's jaw is set, his eyes hard – clearly, he's been rehearsing this moment for hours. Behind me, I hear Kettering's footsteps on the stairs.

"I've changed my flight. It's leaving late tonight," Dennis says. "One last chance, Alva. That's the only reason I'm still here. Rebook your flight." He thrusts his phone at me, the screen's glow harsh in the dim hallway. "Do it now."

I freeze, staring at the phone. Behind me, Kettering clears his throat. Dennis shoots him a deadly stare past my shoulder.

"Let's just go back inside and talk about this, okay?" I plead with Dennis.

"I would love to do that, I would. But *she's* in there."

"Who?" My eyes dart to our room door, blood rushing in my ears as I push past Dennis, fumbling with the doorknob.

The door swings open, and there she is.

"Surprise," Sofia drawls, sprawled across our bed like a cat, the tinny sounds of *Britain's Got Talent* filling the room from the TV.

"What are you doing here?" I stammer.

"Watching a bit of telly. And who is this?" Sofia asks, eyes on Kettering in the hallway.

"He's... nobody." I brush my hands through the air as if the druid were a stickman on a chalkboard I can simply wipe away. "Look, I'm thrilled you came to see me, but could you please do me a favour and just wait outside for a while? There's a pub across the street. I'll come meet you there soon."

Sofia swings her legs off the bed dramatically. "Fine, fine. I know when I'm not wanted."

"Hey, but don't you go anywhere, okay?" I call after her.

To my relief, she pauses once more at the door. "As long as they serve old fashioneds, I tend to remain rooted in one spot."

I turn to Kettering next. "And you, go to your room, close the door behind you, and turn on the TV so I can hear it through the wall. You have no business overhearing our conversation."

"He moved into the hotel now?" Dennis asks.

"Yes, he did. Now you – come with me."

At last, the door thuds closed behind Dennis and me. I stand by the window, while Dennis sits on the bed. Next door, the TV springs to life, a weather forecast droning through the wall.

"I'm so sorry," I say, "This is turning out to be an absolute nightmare for you. Sofia can be a bit intense. I hope she hasn't been rude to you."

"Well, she called me 'Baron von Boring'. Other than that,

let's just say there's a reason why I waited out in the hall and not in the room... the over-expensive room that *I* paid for to be with you, mind you."

I look at him, seeing the disappointment in every line of his face.

"Come with me," he pleads. "We don't belong here. And you don't need these people. Let's just... let's go home."

The word 'home' sticks with me, and part of me wants to do it. To run, to feel safe in the familiar. But that part is small, a pebble compared to the mountain of life – *my* life – waiting for me if I stay.

I turn toward the window, watching Sofia cross the street below, sauntering through a red light, unfazed by honking cars, then slipping into the pub.

"I can't," I say, the words escaping before I lose the courage to say them. I turn back to Dennis. "I'm so sorry, but I can't."

Dennis nods, resignation on his face. Beneath it, I can already see his anger simmering. He grabs his jacket, shrugging it on more forcefully than necessary. At last, he explodes. "What was I to you, really? These past three years. Was I just a-a-a... placeholder? And the life we've built together? Was that all a lie?"

"You were never a placeholder," I insist, meaning every word. I approach him, reaching out a hand but he won't take it now. "But I did lie to you," I confess. "I never was who you thought I was. And I'm sorry about that. I didn't think this was going to happen. I never thought I would get back what I've lost."

His face contorts with rage, a side of him I've rarely witnessed. It reminds me of the time he discovered someone had been poaching on the reserve – his fury then had been terrifying.

"You are making a huge mistake, you know that?" he spits.

"And when you realise it, don't you come crawling back to me to pick up the pieces."

He storms out, slamming the door so hard the walls shake.

I slump onto the bed, regret bubbling up inside me at how poorly I handled that. The TV in the next room switches off only seconds after Dennis has left.

"Thanks for pretending, Kettering..." I yell at the wall.

* * *

The pub is warmly lit, a cosy sanctuary from the chaotic London night. Rich mahogany walls are adorned with intricate gold leaf designs and ornate glass panels, giving the place an air of timeless elegance. Sofia perches on a high-backed wooden chair at the bar, swirling a drink.

I slide onto the barstool next to her, snatching what remains of her drink, downing it in one go, then grimacing at the alcohol burn in my throat.

"Easy there, tiger." Sofia chuckles.

"I never drink alcohol," I gasp, wiping my mouth.

"How do you get through the day?"

"Not well – clearly."

A beat of silence passes between us.

"You want to go for a walk?" I suggest.

"Love to."

As we exit the pub, Kettering is waiting. Of course, he's waiting.

Sofia eyes him. "You move quick, sis, I give you that."

"Who? Him? He's not a conquest; he's a druid. And he's ordered not to leave my side, unfortunately."

"A druid?" Sofia snorts. "Shouldn't you be off boring people with your battle stories from the French Revolution, grandpa?"

I can't help but smirk. "I'd say you get used to him, but you don't, really." Turning to Kettering, I lay down the law. "Look, we're going for a walk now. If you're coming – which I have no doubt you will, regardless of what I say – you stay ten paces behind, understood?"

Kettering barely flinches, but his eyes burn with spite.

Sofia and I make our way into Hyde Park, leaving the city to fade behind us. Moonlight filters through the trees as we walk, casting dappled shadows on our path. The traffic noise is muted here, replaced by the rustle of leaves in the wind and the crunch of our shoes on the gravel.

"So, what's with the bodyguard?" Sofia asks, jerking her head back at Kettering.

"Well, you heard what happened at the Assembly – apparently, I'm deemed unsafe, thanks to our wicked grandmother pushing into my consciousness at the most inappropriate moments."

"Well, personally, I'm offended that *you're* the twin who's deemed special. I've got my own hotline to the past." She pokes me in the side. "Who sent the fossil, anyway?"

"Gathoni Nyong'o."

"*That* woman..."

"You know her?"

"Everyone does. But aside from being the Assembly's head elder, she's also the chancellor of Chyulu Academy. Single-handedly kicked me out earlier this year."

"You went to *Chyulu?*" A bout of envy overcomes me. The Chyulu Academy of Higher Magic in Kenya is the pinnacle of magical education. Only the most gifted and promising students are invited to study there. I'm both proud and a little jealous when I realise Sofia must have become a truly powerful witch – expelled or not. When we were kids, I was usually the one to get the hang of a new spell first. Now the difference in our magical skills suddenly feels like a chasm, and I feel left behind.

"And why did you come over tonight?" I ask her, kicking an acorn across the path.

Sofia deftly kicks it back. "I wasn't going to," she confesses.

"What made you change your mind?"

"Not what – *who*."

It occurs to me then that she might be talking about her foster father but just when I'm about to raise the alarm bells once again, Sofia seems to catch my sentiment and adds, "Pippa, my PA. Turns out she has quite strong opinions on repairing family bonds in a world that's about to be turned upside down."

Relief washes over me. "I like her," I say.

"Yeah, she has her way of getting under your skin, whether you want her to or not. She would also like to inform you that the weekly Venus in Fur coven meet-up is tomorrow."

"*She* would?"

"Well, as the coven magistrate it is my pleasure and my duty to invite you, of course. Five in the afternoon tomorrow. We're at the old Gin Distillery in Shoreditch. Black warehouse on the corner of Brick Lane and Woodseer Street – you can't miss it."

"Thanks, I'll be there."

We come across a playground, and without a word, we both move towards it, muscle memory from childhood taking over as we settle side by side on two swings.

"I don't blame you for it," Sofia says suddenly, her legs dangling. "The accident."

I nod, trying to speak past the lump in my throat, but no words will come.

"I miss them," she says.

"Me too."

"Hey, you ever wonder what she would make of everything, the reveal and all?"

"Mama?"

"Yeah. I reckon she would get a crack out of it, don't you? She'd be at the forefront of the entire movement, join every committee, probably start a magical advice column via the Resonance Network." Sofia laughs.

"Oh god, yes. And Dad would be right there with her, trying to explain magic using quantum physics or something," I chuckle. "Do you remember that time when she nearly exposed her magic to that one neighbour? She'd used a growth spell on her tomatoes, and they grew big as watermelons. And when old Herr Peters marvelled at their size—"

"She blurted out something about 'experimental fertiliser,'" Sofia finishes my sentence. "Spent the next month concocting those bizarre mixtures of compost and kitchen scraps to keep up the charade, and the—"

"The whole street smelled like rotting vegetables for weeks," we finish together, and both crack up laughing.

Eventually, Sofia jumps off her swing, and I follow her.

"What happened to you?" she asks as we weave through a cluster of teenagers, cigarette smoke mingling with the hip-hop beats coming from their phones. "After the accident, where did you go?"

And then I tell her about Haus der Hoffnung, how the other foster kids thought I was weird (Ember nods knowingly at this), and how I lived homeless in the German woods for years. The latter draws a serious look from her but also a pinch of respect.

As we stroll, I find myself constantly scanning the park, my eyes darting from shadow to shadow, searching for any hint of a threat.

"Someone tried to kill me – twice, actually, over the past twenty-four hours," I say abruptly.

Sofia stops in her tracks. "Are you sure?"

"Well, unless you'd consider hexing me with a freeze spell

and making a giant tree fall right where I was standing two unlucky coincidences, then yes: I'm sure."

"Who?"

"I don't know who she is. I don't even know if it was the same witch both times. All I know is that," – I stop, remembering Sofia's previous reaction when I so much as mentioned her foster father – "Gathoni warned me of him – Mardequai."

"Of course, she did."

"Well, she must have had a good reason."

"Listen, you've only just re-entered this world, so there's a lot you don't know. But basically, those two have been on opposite ends of the spectrum ever since the referendum was first announced. And quite frankly, not everyone is as excited about the Reveal as she is."

"Including you? How did you vote?"

"That's private."

"Come on, who am I going to tell?"

Sofia sighs. "Fine. I voted in favour. But only because I'm tired of pretending my success comes from 'daddy's money' when I can literally charm my way into any VIP event with a flick of my wrist. I'm done dimming my light. *However* – that doesn't mean I'm subscribing to the whole kumbaya bullshit the head elder's posse is trying to spread. Anyone who thinks humanity will take kindly to us clearly has never read a history book."

"Does he know how you voted? Mardequai?"

Sofia scoffs. "If he knew, he'd probably disown me."

I shove my hands in my pockets, contemplating whether or not to say what I'm thinking. But then I can't stop myself.

"Look, I know he took you in and looked after you and all that. But I don't trust him. And I think neither should you."

Her eyes flash dangerously. "I'm sorry, but you are in no

position to say that to me. I know him, alright? Probably better than anybody."

I fall silent, searching her face. Frankly, I find it hard to believe that a twenty-six-year-old would be the one to best know a man who's lived through the rise and fall of empires. And Sofia's next words reveal cracks in her own certainty.

"Why would he try to harm you? What possible reason could he have?" she asks, slumping down onto a park bench.

In the distance, I spot Kettering. He's standing stock-still, head tilted back, peering up into the canopy of an oak, probably marvelling at some owl. Despite all his grumpiness, I'm glad he's here. Not that he could defend me exactly, should a witch come charging from the bushes. But it's a lot less likely one might try, as long as one of Gathoni's watchdogs is around.

"I don't know," I say softly, taking a seat next to Sofia. "He was perfectly nice to me before the Assembly. But after he questioned me, after I spoke out in favour of the Reveal, his manner shifted."

Sofia shakes her head as if to stop the truth from getting in. "I just don't see how he could be so short-sighted. It's not like him. You don't understand: he is smart. He is the definition of cunning and foresight. And to assassinate the most important figure in this Reveal, maybe with the exception of Nyong'o, a day after he publicly attacked you? That's just not his style, I'm sorry. Mardequai operates from the shadows, and he's usually three steps ahead of everyone else."

I look down at my hands, waiting one, two, three beats. "I must have missed the part where you tell me your foster father is a kind and loving man who'd never hurt a fly, let alone kill somebody," I murmur.

Sofia turns to me with a hint of pity. "I envy your innocence, you know that? But I hate to break it to you: the magical world isn't the beautiful fairytale Mama made it out to be when we were kids. It's complex, often brutal, and rarely black and white."

She stands up, taking a few steps away. "Look, if you want to be a part of my life, there's one thing you need to understand, alright?"

"What's that?" I ask, still on the bench.

"I have changed and... and I *want* change, for witches, for our future. But change – *real change* – never comes without sacrifice. The old world has to burn for the new one to rise from its ashes. And sometimes, that means making hard choices."

She almost sounds as if she needs to convince herself, not me. Either way, I'm alarmed at the heavy undertones.

"What exactly are you saying?" I ask.

She turns back to me then, a new determination in her stance. "I'm saying that the world is about to get one hell of a wake-up call. And we need to be ready to seize the opportunity when it comes. No matter the cost." I can hear the passion in her voice, the conviction, but there's something else too – a hardness that wasn't present when we were children.

"What does that mean?"

Now Sofia's eyes flash with a fierce light. "It means, when this Reveal happens, I will make sure that witches come out on top. Our kind has been hunted, persecuted, and forced into hiding for centuries. But no more. I will fight tooth and nail, and so will the witches in my wake. We will stand up against anyone who tries to cage us again. And Mardequai? I hate to break it to you, but he's the one you want on your side when shit hits the fan, *trust* me."

With that, she begins to walk away.

"You know who used that kind of rhetoric?" I call out, hurrying after her. "Ruth, that's who."

Sofia freezes mid-step, releasing the breath she's been holding.

"He's manipulating you," I say, somewhat softer now. "Can't you see that?"

She picks up the pace again. "Don't go there, Alva. If you know what's best for you, stop it right now."

"Ask him about the accident," I blurt out. It's a shot in the dark, a bold assumption based on nothing but my dislike of the druid. But it's also a gut feeling, and rarely have I been wrong about those. "Ask him what happened that night."

Slowly, Sofia turns back to face me, the light from a streetlamp casting half her face in shadow. "I *have* asked him. He had nothing to do with it, he swore it to me."

But now I can clearly see the conflict in her face – there's loyalty to Mardequai, no doubt, but my words are having an effect on her, too.

"And you believe him?" I ask gently, sensing an opening.

Her silence is more telling than any answer could be. She looks almost lost, vulnerable – so unlike the rebellious witch of moments ago.

"I do," she says, a little too late. "He has been there for me, he gave me a new life the day my old one went up in flames, and today I am *his* daughter just as... just as much as I was theirs."

And then it hits me, the detail that felt off in the car yesterday morning when Mardequai told me he was the first to arrive at the crash site. His words struck a false chord then, and now I understand why.

"Then riddle me this," I say, the thought forming in my mind at the same time I voice it. "Up until the moment I reached out to you three weeks ago, he presumed me dead, right? He thought I'd died in that crash thirteen years ago, together with Mama and Dad. And for reasons I have yet to uncover, no one from the Elster Coven told him I was still alive, and that I had confessed it was *my* loss of control which caused the accident."

"I suppose." Sofia folds her arms in front of her chest. I close the gap between us, my eyes drilling into hers.

"Then why did he ask me – the morning *before* I admitted it publicly, mind you – if I still feel guilty for it? How could he have known, Sofia? How could he have known *I* caused the accident? You go and you ask him *that*."

Chapter Eighteen

The Belgravia mansion looms before Ember, its white brick walls perfectly illuminated against the evening sky. She approaches the front door, and after a firm knock, the door swings open to reveal Michaela, a witch and Mardequai's long-time housemaid.

Michaela's face, etched with the wrinkles of her seventy odd years, softens at the sight of Ember. "Miss Wild, what a pleasant surprise. It's been quite some time," she says, her tone welcoming despite the late hour.

"Hello, Michaela. Is he here?" Ember asks, stepping inside.

"He is, but..." Michaela says, "he's currently, well, *occupied*. He is painting in the drawing room."

"That's fine. I'll wait." As Ember makes her way down the familiar corridor, lined with ancient tapestries and paintings that cost a small fortune each, she can't help but wonder why Mardequai still bothers with it all. The schemes, the power struggles, the politics.

What would *she* do if she could live forever?

Every druid finds a different answer to that question. Some choose to dedicate their endless years to the pursuit of knowledge, amassing libraries, travelling the globe to uncover its last secrets. Others immerse themselves in nature, becoming one with the wilds they call their friends. Many eventually choose a spiritual path, joining one of the druid monasteries, hidden in secret locations around the world. And while it is true that they cannot die, eventually those who go there become as good as dead, like rocks or mountains – alive but not.

Mardequai, as far as Ember knows, has a multitude of lives set up in countries of his choosing. Houses, wardrobes, names he can take with ease whenever it becomes apparent that he's not aging. As Ember approaches his study, she wonders what they might look like, the lives not yet lived by her foster father. In New York, he could be a reclusive painter with a penthouse overlooking Central Park. In Tokyo, he might be a tea master, his traditional home a haven of tranquillity. And in a remote village in the Andes, his humble abode would be filled with rare orchids, strange plants, and ancient artefacts.

One thing she knows for sure: while well connected in the highest circles, he tends to keep a low profile, never photographed and rarely seen in public.

His current identity revolves all around the arts. Mardequai has established himself as an enigmatic collector, known for having deep pockets and eclectic tastes. His townhouse reflects this obsession; he has turned every wall into a distinct gallery. The entrance hall, for example, showcases a rotating exhibit of German Renaissance painters, while the dining room is reserved for the Baroque period. His study houses a collection of unique texts from the Alexandria library, which he would probably have acquired firsthand before it burned down.

The secret heart of his collection is his drawing room, a

perfectly designed space with soaring ceilings and north-facing windows. Here, Mardequai indulges in his own artistic endeavours. However, none of his works ever leave the room.

As Ember moves toward his holy space now, a debate rages in her mind. She had left Alva back at the shabby hotel, adding a protective charm to her door, just in case. The charm won't be able to ward off a full-on magical assault on her life, but at least it should alert Alva to any danger looming throughout the night.

Ember hadn't wanted to come here tonight, but in the end, her need for clarity had been too nagging. He would have a perfectly reasonable explanation for all of it anyway, she thinks to herself. He always does. However, it certainly would have been easier to dismiss Alva's accusation altogether if it hadn't indeed revealed a missing piece in the tales he told Ember, too: how *did* he know Alva had caused the accident?

Ember reaches the door to the study and knocks until Mardequai's voice resounds from within.

"Yes, what is it, Michaela?"

She opens the door. Candlelight spills into the dark hall, casting flickering shadows across the walls. Inside, Mardequai stands behind an easel while classical music plays softly in the background. Mozart. Across from the druid is a scene like something straight out of a Roman orgy. Half a dozen naked people recline on ottomans or stand like marble statues, holding wine chalices or engaging in pretend conversation while standing perfectly still.

"Oh my... I am so sorry, I didn't know..." Ember stammers, her face flushing.

Mardequai glances at her without surprise. "Ah, Ember. How wonderful that you've come to see me. I was planning to call on you in the morrow," he announces, practically cheerful. "In fact, I'd appreciate your assistance, child. I am encountering some difficulty portraying their features in this dark light, especially since they keep twitching and fidgeting. Would you mind freezing them for me?"

Ember shoots an irritated look at both Mardequai and the models, who appear equally ill at ease at the prospect of being 'frozen'.

"Oh, don't worry, Michaela will make them forget this later anyway, and they have been thoroughly reimbursed," he adds as if to remind his models of the job.

Reluctantly, Ember raises her casting finger when one of the models protests, "Whoa, whoa, whoa. Hang on a mi—" But it's too late. He freezes mid-sentence, his face now a stony grimace of panic. The rest of the models turn immobile as well.

"Well, we can't leave it like that now, can we?" Mardequai steps forward, adjusting the model's features as if moulding clay. "What brings you here tonight?" he asks, busy forming the lips of a blonde woman into a pout.

"I went to see Alva tonight," Ember says, stepping further into the room.

"How lovely. A sibling reunion at long last."

"She said someone has been trying to kill her ever since the welcome ceremony at Arcadia House."

"Oh my. How terrible." Mardequai returns to his easel. "However, I must say, I'm not entirely surprised. She caused quite the outrage, that sister of yours."

"Not entirely unprovoked, I take it?"

"I merely showed the Assembly her true colours. Your sister is a dangerous witch, responsible for the loss of countless lives. If I were to guess, I'd say that many members of our community still hold a grudge against her. It's like finding out that Hitler is still alive."

"Except Alva *isn't* Ruth," Ember reminds him. "Our grandmother was burned at the stake in 1956. She *was* brought to justice."

Mardequai continues painting as if Ember hadn't spoken.

"You shouldn't have exposed her like that," she dares to add. "If there is someone out to assassinate her now, that's on you. No matter if directly or indirectly, you had a hand in it."

Mardequai looks at her across the easel. He appears almost bored. "Is that why you have come tonight? To lay the blame on me?"

"No, I... I came because I need to ask you something."

Mardequai resumes his painting. After a long pause, he finally meets her eyes, as if he's been waiting for her to speak all along – an old power play he's been employing since she was a teenager. "Well, I am listening," he says, fluttering his eyelashes.

"When did you find out Alva was still alive?" asks Ember.

"The day you told me so," he replies, pointing his paintbrush at her.

And Ember tries to read that face, searching for any sign of a lie, but as always, it perfectly matches his words.

"And after the accident, the Elster Coven simply agreed that I should stay with you – a complete stranger?"

"You seem to forget that it was *you* who would not leave *my* side, remember? And yes, the Elster Coven was quite relieved to have found a solution to the problem of what to do with you, to be honest. You also seem to forget that my foundation has a long-standing history of supporting orphaned witches."

Ember can't help but acknowledge that this much is true, recalling the many women Mardequai's foundation has helped over the years.

"Alva also said the Elster Coven leader sent her to a foster home, and that she disappeared when she turned eighteen."

At those words, the paintbrush hovers as if forgotten in

Mardequai's hand, a subtle hint that *this* is indeed news to him. "Is that so?" he asks, his interest piqued.

"Why would they have kept that from you?" Ember presses. "Why would they have entrusted *my* care to you but withheld the fact that Alva survived – and that she caused the accident?"

"I'm on the cusp of that discovery, trust me."

His reaction, however controlled, shows that this indeed vexes him, a chapter of the story he is not privy to. However, it's not the coven's secrets that concern Ember right now – it's Mardequai's own, and she just made him admit to them, too.

"How did you know the accident was Alva's fault, then?" she dares to ask, her heart rate picking up.

"What now?"

"You always told me Alva wasn't even there when you arrived at the crash site, and for the last thirteen years, you presumed her dead. Which means, you couldn't know that she admitted to have caused the crash, either." Ember turns to face her foster father. "In fact, there was no way you could have found out about her loss of control *after* the accident. So, you must have known about it *before*."

"Don't be ridiculous, child. You don't know what you're talking about."

And then, Ember's world tilts on its axis. It's as if a veil has been ripped away, revealing what she can no longer unsee. Her chest constricts, each breath a struggle as the truth of Mardequai's betrayal becomes apparent.

Her voice cracks through. Fury on the surface, something sourer underneath. "How did you do it? Did you order one of your acolytes to hex Alva? What was in it for them? How much did you pay to have my family *murdered*?"

The frozen models seem to stare at Mardequai like a jury in a court case, but he won't give them a confession.

"You're being hysterical. Here, have a sip of wine, that'll calm you down." He hands Ember his glass.

Ember takes it but instead of drinking, she tosses it across the room, using Anima to splinter the glass in mid-air. She directs the shards until they hover just in front of Mardequai's chest, poised to strike the heart.

"Tell me the truth!" she demands, tears welling. "Did you want *me* dead as well?"

Still, Mardequai remains calm, almost condescending. A different kind of power, but no less effective. "What do you think you're doing? You know you can't kill me."

It's another long-established routine she has learnt never to challenge. She might be the witch, but he is still the one holding all the power, her spells ricocheting off his immortal body like raindrops against a windowpane.

Ember's resolve falters, and she lets go of the shards, which fall to the floor. "I hate you," she whimpers.

"Why? Because I knew someone wanted to murder your family? The Hausmann name was among the most notorious magical family names in all of Europe! That only worsened when news of Alva's connection to Ruth became public knowledge. A witch with a memory beyond her own lifetime? Many, many of my brothers would regard that as a threat."

"But not you?"

"*Think*, Sofia. If I was behind it, why would I have left you alive? You, who showed a similar ability?"

Ember sinks toward the floor. "I don't know," she whispers.

"All it takes to spread a fire is one wild ember, have you forgotten?" says Mardequai, now using his fatherly voice. "You are my ember. You and me, we were destined to find one another, remember?"

"Do you swear it?" Ember asks then. "Do you swear you didn't have anything to do with it?"

Mardequai opens his arms, a rare gesture for a father so aloof. "Come here."

Ember waits for a long moment, rage warring with the need for his approval. But as always, that craving for affection wins out. She picks herself up, stepping into his waiting arms. Like iron to a magnet, she moves towards him, years of yearning for these fleeting moments of affection overriding her better judgment.

"How could I have wanted you dead, hm? How could you even think that? You and I are going to change the world together," he murmurs into her ear. "You and I are meant for greatness."

Mardequai envelops her, and it feels both reassuring and restricting, the embrace a perfect metaphor for their relationship. Ember is a sparrow in an eagle's eyrie, protected yet dangerously trapped.

There's a pause as Mardequai's grip tightens, his lips moving closer to her ears until he whispers, "And now... now I need you to proceed with the next step." The words are as unexpected as they are chilling, like a gust of winter wind in midsummer, reminding Ember that with Mardequai, every gesture of affection comes at a price.

"What do you mean? What next step?" she asks, wiping her face.

Mardequai cradles her face in his hands, his touch gentle yet somehow commanding at the same time. "Tomorrow, when you're meeting with your coven for the full moon, I want you to gather in a public place, then I want you to reveal your magic to the world."

"What do you mean? The reveal isn't due until Wednesday."

"I need you to pre-empt it."

"*Why?*"

"Because, dear child, to wait would suggest we are content to follow the head elder's lead in the years to come. She would have us kneel in front of the politicians, so we are not a threat. But we are. And you need to show them that witches won't be moulded into whatever shape they find least threatening."

As Mardequai speaks, the dots finally connect in Ember's mind. She sees now how everything fits into his grand scheme, a plan long in the making. By forcing an early, chaotic reveal, he's not only challenging the head elder's authority – no, he's sowing the seeds of discord between humans and witches right from the start.

Because, if witches were to be perceived as peaceful and cooperative, Mardequai would lose his chance to divide and conquer. He needs fear, needs that chaos. Only then can he step in to present himself as the solution to a problem he himself created. It's a masterful move, she must admit, one that paves the way for his ultimate goal: becoming the puppet-master of all.

"They're going to send me to Saltholm," Ember interjects.

"I will make sure that won't happen."

"And I am to take your word on that?" She steps away from Mardequai, looking out the window onto the dark street. "No," she says firmly. "I won't do it. I won't become the face of this."

Mardequai doesn't even appear to have heard her. "Why do you think I asked you to rally the youth behind you? Make a name for yourself through the anti-assembly movement?"

"I won't do it. Find another witch to manipulate." Ember tries to summon all of her courage, but her voice is already cracking.

She turns around, finding Mardequai back with the models, busy forming one of their hands into a fist, then aiming it at the jaw of another. "Pity. Such a pity. Because, you know, there are always ways to *make* you do it."

"What do you mean?" Ember asks, now alarmed.

"Those attacks on your sister?"

"What about them?"

"If you wish them to stop, you best do as I say, child."

"So you *are* behind them."

"I didn't say that." Mardequai picks up an antique dagger from a shelf, running his finger along the blade, the steel glinting in the candlelight as he places it into the hand of the model being struck. "But what I *did* say is that I am the one who can make them stop."

Chapter Nineteen

"I assume you told Gathoni about my mishap in the forest?" I ask over the rumble of the London Tube, gripping the metal handle above me as I sway with the train. The scent of brake dust and too much perfume (or, in some cases, too little) hangs in the air, mixing with the lingering traces of Dennis's aftershave that still cling to my skin, my clothes. I've spent the whole of Sunday in my hotel bed, licking the post-breakup wounds, listening to Kettering moving in the room next door. I had tried to slip away quietly when it was time to make my way over to Shoreditch for the coven meet-up, but no such luck: the druid was on my case no sooner than I touched the doorknob. Now, packed like sardines on the train, I can't escape his vexing presence.

"She receives my daily reports," he responds, his stoic face barely moving.

"What did it say? Your report from yesterday?" I press, inching closer as a bunch of school kids squeeze past us. And now I'm practically nose-to-chin with him.

"That is none of your concern."

"Just spit it out. You know I won't stop asking until you tell me. What did you write about me?"

"The truth." His words are cold, at odds with his breath, hot on my forehead.

"The truth according to the druid who still holds a grudge against me because he believes I'm my evil grandmother," I reply just as the train screeches to a sudden halt. Before I can stop myself, I'm lurching forward, straight into Kettering's broad chest. His arm instinctively wraps around my waist to steady me, and for a split second, we're frozen, my fingers splayed against his chest, his hands firm on my hips. But as soon as I've found my footing, he releases me and moves to the next handle.

When a slightly strange ping resounds over the rumble of the Tube car, I glance around, wondering where it might have come from. The sound repeats, louder this time, like a smart-phone alert, but much more annoying. I grimace as the pinging persists, growing more frequent. It's starting to grate on my nerves, and I notice a few other passengers getting annoyed as well. Just as I'm about to snap at the invisible noisemaker, Kettering leans over and says, "You have a message."

"What? From whom?"

The druid sighs. "On your RN app. I recognise the sound."

There it is again – *ping*.

"Oh God, that *is* me!" I fumble for my phone, the looks of the other passengers burning my cheeks. After a lot of confused swiping on my part, I look up at Kettering, lost.

Rolling his eyes, he takes the phone. His fingers move across the screen, navigating to the Resonance Network app I managed to download this morning. Another clever bit of magic, it appears only on phones of ICAG-registered witches and druids.

"Here," he says, handing it back. "But you really shouldn't be using this."

"Why?" I ask. I was elated that I finally got to receive daily magical news again.

"It's... outdated," he replies cryptically.

I squint at the screen. "It's from the head elder. She requests my presence at the Resonance Network Operations Centre beneath Blackfriars Pier tomorrow. I'm to stand by her side during the collective cleansing of the Thames." I blink in surprise. "Is she sure about that?"

Kettering's response is friendly as always. "I don't know, witch. I suggest you ask her about it when you see her."

"Alright, sorry." I hold up my hands in mock surrender, almost losing my balance again. "I thought you worked for her."

"I don't work for the government."

"Who, then?"

"That is none—"

"Let me guess, it's none of my concern."

We exit the station, emerging into the bustling streets of London. I'm momentarily disoriented by the flood of people and the unfamiliar neighbourhood. At a crosswalk, I look left out of habit when, suddenly, Kettering clamps down on my arm, yanking me back just as a red double-decker bus whizzes past, mere inches from where I just was.

"Is it too much to ask that you at least keep your eyes open when you walk?" he growls.

"My eyes were open. The traffic here confuses me. It's all on the wrong side."

"Is it the traffic that's wrong or is it you?" Kettering asks, already striding ahead.

We meander through the streets of Shoreditch, passing colourful street art, quirky boutiques, and trendy cafes. I pause repeatedly, checking for street names and backtracking. Kettering, however, maintains a brisk pace.

"Are you lost?" he finally asks.

"I'm not lost. I just... don't know where I'm going."

"That would be the literal definition of being lost."

I'm about to come up with a counter but when we round another corner, my eyes are drawn to a sleek black Range Rover across the street, and I know I'm no longer lost when the back door opens, and Sofia alights. She's wearing a raven black blazer over a forest green silk blouse, paired with skinny jeans and her signature stiletto heels.

"Hey, Miss Wild!" I call out, darting across the street without thinking. I narrowly avoid colliding with a cyclist, who swerves with a string of lovely British curses. Behind me, I just about hear Kettering's annoyed groan.

Sofia turns around with a grim, annoyed expression, probably expecting a fan or a paparazzo. But when she spots me, her face does not light up.

"Oh hi, what are you doing here?" She looks up and down the pavement as if I shouldn't be in this part of town.

"Five p.m., right?"

"Right, I invited you, didn't I?"

"Yes, you did. But I mean, if you changed your mind, that's fine..." I say, unable to hide my disappointment.

"No, no, it's cool. I suppose. It's – whatever. Hey, how about I introduce my shadow to your shadow?" she says quickly when Pippa returns from the parking ticket machine, her khaki cardigan hugging her athletic form.

"Hi, Alva. Nice to see you again," she greets me with kisses on both cheeks. Shifting her tablet from one arm to the other, she reaches out a hand to Kettering. "And another new face. I'm Pippa Watson, how do you do?"

"Cornelis Kettering," he replies with a curt handshake.

"Kom je uit Holland?" Pippa asks, smiling, which draws a look of surprise from my sister's face.

As a reply, all Pippa gets from my shadow is something that

resembles a nod. I must say, I'm a little relieved to see that not even a sunshine like Pippa can brighten his mood.

"You speak Dutch?" Sofia asks, admiring her assistant.

"I happen to be fluent in six languages," Pippa says. "Hey, I was going to get a cup of tea at Smither's while these ladies do their thing. You're welcome to join, Cornelis."

"I will be fine right here, thank you." Kettering folds his hands in front of his body as if he's about to descend below ground.

"Why, he's a charmer, isn't he?" Pippa murmurs in my ear as she parts with us. "Catch ya later, call me if you need me."

"Why do you allow him to follow you around all day, again?" Sofia asks, nodding subtly towards Kettering, who trails behind us at a distance.

"I don't exactly have a choice. He's like a leech."

We turn off Brick Lane onto a side street, the bustling noise fading. "And to be honest," I say, lowering my voice, "it's also kind of nice – well, not *nice* but, you know, *comforting* – to have someone around after what's been happening."

Sofia casts me a glance as we approach a towering black brick building, most of its windows broken. "Do you fancy him?"

"*What?* No," I say, reflexively tucking a strand of hair behind my ear as I look over my shoulder at Kettering again.

Sofia's eyes light up. "You totally do! You wanna know how I know? Because you're doing the hair-behind-the-ear thing, and you're denying it just like you denied fancying Kevin Kreisel in fifth grade!"

"I do not!" I protest as we reach the entrance of the old distillery. Sofia produces a key from her pocket and unlocks the massive door.

As the two of us step inside, Kettering stays behind on the pavement. I'm tempted to put out a bowl of water for him, or at least make a joke of that sort, but I'm not going to give my sister any more reason to tease me.

Inside the building, a bunch of old machinery, crates, and broken glass awaits. As we walk past ancient-looking copper stills, I breech the one topic we've both been dancing around until now.

"So, did you ask him?"

"Ask who?"

"Come on, you know who – Mardequai. Did you ask him about the accident?"

"You know what? I did." Sofia's fingers worry at the edge of her sleeve. "And it is as I said: he had nothing to do with it."

"Then how did he know?" I ask. "How did he know I caused the accident? Why did he ask me if I still feel guilty for it? You did ask him that, right?"

"I did."

"And?"

"And he said lots of people suspected an attack on our family was imminent back then. But that doesn't make *him* a murderer, Alva."

"That doesn't answer my question though, does it?"

"Listen, you need to let this rest, do you hear me? I get that you'd feel the need to, like... *rid* yourself of the guilt." She rolls her shoulders back and lifts her chin. "But if you know what's good for you – for us – you'd better stop attacking him, alright?"

We reach an ancient-looking elevator, its metal grate screeching as Sofia pulls it open. But I can sense that she herself has closed off again. And so, I try a different approach.

"I'm sorry," I say. "I didn't mean to upset you. I'm so grateful that I found you, you know that. And, for what it's worth, I'm grateful that he invited me to come to London. I've been given a chance here to redeem myself and to get back in. I won't jeopardise that."

"Back into what?"

"You know, the sisterhood. This whole new world we're building now. I want to be a part of all that."

Sofia softens slightly. "I suppose that answers the question of how you would have voted, huh?"

"You guessed it," I reply. "Don't you see? It's exactly what Mama always taught us: with great power comes great responsibility. Witches and druids are meant to be guardians – are meant to be the *healers* of this world."

"Sounds pretty kumbaya to me…" Sofia mutters.

"Don't," I say. "Don't ever do that. I respect that you've moved on – that you're *his* daughter now, like you said. But don't you ever forget that you were *hers* once. Don't ever mock what you know she so firmly believed in."

A tense silence falls over us as the elevator continues its climb. After a moment, I decide to break it. "And since when have you become such a cynic, anyway? You used to be all over this stuff, you little hippie."

Sofia smiles but doesn't respond. Instead, she studies my face intently, becoming almost wistful.

"You look so much like her," Sofia says quietly. "When you get passionate like that – it's like she's standing right here."

"Then so do you," I reply with a small smile.

Sofia shakes her head. "No, it's different. I may have her face, but you… you've got her spirit. Her conviction. Always did."

She falls silent then, her gaze drifting somewhere far beyond me, beyond the elevator, beyond London itself. There's a shift in her, subtle but unmistakable, as if pieces of a puzzle were settling into place. For a fleeting moment, she looks not like the hardened woman Mardequai moulded, but like the sister I remember. Something resolves in her face then, though I don't understand what it means.

"He doesn't own you, you know?" I add when I see an opening. "Mardequai. I know he was there for you, raised you, whatever. But I don't think Mama would have seen eye to eye with this guy."

The elevator comes to a stop, and I notice something darker pass over Sofia's face then, a shadow of that same something she doesn't want to share. She pulls open the gate and steps out before I can discern what it might be. "You're terribly annoying, you know that?" she says, avoiding eye contact. "My life was a lot easier before you came back into it."

"You and Kettering should start a club," I jest, following her out.

"You like that dinosaur, admit it!" Sofia teases, some of her tension dissipating.

"I do not," I insist. "Now, tell me the names of the other coven members. I want to make a good impression."

We walk towards a rusty metal door at the end of the hallway, but then Sofia turns to me once more. "Speaking of names, could you be a darling and call me Ember when we're with my tribe? I kind of have to keep up with appearances."

I nod. "Sure, you got it."

And then it's time to face the firing squad.

Chapter Twenty

"What's up, witcheeees?"

Sofia slams open the door that leads onto the rooftop of the old distillery, and I follow her at a distance, shy like a mouse as I study the gathered coven members, who cheer and whistle as their magistrate makes her entrance.

Up top, a sprawling urban garden awaits, the pink and russet colours of beautifully kept flower beds creating a soft backdrop to the industrial Shoreditch architecture. I recognise the purple leaves of sedum matrona, yarrow cerise queen, the foxglove-like flowers of penstemon garnet, and some type of feather grass, standing tall and shielding the terrace entirely from view, save from the skyscrapers of London's financial district on the horizon. Judging by this charming rooftop meadow, someone in the coven must have an exceptionally green thumb, and as I step out of Sofia's shadow, I look around, wondering who it might be.

"Listen up, everybody, we have a new member." Sofia lights a cigarette and lowers her voice, giving it a hint of cool boredom. "This is my sister, Alva Hausmann. Don't let the German accent throw you – she's actually not bad company once you get to know her. Alva, this is everybody."

Overall, my sister suddenly seems a lot more... *enigmatic*. I suppose that's what she meant about 'keeping up appearances'. I don't blame her for it. I have long thought that a person is really several people, depending on who they spend their time with. Take me, for example: for the last three years I've been 'domestic Alva', washing laundry, cooking meals, and spending each weekend at the archery range, convincing myself I enjoyed hanging out with Dennis's high school friends.

My coven introduction is met with an awkward silence and lots of blank stares.

"Hi," I say with an even more awkward hand wave, but no one replies.

My infamous appearance before the Assembly has made its rounds, then.

"Come on now, is this how I raised you kids?" exclaims Sofia, making her way to a small bar cart, stocked with an array of spirits and mixers, where she fixes herself a drink. "Where are your manners? Introduce yourselves."

At last, a young witch no older than nineteen approaches me. Her ginger hair is braided into an impressive arrangement draped over one shoulder, her features still somewhere between teenager and grown-up. "Hi, I'm Saskia Antonov," she says and offers me a hand.

"Nice to meet you," I say, a small relief spreading through my chest at this tiny crack made in the ice.

"Adanna McClendon," says a tall, dark-skinned witch with micro-braids standing by a vintage record player atop a weathered trunk, busy selecting a vinyl record from a stack nearby.

"Cool shirt," I say, gesturing at her T-shirt of the famous Andy Warhol soup can, which she wears under a floor-length crimson wool cardigan.

"Cheers," Adanna replies – and did I also see a friendly wink there?

My confidence rising, I follow Saskia, taking in my first ever covenstead.

The terrace is adorned with strings of fairy lights criss-crossing overhead, casting a warm light as day fades to night. Trailing ivy twines along a wooden pergola, creating a natural canopy for a plush sofa in the corner, piled high with tasselled pillows in rich purples and magentas.

There, two witches sit, introducing themselves as Inaaya Bajwa and Minnie Allen. The first one eyes me sceptically, the second one breathes a gentle 'Love your aura' in my direction as she reaches for a pack of matches on a low table, lighting an assortment of mismatched candles.

At the far end, on a long bench tucked away in the corner by what looks like an extensive herb garden, the last witch remaining introduces herself as Eun-Ji Jeo.

"I'm just picking some leaves for a fresh brew of Korean mint tea," she says. "Would anybody like some? Alva, how about you?"

Bingo – I've identified the green witch of the coven.

"Love some," I reply and shove my hands in my pockets for lack of knowing what else to do with them.

"Where is Zara?" asks my sister, now sprawling on a Moroccan rug on the floor, elbow poised on a pouf, ice cubes tinkling in her glass.

"Running late, as always," replies Adanna.

"Never misses an opportunity to challenge my authority, that one. Fine. We'll start without her. Come, come and gather, my favourite misfit magical creatures. Let's get this party started."

At my sister's word, everyone gets up from their seats to join her in a circle on the rugs. I follow their lead and sit cross-legged next to her, relieved when Eun-Ji settles in right beside me, even though there were several other open spots. She smiles at me, setting down a tray of clinking glasses and a cast-iron teapot on a coffee table nearby.

Adanna's music selection, a chilled Indian sitar instrumental, resounds from the record player. When everyone has joined the circle, Sofia places both hands on her knees, palms faced upward, and the other witches follow her lead, taking one another by the hands. I hesitate but before I know it, Eun-Ji's palm rests atop my own, and Sofia, to my left, grabs my hand with an amused side glance. She takes a deep breath, closing her eyes, and then a low hum reverberates from her core, augmented by everyone else in the circle.

I, too, close my eyes and begin to hum, tears welling as I'm overcome by a profound sense of reverence. I'm really back. Back where I belong.

Our collective vibration fills the circle and as it rises, so does the Anima I feel coursing through me from both Eun-Ji and Sofia's hands, a closed loop of pure, feminine energy that seems to repair something deep within my chest I had no idea was broken.

As the humming fades away and we open our eyes, Sofia lets go of my hand with a gentle squeeze. I casually raise a thumb to my cheek, wiping away the wet of my tears.

"Right," Sofia addresses the circle. "Welcome to the third full moon gathering of the Venus in Fur Coven. As always, I am delighted to have you here, and I'm also delighted to have my sister here – Alva." She gestures at me, suddenly a little awkward, and then she seems to have lost her train of thought. Indeed, there's a crack in her composure, something that troubles her mind and steals her focus.

"Um, now... what shall we do first? I suppose a bit of house-keeping." She rummages around in her pockets, drawing out her phone. "The ICAG has sent some guidelines and reminders via the RN on what is going to happen post Reveal, and how we ought to behave once magic is on the loose. And I... I'm going to read them to you now."

Just then, the rooftop door bursts open, and a woman with long, silky blonde hair falling smoothly past her shoulders marches across the terrace.

"Sorry I'm late," she announces, but it doesn't really sound like she is. She's dressed in black jeans and a matching crewneck sweatshirt, with dangling teardrop earrings that match the piercing blue of her eyes. Her makeup is impeccable, with a subtle smoky eye and lips painted a soft pink that give her an appearance of innocence, which somehow seems at odds with her entire energy.

Flopping into a beanbag, she joins the circle between Adanna and Inaaya. "Who is this?" she asks, casting me a less than friendly look.

"This is Alva, my sister and newest addition to the coven," Sofia replies. I can hear the annoyance flaring underneath her words. "Alva, this is Zara Thorndike. She joined our little band of rebels shortly before you did."

"Must have missed the memo where we voted on her admission..." Zara scrutinises me from head to toe, which makes my cheeks flush.

"Why, I didn't take you for such a traditionalist but if you insist, we shall vote right now," Sofia says. "Those in favour?" She raises her hand, her gaze burning through the circle of women. Saskia's hand shoots up without missing a beat – whether out of sympathy for me or fear of her magistrate, I can't quite tell. Eun-Ji follows quickly thereafter, then Minnie and Adanna. Inaaya's hand rises last, and with some hesitation.

"Zara?" Sofia challenges.

"Guess I abstain from this one," Zara replies through gritted teeth.

"Just as well." Sofia nods curtly. "Now that's off the table, let's proceed to more important matters. ICAG ground rules for the Reveal. Let's hear them." Once again, she reaches for her phone.

I notice how tense she is as she begins to read and wonder if Zara Thorndike brought this on. But then again, Sofia has been on edge ever since I ran into her outside the building.

She clears her throat, then announces: "All witches are reminded that the disclosure of magic will be gradual. Refrain from open displays of your powers for the first month after the Reveal, allowing time to gauge public reaction and anticipate varied responses. Be prepared for a range of sentiments, including curiosity, fascination, fear, and scepticism. Some may react negatively or with hostility."

"Yeah, you bet," interrupts Inaaya, looking down at her fingernails. "Can't wait for the chauvinists to enter the chat."

Sofia scoffs, then continues, "Therefore, it is vital that every witch participate only in pre-approved, organised demonstrations until further notice. A list of sanctioned events has been provided via the Resonance Network. Next point, media interactions: there are witches among our community who might, due to previous oversteps or salient behaviour, be approached by journalists. Those individuals are encouraged to direct all media inquiries to their coven magistrate, who will get in touch with the designated spokespersons. Please avoid impromptu interviews or magical displays for journalists at all costs."

"And what if the overstepping individual *is* my coven magistrate?" quips Saskia Antonov.

"They probably put that in there just for you, Em," adds Adanna, which causes a flash of my sister's eyebrows but none of her usual witty banter.

"Social media guidelines," she reads next. "Refrain from posting magical content on personal social media accounts until official channels have begun to do so. Workplace conduct: continue to perform job duties without magical assistance unless explicitly authorised by regulatory bodies. Educational outreach: every witch and druid is strongly encouraged to participate in community education programs to demystify magic and address common misconceptions. Cultural sensitivity: be mindful of diverse cultural and religious beliefs regarding magic and avoid practices that might be seen as culturally insensitive or blasphemous. Legal compliance: familiarise yourself with new laws and regulations regarding magical practice. And lastly, emergency protocols: in case of far-reaching negative sentiment and/or violent incidents, follow established emergency procedures and contact MIRT, the Magical Incident Response Team, immediately."

"So basically, there will be a reveal, but we still have to keep a lid on," concludes Inaaya.

"I think I'll disappear in my den until this shitstorm has blown over. I can't handle that much heightened emotion," whispers Minnie, her face already etched in pain.

"Minnie is one of the last remaining true clairvoyants in the world," murmurs Eun-Ji in my direction, and I nod appreciatively, taking the glass of steaming mint tea she pours for me.

"They also suggest that on this full moon, every coven engage in a lively discussion about the future," says Sofia, tucking away her phone. "So, this is your opportunity to share any concerns or suggestions you may have, darlings. Let's start to my left. Adanna, what's your take?"

"Well, quite frankly, I still find it ridiculous to think that magic is supposed to fix what centuries of industrialisation and colonisation have fucked up," Adanna declares, her words followed by a collective nod. "I get that Anima is waning and all that, but to think that the whole of humanity can be redirected is so naïve. If anything, they'll look at us *literally* as this magical bullet that will somehow solve a global ecological crisis – which, mind you, *they* have caused – all without them changing their habits one bit." Adanna's words have an angry edge to it. "But I suppose, what's done is done. I'm just along for the ride at this point. My family has secured spots at Hudspeth's bunker, just in case this Reveal *does* go up in flames," she finishes, leaving my mind reeling with fascination at everything she's just said. I feel like I've been dropped in some movie – that there's no way this is reality playing out in front of me. There are so many angles to this Reveal I hadn't yet considered, and I'm dying to learn more.

"What about you, Zara?" Adanna turns to her left, where Zara leans forward in her beanbag. "Look," she says, framing her words with her hands, her elbows resting on her thighs. "I'm not going to sugarcoat it: I voted in favour – you all know I did – not because I'm particularly fond of a collab between us and the plain-folk, but because I believe it's about time we show them what we're made of. It's time we take our rightful place in this world as the most powerful fucking creatures ever to walk upon it, and I personally cannot wait for that to happen."

I glance at my sister as Zara's words echo across the rooftop, not surprised to find her jaw clenching. Ember Wild's reasoning would take on very similar rebellious undertones, I'm sure. It's almost as if Zara intended to beat our magistrate to the punch, the rivalry between them brewing hotter than Eun-Ji's tea.

Up next, it's Inaaya's turn, and she shares a perspective that, quite frankly, blows my mind. "Has anyone considered the impact on global economics? I predict that magical solutions – real and fake – will pop up like mushrooms over the months to come. The Reveal could render entire industries obsolete overnight. We might inadvertently trigger a worldwide economic collapse, and then what?"

"Well, I reckon that will be inevitable, and it would be a good thing," Sofia joins in. "We're talking about a gargantuan seismic shift here; a whole new world will emerge from this. Out with the old, in with the new, you know what I'm saying? We need to break the wheel."

Murmurs of agreement ripple through our circle, and my heart rate picks up when a thought I'd like to share forms in my mind. But I'm too scared to speak unless spoken to, deciding to wait my turn.

"Saskia, what's your take?" Sofia addresses the youngest in the group.

"I just think it's going be so important that we all stick together through the entire thing, you know? Many of you know this of me, but I've had my fair share of, like, exploitation and abuse growing up." She says this with a detachment that I can only guess is her way of coping. Turning to me, she explains, "You see, I grew up in a travelling menagerie after my mother passed away. No one knew I was magical, but alas, I was still their child prodigy. The more daring and inexplicable my performances, the more food for everyone on the table. People will try take advantage of us, and we won't make it if we don't show a united front."

Minnie Allen echoes the sentiment, raising the importance of kindness and patience in the years to come, and says that she hopes the Reveal brings us all closer together.

I twitch my fingers nervously when it's Eun-Ji's turn to speak, knowing I'll be next. She raises such a valid point, mentioning the potential to heal the 'sister wound,' the depth of her soul shining through her eloquent, thoughtful words. "By stepping into the light, we can demonstrate the true power of sisterhood. Magic means so much more than spells and potions, it also means – *this*." She gestures at our circle of gathered women. "It means connection and trust and friendship, and I really think the Reveal might inspire all women – and men, for that matter – to return to this sense of community."

"Alva?" says Sofia next to me, and I briefly clear my throat before I voice my rehearsed thought.

"I agree with everything that's been said, and it's so fascinating to listen to all of you. You must know, I haven't been a part of the sisterhood for many, many years, so I'm still learning, obviously. But I was wondering if anyone has considered how the sudden spike in magic might affect the natural resources of Anima. Like, I'm sure someone has already written a whole report on this, and I obviously wouldn't know about that, but what if the Reveal disrupts the balance even further, because suddenly we'll all use more Anima? First, because we are now free to openly do so, but also second, because the demand will be higher, as we set out to undo all the damage?"

"That is *exactly* what my mum fears is going to happen," Adanna pipes up from across the circle. "Too much demand, too few resources. The Reveal could expedite the crisis. It's a real concern – you're spot on there, Alva."

"So, when I was at Chyulu, there was a lot of talk about this exact problem." Sofia turns to me. "You see, they've been preparing for this for the last decade or so, and the Academy was obviously at the forefront, coming up with many of the solutions the ICAG has now implemented. The idea is that tackling those gargantuan global tasks, like cleaning up the oceans and whatever, will require – well, let's call it slightly *darker* magic."

"Darker, how?" I ask. Instantly the sheer notion stirs something – or someone – within me. It's like the moment someone so much as mentions dark magic, Ruth rises to the surface. I swallow, hard, as if that could sink her back to the bottom, focussing on Sofia's next words.

"There are tools. Rare, ancient tools witches and druids have employed since the dawn of time. They were mainly used for magical warfare during the time of the Crusades, and since deemed unsafe. But desperate times call for desperate measures, and now they could actually be used for good."

"I don't quite understand," I confess.

"They're called Celestial Stones, actual pieces of the Solantha Comet. They're like magical enhancers," explains Minnie. "Instead of drawing Anima from the environment, those trained in wielding them may gather energy from within the stones."

I nod, recalling the origin stories every child witch learns. The Solantha Comet's ancient passage, brushing past Earth and, so the legend goes, awakening magic in a chosen few women while bestowing immortality upon some men. Since those days of old, magic passed through bloodlines, mother to daughter. But immortality proved to be a rarer blessing, granted every one-hundred-and-eight years when the comet returns — and that return comes next year.

"The stones also aid in counter-balancing big spells," adds Sofia. "It's a huge part of the curriculum at Chyulu. They're raising an army of 'eco-warriors' up there in the mountains, if you will."

"What does it feel like, to have that much power?" I ask, a strange longing burning in my solar plexus.

"Fucking amazing," confesses Sofia. "But, I don't know, also kind of scary, to be quite honest with you. There are a lot of rules and stipulations around them."

"Such as?"

"Such as who may use them, and under what circumstances. You're also never supposed to use one on your own, only with another witch as your proxy. Someone to stand guard in case the witch with the stone loses control. Oh, and during the Solantha Comet's passing, they may not be used at all. Something about the proximity to their source that can cause serious damage.

Let's put it this way: it's no wonder they are kept under strict lock and key."

"And why couldn't these magical tools be used in secret? If they're so powerful, why is the Reveal necessary at all?"

"Because," replies Sofia, "there's no chance of pulling off something of that scale without being detected. So, the Reveal is designed to get out in front of the story. Control the narrative, you know?"

I nod, still processing.

"Alright, enough with the heavy," she concludes, snapping her fingers. "Let's move on to the fun part of tonight's soiree, ladies."

She's about to stand, when Zara speaks up, her tone bearing yet another challenge. "Why did you want us to clear our schedules for the whole evening, then?"

"Yeah, I had a spa appointment at the Dorchester at eight," concurs Inaaya.

A flash of distress crosses Sofia's features as her eyes meet mine. "Well, I wanted to take my ladies out for a celebratory drink tonight," she announces, reverting to her usual exuberance. "So many reasons to celebrate: this full moon marks our three-month anniversary, it's our last gathering in hiding, and we have a new coven member."

"That's it? Just another party, yeah?" says Zara, studying my sister as if she were the clairvoyant of the coven.

Sofia's jaw tightens almost imperceptibly. "Do you have a problem with that?" She tosses back her drink in one smooth motion, eyes barely leaving Zara's.

"Nope." Zara shrugs one shoulder. "Just thought we might actually be doing something purposeful for a change. All you ever do is get off your face and call it 'coven bonding.'"

Sofia leans forward. "If you're looking for purpose, Zara darling, maybe you should join a book club instead. My coven, my rules. And tonight," – she raises her glass in a toast – "I rule that we drink until we can't see straight."

"Hang on, nobody goes anywhere before we do my favourite full moon thing," says Saskia, moving toward the record player.

"Never," says Sofia, and I can sense the soft spot she holds for her youngest coven member.

The witches begin to stir, Inaaya mixing what look like mojitos for everyone, the rest clearing surfaces and rearranging poufs to free up space.

Sofia, however, remains strangely offside, pivoting toward the balustrade, where she looks out across the city, lighting a cigarette. It's a crystal-clear autumn night, and beyond the skyline, the full moon edges slowly over the horizon.

"Are you alright?" I come up next to her, watching as the silver disk rises behind the rooftops. "You seem kind of, I don't know, *distressed* tonight."

"What? No, m'fine. Of course, I'm fine. Peachy, actually." But her eyes drift over my shoulder, narrowing slightly as she spots Zara apart from the group, hunched over her phone as if this was all beneath her.

I follow her gaze. "Whoever voted yes on *her* admission, anyway?"

Sofia puffs out some smoke. *"Right?"*

Meanwhile, Saskia has selected an album: a live concert by Stevie Nicks, which prompts everyone else to dance and sing with reckless abandon, the mellow tunes of 'Gypsy' echoing across Shoreditch like an anthem.

"But listen, I've been thinking," says Sofia, her voice now raised over the music. "I quite like Minnie's idea to lie low for a while. You know, until everything settles. How about you and I go somewhere together?"

"Like where?"

"I don't care – you choose. Some full-on sister trip, somewhere they can't find us."

"Who's they?"

"You know, Gathoni, Mardequai, the elders, the ICAG – let them deal with this whole mess."

"I'd love to – of course I would – but I don't know if I can. Gathoni wants me by her side throughout the Reveal. In fact, she has summoned me for that Thames River cleanse thing tomorrow."

"Oh, *fuck* the Thames, and fuck her. She's not the boss of you. If it's sisterhood you're after, I've already given that to you – I mean, will you just look at that?" She gestures at her coven, dancing like wildflowers in the wind.

"You don't need her approval. You don't need *anyone's* approval! You're free now. Best get used to it," Sofia reminds me, then she joins the dance, arms raised to the stars, sweeping like a dervish. "Come, fly, little birdie! You're free, come fly away with me!" she lures me, pulling me by the arms until I finally give in.

"Fine," I call out over the music. "I've always wanted to go to Morocco!"

"Mabon in the Sahara Desert, what a splendid idea," replies Sofia. "I'll have Pippa make the travel arrangements. Brace yourself, Marrakesh, the Hausmann twins are coming for you!"

She grabs me by the hands and starts flinging me around, and suddenly, I'm swept away in a whirlwind of joy. Each twirl feels like coming home, each laugh that bubbles up from deep within makes my heart swell with an overwhelming happiness I haven't experienced since we were kids.

When the song reaches its peak, the others all sing 'She was just a WITCH, she was just a WITCH...', and I find myself shouting along. And while we spin and sway, I feel a profound connection, not just to Sofia, but to something larger. It's as if everything around us is suddenly charged with sisterhood and magic. And it warms my heart to think that right now, all around the country – all around the earth – women, magical and non-magical alike, might be doing this exact same thing, dancing to Stevie Nicks under a full moon.

And there's a lot of hope in that.

Chapter Twenty-One

Ember downs another shot, the alcohol burning a path that does nothing to quiet the storm in her mind. The coven has migrated to Old Street Records, the dimly lit bar pulsing with an electric energy, a fusion of industrial chic and underground grit. Exposed brick walls loom overhead, their raw textures softened by the warm glow of Edison bulbs strung along the ceiling. Dark leather booths nestle in half-circles along one wall, the bar dominates the opposite side, and at the far end, a band performs on a small stage, entertaining the crowd with live versions of all the throwback classics.

The coven's table is packed with every pizza from the menu, but there's a clear divide in the booth now. Ember and Alva are seated in the middle; to Ember's right, Minnie and Adanna are roaring their lungs out, singing along to 'Mr Brightside'. To Alva's left – this being the reason for the divide – sits Zara, her back ostentatiously turned toward the Hausmann twins, still immersed in her phone, while Inaaya, Saskia, and Eun-Ji are chatting away in their corner of the booth.

Ember picks at the crust of an untouched pizza slice, her

appetite long gone. Just hours ago, she'd been ready – resolved even – to follow Mardequai's plan to the letter. Control the narrative; create the chaos, but on her terms. She would be the face of what was to come, the harbinger of a new reality. And most importantly, Alva would stay alive. Mardequai's threat had been crystal clear: perform the pre-empt or watch her sister die.

But somehow – annoyingly, really – Alva's words in the elevator had pierced through years of Mardequai's conditioning like a silver needle through cloth. "It's never too late to do the right thing." Such a simple phrase, yet it had unravelled everything. Ember had seen her mother in Alva's eyes – the guardian, the healer who believed magic existed to mend the world, not shatter it. For so long, Ember had convinced herself that Mardequai's path was strength, that her mother's idealism was weakness. That Sofia was weak. That Ember was strong. But standing in that elevator with her sister, the name 'Sofia' had stirred in her chest like a dormant ember coming back to life – ironic, considering the name she'd chosen to escape it.

She glances now at Alva, who's nursing her soda, eyes darting occasionally to the druid. *Morocco.* Ember can't shake the feeling that settling into the seat of that plane tomorrow won't be an escape at all. It will be the beginning of another hunt. How far – how long – can they really run from a man who has eyes in every shadow? Every flicker of Alva's smile sends a knife of fear through her chest. She'd called off the pre-empt, but has she just damned them both as a result? Mardequai isn't a man who accepts betrayal. He isn't a man who lets his possessions walk away. And make no mistake, that's how he sees her: as a possession, a tool, a particularly clever attack dog who's about to go off-leash.

"And what are we going to do about *him*?" Alva shouts over the music into Ember's ear, nodding at her druid. Sitting awkwardly straight on a barstool close by, his overall demeanour seems entirely at odds with the relaxed vibes of the bar. Just as the sisters speak of him, a couple of women gravitate towards his table, their body language suggesting they're asking about the empty seats. Even across the crowded room, his response is unmistakable, his lips forming a single word – "No" – which sends the ladies back from whence they came.

"What about him?" Ember shouts back, biting into a slice of pizza after all.

"Well, I don't think he'll just let me jet off to Morocco like that."

"Do you two have some sort of a bondage arrangement?" Ember quips. "Does he tie you up at night and give you a good go-around, is that what's going on here?"

"What? No!" Alva covers her face in her hands, flushing.

Ember smirks despite herself, delighted that she can still ruffle her sister's feathers after all these years.

Alva nips on her soda water, the unsullied soul. "I'm serious though: how do we get rid of him?"

"Just tell him his services are no longer required." Ember shrugs. "And if he won't listen, you have the means to *make* him listen."

"Like what?"

"Well, are you a witch or are you not a witch? You are way more powerful than him; I'm sure you'll figure something out."

"Excuse me, ladies, but can I ask something, please?" Minnie, visibly trollied, leans across Ember's lap, addressing Alva.

"Sure, go ahead," Alva replies.

"Adanna and I were just talking about you and we were wondering if you believe in reincarnation. Like, is that what's going on with you, you think?"

Ember leans back into the soft leather, nervous to witness how her sister will handle this.

"I don't," Alva replies firmly, her face hardening.

"Huh, that is surprising."

"Why is that surprising?" There's a hint of a challenge in Alva's voice. Good for her.

"Well, you know, given your... *condition*."

Now Adanna joins in as well, one arm around Minnie so she can lean in closer. "There's a transcript of your Assembly hearing on the RN. It's making the rounds at the moment."

"The other girls are so kind to keep me updated on the latest, you see," explains Minnie. "I don't use the network; it's messing with my aura somehow."

Ember turns toward her sister, rolling her eyes.

"So, do you?" Minnie persists. "Believe in reincarnation?"

As if reaching for courage, Alva grabs Ember's negroni and has a long sip.

"Easy now," Ember mumbles.

"I don't believe in reincarnation because that would mean that I am... *her*, and I am most certainly not her," Alva declares, setting the drink down a bit too hard.

"How do you know?" Minnie asks as she and Adanna both look at Alva sceptically.

Ember jumps in, a lioness ready to defend her sister. "She knows because she's her own person, alright? These visions, these memories we receive, they're very much detached from us. It's as if you're watching a movie on a screen."

"Why'd you say *'we'*?" asks Adanna.

"Because I get them, too. Mine are from a different witch, from a different time, and they are less frequent or vivid, but it's the same thing."

"Fascinating. Why do you think this happens?" Minnie asks, the topic clearly right up her clairvoyant alley.

"Alva and I are special that way." Ember folds her arms in

front of her chest, mimicking her sister. "We've got our own connection to the past."

"Gotcha," Minnie replies, and the conversation ends when Adanna begins belting out the lyrics to 'I Love Rock 'n' Roll' into Minnie's ear as the band launches into Joan Jett's famous chorus, and Minnie joins in.

"Thank you," Alva murmurs to Ember, but she's visibly distressed. Lost in thought, she reaches for Ember's drink again.

"Careful now, you're crossing over to the dark side," Ember jests.

"This is good stuff, turns out," adds Alva, lifting the cocktail glass to her mouth once more.

"How about you get your own?" The words have scarcely left Ember's lips when, out of nowhere, Kettering lunges at their table, shoving it aside with surprising force, smacking the drink from Alva's hand and launching the glass across the room, where it explodes against the wall in a spray of shards and liquid.

"What the actual fuck?" Ember blurts out, as Alva pushes back into the booth.

"Nothing to see here, folks," announces Adanna, not missing a beat. "Just an accident." The druid's tackle has drawn the attention of the surrounding booths, heads turning and necks craning to see what's going on.

"She put something in your drink," Kettering declares, catching his breath and pointing at – Zara.

"*What?* How dare you?" Zara exclaims, shooting up from the booth.

"Who even is this guy?" Inaaya defends her friend, eyeing Kettering head to toe.

Meanwhile, Eun-Ji moves across the room towards the broken glass, stopping the bartender from cleaning up the mess and sending him away – with a subtle hex, for sure. Using only the tips of her fingers, she picks up the bottom half of the glass, which is still intact, carrying it over and sniffing the remaining liquid.

"Poison hemlock," she concludes.

"I-I didn't do this!" Zara insists, pointing at the glass, which Eun-Ji now neutralises, vaporising the liquid until it's all but disappeared. "Come on, I'm not *that* stupid."

"Minnie." Ember gestures to the clairvoyant, who immediately offers her hand for Zara to take.

"This is ridiculous," Zara says, but she does present her own hand. "Fine," she says through gritted teeth. "I got nothing to hide."

Gently, Minnie clasps both hands around Zara's, closing her eyes, searching. The loud guitar riffs from the stage, the singing, the partying suddenly seem at odds with the group, who stand detached in their tense corner of the bar. After a long while, Minnie opens her eyes again.

"She did it," the clairvoyant announces, a mix of disappointment and recognition on her face as she looks at Zara.

No sooner has Minnie said the words, than Ember springs into action, her powers erupting as she draws Anima from the lightbulbs overhead and the guitar amps on stage. Electrical Anima, always a fickle beast, gathers at her fingertips – but Ember's ample experience steadies her grip.

Zara, a capital witch through and through, responds in kind. Urban Anima has been her lifelong companion, and it answers her call instantly. The two witches engage in their standoff, and the bar plunges into darkness, every light, every electrical device sucked dry of power. A small mercy – at least the humans won't witness what's about to happen next.

In the pitch black, the witches move like predatory cats at night, their heightened senses guiding them around tables and chairs, shielding against any magical blasts that sizzle through the air. The rest of the coven scrambles to intervene, but their voices are lost amid those of the confused patrons.

Ember weaves a thread of Anima tightly in her fist, and with a fierce blow, she unleashes it directly at Zara's chest. A crash echoes through the darkness, followed by a pained grunt. She got her.

"Stop it, Em," Adanna's hands find Ember's arm in the dark, holding her back.

Now smartphones begin to light up again, and in the scattered beams, Ember catches a glimpse of Zara as she bolts out the door and into the streets.

Adanna, not hesitating, is the first to rush after her. Ember follows, with the rest of the coven close behind. But Adanna is by far the fastest, tearing after Zara like a fox chasing a hare.

Out on the street, Zara bolts through the late-night crowd. Adanna is onto her, but Ember struggles to keep up. She pushes through pedestrians, her eyes locked on Zara vaulting over a street vendor's cart, scattering soda cans and souvenirs across the pavement.

Through winding alleys and across bustling intersections, Zara's magic lashes out, now desperate, toppling bins, forcing her assailants to hurdle over the debris. A fire hydrant bursts, sending a geyser of water into the air, momentarily stopping Ember. She shields her eyes from the spray, losing sight of Zara. Adanna is still running, but now Ember's lost her, too. Still, she pushes on, narrowly avoiding a taxi that screeches to a halt, the driver's curses lost on her. At last, she catches up with Adanna, who's come to a halt in a quiet square, panting.

"She... she's gone... I lost her at the intersection," Adanna gasps, holding her thighs as she catches her breath. "She must have jumped into a taxi or... I don't know, disappeared in the crowd somehow."

"Fuck's sake!" Ember curses, kicking a lamp post, which causes its bulb to go out.

The rest of the coven catches up, a bunch of upset finches, rattled by a snake in their midst.

"Did you catch her?" asks Saskia.

"Does it look like we did?" replies Adanna.

"So, what now?" Eun-Ji asks, and everyone turns to Ember.

"I don't bloody know, alright? She's out of the coven, obviously." Ember paces up and down the pavement, her mind racing. *Mardequai.* Zara's but another one of his puppets, his eyes and ears planted right in the midst of her coven. She should have known. Maybe she did. Just like with Alva, he'd overruled coven law to force Zara's admission – another reminder of how little actual autonomy she had, how much his fingers still pulled her strings. "Go home," she orders abruptly, desperate to be alone. "You can all go home now. And should she make contact with any of you, it is your duty to report it – not just to me, but to the authorities, mind you. That witch is going straight to Saltholm, trust me."

Ember walks off, her mind roiling from a violent concoction of rage, alcohol and – panic.

"Well, good night, then," calls Saskia hesitantly.

"Anyone wants to share a taxi?" asks Inaaya.

After a little shuffle and a bunch of hugs, the coven disperses, leaving only Ember, Alva, and Kettering behind.

Ember makes her way toward a small grassy area in the middle of the square, slumping down on a park bench, where she lights a cigarette. The park is empty save for a solitary dog walker. The autumn wind carries fragments of her sister's conversation with the druid. Though most words escape her, "Thank you" rings out clearly.

Moments later, the sound of shoes on gravel announces Alva's presence.

"Got your coat," she says gently and sits down beside Ember, who slips into her blazer.

"So, what you reckon? How bad is that stuff, medically speaking?" Ember asks, taking a drag.

"As in: would I have died, had I downed a hemlock negroni?" Alva crosses her legs. "Well, let's put it this way: there are reports of children suffocating because they used hemlock stems as whistles. The main toxin is coniine, and that stops the nervous system from working properly, which can lead to rapid suffocation."

"So, total failure then," Ember concludes, flicking her cigarette.

"*Totalausfall,*" Alva agrees in German.

They go quiet for a beat before one sister voices exactly what the other feared she would.

"You... you do agree that she didn't do this of her own accord, don't you?" Alva says.

Ember rises, avoiding eye contact, her hands gripping the iron park railing as if to wrench it from the earth. "I don't know," she sighs. "To be honest, Zara's been fighting me ever since she joined the coven."

Now Alva stands, too. "Why are you still defending him?"

Ember interlaces her fingers behind her nape, tousling the shorter strands at the base of her hairline as she buys more time to think. "We don't know he's behind it," she says at last. "We don't know that. After all, it was *my* drink she spiked – not yours."

"*So what?*" Alva bristles with irritation. "She probably wouldn't have minded if she'd taken us both out. You said it yourself; she has a problem with your authority."

"But *he* wouldn't hurt me!" Ember exclaims, her words cracking like brittle sticks. "You don't understand, he would never risk losing me."

However, even as she says this, Ember feels the betrayal crawling in, a treacherous, malignant scorpion. The call was just too close, the blatant disregard for her own safety too hard to ignore.

"But he would hurt *me*," argues Alva.

There's a part hidden deep within Ember that still refuses to believe it. A part that still clings to the naïve notion that she is in control of her own life, that she calls the shots here. But who's she kidding? She probably never has.

And of course, Alva is right. If anything, the proof lies in the timing: the moment Ember refused to do Mardequai's bidding – the moment she called off the Reveal's pre-empt – her foster father unleashed the threat. Tentacles firmly in place like an octopus, he'd planted a killer within her own coven, ready to deliver immediate results, should Ember decide *not* to. Zara on her phone all night wasn't just rudeness – it was reporting back. She'd likely texted him via the RN the moment she realised Ember had changed course. By now, Mardequai would know everything.

As much as it pains her, there *is* no other way to see it.

"I've got no choice," she utters as the realisation hardens in her mind: her pre-empt of the Reveal is back on.

"What do you mean?" Alva edges closer, a softer tone, a gentler touch on the shoulder.

But Ember breaks away. "I've got to go now," she says, but the distance between them is not easily increased. "I suggest you do the same."

"What's that supposed to mean?"

"Go home, Alva. Go back to that boring boyfriend of yours and live your boring old life. And I mean that in the best sense of the word: boring and predictable is exactly what you'll want in the days to come."

Ember fishes for her phone, dialling Pippa's number as she

exits the park, brushing past Kettering, who stands glued to the pavement as if his feet were rooted in concrete. "Yeah, can you come get me, please?" Ember says as soon as Pippa picks up. "I'm just around the corner." She finds the nearest street sign. "Hoxton Square."

"But... what about Morocco?" Alva's voice comes up from behind.

"Morocco is off," Ember says, then strides across the tarmac to a spot where Pippa can easily collect her.

"What on earth does he have on you, Sofia?" Alva calls after her.

"Stop calling me that. I'm *Ember*, alright? Sofia died in that crash thirteen years ago."

The Range Rover turns the corner and comes to a stop between the twins. Ember opens the back door, about to get in, but then she pauses, sighs, and walks back around the car. Standing before Alva, she takes her by the hands. "Just... fly home, okay? No matter what you hear, you get the hell out of this city as soon as possible. Let Kettering drive you to the airport. Clearly, he cares about your safety."

"Why are you telling me this?" Alva shakes her head ever so slightly, the movement dislodging a solitary tear. Ember's fingers twitch, fighting the urge to brush it away.

"It's better if you don't know, trust me."

She wrenches herself free, bolting for the car. "Let the druid take you home, alright? Don't walk alone," she urges over her shoulder. Then, barely audible, she murmurs to herself, "I just need a little more time. Please, just give me until tomorrow..."

* * *

Pippa's eyes are trained on Ember in the rearview mirror as they leave Hoxton Square behind, a question poised on her lips.

"Didn't they need a lift?"

"Nope, they prefer to walk," Ember replies absentmindedly, elbow perched on the armrest, fingers covering her mouth.

"And where to now, Your Ladyship? The Cauldron? The night is still young for you, I suppose?"

"The townhouse."

"As you wish." Pippa clears her throat. "But just so you know: Mr Guise won't be there."

"How do you know?"

"He left a message earlier this evening. He's off to Dunmorrough. He said, and I quote: 'Do not disappoint me again, Ember,'" Pippa says, mimicking his voice.

"Right. Back to the Mandrake, then," Ember replies as if on autopilot. Her insides, however, are roiling with nausea.

Pippa nods curtly, merging with the evening traffic on Old Street. Stopping at a red light, she picks up the conversation again. "What was he referring to, if you don't mind me asking?"

"You'll find out soon enough."

"Bit snappy tonight, are we?"

"Do you make it a habit of speaking to all of your employers like that?" Ember snaps. Realising it, she softens her approach. "I'm sorry. Got a lot on my mind tonight. Just get me there as fast as possible, yeah?"

"Yes, ma'am."

A half hour later, Pippa drops her off in front of the Mandrake. The boutique hotel's striking black exterior stands out against the otherwise muted facades of Fitzrovia. A soft drizzle patters on the windshield, the rhythmic sound of the wipers the only sound in the car.

"Thanks, Pippa darling. You can drive yourself home now. And... take the day off tomorrow, alright?"

Pippa turns around, her hand resting on the back of the passenger seat. "Are you sure?"

"Yeah, you deserve it. Just... just fetch the cat in the afternoon and make sure you'll be at the townhouse from, let's say four o'clock? Would that work for you?"

"Of course. Whatever you need."

"Excellent," Ember says, stroking Pippa's hand.

Seizing the moment, Pippa gently clasps Ember's wrist. "Hey, are you alright?"

"Of course, pet, why wouldn't I be?"

Pippa's eyes refuse to leave Ember's, searching, questioning. "You're lying. Something's off with you, I can tell."

"You sure can." Ember smiles sadly. "You always can. One of the few annoying qualities about you, Miss Watson."

For two swishes of the wipers across the windshield they sit motionless, eyes meeting, hands still joined in the quiet car.

"Hey, you still want to run away together?" Pippa quips, interlacing her fingers with Ember's. "I hear Tokyo's autumn foliage is stunning this time of year."

Ember chuckles. "I'm afraid that plane has left without us, angel." She strokes Pippa's thumb. "Good night."

And with that, she pulls away and steps out of the car. Crossing the pavement, her knuckles graze her nose as she sniffles softly, catching the lingering notes of Pippa's perfume on her skin, light orange blossoms and deep magnolia undertones.

The hotel's entrance is understated, marked only by its mystical emblem – a stylised all-seeing eye – hovering above. Ember slips inside, collecting her key card from reception.

This place couldn't be more suited to her if it tried. Drawing inspiration from its namesake, the mandrake root, a potent hallucinogen steeped in witchcraft lore, the hotel sprawls across four floors, beckoning guests into an alternate reality of bizarre décor and eclectic vibes. At its core lies an evergreen sanctuary: living walls of cascading jasmine and passion flowers, their tendrils reaching down from the ceiling.

Ember traverses the courtyard, unfazed by the guests surreptitiously filming and snapping photos (such attention is old hat to her now). She makes a beeline for the Waeska Bar, slumping down in her usual seat by the counter. Portishead's 'Glory Box' resounds from the speaker, Beth Gibbons singing about giving her a reason to love you before the hauntingly dark guitar solo sets in. Ember orders a whiskey neat, then fishes out her phone to dial Minnie.

"You still awake?" she asks when her friend picks up.

"Sure, I was just starting a seance to connect with my spirit guides," Minnie says. "How are you doing after tonight?"

"Yeah, I'm fine. Listen, we need to start the coven phone chain, save for Zara, of course."

"Of course. I'll call Saskia right away. What's the message?"

Ember downs her drink, signalling for the barkeeper to refill it straight away. She thinks for a heartbeat, tracing patterns on the condensation of her glass. "We're meeting tomorrow at three o'clock, St. James's Square. Tell them to bring their cloaks."

"What for?"

"I'll explain tomorrow."

"Alright." Minnie doesn't sound too concerned, probably floating in a different realm after smoking her blue lotus pipe. "See you tomorrow, then. Oh, hang on – who's going to call Alva? We don't have her number."

"Alva's not coming," Ember replies, then hangs up the phone.

The barkeeper has returned with the bottle, about to refill her glass, when Ember takes it off his hands. "Actually, I'll have the whole bottle – thanks, Aaron."

Aaron doesn't so much as blink at her decision; it's not the first time she's done so, and he knows she's good for it.

Ember picks up her phone again, her fingers hovering over

the screen for a moment before she decides to record a message for Mardequai.

"I didn't think you could do it. I really believed you when you said I was your... that I was your ember." She swallows hard, the betrayal festering in her chest. "But I guess you've found your replacement now. Next time, just make sure she doesn't try to use poison for the job."

She hits send, watching as the message is transcribed and then delivered through the RN app. A green checkmark appears, confirming its receipt.

Clutching the bottle, Ember glides towards the elevator, a subtle hex freezing a nearby couple in their tracks before they can step inside with her. As the doors part, she stumbles in, taking a swig straight from the bottle. She holds onto the wall, teetering on her stilettos as she peers out through smouldering dark eyes. Outside, a man's camera flashes, capturing the infamous Ember Wild just as the doors begin to close.

Little does he know that snapshot will fetch a pretty penny by this time tomorrow.

Chapter Twenty-Two

When Sofia and I were kids, I was always the scaredy pants.

I'd freeze at the top of the slope, while she zoomed down on her sleigh. Playing hide-and-seek, I'd always pick the boring spots, while Sofia would squeeze into the creepiest corners, where no one found her until she chose to come out. At the beach, she'd dive into the waves headfirst before I even had a toe in the water.

And to this day, nothing terrifies me more than a thunderstorm in full force. It doesn't matter how many times someone explains to me how it works, or how low the chances are of actually getting hit by a bolt of lightning – as soon as I hear thunder cracking, I turn into a dog, hiding beneath the furniture.

Indeed, my fear of thunderstorms was so notorious growing up, our dad decided something ought to be done to help me deal with my fear. One afternoon, as another mighty storm thundered closer, he sat Sofia and me down at the kitchen table and began to weave a tale.

"You know" – he pulled out his pocketknife and a small

block of wood and began to shave off delicate curls – "I heard a crazy thing about thunderstorms once."

His eyes flicked between his handiwork and our faces as he continued. "Imagine this, a storm is brewing on the horizon. Dark clouds roll in, swollen with rain and thunder and lightning."

I remember simply picturing that scenario was enough for me to huddle up next to Sofia on the kitchen bench.

"Now, as the storm approaches, all the animals on the ground and all the birds in the sky are seeking shelter – they disappear into their burrows or fly into the trees, where they huddle in their nests. But one of them is different."

He brushed away some shavings from the table. The wood was slowly taking shape as he spoke, but I couldn't quite make out what it was becoming yet.

"Do you know which animal it might be?"

"A fox?" I asked.

"No, it's gotta be a horse!" Sofia guessed.

"Good guesses, very good guesses. But it is, in fact, the eagle that does something truly remarkable. Instead of hiding, the eagle spreads its mighty wings and takes to the sky."

As if on cue, the wood in his hands began to resemble a bird form, wings starting to emerge.

"The winds pick up and the rain starts to fall, but the eagle doesn't fight against it. It doesn't even try to escape it. Do you know what the eagle does instead?"

Sofia and I both shook our heads, our eyes darting between his face and his busy hands.

"It uses those very same winds that frighten other animals to death to *lift* itself higher and higher, until it soars above the storm clouds, rising to where the air is calm and the sun is shining."

His knife moved more precisely now, adding details to what was clearly becoming an eagle figurine.

"While the world below is dark and scary, the eagle finds peace by facing the storm head-on and using its strength to come out on top."

Dad leaned forward as he put the finishing touches on his carving. "So, you see, sometimes the very thing we fear most can become the force that lifts us up. We just need to learn how to spread our wings and ride it out."

With that, he handed me the beautifully crafted wooden eagle. "Always remember, Alva," he added, "you have the strength of an eagle inside you. And you can rise above *any* storm."

"I have eagle strength, too, you know?" Sofia announced, not missing a beat.

"Indeed, you do, darling – and lots of it," Dad said with a chuckle. "Which is why you don't need a reminder – you *are* a reminder for all of us to be a little more daring sometimes."

I still carry that whittled eagle with me today. But it was actually Sofia who would relate to Dad's story in a much more literal way: from that day on, whenever a storm brewed on the horizon, she'd built a blanket fort so I could hide, making sure I had my eagle figurine with me. But once I was safe, she would run up to the attic, open the window and spread her arms, rain pelting her face as she pretended to be an eagle, facing the storm, ready to soar above it.

But that was then, and this is now.

As I watch my sister drive away, leaving me behind in a dark London street with nothing but questions and a grumpy immortal, I make my choice: I won't do as she says. I'm not going to leave. I'm not going to run away while she faces whatever she thinks she must face alone. This is a storm I will not ride out beneath the blankets.

This time, *I'm* going to be the eagle.

The next morning finds me tired an exhausted and – late for the damn river cleanse. After a sped-up bathroom routine, I slip into the same outfit from the day before, throw on my coat, and rush down the hotel stairs with silent prayers that I haven't missed breakfast yet. But as I turn the handle to the breakfast room, it's locked. Swearing under my breath, I check my phone for the time – it's ten fifteen. According to the GAAG schedule, that leaves me with forty-five minutes left on the clock to get to... damn it, I have no idea where I need to be.

"Morning."

I spin around to see Kettering by the hotel entrance, holding two paper cups.

"I, er, I pressed the wrong button on the coffee machine," he says, offering me one of the cups. "I wanted black, but it spat out a cappuccino. Do you want this?"

"O-kay? Thank you. That is... unusually nice of you." I take the cup from his hands, my fingers briefly brushing his.

"Didn't want it to go to waste, that's all," he replies, tossing his empty cup in a waste bin. "You ready to go?"

"Yes. Do you know where to?"

"Follow me." He swings around and steps into a sunny autumn morning.

A coin-sized cookie sits on the lid of the coffee cup. Although I'm tempted to question the druid about it, I pop it into my mouth, stifling a smirk as I fall into step beside him.

Kettering suggests we walk instead of taking the Tube, and I'm grateful for the fresh air – and the opportunity to buy a sandwich and a second cup of coffee from a cart in Hyde Park.

At exactly eleven o'clock, we arrive at a nondescript flight of stony stairs.

"You're sure this is where we need to be?" I ask. Granted, we are by the riverbank, but it seems like way too busy a place for any kind of magical demonstration. The pavement is bustling with pedestrians, starting another week of regular nine-to-fives.

"Let's find out, shall we? After you, madame," he says, gesturing for me to descend.

I go, but not without a comment that's been on my tongue since the cookie. "Why are you so nice to me today?"

"Maybe I've just grown tired of hating you."

"Well, whatever the reason, I much prefer 'madame' over 'witch'," I say, managing just a single slip on the wet stairs. Kettering quickly steadies me, albeit with a curse.

We step onto a gravel beach, the murky Thames water lapping as a boat chugs by, disappearing below the red-and-white arches of Blackfriars Bridge. Rounding the stairwell reveals – another flight of stairs, this set leading into a dark abyss.

"What's stopping regular people from snooping down there?" I ask.

"This your first time being a witch, is it?" Kettering quips. "Protective wards, of course."

"Ah, figures," I reply when I spot the faint traces of runes carved into the ancient stone walls.

Descending into the pitch blackness of underground London, I use my smartphone to light the way until I can see warm light spilling through a distant archway.

At the end of a long tunnel, we pass this arched entryway, its bricks patinated with age and water vapour, its curves echoing the flow of water below. Stepping onto a wrought iron walkway, I'm met with a sight that takes my breath away: we're standing above a subterranean river, a vast chamber unfolding before us, its vaulted ceiling soaring to impressive heights, lit by dancing torchlight. More runes, etched into the brickwork, shimmer in the water's reflection. Shadowy alcoves house arcane devices, a rusty blend of industrial machinery and magical artefacts.

Further down the walkway, a large group has gathered, their voices carrying across the water.

"What is this place?" The question escapes me as I look around this enormous magical secret, hidden directly beneath central London.

"The Blackfriars Pier Water Chamber, the birthplace of the Resonance Network," replies Kettering from behind me. "Elias Klein built it during the Victorian era. It connects directly to the Ley Line Confluence beneath St. Paul's Cathedral."

"Elias Klein? The Silicon Valley druid?"

"The very same. Although back then, he still went by his birth name, Fenwick Martin."

I touch a pillar as we pass another archway, the bricks cold and wet against my skin. "How does it work, exactly?"

"A combination of several forces." Kettering's voice echoes above the river's rush, and I detect a hint of something darker in his tone I can't quite place. "Fenwick Martin claims the location is the crucial part: like all RN operation centres, this place sits at a confluence of ley lines, and its power is enhanced by the proximity to a large river like the Thames, he says."

"What are ley lines, anyway?"

"According to him, they are Earth's magical highways, similar to a forest's root network. Invisible threads of energy running under our feet that connect high-frequency places around the world."

"So, the ley lines transmit the messages and the river's Anima fuels the network?"

"Something like that."

"And Elias – I mean Fenwick – he built all this?"

"Well, not by himself. He'd been working on the concept for several decades, determined to make resonant communication accessible for the entire magical community, not just the privileged few. Eventually, he said he figured out that the low-frequency polluted waters of the Thames were to blame for his failed attempts. He'd gone to build a test site in the Scottish Highlands, where the water was crystal clear, and there, he said it worked flawlessly. So, he came back to London, trying to convince the government to tackle the river's pollution – to no avail. It was not until the summer of 1858, when the infamous 'Great Stink' befell the city, and thousands died of cholera, that Parliament hired Joseph Bazalgette to revolutionise London's sewage system. Fenwick Martin began working under him and secretly built his own channel. He diverted water from the Fleet River, a tributary of the Thames. The Resonance Network henceforth worked independently from any non-magical systems. It's probably the only truly clean water source in the whole of London. But the city's overall pollution still dampens the RN's effectiveness, he claims. Hence, our little gathering today."

I turn around to Kettering. "How do you know all this?" I ask, searching his face.

"I was born in the eighteen hundreds," he replies simply. "In Amsterdam, for what it's worth. But my father took me to London for the opening. The RN was *the* revolution of the century."

"How did it work back then?"

"Telegraph keys, connected to these same water-filled resonance chambers. Magical Morse code, basically."

"And your father? He'd be a druid, too, then?"

"Naturally."

"Where is he now?"

"I think this question-and-answer session has come to an end," he says and nods at something ahead of us.

We've come within earshot of the other people now, and as I swing around, Gathoni Nyong'o approaches me, arms spread as if to embrace me. She's dressed in a flowing, olive-green kaftan, wide sleeves billowing as she walks.

"Ah, Alva Hausmann – the woman of the hour," she greets me. She lowers her arms, however, and opts for a formal hand-shake instead of the embrace I perhaps expected. "We are delighted you could make it."

I shake her hand, managing a smile. Yet if I'm being honest, I don't love the fact that she's singling me out the way she does. I'm much more of a drop in the river kind of girl; I don't enjoy being the centre of attention.

Gathoni's eyes suddenly widen as they land on the druid. "Cornelis," she says with surprise. "I wasn't expecting to see you here."

The unexpected tension between them catches me off guard. I glance between them, sensing an undercurrent, but I don't know what it's about. Gathoni, however, quickly refocuses on me. "Well, are you ready to cleanse some water, dear?" she asks, the people on the other end of the walkway craning their necks to get a good look at me. There aren't as many participants at today's gathering, probably due to the confined space. No more than two dozen people have lined up on the walkway. Behind them, another tunnel leads into darkness. Above its entrance, an ancient signpost bears the inscription To St. Paul's Cathedral in weathered letters.

"Listen, it's not going to be a big deal," Gathoni says with a conspiratorial murmur, clearly sensing my unease. "I will do everything; you just stand beside me as my proxy. That's the law, a safety protocol when using a Celestial Stone. But I've never needed my proxy, not once. So don't you worry about anything."

"A Celestial Stone?" My eyes widen when I remember last night's coven chat on the rooftop. I didn't think I'd see one in action this soon. Then, to my dismay, something else inside me springs to life – dark thoughts taking over my mind, and the strange but thronging urge to tear at the head elder's clothes, to search for, to *grasp* that powerful element I can practically sense on her. A shiver courses through me as I fight Ruth off. I pull my coat tightly around me, as if to trap within its folds the darkness I harbour.

It cannot happen. It *must* not happen. Not now. Not today. I've finally managed to get Kettering to at least consider the possibility that I might be a good person. And under no circumstances must I disappoint the head elder. Clearly, she's throwing me a bone here – regardless of whether it's to save her own skin, mine, or both.

But there's another reason why I must not screw this up, and it reveals itself when I notice several of the bystanders reaching for notebooks and pens, cameras and recording devices. These are not mere Assembly members – these are *journalists*, witches and druids with covert positions in the human media.

Clutching my throat, I pull my coat even tighter and trail after Gathoni, eyes glued to my feet. Kettering hangs back, but when I cast a glance over my shoulder, he offers an encouraging nod.

The walkway broadens at its centre, forming a metal-grated platform where the group assembles in a semicircle. One man stands apart from the rest, perched over a tablet, absorbed in whatever he's reading there. I place him instantly – a face from my first day at Arcadia House. Yet now, coloured by Kettering's tales, it's as if I'm seeing the man for the first time.

"Have you met Elias Klein?" Gathoni asks when she catches my look. But she doesn't wait for my reply, already addressing the druid. "Elias, come meet Alva Hausmann."

The druid glances up with a brief smile as he walks over to us. It's hard to believe the man has been around since before the Victorian era. He looks no older than forty.

Our introduction feels like a charade, all camera flashes and fake smiles as he slides his tablet into his bag, then takes my hand in both of his.

"What a pleasure," he says to me. However, he won't meet my eyes, and his demeanour clearly betrays discomfort. At first, I think it's the usual Ruth Hausmann prejudice – that judgmental look, mixed with a strong dose of trepidation. But Elias Klein doesn't seem scared. If I didn't know any better, I'd say he looks deeply troubled. Contrite, even.

When the photo op is over and done with, he is quick to excuse himself.

"Well, I...I'd best make my way to the control room now," he stammers. "See what metrics will show up after the cleanse. Good luck."

The druid disappears, making his way toward St. Paul's Cathedral.

"Welcome, welcome, everybody," Gathoni addresses the small crowd. "Thank you kindly for being here with us today, and for agreeing to use your respective positions in the media to spread the important story we hope to tell here. The Reveal is a mere forty-eight hours away, a momentous achievement our entire community has been working towards for many, *many* years."

A melodious hum rises from the gathered, resonating through the water chamber.

"To show our non-magical brothers and sisters that we come in peace, that we are sharing our gifts with them to help them on their path of renewal, of reconnection with the natural world, we have planted seeds of hope all across the country, living proof of our good intentions. With your help, these good deeds will spread over the coming days. And we have gathered here today to add the final stroke to our masterpiece: the crowning jewel of our preparations will be a thorough magical cleanse of the Thames River, achieved by the use of a Celestial Stone."

The head elder presents the object, cradling it in her cupped palms. I strain to peek over her shoulder, but her fingers close around it before I can catch a glimpse. The missed opportunity stirs a dark hunger within me, one I struggle to tame.

"But let it be clear: this is but a temporary measure. Our magic, potent as it may be, serves merely as kindling, a catalyst to foster and propel permanent solutions. Under no circumstances must humanity believe that they needn't change, that our powers are a silver bullet. May this cleanse be a nascent star of hope in an ever-darkening sky," Gathoni finishes her speech, and more humming resounds from the gathered.

Exhilaration buzzes through my veins when she turns away from the journalists, casting me a reassuring glance as she comes down on her knees at the water's edge. Her right fist clasped around the stone, she presses it against her third eye and begins to murmur an incantation in what must be her native tongue – Swahili if I were to take a guess. Quiet at first, then growing louder and louder, until her voice echoes all across the chamber, bounces off the water, and resonates deep in my marrow, a haunting fusion of words and melody.

In the midst of her chant, unexpectedly, she grasps my hand, and then a surge of energy floods my palm – so potent, so fierce, darkness swallows my vision, and I momentarily lose balance.

But Gathoni's grip on my hand remains strong, her other hand now shaking from the Anima that must be accumulating in her fist, until streaks of light seep through the cracks between her fingers. At last, she releases an eerily beautiful sound, and with a deliberate gesture, she submerges the stone in the river, tugging my own arm and forcing me to my knees beside her.

The instant the stone touches the surface of the water, its magic erupts. Light beams race across and below the water, illuminating the depths below us in a rush of golden tendrils that quickly reach the edges of the chamber, finding tunnels and cracks to seep through into the city.

And for a moment, all seems well. I bask in the warmth of Gathoni's powers, amplified by the stone in her hand. The feeling surges through our joined hands, racing up my arm, and suddenly, I *am* the river. Fluid, free, and boundless.

But as soon as the Anima reaches my chest, horror dawns. Something within me awakens, and it is equally potent. I feel Gathoni's magic recoiling from my core, and like two magnets repelling one another, a war erupts in my body. To my dismay, Ruth breaks loose, urging me to seize that power, to claim the force coursing through me. *Let me do it... let me have it. I must have it...*

I've always known Ruth was evil – dark and wicked, capable of unspeakable crimes. But *this*... this exceeds even my worst nightmares. Her true strength emerges, terrifying in its magnitude as her words erupt from my own mouth: "I must have it!"

A dark force surges back through my arm and into Gathoni's body, coursing through her and then further still, into the river. Now pitch-black threads streak the water, a noxious ink dissolving Gathoni's golden good.

"Stop it, Alva – what are you doing?" Gathoni's panic pierces through to me, but I can't do anything to stop this. Gathoni seems to realise it, too, instantly switching gears. "Ruth – *Ruth Hausmann*, I implore you: stay away!"

Gasps and shouts erupt behind us, as the dark threads in the river begin to spread at an alarming rate, reaching the chamber walls, almost free. I'm trying – truly trying – to halt them, but I can't, and what terrifies me most is that I'm not sure I want to.

Suddenly, strong arms encircle my waist, wrenching me away, severing the connection between the head elder and me. The dark threads snap back into my body and the river returns to gold, then to its natural hue. But Ruth isn't finished – she craves that power, she wants it back.

My body struggles against the person holding me, who I now realise is Kettering, but he's relentless, dragging me away despite my resistance. Back on the walkway, Ruth (or is it me?) manages to fire off a spell against his hand, briefly freeing me. But he persists, seizing me again, hauling me away from the cameras and into the dark corridor leading to St. Paul's.

At last, he slams the door shut behind us, locking it and plunging us into near darkness. Only a distant light trickles down the hallway from the other end, casting shadows across his shocked face. My breath steadies as I gradually reclaim myself. I brace for Kettering's fury, for him to call me by *her* name again. But he doesn't. For a heartbeat, he remains motionless, propped against one wall while I sag against the other.

Then, out of nowhere, he lunges at me, clawing at my coat, nearly ripping it off.

"What are you doing?" I demand, my throat constricted by my own guilt.

His hands sweep my body, delving into my jean's pockets. Finding nothing, he turns to my coat, his movements frenzied until – he freezes. One hand deep in my coat pocket, his eyes lock onto mine. With agonising slowness, he extracts what he's found. It's the obsidian rock, the talisman I've carried with me since the day of the accident, thirteen years ago.

"I knew it," Kettering drones. "You've got one."

"I've got – *what?*" I ask as my eyes wander between his face and the rock in his hand.

"You've got a Celestial Stone."

Chapter Twenty-Three

I stare at the rock nestled in Kettering's palm as if seeing it for the first time.

"That's not what this is," I hear the words tumble from my mouth. "It can't be. This is... this is just a rock. I've had this half my life."

Kettering leans in, bracing one hand against the wall beside my face. His eyes pin mine. "Who gave it to you?"

"Nobody. I... I found it," I stammer, shrinking back against the wall.

"You *found* it? *Where?*"

I shake my head, trying to clear the fog, but it only spawns more confusion. "How do you even know this *is* one?"

"Because of what just happened in there," he says, his gaze wandering to the door, then back to me. "That tug-of-war between two equally powerful sources? I've seen it happen before when these stones were tested for safe use. Don't fool me, witch. I've got you figured out. No point in denying it now."

"I'm not denying anything!" I exclaim. "I had no idea this was a Celestial Stone! I've never even used it before."

Only that isn't exactly true, is it? If I'm being honest, I might have felt the effects of the stone before. Many, many times before. Could it truly be? Could it be the stone which has been responsible for my misadventures with Anima over the years, from hexed soaps to inexplicable bouts of rage to wilting trees? I run a list in my head of the countless times when my magic had gone awry.

Kettering closes the distance between us, his face mere inches from mine now. He holds the stone up, level with his eyes, which burn with an intensity that forces me to look away.

"Swear to me," he urges. "Swear this isn't yours. Swear you had no idea what it was until now."

I meet his stare. "I swear it."

The change in Kettering is immediate. He steps back, the tension visibly leaving his body. His hands clasp behind his head, fingers interlocking as he lets out a giant sigh.

"This entire time I thought it was your grandmother causing you to lose control, to overstep the line into darkness whenever you attempted a spell. But... it's not her." His eyes find mine again, but this time, there's something different in his gaze. It's as if he's truly seeing me for the first time – not as a reflection of my grandmother, not as a potential threat, but as myself. "You are not her."

"Well, I kind of told you that all along." I take the stone from his hand, its familiar weight taking on a new meaning as it rests in my palm. As I've done countless times before, I examine it closely, but this time, it's different, and I don't know why. The moment my fingers brush its surface, something awakens again. Power surges from the stone, maybe because it was recently activated, latching onto my skin and then racing through my body like the nearby river. I quickly slip it back into my pocket, scared its power might lure Ruth back to the surface.

"Where *did* you find it?" Kettering asks, now gentler.

"I... I don't remember. It was after the car accident. When they discharged me from the hospital and returned my belongings, it was just... there, in my pocket."

"Why didn't you tell anyone about it?"

"I never thought it mattered," I admit. "Everything after the crash is a blur. I assumed I'd picked it up that night, somehow. It was just one more piece of the puzzle I couldn't fit together. I kept it as a... talisman, I suppose. To honour them."

"You do realise what this means, don't you?" Kettering asks.

I look up at him, confusion clouding my sight. "What *what* means?"

He takes my hand with both of his. "Don't you see? Someone must have slipped you that stone, knowing it would wreak havoc on your magic. So, the accident wasn't your fault."

"*What?*" I'm struck dumb, stunned into stillness.

"And it probably didn't just affect *your* magic," the druid says. "If you toyed with this in a confined space like a car, with two other witches present, it would have disrupted all of your powers, I'm certain – especially your mother's. It takes years of training to master a Celestial Stone. In the hands of a child witch, it would be a stick of dynamite."

My breath catches when his words sink in. What he's suggesting is almost too much to comprehend. For years, I've carried the burden of guilt around me like I have that stone. It's shaped every decision, tainted every memory. The idea that there might be another explanation, another truth behind that night, is as freeing as it is unsettling.

I close my eyes, allowing memories to come – the screech of tires, the shattering of glass, the numbing silence that followed. Could it all have been different than I thought? A tremor travels through my body. I'm about to say something when a pounding on the door jolts me back to reality, a cacophony of voices resounding from the other side.

"We need to explain this to them," Kettering says, already reaching for the handle.

"No!" I yank him back. "Please, I... I can't go back out there."

"Come on. This is your chance to set the record straight. Why would you even hesitate?"

"Because who is going to believe me? Who's going to believe that I just happened to come across one of the most powerful magical artefacts by chance? *Think*, Kettering. They'll conclude I got it from *her*." And we both know who I'm referring to. "They'll conclude that I *am* her."

"But they already do, after what you just did." Kettering gestures at the door.

"Then let's not make it worse. If they find a Celestial Stone on me, they'll probably lock me up at Saltholm. Possession of an unregistered magical item would be just the beginning. They'd likely slap me with malign intent, or even worse allegations."

"Running looks like an admission of guilt."

"That's my choice to make. Please, Cornelis. Let me make a plan first before I face all that."

Kettering sighs, thinking for a beat.

"Fine," he says at last. "Let's go this way."

He seizes my hand and pulls me towards the distant light at the other end of the corridor – the passage leading to St. Paul's Cathedral. I follow him as we pitter-patter down the wet tunnel until a thunderous crack echoes behind us.

"There goes the door," says Kettering. And then our pace picks up to a sprint.

At last, the entrance to St. Paul's RN control centre looms ahead, bathed in an ominous red glow that sweeps across our path like a lighthouse.

"Quick, this way," Kettering hisses, veering left into a smaller tunnel, shrouded entirely in darkness.

Overhead, corroded pipes weep, occasional drops landing on

the floor and on our heads. A low rumble builds, swelling into a roar as a subway train hurtles by somewhere close, the ancient stonework around us trembling. Footsteps approach, and Kettering freezes, his hand clamping over my mouth as he drags me into a shadowy alcove. There, we press against each other, hardly daring to breathe. The footsteps grow louder, lingering for an agonising moment before fading into the distance.

"I think they're gone," Kettering whispers, removing his hand from my mouth. For another two breaths, we inhale the same air, our bodies rising and falling as if made from one piece. The eerie red light illuminates his angular features every once in a while. He's so close to me, I can see a tiny scar next to his left eye, can feel the pounding in his chest. I suck in air through my mouth, parting my lips, about to say something, or perhaps do something, when—

"I swear to you, mister, no one else came with me..." A voice comes from the far end of the tunnel we've slipped into, emanating from the shadows.

Kettering and I spring apart, eyes straining against the dark. I fumble for my smartphone, my hands shaking.

"Who's there?" Kettering demands, positioning himself between me and the potential danger.

A figure slowly emerges from the dark tunnel. As my eyes adjust, I make out a woman. Her hair hangs in messy strands around her face, and thick-rimmed, broken glasses sit crooked on her nose. Her clothes are in complete disarray – a dirty blouse, partially untucked, a lumpy old skirt, twisted awkwardly. I notice, to my horror, that her temples bear fresh scars, resembling cigarette burns. She stumbles towards us, jerky and uncertain.

I grip Kettering's arm, cold fear crawling down the length of my spine like a drop from the ceiling.

"I didnae mean tae do it," the woman mumbles, her words

tinged with a Scottish accent. "I know that now, mister..." Her unfocused eyes dart around the dimly lit tunnel. She wrings her hands but hasn't even registered we're here.

Suddenly, her head snaps up, and the abruptness of the movement causes me to flinch. Her eyes lock onto Kettering, and the change in them is instantaneous. Sheer terror warps her features, and she stumbles back, hands flying to her ears, pressing hard against them.

"It willnae happen again," she whimpers, pacing up and down like a caged rat. "It will never happen again, I'll be a good girl now, mister. I swear it to you."

Her words tumble out in a chaotic rush, a desperate mumble that's hard to understand. She rocks back and forth, but her eyes never leave Kettering, who looks back at her with deep worry.

He and I exchange concerned glances, then I take a step forward. "What won't happen again, dear? And what happened to you?"

As I reach out to touch her shoulder, she grabs my arm, her fingers biting through the fabric of my sleeve. "Dinnae let him take me away!" she pleads, her eyes unfocussed. "They'll hurt me if I go back there!"

"Back where? *Who* will hurt you?"

"The king o' the castle," she lisps.

I'm about to dismiss her ravings when she speaks again. "Dunmorrough Castle, that's where I was. That's where they keep them..."

Shock courses through me when I recognise the name. "Dunmorrough Castle? *Mardequai's* estate?"

"Hush!" She pulls me close again, her breath now hot against my hair. "I'll tell ye a secret. I found a wee hole in the fence." A giggle escapes her lips. "It's still there. I didnae tell them where."

Her grip on my arm tightens even more. "Ye must go back.

Save them. There's an auld shed by the Oakwoods. That's how ye get in unseen..."

Her focus drifts back to Kettering. Once again, something in her snaps, and a new wave of panic sends her pacing again.

"Please," I beg. "What's your name? Tell me your name."

A weird and scary sing-song creeps into her voice. "Effie, Effie, two-by-four, cannae fit through the kitchen door..." She giggles again. "But I *did* fit through that fence, didn't I?"

"Effie? Is that your name?" I implore, searching her face for any sign of recognition.

"Effie Bell, Effie Bell, tripped and fell down the well, soaking wet and smelling yucky, Effie Bell's not very lucky..."

A rusty door screeches in the distance, the sound echoing off the damp stone walls. Footsteps follow, their approaching rhythm painting the girl's features with terror.

"Must go now," she hisses, her eyes darting towards the sound of the footsteps. "They cannot know I ran off again..."

And with that, Effie Bell tears herself loose.

"Hey – *wait!*" I call after her, but she's already running, melting back into the shadows. Another train rattles past, its thunder vibrating through me as it muffles the sound of Effie's retreating footsteps.

Suddenly, a beam of light cuts through to us, painting us in stark contrast against the mouldering walls.

"Who's there?" a familiar voice calls. Kettering and I spin around, moving closer to the light source. As we approach, the beam illuminates the face of Elias Klein.

"What are you doing down here?" Klein demands as he surveys the dank tunnel. "Is the ritual over?"

Relief floods me when I realise, he doesn't yet know what transpired back in the water chamber.

I gesture in the direction Effie Bell ran. "There... there was a g—"

"There was a great little alcove we thought might be perfect for a moment of privacy," Kettering interjects smoothly, taking my hand, which causes Klein's eyebrows to shoot up, embarrassed. "Oh! I... My apologies. I... I... didn't mean to intrude." He fumbles with his flashlight, switching it off as if to prove his discretion.

"No harm done," Kettering assures him. "We were... wrapping up here anyway, weren't we, madame?"

I nod, clearing my throat. "Yes, quite."

"Mr Klein, would you mind guiding us out? I'm afraid we've lost our bearings."

"Of-of course. This way, please."

Klein takes point, leading us through his underground maze. Kettering and I fall in step behind him, with me bringing up the rear. I can't help but glance over my shoulder, again and again, searching for any sign of the mysterious girl, but the tunnels remain empty.

Only the beam of Klein's flashlight moves across the curved ceiling, revealing nothing but wet bricks and rusted pipes.

"Say, I know you from somewhere, don't I?" Klein asks, studying Kettering's profile.

"Well, the druid community is rather tight knit, isn't it? We have come across one another at an event or two, indeed. I'm honoured you remember me."

Klein shakes his head as we round a corner. "No, no. It wasn't at an event. I think I knew your father... Kettering, isn't it?"

"That's right, yes."

"Brilliant man. You look just like him. You two came to see me here, didn't you? Back when the facility first opened?"

"Indeed, we did. I can't believe you remember that. It was almost two hundred years ago." Kettering deftly sidesteps a puddle as I suppress a chuckle. Druid chit-chat. Gotta love it.

"Well, memory *is* the cement druid eminence is built upon." Elias shrugs. "Does he still work as a lawyer, then?"

"No. No, he has moved on from that, last time I checked."

"What a shame. He was absolutely brilliant at it. Gave me some good advice back then. What is he doing now?"

"I'm not entirely certain," Kettering admits.

"You two aren't in touch?"

"Oh well, you know how it is with druid fathers and sons: a few decades may easily pass without any contact. But I'll be sure to send him your regards next time I drop in on him."

"Well, please do. Brilliant man. Ah, and here we are now, back at the surface." Klein pushes open a heavy iron door, and harsh daylight floods the corridor, forcing me to shield my eyes.

As our vision adjusts, we find ourselves in a quiet, red brick courtyard. The muffled sounds of street traffic reach us from nearby, while bushes and trees provide cover for the inconspicuous entrance to Klein's secret burrow.

"A pleasure meeting you both," Klein says, shaking our hands. "Alva, thank you for your assistance today." With that, he retreats rather quickly into the tunnel, the door closing behind him with a resonant thud.

"You don't like him very much, do you?" I ask Kettering the moment we're alone.

"Not particularly, no," Kettering admits, scanning our surroundings. "Come on, we need to get you off the streets — they'll be looking for you."

He seizes my hand and before I can gather my thoughts, he's already dragging me around the corner, flagging down a passing taxi. But as I slide into the back seat, I can't shake the image of Effie Bell disappearing back into the shadows.

Chapter Twenty-Four

The autumn sun slants low across London as Ember leads her coven down Regent Street toward Piccadilly Circus. The pink cloaks started as a jest for one of the Cauldron parties; today they'll be their battle dress. Dramatic, eye-catching, impossible to miss. Perfect for what they're about to do.

"Everyone remember the plan?" Ember calls over her shoulder, her stride more assured than she actually feels. Adrenalin courses through her veins, making her fingertips tingle with Anima waiting to be unleashed.

"Yes, Em," Saskia replies, her usual cheerfulness tempered by nervousness. "We've gone over it three times."

Ember nods, not daring to look behind her, where five witches follow in perfect step – Saskia, Eun-Ji, Adanna, Minnie, and Inaaya, trusting her in the lead.

Hours earlier, they had gathered at St. James's Square, huddled in a tight circle as Ember revealed her audacious plan.

"We beat them to it," she'd insisted, eyes burning with conviction. "That's all I'm proposing. It's going to happen, anyway. But if we pre-empt the official magical reveal, we control the narrative. Not the elders, not their chosen representatives – *us*."

The debate had been heated, with Eun-Ji and Adanna voicing the strongest concerns.

"This is reckless," Adanna had warned. "There are reasons for protocols. They're going to send us all to Saltholm."

"What do you think is going to happen once magic is revealed?" Saskia jumped in, forever having Ember's back. "Witches all across the world will erupt like bloody volcanoes! They can't arrest *everyone*."

And in the end, Ember's passion had been persuasive. "Don't you see? This is so much bigger than us. For centuries, others have decided when and how witches could use their gifts. We have a chance here to shape history in our image, to become modern legends, like we always said we would. I've been clear about this right from the start: *That* is the reason I founded this coven. Now is our moment to prove it."

The coven vote had passed four to two, narrowly tipping in Ember's favour. But what none of them suspected was the truth behind her fervour. That Mardequai's threats against Alva had forced her hand. As they donned their pink cloaks, Ember had led them forward with a confidence that masked her guilt, knowing she had gambled their trust on a betrayal.

"Almost there," she announces as the roar of Piccadilly Circus grows louder. Tourists crowd the pavements, locals hurry past, everyone clutching shopping bags or phones, unaware that in minutes, their understanding of reality will shatter.

Ember feels a flutter of doubt. This isn't what she wanted. Not really. This was Mardequai's plan. His manipulation. His ultimatum. Alva's life for Ember's loyalty.

But there's a twisted joy in it too – the imminent release after years of hiding. The chance to be what she truly is, conse-quences be damned.

"Remember," she says, slowing her pace as the iconic screens of Piccadilly come into view, "once I start, don't stop until I give the signal. No matter what happens."

The others murmur agreement, their faces shadowed beneath their hoods. Too late for second thoughts now. Too late for anything but forward motion.

They pause at the edge of the Circus, blending momentarily with tourist groups. Ember takes a deep breath, scanning the crowded intersection. The perfect stage for their debut.

"Now," she whispers, and steps into the street.

Traffic slows, then stops altogether as six women in bright pink cloaks fan out across the pavement. A few pedestrians laugh, assuming this is some kind of performance art or publicity stunt. Others reach for their phones, already filming.

Perfect, Ember thinks. The more cameras, the better.

She raises her hands, feeling the familiar rush of power building beneath her skin. For a moment, she thinks of Alva. She thinks of her mother, who would have hated this spectacle. She thinks of Mardequai, watching from somewhere, his puppet strings pulled tight.

Then she pushes it all away and focuses on the magic.

The first spell hits like a thunderclap inside her chest. Ember draws Anima from the air, the ground, the electricity humming through the billboards overhead. The massive screens flicker and die as she redirects their power, channelling it down through her fingertips and into the concrete beneath her feet.

The pavement cracks like shattered glass, fissures spreading outward. People shout in alarm, backing away. And then – life. Green shoots burst through the broken concrete, unfurling with impossible speed. Vines climb lampposts, flowers bloom in bril-liant purples and blues, grass replaces asphalt.

The rush is intoxicating. All those years of controlled, hidden magic, and now –freedom. Ember lets out a laugh that's part exhilaration, part defiance.

"More!" she calls to her coven, who respond instantly.

Eun-Ji gestures at a nearby tree, which bends toward her like a courtier bowing before royalty. Its branches stretch and twist, leaves rustling violently without wind. Adanna and Minnie work in tandem, drawing water from underground pipes to create a fountain in the middle of the street. Inaaya raises her hands, and butterflies appear from nowhere, hundreds of them swirling around her in an impossible kaleidoscope. Saskia freezes a row of tourists in place – she doesn't harm them, just holds them motionless until Minnie guides the rushing water into safer streams.

Behind them, traffic has ground to a halt. Ahead, people flee or stand transfixed. Every phone is trained on them. Every eye witnesses magic made real.

And in the centre of it all, Ember feels something tear loose inside her chest –something that's been caged for too long. She's terrified and triumphant and furious all at once. Furious that this is Mardequai's victory, not hers. That she's saving Alva by doing exactly what he wants.

But she's also, Mother help her, *having fun.*

The coven forms a circle as rehearsed. Together, they channel energy downward, focusing on a single point at the centre of the chaos. The ground trembles, then splits open. From the fissure, a sapling shoots upward, growing with magical speed until a massive oak stands where there was once only pavement. Its roots buckle the road, sending cars tilting at odd angles. Its branches spread wide, casting giant shadows across the chaos below.

Ember breaks away from the circle, approaching the nearest news camera that's appeared on the scene. She lowers her hood with a flourish, letting them see her face clearly. The face that will be on every screen worldwide within the hour.

Phones flash. People scream. Somewhere, sirens begin to wail.

And despite everything – despite knowing she's Mardequai's pawn, despite the chaos she's unleashing and the witch hunt that is sure to follow – Ember feels a savage thrill coursing through her veins as she stares directly into the camera lens and says:

"Ding dong, the witches are back."

Chapter Twenty-Five

The taxi pulls away as we walk toward the old familiar Bowery Arms. The hotel's main entrance stands open, spilling warm light onto the pavement. Through the doorway, I can see the tiny lobby, where the receptionist is engaged in conversation with a group of tourists.

Just as I'm about to step inside, Kettering's hand closes around my arm, pulling me back.

"Listen, you're not going to do anything stupid, are you, Sherlock?" His shoulders tense as he moves nearer, speaking just loud enough for me to hear over the lobby's background noise.

I turn to face him. "Like what?"

"Like a trip to Scotland, to see if there's any truth to the girl's story?"

"What's it to you?"

Kettering pulls me closer, his grip tightening.

"Listen to me," he hisses, his breath warm on my nose. "I don't want you going there, do you hear me? I can't... I can't *keep rescuing* you."

"Nobody asked you to," I reply, searching his face.

He steps back and lets out a deep sigh. "This was so much easier when I thought you were pure evil," he mutters, shaking out his hands as if to prepare for a fight.

A guest brushes past us then, dragging a suitcase down the stairs, which momentarily drowns out any chance to speak.

"It was him, you know?" I say once we're alone again, and the druid turns back toward me.

"Mardequai," I say. "I know it was him who slipped me that stone."

"How can you possibly know that?"

"I think you know it, too," I reply, my words nearly lost in a sudden burst of laughter from the reception.

Kettering exhales, a sigh so deep it's as if he's trying to release decades of secrets from his body. He presses the fingers of both hands against the bridge of his nose, his palms covering his mouth like a face mask.

With slow steps, he moves towards me again. His hand lands on the doorframe above my head, his arm forming an arch over me. His positioning is both protective and constricting. For a moment, I'm tempted to lean into him, to seek the comfort and safety he seems to offer.

"Promise me you won't go snooping in Dunmorrough, no matter what happens," he implores. "Promise me you won't do anything reckless."

I shake my head, my lips parting as I search for words of protest.

"*Promise* me, Alva."

The sound of my name startles me. It's the first time he's used it.

After a long moment, I finally give in. "Alright, I promise."

A sudden commotion erupts inside the hotel lobby, drawing

our attention. People rush towards a small TV nestled above the fake fireplace in the corner.

"Bloody hell, what's happening?" someone calls out.

The receptionist fumbles for the remote to turn up the volume. A sense of foreboding creeps into my stomach as I tear myself away from Kettering and we move towards the growing crowd around the tiny TV.

The scene that unfolds on the screen is surreal. "WITCH-CRAFT IS REEL!" reads the caption, the spelling mistake hinting at the haste with which it was written. And there, at the head of six women dressed in daring pink cloaks, walks – Sofia. Marching down Piccadilly Circus, their magic transforms the London landmark into a demonstration that was supposed to wait until Wednesday.

But now, the iconic Ember Wild leads the way and as she moves down the street, trees bend towards her like bowing subjects, their leaves rustling violently. Behind her, the other witches move in perfect synchronicity, their hands outstretched, their faces hidden beneath their pink hoods – though I know it must be Saskia, Eun-Ji, Adanna, Minnie and Inaaya. Wherever they pass, flowers sprout from the pavement, bursting into sudden bloom, new growth magically transforming the city into a jungle. Onlookers gasp and stumble as they film with their smartphones, capturing how the Venus in Fur coven draws Anima from their surroundings. The renowned billboards flicker and die, their electricity redirected to fuel the witches' display of power.

In the centre of the square, they form a circle, channelling energy until the ground beneath them cracks and a small sapling bursts forth, growing at an unnatural speed into a massive oak.

My sister breaks from the group, approaching the nearest camera, a wicked grin on her face as she lowers the pink hood of her cloak. Her voice booms with audacity through the TV speaker: "Ding dong, the witches are back."

As I watch, transfixed yet horrified, I feel Kettering's hand on my shoulder, gripping tightly.

"Safe to say no one will have time to come looking for you now," he murmurs.

Unbidden, my hands press against my lips, covering my mouth in shock. The promise I just made to him suddenly feels impossible to keep.

The reporter on the scene is wearing a Manchester United shirt, his hair is unkempt, his eyes betray his troubled state, yet he speaks with a detached professionalism only journalists can pull off.

"Scenes of panic and disbelief are unfolding here at Piccadilly Circus, where about fifteen minutes ago, a group of six women brought inner city traffic to a standstill when they revealed what can only be described as magical abilities."

The screen switches to the images recorded only moments ago, when Sofia and the coven gathered in a circle, a wall of pink fabric shielding them before they seemingly disappeared into thin air, leaving nothing but their cloaks behind, billowing then falling flat to the ground – an accelerating spell, I'm sure. If they slowed down the footage, they'd probably find six witches dispersing in all directions like autumn leaves.

"The women uprooted entire trees, made new ones grow to full size within seconds, controlled the weather and the elements, even froze rows of people," continues the reporter.

My eyes still fixed on the tiny TV screen in the lobby, surrounded by more people than the hotel has room for – passersby have since come in to see what the commotion was about. Sofia's words from the night before ring in my ears, the final brushstroke to complete the picture: *It's better if you don't know...*

So, that's what Mardequai had on her. She did this to stop me from being killed.

"I need to go to her," I say, tearing my eyes away from the screen as I make for the exit again.

"Remember when you convinced me in the tunnel that you wanted to make a plan first?" Kettering warns from somewhere behind me.

"*So?*"

His fingers wrap around my wrist. "If *ever* there was a time when it's crucial to have a plan first..."

He pulls me away from the lobby, leading me up the cramped staircase instead. Maintaining his grip, he fumbles in his pocket with his free hand, producing his key card. The door to his room yields with the electronic chirp.

Inside, it's as if nobody has even checked into the room. The bedsheets are as crisp as if no one has ever slept in them and the coffee station is unused. Only an old-school leather suitcase in the corner – the kind that Paddington Bear travels with – hints at a patron currently occupying the space. That, and the distinct scent I've come to know as Kettering's over the past days.

The druid closes the door, then turns to face me. He rotates his hands, palms out. "What are you going to do? Rock up at Piccadilly Circus right now? That's not a plan, that's crazy. The whole city will be drowning in chaos tonight." As if to prove his point, a police siren blares down the street outside. "Besides, she'll be long gone by the time you get there."

"I still have to try." I make my way toward the window, brushing the curtains aside. Night has settled over London, and the street down below is gridlocked. "You don't understand," I sigh and turn toward Kettering, coming to lean against the windowsill. "She didn't have a choice. Mardequai blackmailed her. You see, she did this to *save* me."

"Then you should honour her sacrifice by actually *staying*

safe, don't you think?" Kettering engages the safety chain and bars the door, which vexes me.

"What do you think you're doing?" I ask, taking two steps toward him. "You can't keep me here. I'm a lot more powerful than you."

"And what are you going to do about it?" His steps mirror mine as he crosses the room, closing the distance between us. Now he towers over me, our bodies nearly touching, his gaze down his nose meeting my eyes. *"Kill me?"*

I narrow my eyes when a wicked idea takes root. My fingers curl around the stone in my hand, gathering Anima directly from its core. With deadly precision, I unleash a blast that slams into his chest. His body hurtles backwards, crashing into the built-in wardrobe with a satisfying thud of splintering wood – and probably some bones.

An eerie silence fills the room, and for a beat or two, I panic when he doesn't move.

"Kettering," I say, placing my hands on my hips. "Kettering, come on."

At last, his groan breaks the quiet. His fingers twitch, then his arm. Slowly, he stirs. His neck, twisted at an unnatural angle, rights itself with a series of sickening cracks. Bones shift beneath skin, while his shattered legs realign. Finally, he coughs heavily and then his eyes, burning with rage, lock onto me.

"You just killed me!"

"You cannot die."

"That doesn't mean it didn't *hurt*." He rubs his chest and comes back to standing. "You're going to pay for that, by the way." He gestures at the pile of splintered wood that used to be the wardrobe.

"*Fine*, now if you'll excuse me." I brush past him, but he holds me by the arm once again, his grip firm but not too forceful.

"Look, we can do this all night long, but I will keep you from leaving this room, do you hear me?"

Tension floods my muscles; I'm about to launch another blow.

"It's madness out there right now," he insists. "You... you would not be safe. And you don't even know where she is at the moment. Wait until the morning. Until things have settled a bit. Please, Alva. Please stay here tonight."

I release a weary breath, and with it goes my resolve, melting away like snow in hot water.

He reaches for the TV remote on the desk next to him and presses the on button – a cheeky distraction to keep me here, but the moment the news flickers across the screen, I slump down on his bed, elbows on knees to steady my chin as I watch, holding my breath.

The same reporter, now shown on the righthand side of a split screen, is in conversation with a TV host in a studio on the left side.

"And who are these women representing, do we know, David?"

"Well, as of now, the terrorists have not pledged themselves to any cause or religious group, Terry..."

"Terrorists?" I exclaim, jerking my head back.

"... but we have since been able to identify the leader of the group. The woman who so boldly declared that, and I quote, 'ding dong, the witches are back' appears to be a notorious London socialite who goes by the name Ember Wild. Wild has recently risen to fame, causing scandalous scenes at major events in London high society. She's rumoured to be the foster child of Mardequai Guise, a reclusive art collector rarely seen in public. Her Instagram account, ironically, features viral posts and videos of her seemingly performing magic tricks – tricks that, as of this moment, Terry, we must assume are no tricks at all."

"Why would she do this, so close to the actual Reveal?" Kettering gestures at the screen, now showing recordings of Ember Wild's Instagram reels.

"I told you, this isn't *her* pulling the strings, trust me. He's forcing her hand in this. So, *you* tell me what your 'brother'" – I air quote the word – "is cooking up here."

"Well, whatever it is, I'm sure we'll find out soon enough."

"Holy shit, holy shit, turn up the volume – turn it up!" I exclaim, as the TV switches to the next story.

"We're receiving breaking news of another inexplicable incident unfolding in central London. Witnesses at Trafalgar Square report a sudden, violent whirlwind materialising out of thin air. The vortex appears to be lifting cars, uprooting trees, and scattering debris..."

The camera pans to shaky mobile phone footage of Trafalgar Square, where a swirling mass of wind sweeps over the streets. As onlookers flee in panic, the whirlwind picks up a double-decker bus, suspending it in mid-air before gently setting it down atop the National Gallery.

"Authorities are baffled by the controlled nature of this phenomenon," the reporter says. "Despite its intensity, there have been no reports of serious injuries. The whirlwind seems to avoid people deliberately, while manipulating large objects with impossible precision."

"This is only going to get worse throughout the night," says Kettering. "Witches have been waiting for this moment for months. We're going to see a lot more magical outbursts tonight. It's like kids finally lighting their firecrackers on New Years Eve."

"Well, this is it then, the cat's out of the bag," I say, settling in.

What follows can only be described as the most surreal night of my life. I sit next to an immortal in a shabby hotel room, a spread of crisps and chocolate bars from the vending machine and drinks from the mini-bar before us, watching spellbound as the story breaks around the globe. The tiny TV flickers with images of inexplicable events occurring everywhere, each more unsettling than the last.

In downtown New York, every bodega cat in the city – those beloved guardian spirits of corner stores – suddenly abandons their posts and streams toward Central Park, revealing themselves as witch familiars as they form a massive circle to amplify their witches' power for the first public magical broadcast in the city's history. Footage from a Rio de Janeiro favela shows a young girl on a rooftop during a storm, creating a pocket of brilliant sunshine above her space while directing the surrounding rain into precise streams that fill her water barrels and nourish her potted plants.

Another shaky smartphone video from Nairobi captures a street performer seemingly controlling a swarm of locusts. The insects form mesmerising shapes in the air before descending on a nearby marketplace, devouring only specific items from male stall owners.

And in Moscow's Red Square, security footage shows a group of university students linking hands, causing every electronic device within a hundred-meter radius to play the rebellious song "I want changes" by the former Soviet rock band Kino, its lyrics a forbidden anthem for political reform in Russia. As authorities rush to respond, the students vanish into the crowd.

All the while, I'm bracing myself every time the TV switches to a new story, expecting at any moment to hear of Sofia's arrest. But while reports state that the entire London police force is out looking for her, she remains missing. I've tried calling her what feels like a thousand times, left messages on the RN and her Instagram, the latter having turned into a digital madhouse as every one of her followers tries to do the exact same thing – anything to get her to respond.

Just before midnight, Gathoni Nyong'o appears on national news, still wearing the kaftan she wore at the water chamber, delivering the gist of what was likely going to be her speech at the climate summit on Wednesday. But as she replies to the news anchor bombarding her with questions, her words strike strangely off; they're mere damage control in a world that has just come off its hinges. It physically pains me to watch her taking the blame for all that's been happening. Years of preparation have been destroyed in mere minutes, and now the uncontrolled wrath and fear of the people seems to unload on one single witch.

"Good evening," the news anchor begins, barely controlled. "With us tonight is Gathoni Nyong'o, who claims leadership of the... creatures responsible for the global chaos. Ms Nyong'o, let's cut to the chase. Are our children safe?"

Gathoni leans forward. "I assure you, children are absolutely safe. Our abilities are entirely rooted in nature and—"

"*Nature?*" the anchor interrupts. "We've seen cars floating in Central London. Is that natural to you?"

Gathoni sighs deeply. "Those incidents were uncontrolled shows of power by individuals who—"

"H-hold on now," the anchor interjects. "You're telling me these events are beyond *your* control? Then what assurances can you give that we won't see more of these attacks?"

"They're not attacks," Gathoni insists. "These are isolated incidents, caused by frustrated individuals of our community who are not representative of what we stand for. Our aim is to work with human authorities to establish an open and peaceful integration of our abilities to benefit modern society."

The anchor leans back in his chair as if to shield himself from her words. "An *open* integration, you say? Are you admitting, then, that witches have been secretly manipulating world events until now?"

Now Gathoni struggles to maintain her composure. "I understand your concern, sir, but I assure you, we haven't been manipulating anything. Nor are we planning on doing so. Our goal is to address global challenges like climate change and—"

"Now wait just a minute," the news anchor cuts in again. "Are you suggesting witches have the power to affect weather patterns? What about natural disasters? And the recent spike in plane crashes – is your community behind those, too?"

"No, quite the contrary," Gathoni says. "We're as concerned about climate change as anyone, as it affects our magic, too. I know these revelations are frightening, but fear and suspicion will only make things worse. We need to work together now, and I'm here to tell you that we have come in peace."

"I'm afraid our viewers will have a hard time believing that, given what we've been seeing all night."

"Fuck's sake, I want to strangle that guy!" I burst out. "He won't even give her a chance!"

Kettering shifts beside me. "She's doing remarkably well, all things considered," he says, his eyes fixed on Gathoni's composed face on the screen. "But I'm afraid it won't help her much."

Gathoni continues to answer every question with the patience of a saint, promising full cooperation with the UK government and other global leaders. Her voice remains steady, her demeanour calm despite the anchor's increasingly frantic reactions.

When she mentions the referendum, however, his eyes almost fall from their sockets. "Hang on. You're saying there was a *vote*? An organised decision to reveal yourselves?"

Gathoni nods. "Yes, like you, we operate by means of democratic processes."

"But that would mean…" the anchor sputters, his professional facade cracking to reveal raw surprise. "How many of you are there? How long have you been – well – *organising?*"

I'm reminded of Dennis's reaction when he first learnt magic was real – that same struggle to grasp the scope of what he was hearing. But where Dennis had time to process, this anchor is live on air, his every reaction broadcast to a world already teetering on the edge of collapse.

Gathoni tries to steer the conversation back to reassurances, but the damage is done.

Kettering sighs softly beside me. "And so it begins," he murmurs.

We remain glued to the TV for the remainder of the night, while outside we hear the blare of sirens, shouts from passersby, and even the disturbing sound of explosions.

At about three a.m. the reports seem to settle down a fraction; instead of new images unfolding, the same footage seems to repeat, and instead of breaking news, many channels have switched to expert interviews and discussions – priests, professors, and occult historians proffer advice and elaborate on their theories.

Reactions from important figures across the globe plaster the captions: the Pope has issued a statement, warning people to stay at home and stay safe. The UN Secretary-General calls for an emergency meeting to address the global crisis. The Dalai Lama urges compassion and understanding in the face of these unprecedented events. Meanwhile, Elon Musk has already posted about integrating magic into sustainable energy solutions, causing his company's stock price to surge.

British Prime Minister Nigel Hall delivers a rather belligerent address to the nation, condemning the witches as a threat to Britain and mobilising the military to aid the police force. He's quick to promise a zero-tolerance approach to witchcraft and sorcery, hinting at potential legislation to criminalise any magical practices. His aggressive stance draws criticism from opposition parties but clearly resonates with his right-wing base.

US President Linda Warren, on the other hand, takes a more neutral approach, assembling a task force of scientists and high-ranking military officials to investigate the global phenomena.

Throughout all this, a strange sense of calm settles in our small space of the world, as both Kettering and I become more and more exhausted by the unfolding news. We find ourselves sprawled across the bed, eyes heavy with fatigue. The flickering light from the TV casts eerie shadows on the walls, the discussions now fading to a mere background hum.

I lie on my side, one arm draped across my belly, fighting against the overwhelming urge to sleep. My eyelids feel as heavy as if I haven't slept in weeks, each blink a battle against the darkness of the room. I struggle to focus on the TV, willing my eyes to stay open, but they win each time, closing for longer and longer periods.

Kettering beside me breathes slow and steady. I turn slightly, seeing his edgy features illuminated by the TV's glow.

"I'm sorry I killed you, by the way."

"Don't mention it," he murmurs.

"You know, for a moment there, I thought you were actually dead."

"It takes a while until we learn to speed up our recovery. Doing so requires – well – *dying* quite frequently, to train the body. I suppose I never saw the point. I like the pain and the darkness that follows."

I sit up, frowning. "You *like* the pain?"

"Never mind," Kettering replies. He grabs a bottle of water, unscrewing the cap.

"No, please. Tell me."

He clears his throat and has a long sip. Setting the bottle

down, he says, "This might be hard for a mortal to understand, but when you cannot die, the one thing you will forever crave is..."

"Dying?"

He shrugs, then adds after a breath or two of silence, "Don't you ever wonder what it's like, on the other side? Don't you want to know what happens – *after?*"

I take a moment to consider this.

"I guess I have thought about it," I muse. "More so in the immediate aftermath of the car accident. I suppose, back then, part of me found solace in the idea that my family might still exist somewhere, reunited, waiting for me, watching over me from afar. But another part – the one that usually won – simply couldn't bear the idea that they were still out there, potentially blaming me for what I'd done."

Kettering gives a confirming grumble, just when a subtle vibration draws his attention. He reaches for his phone, the blue light illuminating his face. His eyes scan the screen, brows furrowing slightly as he reads.

"More bad news?" I manage to ask.

"No, just... same old, I suppose." He slips the phone back into his pocket. "Why don't you try to get a bit of sleep? I'll wake you if anything happens." He reaches for the remote and mutes the TV, plunging the room into a sudden quiet.

"But what about you?" I murmur, pushing through my exhaustion.

"I'm not tired," he assures me.

And despite my best efforts to stay awake, my eyelids grow ever heavier, and I drift off. The room becomes a hazy blur, sounds muffled as tiredness overcomes me.

At some point during the night, I become vaguely aware of movement in the room, and I hear the rustle of fabric and the thuds of careful footsteps. Kettering moves across my field of vision, reaches for the curtains, drawing them closed with a gentle swish. The room darkens even further, and I feel myself slipping into a deeper sleep, comforted by Kettering's soft touch, pulling the blanket over my shoulder, stroking my cheek – if by mistake or on purpose, I'm too tired to discern.

Chapter Twenty-Six

Ember moves through dark alleys like a thief, her features lost in her jumper's oversized hood. Avoiding the bustling main roads, she weaves through a labyrinth of mews, parks, and hidden courtyards. Like a cat on the prowl, she slips from one patch of darkness to another.

Her phone vibrates persistently, her fingers twitching with each new message coming through, resisting the urge to check. Finally, she relents, fishing the phone from her pocket as she hurries onward. The screen illuminates in her hand, revealing a flood of Instagram notifications, intermingled with frantic messages from both Pippa and Alva.

Just when she rounds the corner onto Belgravia's Wilton Crescent, the one message she's been hoping for arrives. The RN app pings, finally displaying Mardequai's approval: "Good girl. You know where you'll be safe. Go there now and await further instructions."

Ember's pace quickens until she finds herself in the shadow of his mansion. Darkness has now fully settled over the neighbourhood, but a warm light spills from the open doorway where Pippa waits, Janis Joplin cradled in her arms.

"What have you done?" her assistant sighs as Ember pauses before her.

"What I had to," she replies, giving Pippa's arm a gentle squeeze and Janis a quick ruffle, before brushing past them into the hallway.

As if summoned, Michaela emerges from the kitchen. Her face betrays her ignorance of the unfolding mayhem. Clearly, the house manager hasn't watched the news tonight.

"Miss Wild, what an unexpected pleasure," she says. "But I'm afraid Mr Guise is currently—"

"Yes, I know where he is, Michaela," Ember cuts in. "Listen, he asked me to send you home. Your services won't be required here for the next few days."

"But – I am home. I live here."

Michaela's response catches Ember off guard. "That's right," she recovers quickly, fishing out her Mandrake key card. "Take this. You're moving into the Mandrake penthouse, courtesy of the Guise corporation." She presses the card into Michaela's palm. "Enjoy yourself. Order anything you like on the company dime. Live a little, old girl." And with a clap on the top of Michaela's hand, Ember manoeuvres the house manager out the door.

As soon as Pippa and Ember are alone, her demeanour shifts. She turns on her heel, striding straight towards the library.

"So, what now? What do we do?" Pippa hurries to keep up, the ginger cat still in her arms.

But Ember doesn't reply, her eyes scanning the library shelves, her hands grazing the spines, searching, searching.

The silence continues, broken only by the rustle of Ember's movements and the cat's meows.

"You're scaring me, Sofia," Pippa says, pressing Janis Joplin to her chest.

Just then, Ember stills, and a victorious gleam flashes in her eyes as she grasps a particular book. But instead of pulling it out, she tilts it back, and a satisfying click resounds, followed by the groan of the ancient mechanism springing to life.

Before Pippa's flabbergasted eyes, a section of the shelf swings inward, revealing a dark tunnel. Ember grabs Pippa's free hand and pulls her towards the opening.

"Come on," she urges, and her assistant stumbles forward, dumbfounded as they cross this secret threshold.

The tunnel stretches beneath the streets, a secret path leading them away from danger. Ember guides Pippa, who has gone quiet, stumbling behind her. After what feels like an eternity, they emerge into the basement of a townhouse just three doors down from where they started.

Mardequai had shown Ember this place weeks ago – an act of trust that now takes on a whole new meaning. As they ascend a creaking staircase, Ember's mind races. Clearly, he's been planning for this to happen, preparing her for this very outcome.

They step into a small but neat living room. Pippa finally sets the cat down, and she immediately winds her way around Ember's legs, purring, then inspecting her new surroundings with sceptical eyes.

"What is this place?" Pippa asks, gazing around as well.

"One of Mardequai's safe houses," Ember replies as she moves around, still frantic, her eyes darting from one corner to another, her arms pulling the curtains closed with sharp tugs. The room, despite its modest size, exudes an air of unexpected luxury, fine-tuned to Mardequai's tastes.

The usual richly upholstered furniture and the well-stocked bookshelves, a state-of-the-art entertainment system, and a small but fully equipped mini-bar. Everything a person might need for an unexpected stay is perfectly arranged in the compact space. It's the ideal hideaway, and a testament to her foster father's paranoia. Or perhaps, his foresight.

"Can you stop stalking around?" Pippa's exasperated voice cuts through her thoughts. "You're driving me mad. Will you please tell me what's gotten into you? Why did you do that?" She gestures at the window as if Ember's dark deed had happened right outside the glass.

Ember pauses, her hand resting on the back of the sofa. "I had no choice," she says.

The tension in the room rises as the two women gravitate towards each other, eyes locking, breaths synchronising. And before either of them can even make the decision, they both reach out, Ember's hands cupping Pippa's face as Pippa pulls her close at the waist. And then their lips meet in a hungry, passionate kiss that doesn't feel entirely earned for Ember, but it's long overdue, nonetheless.

Time stands still as they melt into each other like they did the first night they met – the night Pippa can't remember, the night Ember wishes she'd never erased from her assistant's mind. As if all those regrets and stolen moments were just detours leading to this exact place – now everything around them fades away. The safe house, the pre-empt, the whole damn world out there. Ember hungrily threads her fingers through Pippa's hair, and Pippa pulls her even closer, pressing her body against Ember's. The kiss deepens, suppressed desire pouring out until they part for air, then go again. At last, their eyes lock for a burning second, and Ember's lips part to speak, but Pippa silences her with another kiss, this one softer, but no less hungry – maybe even more so.

Only the sudden, harsh whir of some machine close by finally startles them apart. They jump, hearts pounding for an entirely different reason now, as a fax machine in the corner springs to life. Both flushed, they stare at each other for a beat longer, the pressure of the kiss still lingering on both their lips. As if snapped from a dream, Pippa is the first to move. She rushes to the machine, snatching the paper.

"It's from him. Mr Guise." Pippa's eyes narrow as she reads. "But it's... it's not addressed to you, it's..." She looks up at Ember with utter disbelief. "It's addressed to *everyone*. The entire magical community."

Ember strides across the room. She takes the paper from Pippa's hands, her eyes darting across the words. Breathlessly, she begins to read the pronouncement aloud:

Notice to all druids and witches. In light of the shocking and audacious public display of witchcraft witnessed tonight, the Druid Council has called an emergency meeting to address this unprecedented situation. After careful deliberation, the Council has decreed that druids will not be part of this magical reveal. Our position on this matter is absolute and non-negotiable.

Furthermore, we must emphasise that any claim about druid immortality will be staunchly denied. In this new paradigm, witches will henceforth stand on their own. The druid community can no longer align itself with those who choose to expose magic to the world at large.

Effective immediately, druids will cease all cooperation with humanity. Instead, we will form a separate union, isolated from the complications that this reveal will undoubtedly bring. However, we extend an invitation to any witch who shares our vision. Those who recognise the wisdom in maintaining our secrets, and the dangers brought upon us by human folly, are welcome to join our ranks.

All druids, without exception, and those witches sympathetic to our separatist movement shall register their names via the RN frequency 3.234. Following registration, all individuals must report to their nearest druid authority within the next forty-eight hours. For those residing in or currently visiting the United Kingdom, your instructions are to make your way to Dunmorrough Castle in Argyll, Scotland. This location will serve as our central gathering point, where further instructions will be disseminated. The time for action is now. The survival of our way of life depends on swift and decisive leadership. Let there be no doubt: the path we have chosen is necessary for the preservation and the safety of our way of life.

Signed, Mardequai Guise, elected leader of the Druid Council.

Ember's fingers release the paper, which floats to the floor.

"That son of a bitch," she breathes as all the pieces of Mardequai's plan finally click into place.

Chapter Twenty-Seven

I stir awake, morning light breaking through a gap in the curtains. My eyes instinctively turn to the TV, worried about what I might have missed while I was asleep. But this morning, the coverage is slightly more light-hearted, showing footage of otters and dolphins playing in the Thames. The headline reads: "Ocean wildlife frolics in Central London: Thames sees biodiversity explosion amid witch reveal."

"Huh, I guess at least the river cleanse worked out," I mumble, stretching my limbs.

But then I become aware of the room's emptiness. Sitting up abruptly, I scan the space, but Kettering is gone. Even his suitcase has disappeared. A pang of worry hits me. Where did he go?

I peel myself out of his bed when a fresh headline scrolls across the bottom of the screen: "Could witches be telling the truth? Reports of healing nature flood social media." But it's the next headline that jolts me fully awake:

+++ Breaking News: Foster father denounces Ember Wild's actions, pledges to assist authorities +++ Belgravia mansion searched +++

A fresh bout of fear for Sofia surges through me, but it's quickly replaced by a sense of opportunity. This is my chance. Without Kettering constantly hovering over my shoulder, I'm free to go to Sofia, or at least try to find her. Grabbing the remote, I flip through the channels, searching for more information about this Belgravia mansion. But nothing more specific appears. I snatch my phone, fingers tap-tap-tapping as I search for "Mardequai Guise address" and many variations thereof.

Frustration mounts as each search draws a blank. Then, an idea blooms in my mind like a sudden spring: the invitation!

I rush back to my own hotel room, fumbling with the key card in my haste. Once inside, I dive for my bag, rummaging around its contents until I brush against the rough parchment of the ancient envelope. I pull it out, turning it over.

Bingo! There, in the top left corner, is Mardequai's Belgravia address. A sense of victory courses through me and I hastily grab my coat. Heart pounding, I rush down the stairs, leaving the hotel without even a thought about breakfast.

The revolving door spits me out onto the sidewalk, where the autumn air nips at my cheeks. I look both ways down the street, scanning for any sign of my normally constant druid shadow.

Nothing.

Just the usual London bustle as the day begins. I don't know if I should be unnerved or content about his disappearance. I raise my arm like they do in the movies, almost surprised when a black taxi appears almost immediately, coming to a stop for me. One last, furtive glance over my shoulder, then I climb in.

"Belgravia, please," I tell the driver, my hands gripping the door handle tighter than necessary at the thought of being off on my own again, and what I might find once I get there.

Mardequai's mansion is under siege. A swarm of paparazzi and onlookers crowd the pavement, cameras flashing constantly, voices rising in a cacophony of shouted inquiries and the latest gossip. The house, however, is barred by police; no one can get in or out. Defeated, I turn on my heel and begin to walk away, the noise of the crowd already fading slightly as I put distance between us. But then I hear a soft *Pssst*, barely audible above the commotion. I glance around until my eyes land on an unassuming doorway set back from the street. There, partially concealed by the hedges, stands Pippa. Her eyes dart between me and the policemen as she gestures urgently for me to come over.

"Quick, quick!" she whispers, ushering me towards an unassuming building three doors down from the besieged mansion. I follow her lead, slipping through the doorway.

"She's through there. But I warn you: it's not pretty..." Pippa announces, pointing me toward a door off the small hallway.

As I enter a dim living room, I find my sister lying sprawled on the sofa, her usually impeccable appearance now completely dishevelled. The air is clouded with cigarette smoke that stings my eyes and catches in my throat.

Empty bottles – wine, spirits, mixers – litter the place, scattered haphazardly across the coffee table and the floor. The scent of spilled alcohol mingles with the smoke, and the blare of the TV is uncomfortably loud. On screen, a live news report shows footage of the search happening at the mansion, where reporters and police swarm the garden.

"A bit early for cocktail hour, don't you think?" I say, and Sofia's face distorts with annoyance as soon as she spots me across the armrest. "What are you doing here? I told you to go home, goddammit. *Pippa!*" she yells out into the hall. "Call Alva a taxi, please?"

"Pippa, you will do no such thing," I instruct my sister's PA.

"You forget that she works for *me*." Sofia simply nods at

Pippa, who has shown up next to me and follows suit, already dialling the number.

"Yes, I'd like a taxi, please. Wilson Crescent number five, on the corner of..." Pippa's voice gets lost in the hall, just as the TV shifts to a press conference featuring the prime minister, his tone grave as he addresses the nation: "We cannot allow these bitches – I'm sorry, I mean these *witches* – to terrorise our society. Their very existence makes them a threat to the citizens of our great nation."

"He made you do this, didn't he?" I ask. "Mardequai. He forced you to reveal yourself and he used *me* as leverage."

Sofia reaches for an almost empty wine bottle, refilling her glass with the remains. "Well, it's done now, so no more need to fret your little head over it. The world stands divided, and I'm the one who parted the seas, so to speak..."

"What are you talking about? Surely, we can still turn this around."

Sofia takes a long drag from her cigarette, exhaling smoke towards the ceiling. "Have you not heard? The druids are out. They're gathering at Dunmorrough right now to establish a new union strongly opposed to Gathoni's stance." She rummages around on the floor, picking up what looks like a fax, which she hands to me.

"*What?*" I hastily scan the paper.

"Yup, turns out the old man had an evil master plan all along."

"So you finally agree with me that he's evil, do you?"

Sofia's eyes wander to the TV, then back to me. "The man coerced me into becoming Maleficent in the public eye to prevent my sister's murder, then fed me to the dogs, so yes: I'm well-acquainted with his lack of morals."

"I'm afraid it's about to get worse... I came here to tell you something."

Sofia raises the glass to her lips. "Whatever it is, it can't possibly be worse than..."

Wordlessly, I place the Celestial Stone on the messy coffee table.

Sofia stares at it, thunderstruck. Her glass slips, spilling wine onto the cluttered surface. "Where did you get this?" she manages at last. She reaches out for the stone, but I remove it before she can get her hands on it.

"I've had it for the last thirteen years, since the night of the accident. Mardequai must have given it to me. I suspect one of his witches meddled with my short-term memory, and that's why I don't remember it."

"That's a wild accusation," Sofia says, suddenly becoming very interested in smoothing out a wrinkle in the tablecloth. Her fingers work over the fabric. And while her words challenge me, her deliberate avoidance of eye contact tells a different story. It's not like she's denying the truth of what I've just said.

I hold out the stone, and that catches her attention. "He slipped me this stone. You know he did. Which means, he wanted us dead, all of us – including you. He would hurt you. He *has* hurt you."

Sofia dismisses this, pushing my hand away. "But *why*? Why would he do that? He's got no reason to kill us! If he did, I wouldn't be alive today. Why don't you get that? In fact, the only reason I'm not at Saltholm right now is because he is holding a protective hand over me. He might have fucked me over in the eyes of the public but he hasn't told them about *this* place. And as long as I do what he says, he will leave you alone, too."

I consider that. She has a point. The full picture still eludes me, and the burden of proof does rest on my shoulders. I've yet to uncover Mardequai's true motives.

My eyes drift back to the TV. But then a grim determination

settles over me. Proof or no proof, one thing is for certain: Mardequai is dangerous.

"But what if it's bigger than you and me?" I dare to suggest. "What if he is dangerous, Sofia? And not just to me, but to witches in general?"

"What are you talking about?" Sofia leans forward, ashing her cigarette.

I sigh, framing my next words with my hands. "Look, I ran into this girl at the RN operations centre beneath St. Paul's Cathedral. She said there's something terrible going on at Dunmorrough.... Something Mardequai must know about."

Sofia scoffs, reaching for her wine glass. "I spent all my teenage years homeschooled at Dunmorrough. If there was something fishy going on, I'd know about it, trust me."

"It might not have been there when you were around. You haven't been back at Dunmorrough in what? Three years? Or, or... maybe he was hiding it from you all along!"

Sofia lets out a frustrated sound, knocking over a few bottles. "You're in over your head! You've got no idea what you're getting yourself into!"

"And *you* do?" I gesture at the TV, now replaying her Piccadilly Circus act. "I'm sorry, but you're one to talk."

Sofia stands abruptly. "I want you to leave. I'm kicking you out of the coven. Go home, Alva. Go back to Germany. This is not your fight."

"Of course, this is my fight! This is *our* fight. There's no turning my back on this now, no matter where I go, and you know it!"

Sofia, in a surprising move, closes the distance between us and embraces me. "Of course, I know," she says, hugging me so close it almost hurts. "And I'm sorry, but if you get any more involved, it would all have been for nothing. I... I need you to be safe."

"I'm surrounded by people wanting me to be safe these days! How about you all stop worrying about me and start to *listen* to me instead?"

But then our argument is interrupted by the shrill of the doorbell.

"That would be the taxi driver," Pippa's voice drifts in from the hall.

"Come on," Sofia says, squeezing my arms. "You're getting out of here."

"I am not leaving. We're in this together, whether you like it or not," I insist, but she's already at the door. I follow her into the hallway, from where a gruff voice calls out, "Taxi for Watson?"

"Yes, here's your passenger," Sofia announces, pushing me forward.

"Stop this nonsense now, I'm not going anywhere!"

The driver glances up briefly, then does a startled double-take. His eyes widen with recognition as they fix on Sofia. "Hang on, you're the one they're after on the telly!" he exclaims, pointing a finger.

Sofia's demeanour shifts instantly, her features hardening. "Turn around," she commands. "Forget you ever saw me. Take this woman to Heathrow Airport. You will purchase her a ticket to the first available German destination and not leave her side until she's through security. Is that clear?"

"*Hey* – what do you think you're doing?" I protest, but my words seem to fall on deaf ears. The driver's eyes become distant, glazing over as he robotically repeats Sofia's instructions. Before I can react, he grabs my arm and pulls me towards the door.

Sofia steps between us once more, wrapping her arms around me in another fierce embrace, trembling slightly as she holds me tight. "I'm sorry but it has to be this way," she whispers through my hair.

"No, it doesn't. Let me help you," I plead, my hands grasping at her shoulders.

"It's too great a risk to have you here. Please, I just... I just need to know you're safe. You're the only family I have left. And please don't be mad at me."

Then the driver yanks me backward. My fists flail, connecting uselessly with his back, but Sofia's spell proves far more potent than my strength.

Finding myself in the taxi's back seat, I cease my struggle as the driver slides behind the wheel, starts the engine, and drives off. I try everything to break Sofia's spell with my own powers, but it's all in vain. Every bit of magic I try on the man fizzles out like a spilled drink.

As he pulls away from the house, a thought strikes me: if I can't break this spell, perhaps I can work with it instead.

I lean forward to address him. "Look, you don't understand: it was just a joke. She doesn't actually want you to drive me to Heathrow."

But the driver's eyes remain fixed on the road, his voice still robotic. "I must take you to Heathrow Airport, buy you a ticket to Germany, and not leave your side until you're through security..."

Well, if he's compelled to follow orders, maybe I just need to give him the right ones... "Alright, alright, listen – *listen* to me: I hear what you're saying, and we will do exactly that. But you forgot something important in the plan, didn't you?"

His brow furrows, and he looks at me through the rearview mirror. "What's that?"

"Why, we need to go somewhere else first, remember?"

"Where?"

I take a beat, looking outside the window where Belgravia's pristine white facades and black iron railings crawl by in their endless, orderly rows. A realisation settles over me then, and it's pointing in one clear direction. Whatever answers I'm seeking, whatever truth lies at the heart of this whole mess, I'm certain they're waiting for me in Dunmorrough.

The decision made, I turn back to the driver. "We need to go to Scotland first, so you best turn off the metre."

Part Three

Chapter Twenty-Eight

The first leg of the drive passes in silence – once my driver, Horace, is assured we'll get to Heathrow eventually, the thousand-mile detour to Scotland doesn't seem to concern him.

I turn my attention to my smartphone's newsfeed. Today's headlines grapple with the fallout from the "Great Reveal" – the day magic burst into public view. News breaks that Gathoni is currently being held against her will at a London high security prison. A delegation of witches, meanwhile, gathered as planned at the Climate Summit – now repurposed as an Emergency Summit – pleading with global political leaders to free Gathoni and reconsider their stance. On social media, countless viral videos show the newest witchy reveals all across the globe, while the stock market fluctuates wildly as investors try to predict which businesses will boom or bust in this new world. And back in London, a growing group of activists has gathered on the Millennium Bridge, dressed all in pink as a tribute to Ember Wild's witchy coming out.

Halfway through our journey, we stop for fuel (which I

financed) and a quick meal – a sausage roll for Horace and a quinoa bowl for me. Enlivened by the stop, Horace delivers his life story once we're back on the road. A jovial man in his seventies, Horace regales me with tales of his years working as a theatre lighting technician in London's West End. Now retired from theatre life, he drives a taxi to "keep in touch with the people," as he puts it. He speaks of difficult actors and the measly pay but oh, the fun he had whenever they were short of an extra during rehearsals and he got to stand on stage. His profound love for musicals got him into the business, and he is especially fond of *Les Misérables*, which (to my dismay) he decides to recite from start to finish for the remainder of our unlikely road trip.

Ten hours after leaving London, the taxi lurches to a halt on a lonely winding road near Mardequai's estate, just as dusk settles over the Scottish countryside.

The air here is deeply scented, with strong notes of peat and some subtle heather mixed in. Mist clings to the hills that surround us, softening their peaks in the last light, while a nearby stream gurgles its way through the wild landscape.

"Horace," I say, stepping out of the car, "I'm going to stretch my legs for a bit. Would you mind checking the oil before we head to Heathrow? We can't afford any breakdowns on the return trip, wouldn't you agree?"

Once I learnt the right approach, I find him surprisingly easy to direct.

"Most certainly, love," Horace replies and clambers out of the driver's seat. As soon as he disappears under the raised bonnet whilst 'singing a song of angry men', I make a beeline for the imposing wall that shields Dunmorrough from the outside world.

The estate sprawls before me, its true scale dwarfing my expectations. I strain my eyes, searching for any hint of the castle, but not even the faintest outline of a tower breaks the silhouette of treetops.

Armed with nothing but Effie Bell's ravings about a hole in the fence near a shed by the Oakwood, I begin my search. The stone wall becomes my only marker as I trudge over the sodden ground. An icy wind howls across the moor to my left, piercing through my coat and chilling me to the bone. It carries the pleasant scent of autumn, but that does little to ease the nasty gusts whipping my hair and numbing my toes.

At last, a small, dark structure materialises up ahead – could this be the shed Effie mentioned? My heartbeat quickens as I notice the wall giving way to a barbwire fence running alongside a thick line of trees. Scanning the area, I creep closer. Once certain that I'm alone, I turn on my smartphone light and begin to examine the fence. But the barbwire marches forward unbroken as I push deeper into increasingly steep terrain. My shoes, long since soaked by the boggy ground, grow heavier with each step. But just as despair begins to get the better of me, I spot it.

A maw yawns in the barbwire, the metal strands splayed outward like the crooked teeth of a forest monster, rust flaking from the jagged edges. The gap is barely wide enough for a person, but it's what I've come here for, I suppose.

Pocketing my phone, I approach the fence. I slip one leg through easily enough, but as I contort my body to follow, my hair snags on a barb. I wrench myself free with a hiss of pain, losing my balance in the process. I tilt in slow motion, landing in the bog with a squelch, icy water seeping through my clothes as my hands and knees sink into the muck.

Muttered curses escape me, and I heave myself up, now properly shivering from the cold. But I press onward, delving deeper into the Oakwoods.

The forest at night is filled with eerie sounds, but I have

always found solace in the branches creaking and groaning in the wind, and the constant, soft whisper of leaves stirred by the breeze. Indeed, the scent of pine reminds me of home – and 'home', to me, has always been the forest. When I was a child, it turned into the best possible playground. When I was homeless, it provided me with food and shelter. Whenever I had a fight with Dennis, it was my refuge, where I felt seen for who I truly was.

Just as I emerge from the embrace of the Oakwoods, the waning moon breaks free from the clouds, illuminating the scene I had anticipated all along. There, perched on the edge of a perfect Scottish loch, looms Dunmorrough Castle. Its walls, weathered by centuries of storms, stand in contrast to the warmly lit windows dotting its façade, blazing with an amber glow. Turrets and towers reach towards the night sky. Closer to where I stand, about half a mile away, a cluster of cottages nestle in a valley. Smoke curls from their chimneys, unfurling in the moonlight before dissipating into the dark sky. The windows of several cottages spill pools of warm light onto the rugged terrain.

Flashlight still off, I creep forward, trying not to stumble over roots and holes in the ground. The cottages, about twelve in total, are patched with moss and wildflowers. Thatched roofs, sagging with age, crown each of them like shaggy horse's manes.

The nearest cottage has a garden full of the familiar scent of herbs, making me feel treacherously safe. I creep closer to peek through a window when I'm stopped short by a sudden pressure against my back, something sharp piercing through my coat.

"Who are you?" A female voice slices through the night, right behind me.

"D-Denise Marquardt," I stammer, inwardly cringing at the first fake name my mind has conjured.

"And why didn't you respond via resonance?"

The question catches me completely off guard. I blink

uselessly into the night, my mind racing as I try to come up with a plausible lie. "I-I didn't know I was supposed to," I squeeze out.

A firm hand grips my shoulder, spinning me around.

The woman before me appears to be in her late forties, with blue eyes that are sharp, yet tired. Her ginger hair is scraped back with more urgency than care. But what truly captures my attention are the marks on her temples – they're the same ones I noticed on Effie Bell. But hers seem... *fresher*, angry red against her freckled skin.

Her eyes rake over me, lingering on my own temples. "You're new," she says. A comment I can only assume refers to my lack of fresh marks.

"Y-yes, that's right," I say, latching onto the convenient cover story.

The woman's posture relaxes slightly as she folds a pocketknife, slipping it into her jeans. "Did Kate send you down here?" she asks, now softer.

"Yes, she did," I lie.

"Well, alright then. Welcome to the Crossbill Coven. My name is Ellen Jenkins. Let's get you set up."

"Thank you, that is... that is very kind," I manage.

"Which operation centre did you transfer from?" Ellen inquires. There's a tiredness in her voice, an undercurrent of sadness that creeps into her every word.

"St. Paul's Cathedral," I reply, the lies coming easier now.

"Big city girl, huh? Fancy. Is that why you didn't respond to my telepathy? I hear the city's hustle and bustle can make it quite hard to hear each other's thoughts."

"Exactly, I... I'm not used to the silence anymore," I reply, my mind barely in control of my words. Telepathy, really? Before Minnie Allen, I've never in my life met a telepathic witch. And while that might be easily explained away by my thirteen-year absence from the magical world, I know for certain that telepaths have become increasingly scarce. They're like the snow leopards of the witch world – and those who remain have abilities that are a far cry from what telepaths used to be capable of, usually reduced to glimpses into another person's mind, hunches or fleeting feelings. But here walks Ellen Jenkins, telling me telepathic communication is her norm.

"I was just on my way over to the operations centre. Are you feeling up for it? We sure could use the help, with the castle full to the brim tonight."

"Um, sure."

"Where's your stuff?"

"It's still with Kate."

"Right. Well, she's probably going to search it," Ellen replies. "With everything that's been going on lately, don't take it personally."

"So, where are your connection marks?" she asks, and I can feel her gaze back on my temples.

"We, um, we don't use the old connections anymore, down in London. They've come up with a new technology. Wireless or... or Bluetooth or something."

"Bloody hell. *Wireless*, you say? Of course, we're the last ones to see any of that new stuff up here."

We approach what looks like a giant ant hill, overgrown with grass, a massive iron double door barring the way.

"This used to be a protective bunker during the Second World War. The operation centre relocated here from the river in the fifties. Less daylight, but at least it's dry."

"How long have you been here?"

Ellen frowns at my question. "Why, all my life, of course."

She's about to press down the door handle when she turns to me once more. "Listen, you best get used to the silence. I don't know what it was like back in London, but here we're not allowed to talk out loud whatsoever during RN transmission."

"Of course," I say, my heart pounding in my chest as a clearer picture begins to form in my mind.

I'm about to enter another Resonance Network operation centre – the one Effie Bell escaped from – and something tells me I won't like what I will find down there.

For a split second, I panic and consider bolting, worried that, once I'm in, there'll be no easy way out. But when Ellen shoots around, her face searching mine, I mentally slap myself. "What are you rambling on about wanting to run for the hills?"

"Oh, I... never mind. I just... I need to wee."

"Well, no need to head for the bushes, lass. We might be more primitive up here in the north, but we do have washrooms."

And with that, Ellen leads the way into the bunker, while I desperately try not to think, repeating the same sentence over and over in my head. *My name is Denise Marquardt. My name is Denise Marquardt. My name is Denise Marquardt.*

Ellen guides me down a long flight of stairs, then through a dimly lit corridor. As we progress, a distant humming grows steadily louder, like we are in a massive beehive. The sound seems to emanate from the walls, vibrating through the air, settling into my marrow.

With a firm push, Ellen opens another door, and we're immediately assaulted by harsh, artificial light. The humming intensifies, now interwoven with a staccato of clicking sounds, *clickety-click-clickety-click-clickety-click-clickety-click*, like rain pattering on a tin roof.

My name is Denise Marquardt. My name is Denise Marquardt. My name is Denise Marquardt, I repeat over and over in my head. But as soon as Ellen steps aside, showing me the truth of the room, I suddenly find it incredibly hard to focus on my fake name. The sight before me is so utterly unexpected, so profoundly unsettling, that my thoughts slip away like sand through an hourglass.

About two dozen women are perched on simple wooden stools, lined up in front of an enormous switchboard that looks like a relic from the early days of telecommunications, its surface a maze of sockets, plugs, and blinking lights. But it's not the archaic equipment that steals my breath – it's the women themselves.

Every witch in the room is physically connected to the switchboard by two wires. At first glance, I mistake the apparatus for some kind of antiquated headphones. But as my eyes adjust to the harsh light, I realise with growing terror that the wires aren't connected to their ears at all. Instead, they plug directly into the skin along their hairlines, precisely where I had noticed the scars on Ellen and Effie Bell.

Their eyes are closed, faces set in intense concentration. A continuous, eerie hum emanates from their slightly parted lips. Some sway gently on their stools, while others remain perfectly still save for their hands, which move with automatic skill. They ceaselessly connect and reconnect the free ends of their wires to various points on the switchboard, each new connection sending a fresh ripple of clicks through the air.

The realisation is sickening. This, then, is the true nature of resonant communication. Not some mystical, ethereal connection between ley lines and rivers, but a crude exploitation of these women's rare gifts, their temple scars the physical toll of being used as living conduits for others' messages.

My legs nearly give out beneath me as the full load of understanding crashes over me. Every message ever sent through the RN has been carried by women like these. Women with wires piercing their skin, trapped in this underground hell. I think of myself as a child, reaching out through the network to contact my mother when I needed a pickup after a playdate. I think of just yesterday, when I used the RN to communicate with Gathoni, never questioning how my words travelled. The ease of it, the convenience, all built on the backs of these exploited women.

Nausea hits me when I realise: I am complicit. We all are.

My shock and revulsion leave me momentarily stunned, and it must show on my face because Ellen suddenly grips my arm with bruising force, her mind likely probing mine this entire time. Snapping back to reality, I hastily cobble together a thought, praying it's enough to satisfy her telepathic inquiry.

Sorry, it's... very different from London... Much older, I project, focusing on the antiquated equipment. Ellen's frown deepens, clearly displeased by what she perceives as criticism, but it seems to suffice. She turns, moving deeper into the room.

Much older, much older, much older, I repeat, my fingers combing through my hair to obscure my unmarked temples. *My name is Denise Marquardt. My name is Denise Marquardt. My name is Denise Marquardt. I'm from London. St. Paul's Cathedral.* A new strategy forms, and I latch onto it desperately. *I'm shy. I don't talk much. Yes, that's good. I'm shy. I don't talk much. I'm shy. I don't talk much. I'm shy. I don't talk much.*

We stop at an empty stool halfway down the line. Ellen gestures for me to sit, then departs without a word, claiming another vacant spot further down. I survey the switchboard, horrified by the frenzied dance of hands, the relentless *click-click-clickety-click, click-click-clickety-click* forming a maddening rhythm.

The girl beside me, barely out of her teens, catches my eye during a brief lull between transmissions. Her gaze is curious, tinged with sympathy – perhaps remembering her own first day at this bizarre post. I force a weak smile, desperately hoping my mental walls are strong enough to withstand whatever telepathic inspection she might attempt.

I'm shy. I don't talk much. I'm shy. I don't talk much, I think, meeting her eyes with as innocent a look I can muster.

The girl beside me nods towards the wire dangling from a hook in front of my station, then resumes her eerie humming as she reconnects to the switchboard with a flurry of *click-click-clickety-clicks*. My hands tremble as I reach for the wire, guilt twisting my insides. The Resonance Network is used by magical communities *all across the world*. How many more facilities like this exist?

I set the wire down, my movements sluggish as I turn to meet the girl's gaze once more.

I'm sorry, I think, now on the verge of tears. *I'm so sorry*.

Confusion furrows her brow; clearly, she's trying to communicate telepathically. When I fail to respond, a flicker of realisation crosses her face. She disconnects her wires, and twin rivulets of blood trickle down her temples like war paint.

She parts her lips and speaks aloud. "Who are you?" The words emerge as a hoarse whisper, her vocal cords probably atrophied from disuse.

A simple question, a single sentence, but it has the power of bringing the entire operation to its knees. In an instant, the background hum fades to nothing, the incessant clicking silenced as every witch in the room swivels to face me.

I leap to my feet, fumbling with the wire in my haste to hang it up. It slips from my grasp, clattering to the floor with a sound that echoes like a gunshot in the sudden quiet. *My name is Denise Marquardt. My name is Denise Marquardt. My name is Denise Marquardt*, I chant silently, desperately, as I start to edge past the line of women. Their eyes track my movement; stools swivel around as I pass behind them.

Washroom. Washroom. Just going to the washroom, I project, hoping against hope that they might be fooled by this feeble excuse. But as the silence stretches and the tension mounts, I realise with sinking certainty that my cover is blown. Fight or flight instincts surge through me, and I choose flight, my pace quickening as I near the door, two dozen pairs of eyes boring into my back.

"Hey, where do you think you're going?" Ellen calls just as my hand touches the door handle. I whirl around one last time, the grotesque reality of the Resonance Network staring back at me. Twenty-four pairs of eyes directed at me; twenty-four faces I will never be able to erase from my mind ever again.

With a burst of desperate energy, I wrench the door open and slam it shut behind me. The moment it closes, an alarm shrieks to life, emanating from a speaker directly above my head. A harsh red light begins to strobe, bathing the corridor in an ominous crimson glow. My mind races – did Ellen trigger this, or is it an automated response to the sudden silence in the RN? The questions swirl uselessly as adrenalin takes over.

I bolt down the corridor, my footsteps echoing off the walls as I race towards the stairs. Up I go, taking them two at a time, my lungs burning as I climb higher and higher, back to the top, back to the top... *to-the-top-to-the-top-to-the-top...clickety-click-clickety-click...*

Finally, I burst through the iron doors, which shut behind me with a resounding clang. I pause for a moment, gulping down the crisp night air. But my reprieve is short-lived – from beyond a nearby hill, I hear voices and the squelch of hurried footsteps through the bog.

Panic propels me forward once more. I skirt the bunker, moving away from the approaching voices. I make a beeline for one of the darkened cottages, about to sneak around the back, when a pair of strong arms suddenly encircles me from behind, locking me in an iron grip.

Chapter Twenty-Nine

I recognise his scent before I see him.

"*Kettering*, what the—"

But with one large hand he cups my mouth, while the other somehow manages to lock both of my wrists in a vice grip behind my back. "Shhhh," he urges, the sound muffled through my hair as he pulls me back, releasing one hand to open the cottage door. We slip inside and he closes it with a careful thud. Pressing one finger against his lips, he cautions me to stay silent, and I do. Although I'm certain anyone could hear the beat of my heart thumping like a war drum in my chest.

Outside, a group of people with flashlights has arrived, and to my relief, they're heading straight down into the bunker. Kettering and I watch through the nearest window until the light beams dissipate, and the village plunges back into silence.

"I see your promises don't count for anything, Mata Hari." Kettering turns to face me, loosening the scarf around his neck as if my mere presence makes the air harder to breathe. "I told you not to come here, no matter what."

"I did cross my fingers at the time, if it's any consolation," I reply, moving toward the small kitchen, which sports a similar set-up as my apothecary back at the cabin: potbelly stove, an assortment of chairs around a weathered table, a collection of jars filled with herbs and spices. Suddenly exhausted, I pull out a chair and take a seat at the table.

"So, what? You work for him, then?" I ask, folding my arms.

He has come to lean against the kitchen counter, holding his head up with his fist, a brooding gesture that reminds me of a statue in a museum. "No. No, I don't."

"And you expect me to believe that?"

"Do you really think you'd be alive today if I was working for him?"

I study his face, searching for clues, when another possibility dawns. "Oh my God, *he's* your father, isn't he? Mardequai?"

Kettering smacks his lips. "Wrong again. I work for my father, but Mardequai is not him."

Another cryptic – and annoying – response. "Alright then, glad we straightened that out." I'm about to stand up when he decides to give me something, at last.

"I received the druid council decree late last night. I figured it'd be a good idea to come here, see what they're planning."

"You received it via the Resonance Network?" I ask, my newfound knowledge from the bunker fuelling my anguish, which is desperately seeking an outlet.

"Correct," the druid responds.

"Do you... do you *know* how it works?"

"The network?" He shifts uneasily.

"Yes, the network. Because I was just down there in that bunker and let me tell you: it is *fucked up!*"

"Shhh," he cautions me.

"It is fucked up, Kettering," I revert to a whisper. "The whole system relies upon exploiting telepathic witches. They must be under a Whisperlock or something, that's why they cannot leave

or tell anyone or... I don't know." I lean closer, trying to decipher that stone cold face.

"That is a separate issue," he says, avoiding my gaze.

"But you *do* know?"

Kettering pinches the bridge of his nose. "Yes," he confesses. "Yes, alright? I know."

"Of course, you know." My fists land angrily on the tabletop. "You're one of them, so you *would* know."

"Listen, Alva—"

But his explanation is cut short by the sound of voices in the distance. With a warning gesture, he approaches the window, parting the curtains to reveal the dancing beams of flashlights in the blackness. "They're leaving," he whispers.

Back at the counter, his fingers stroke the smooth wood, his eyes following the movement. "I'm going to tell you everything," he says as if confirming an inner choice. "I probably should have done so from the beginning."

I straighten my back, my hands fidgeting with a pestle and mortar on the table as I brace myself for whatever he's about to share with me.

"The truth is," Kettering begins with a deep sigh, "you were right from the start: I do know you. I have known you for a long time. I dare say, I might know you better than anyone these days."

I'm overcome by confusion but also a strange sense of warmth at those words. Since the accident, it hasn't felt like anybody knew me – the real me – at all.

"You already know that your grandmother and I share a dark history." Kettering stands perfectly still, his mouth the only body part that moves. "She... she ruined my life. She took the one thing from me that I loved more than anything in this world. My wife and my..." He chokes. "My little baby girl." Tears build in his eyes, but he doesn't break contact with mine, and I hold his gaze. The guilt it conjures is a vile thing, hitting my chest like shrapnel from a shotgun. Even though I am not Ruth, I am still undeniably her granddaughter. Past life memories or not, her blood runs through my veins. I am because she once was.

"What you don't know is, from that dreadful day on, I made it my life's purpose to avenge my family. I joined the French Resistance. I came close to ending her several times throughout the war. But after the Nazis lost, she managed to disappear. For years, she was nowhere to be found."

Kettering inhales as if gasping for air after a deep dive. "But I tracked her down. I found her. And I brought her to justice."

Images flood my mind, of the day Ruth burned at the stake, that old familiar phantom heat snaking up my legs until I need to shuffle my feet to shake it off. Was he there, on that day? Did he watch her burn?

"But you see, it wasn't enough," Kettering grinds out the words through clenched teeth. "Because she had a daughter, too."

My eyes shoot up at him, a horrible sense of foreboding heating my stomach.

"I wanted to kill your mother," he says, his eyes now focused somewhere on the shelf behind me. "Ruth Hausmann took my daughter from me. So, I came after hers."

I swallow hard, knowing – obviously – that he didn't follow through. But when he goes on to tell me the reason, I full-on choke, forgetting to breathe as he speaks into the quiet.

"But then I met her – and I saw how *good* she was. Your mother was a good person, and to this day I have never regretted *not* killing her. The good she brought to those who knew her, the light she shone onto this world, I would not have wanted to extinguish that."

I nod, brushing away the tears.

"She had none of your grandmother's darkness in her," Kettering concludes.

"But I do?" I don't know how I muster the courage to ask, but now that I think of it, I realise that is *my* question. The one question that defines my life and everything I've done. And I don't know why, but in this moment, his answer matters more to me than anything else in the entire world.

Kettering turns away from me, gazing out the window into the night. "Since the day your parents reported your unusual... *skill,* I have fought with the urge to kill you," he says to the glass, and then, as if on reflex, he swings back around, pain etching his features. "You even *look* like her, did you know that?"

I nod, feeling like the smallest person who ever lived. It's true, I share some of the typical Hausmann features, the thin ridge of the nose, the auburn hair, the strong jaw. But so did my mother, as does my sister. It doesn't strike me entirely fair to hold that against me, but I don't bring it to his attention.

"So, you have been... *around* since my childhood?" I flick through my memories to locate his face but draw only blanks. I still don't understand how all the pieces fit together.

"What do you know of the crash, Kettering? I know you must know *something*."

The room falls silent for a moment, save for our breathing and the howling wind outside.

The druid clears his throat, nodding. "As you grew older, your parents became increasingly worried that people might start to think of you as a threat, that someone might come and take you – or worse. The focus was on you, not your sister, because your visions were so much stronger. It was believed that your twin's faint ability was but a reflection of your own, that she was the moon to your sun. There was an incident when you were five – when you were almost kidnapped."

As those words reach me, fragments of memory flash

through my mind. A playground. A large hand reaching for me. A car door slamming shut. The muffled sound of raised voices. A burst of blinding light. My heart racing, pounding in my ears. The feeling of being lifted, carried to safety. Dad's voice, telling me I was safe now...

"After that, your mother turned to her coven for help, and they requested surveillance from... well, let's call it the 'agency' I work for. I kind of had been around anyway, so I volunteered for the job." He shrugs, sucking some air through his teeth.

"Years later, I was in the car behind you when the crash happened," he tells me, and the truth of that causes the strangest sensation in my stomach. All this time. All this time, he knew.

"Ingrid Brauer, the Elster Coven magistrate, was sitting next to me," he says. "She made the call: she erased your short-term memory, and we took you away."

I grind a few peppercorns with the pestle, my mind returning to that night, the gaps in my memory, the confused jumble of sensations and half-formed images – the *guilt*. Suddenly it all starts to coalesce.

"At that point, we were convinced someone was after you. *She* assumed it was a group of druids because of the whole 'immortal daughter threat' to their own supremacy; *I* thought it must have been someone like me, someone holding a grudge against your grandmother. Brauer decided to hide you, to make you disappear. Your magic seemed to strengthen your visions – that's why she lied to you, telling you that you could never wield Anima again. But it was also essential to the entire scheme. You see – if you're not a member of magical society anymore, you practically cease to exist."

"But if Brauer suspected Mardequai behind the crash, why did she agree to give him Sofia?"

"You don't understand – no one ever suspected *Mardequai*. He was a moral citizen, known for all the good he did in the world. Brauer and I simply swore never to tell *anyone* that you'd survived – least of all Mardequai. Not because we suspected him, but because he was going to raise Sofia. You see, your sister had to believe you were dead, so that she wouldn't come looking for you." Kettering rounds the table, taking a seat in the chair next to me. "It's true, the coven magistrate lied to you. But she did it to save your life."

I let go of the pestle, my hands lost on the tabletop as I desperately try to understand. "And after the accident? What did you do?"

"I decided to remove myself. I needed some distance. Someone else took my place, reported back to me regularly. When you turned eighteen and you were free to leave the foster home, a game of cat and mouse ensued. We tried to stay on your heels, but one day, you just disappeared."

I recall those first terrifying days as a young woman on the streets, learning to spot the signs of danger like a newborn wolf. The constant vigilance, the way I'd scan crowds for anyone who seemed dangerous or too interested. I remember ducking into alleys, changing my clothes, using every possible trick to shake off the feeling of being watched. Had Kettering's replacement been one of those shadows I was running from?

"And that's it, the end. I didn't see you again until the Assembly," Kettering finishes.

"What have you done for the past eight years, then?"

"Other assignments, far removed from Germany – from you." Now his eyes roam over my face with a hunger that makes me want to shrink back and move closer at the same time. His eyes, usually guarded, now burn with a fire that makes my breath catch. His jaw tightens, and I can see the tension in the set of his shoulders.

"Until Gathoni asked you to return to my case?"

"Gathoni and I have crossed paths, and she does consult me

– recently a lot more, thanks to your claim to fame. But she... she didn't send me to shadow you, if that's what you're asking." He forces a guilty sort of half smile. "I kind of sent myself."

"Why?"

"I think because I needed some form of closure. I needed *peace*. And the only way to get it was to find proof of who you really are."

I swallow, my eyes landing on his lips. "How's that going for you?" I ask.

"I don't believe you are her. Not anymore. Any evil that ever came from you was caused by that stone, I know that now." And then, out of nowhere, it's like he gives in to an urge, a natural thing, as he cups my jaw with both his hands, his eyes bearing nothing but sureness, his skin warm, almost feverish at the touch. "You are *good*, Alva, just like your mother was."

Before I can process his words, he leans in and captures my lips with his own. The kiss is passionate, urgent – endless pent-up feelings pouring out in a single moment. I'm caught off guard, but my body responds before my mind catches up.

"No," I gasp, breaking away from him, wiping my mouth. "Not here. Not now." My heart races, and thoughts tumble over each other as I try to steady myself. I move hastily to the other side of the table, switching to where he stood at the counter a moment ago. The physical distance helps me regain some composure, but I can still feel the ghost of his touch on my skin, the taste of his lips on mine.

Gazing out the window, I remind myself *where* we are, and what I've only just found out. "You said you knew about the RN. Tell me about that."

Kettering wipes his face, straightens the scarf around his neck before he clears his throat. "Yes. That was the assignment my father gave me after I handed your case over to another," he replies. "We've long been suspecting dubious machinations behind the network. I've been gathering intel to uncover it for years."

"So how can you still use it, knowing how it works?"

"Because it's how *they* communicate. I don't like it – I'm appalled by the entire thing – but it is my job to surveil it."

"But why haven't you exposed it yet? What are you waiting for?"

"It's not my call to make."

"Whose is it, then?"

"That would be my old man's. One of the reasons we're currently not on speaking terms."

"What *is* he waiting for, Cornelis?"

"I'm not sure," he replies, smacking his lips. "But my father says this is a lot bigger than just the RN. In fact, he keeps arguing the network is but one rotten apple in a giant barrel. He's been on Elias Klein's case ever since that first dreadful machine was built."

"Is that why you came to visit the Blackfriars water chamber in the nineteenth century?"

"Precisely."

And then another piece finds its spot in the puzzle.

"So, the test site Klein built in the Scottish Highlands...?"

"This one right here," Kettering confirms.

"We've got to help these women," I say, and there's a begging quality to my words. "We *cannot* leave them like this."

"I wish it were that easy. But if we do anything now, we will only sound the alarms. That castle is packed with magical folk tonight." He gestures out the window. "As much as I hate to admit it – and trust me, I do – my father is right. We need to keep a cool head, no matter how hard it seems."

"I cannot accept that. I must help them. There's a hole in the fence, that's how Effie Bell got out and—"

"And look how that ended for her!" Kettering reminds me,

then closes the distance between us, holding me by the shoulders. "We *will* help them. We will end this. But it cannot be tonight."

I'm about to protest, when a bell tolls in the distance, the sound drifting through the cracks in the old window frames.

"They're about to start," Kettering murmurs. "Alright, listen. You need to leave now. Climb back through that gap in the fence and bring yourself to safety."

"Why? What's about to start?"

"I don't know, but I'm going to find out." He slides open the cottage door, and I shiver at a sudden gust of cold air.

"I'm coming with you."

"Not a chance. The entire magical community knows what you look like, and it's safe to say at this point, Mardequai wants you dead."

"I'm not scared," I say with eagle courage.

"Well, I am – for you. For your safety."

I take a step towards him, my arm lifting slightly as if to reach for his hand, but I stop myself. "I do not need your permission to go, Cornelis. Look, I'm grateful for everything you told me tonight. But it's still not the whole story. You know it isn't. Mardequai slipped me that stone, of that I'm certain. And you're right: he wants me dead. But I still do not know *why*."

I slowly reach out and take his hand after all. "I need to know why my parents died," I say. "And something tells me, the truth is hidden in that castle. This... this is something *I* must do, to find my peace."

Cornelis stands motionless, his eyes trained on our hands. The silence stretches between us while he thinks, stroking the top of my hand as if he might uncover an answer there.

"Fine. Here, take this," he says at last, taking off his scarf, which he wraps around my neck, covering half of my face. "And... and these, too." He reaches inside his inner coat pocket, revealing an elegant specs case, from which he removes a pair of wire-framed glasses.

"I didn't know you needed glasses," I note, taking them.

"They're for reading, alright?" A hint of a blush colours his cheeks. "Now, let's go, before I change my mind and lock you up in this cottage."

Chapter Thirty

The driveway leading up to Dunmorrough Castle is overcrowded with vehicles. Feet crunching over the gravel, Kettering and I merge with the people, and I'm shocked to see how many witches Mardequai's invitation has drawn. Eight in ten lining up to enter the castle are women. At first, I hope that some of them might simply be curious – or even snooping just like us. But as we get closer to the entrance, I realise that the wheat is about to be sorted from the chaff: three witches, supervised by a young druid who looks barely older than twenty, bar the way while he announces to the waiting crowd, "Everyone who wishes to enter volunteers to undergo a Whisperlock spell. Nothing beyond this point – not whom you meet, nor what you hear – shall be shared with anyone not part of the DA."

"The DA? What's that?" I whisper to Kettering.

"The Druid Alliance. That's what they call themselves now," he replies, then takes my arm, guiding me away from the crowd. "Come on, I've got no desire to let them mess around with my brain. We need to find another way in."

We break away from the line, seeking shelter in the shadow of the building. We sneak along the walls, searching for a door, a window. Rounding a corner, I spot a pair of witches patrolling the gardens. I quickly pull Kettering behind a giant rhododendron.

"This might not be so easy," he says, keeping an eye on the witches while my gaze drifts up the wall.

"You think we can reach that?" I ask, nodding toward the nearest window.

"If I give you a boost, maybe, and you'd need to break the window, then pull me up somehow. But we'd be foolish to think this entire building wouldn't be covered in protective wards." His eyes land on me. "You think you could, you know," – he clicks his tongue twice – "work your magic?"

"What, like, break the ward?"

"Yeah." Kettering shrugs. "I think you could pull it off. However, it would most definitely set off some sort of alarm, so we'd need to be quick."

"No pressure, then." I exhale, my lips buzzing with the rush of air. "Okay, talk me through it."

"What do you mean?"

"The spell. How does it – you know – *go?*"

"Alright, I'll help you up there, and once you're close to the window, you need to gather some solid Anima – not from the wind, that'd be too fickle." He looks around. "Borrow some from that birch over there, that'll do nicely. And then you direct it toward the window, feeling for a weak spot, kind of like the hole you found in the fence, and then, very gently, as if probing a stick through it, you widen the gap. And remember, a little humming goes a long way to help you keep the focus. Oh, and take this, too." He grabs a large rock and hands it to me.

"What's that for?" I ask.

"To smash the window, Einstein." He scans the area again. "Alright, coast is clear. You ready?"

I draw a deep breath, feeling my chest rise with courage. "Alright, let's do it."

But just as Kettering shifts to move toward the building, I grab his coat. "Hang on a second."

"What now?"

"Don't you think I should use the Celestial Stone? You know, for some extra oomph?"

I'm already reaching for my pocket, but he stops me.

"Are you mad?" he hisses, grabbing my wrist. "That's like using a sledgehammer to crack a walnut. You'd blow a hole through half the building and alert every witch from here to Edinburgh that we're here." He shakes his head, exasperated. "Besides, you have no training whatsoever in the use of those stones. It's a miracle you haven't killed anyone yet."

I'm tempted to point out that I did, in fact, kill *him*, but now doesn't seem like the time to split hairs.

"Right, okay. Point taken," I mutter, pulling my hand away from my pocket.

Keeping low, we approach the wall. Kettering gives me a rather awkward leg-up, but I manage to pull myself up onto the windowsill. Sitting on its edge, my chest explodes from the rush and the fear of getting caught, so I sweep the perimeter once more, relieved to see nobody. Then I close my eyes and with a focus on the birch, I dare to begin my humming.

With surprising ease, I can feel my magic reaching out like fingers, stretching, straining until I reach a branch. Connecting to it like a suction cup, then gently sucking Anima from its core, I guide it back to the window, just like Kettering instructed. Like smoke, it billows against the window, which I can feel is covered by a ward, a second skin. Like feet feeling where the ice underfoot is weak, my Anima grazes that skin until I find a spot I might be able to pierce through. Reshaping the Anima, I mould it into a stick and then I start to scrape, gently at first, then, once I'm in, widening the gap more quickly.

"I'm in," I whisper to Kettering and let go of the energy I borrowed, which snaps back into the birch. Taking a swing, I crash through the glass with the rock in my hand – and then the dreaded alarm sounds.

"Okay, here we go," Kettering urges me from below. "Climb in, then pull me up," he instructs, and I do as told, awkwardly reaching through the broken window to find the handle, which opens with a screech. I climb inside, steadying my lower body against the wall while I reach out my arms to the druid.

"Hang on, one second," hisses Kettering.

"What?"

He looks around on the ground, then picks up another rock, which he hurls at the third window to our left. "Decoy," he whispers, then jumps, reaching for my hands to pull himself up.

"Goodness, you're heavy," I groan while he basically does all the work.

Inside the room, we fall to the floor, catching our breaths.

"Alright, now I need you to repair that window," Kettering says, allowing no break.

"How do I do that?"

He nods, his eyes darting to the broken window. "Right, this one's a little more complicated, but you can do it. Focus on the shards lying around. Gather some more Anima, but this time from the air is fine – glass is basically just melted sand, so it's not as fickle as a ward."

He listens for any approaching footsteps before he continues.

"Imagine the glass as something malleable – water, liquid soap maybe. Use your magic to heat it slightly, just enough until it softens. Then guide the pieces back together. The Anima will act as your binding agent. Once everything's in place, cool it rapidly by drawing heat into your Anima. That will set the glass." Kettering glances nervously at the door. "And remember, hum if it helps you focus. But quietly."

I nod. Closing my eyes to concentrate, I reach out once more, finding the glass shards. Anima comes easier this time and feels lighter as it swirls around the pieces. I move them toward the window frame, picture the glass softening, becoming pliable. Humming a little, I guide the shards back into place, weaving them together.

"Good," Kettering whispers. "Now cool it."

I picture pulling the heat from the glass into my Anima, and to my delight, the window seems to shimmer for a moment, then solidifies. The whole thing was surprisingly easy, and I'm a little proud of myself for not screwing it up for once. Relief washes over me, but as soon as it does, Ruth rises within me like bile in my throat, hissing suggestions — *why stop at freezing? Why not shatter it entirely?* — and I have to swallow hard, pushing her influence back down where it belongs.

"Not bad," Kettering says, inspecting my work. "It'll hold up for a casual inspection. Now let's move."

We're about to leave the room when something stops me cold. "Hang on," I say, gazing around the room. The walls are plastered with music posters – The Doors, Nirvana, Janis Joplin. A Fender electric guitar is propped in one corner, a giant mirror draped with pink tulle in another.

"This... this must have been my sister's room," I whisper, the recognition making me choke. This is where she spent all those years I thought her dead.

"That's very touching, Alva, but we do need to run now," Kettering insists, and I follow him reluctantly out the door.

In the dark hallway, we sneak from alcove to alcove, edging closer towards the entrance hall. Outside, people shout angrily.

Clearly, the other broken window has been discovered. But before anyone comes to look for us, we're back with the crowd, melting into a cluster of people at the back of the room who crane their necks to see what's happening at the front, eyes still a little glassy as they recover from the effects of the Whisperlock.

Silence falls from one end of the room to the other when three people ascend a sweeping stairwell at the front. I know all of them by now, my mouth twitching with rage as I spot Mardequai in the middle, accompanied by Orna Morrigan to his right and Ambrose Hudspeth to his left. All three wear the same charcoal robes, Mardequai's parting like a theatre curtain as he spreads his arms, a shepherd welcoming his flock.

"Ah, good people," he sighs, his voice magically enhanced to reach us here at the far end.

"Good, good people. As much as I'm troubled by the circumstances that brought us together on this fateful evening, it does fill my heart with joy to see so many of you have made the journey." He lowers his hands, folding them in front of his body. "As you all know, we have entered a new era. An era many of us – dare I say *all* of us present here tonight – did not wish to enter. But here we are, and here we stand, united in our wish to remain in the shadow of the giant wave about to roll across our world. United in our desire to keep our families safe and our secrets protected."

Thundering applause echoes from the walls, a strange contrast to the humming I've gotten used to during magical gatherings.

"But more than anything," Mardequai says. "More than anything, I would like to applaud the courage and the enormous sacrifice of the witches among us here tonight, whose secession from their mother tree – their sisterhood – was an act of bravery, as much as it was one of necessity."

A low murmur, composed only of druid voices, ripples through the crowd, punctuated by a few "Hear, hears."

"I know our magical sisters must be frightened at this hour," Mardequai says, adopting a gentle tone that makes me want to strangle him. "And I am afraid that fear is justified. It pains me to say that we stand at the precipice of yet another dangerous period in the lives of witches. And it is not fair, I say – it is not *just* – that our magical, beautiful women must suffer so. But let this night be a reminder of one simple and salient truth: you will *not* stand alone in this. We have navigated these waters before, druids and witches, side by side. The Druid was there when the Witch needed him. And when she needed to hide beneath his cloak," – as if to demonstrate his words, he spreads his billowing robe once again – "he opened his arms wide and he gave her shelter, he gave her protection from those fearful of her powers and threatened by her magic."

I hear a snuffling close by and cast a glance at the witch standing next to me, her eyes filled with tears as she embraces a girl I assume must be her daughter.

"And I do not say this to scare you but say it I must: the shadows are lengthening around us. The age of stakes and nooses has passed, but humanity's weapons have only grown more lethal. Where once we feared the sword, the torch, the rope, we now must cower before forces that can unmake the very fabric of this earth. Your hunters have evolved, and you must adapt or perish in this new age of horrors undreamt by those who came before you."

"He says he doesn't want to scare anybody, but that's *exactly* what he's doing," I hiss into Kettering's ear, and he nods gravely.

"But enough of the doom and gloom for tonight." Mardequai switches gears, a put-upon smile spreading across his face as he takes further steps towards the gathered. "Tonight, let us not fear what tomorrow may bring, but let us instead appreciate this union. Let us mingle and share a meal under this roof tonight, and let us strengthen the bonds that..."

Suddenly, Kettering tugs at my sleeve, drawing my attention to a commotion behind our backs. I glance over his shoulder toward the entrance, where two witches escort a third, her hands tied behind her back, her head hanging low between her shoulders. Face covered by locks of blonde hair, she almost stumbles, then looks up, and I suppress a gasp when I recognise her – it's Zara, the coven witch who tried to poison me with hemlock.

"Come on," I whisper, taking off Kettering's reading glasses and pulling him away from the gathering in pursuit of the trio now entering the corridor we just came from.

We trail them at a safe distance, alcove to alcove, as they march Zara down the corridor.

At the far end, they reach a heavy door. With a grunt of effort, one of them yanks it open, revealing a rustic stable beyond. They roughly shove Zara through the door, and she stumbles, falling onto the ground with a whimper before the door thuds closed behind them.

Kettering leans in. "What are they up to?"

"I'm not sure," I murmur back, "but when the witch who tried to kill me suddenly ends up in chains, you can bet it means something, and I don't think it's in her favour."

I sidle up to the door. Ear pressed against the rough surface, I strain to catch any snippet of conversation from within, but the oakwood muffles all sound. I'm about to suggest we search for another way when the sound of approaching footsteps reaches us from behind.

"Dammit," Kettering mutters, then grabs my arm. "This way, quick." Without waiting for a response, he yanks the stable door open and ushers me through.

I tense, ready for a confrontation, but on the other side, we're met with a stroke of luck: we've emerged into a large courtyard, probably once used for horses. Metal rings for tethering are still embedded in the walls, and the cobblestones beneath our feet are worn smooth from decades of hooves. Across the yard, we spot the witches, who have ducked into a stall, where they stand silhouetted against the warm glow of light from within.

Kettering jerks his head toward the left, and we creep along the walls, our palms brushing against lichen and damp stone as we edge closer to the stall adjacent to where the witches disappeared. Reaching the door, Kettering tugs the handle until it slides open with a shriek of rusted metal, shattering the silence and making him freeze.

"Did you hear that?" A voice resounds from inside the next stall, followed by the sound of footsteps from the castle.

As if on cue, whoever we'd been evading in the corridor bursts into the courtyard – it's exactly the distraction we need. In a few seconds of perfect timing, Kettering and I slip through the open door into the dark of the stall, the commotion outside masking our entry.

I ease into the cramped space, gripping the bars of the door, rough and cool against my palms. Inch by inch, I raise my head, my breath held tight in my chest. The top half of my face clearing the bottom of the door frame, I risk a narrow view of what's beyond.

But when I see who has come for Zara, cold terror spreads across my body. Mardequai strides across the courtyard, deliberately slipping the rings off his fingers, one by one, passing them to Orna Morrígan, who follows close behind. His now-bare hands flexing at his sides, Mardequai enters the adjacent stall.

Inside, a choked sob greets his arrival.

Chapter Thirty-One

Silent like two owls in flight, Kettering and I slide along the wall. We press against it, the boards shedding flakes of paint at our touch. A sliver of light catches my eye, revealing a gap in the old wood. I ease forward, positioning myself at the narrow opening, Kettering next to me, peering into the neighbouring stall.

"Zara," Mardequai greets the girl with an almost cheerful clap of his hands. "Zara, Zara, Zara..."

She is down on her knees, a strip of fabric tight across her face, covering her mouth, her shoulders heaving with every suppressed whimper.

"As you can tell from your current predicament, I am... Well, how can I put this?" He taps his lips, a predator playing with his prey. Behind him, Orna lets out a silent chuckle. "I am disappointed, Zara. Truly, I am."

Mardequai walks around her, caressing her hair in an irritating, fatherly way. "When you came to see me, begging me to help you, I was, I must say, truly impressed by your determination, your willingness to go the extra mile for your father."

As he says those words, Zara's sobbing becomes almost frantic, and my own chest constricts, dreading what I'm about to hear next.

"Naturally, we had to stop the payments for his treatment, dear. Dreadful, dreadful thing. But when I give someone a job to do, I expect results."

My mouth puckers as if I've bitten into something rotten. The job she failed to complete was killing me. However, even I am surprised when I hear the next bit.

"Three opportunities you had, three chances to bring down the other Hausmann twin." He shakes his head, clicks his tongue, giving me a moment to process what he means: it was Zara, every single time. That first night, after I left Sofia's club, then the falling tree in the forest, and her last attempt, of course, the poison hemlock at the bar.

"But not only did you fail to finish Alva off. No, you nearly poisoned someone precious to me, didn't you?" Mardequai crouches, his face now inches from Zara's. His fingers brush her temple, the gesture at odds with the rage in his voice.

Behind the wall, I struggle to process what I'm hearing. Sofia was right: he truly cares for her. Zara's failure to kill me is not what brought on his wrath. That makes sense; I bet he's got hundreds more witches in his entourage to do the deed in her stead. No, this, tonight, is about how his daughter nearly fell prey to the very trap meant for me.

"Untie her," Mardequai orders the two witches who have thus far stood silent guard. They do as told, cutting the rope that ties Zara's hands behind her back, then removing the cloth from her mouth.

The moment Zara's tongue is freed, she breaks into a heart-wrenching apology.

"*Please*," she sobs, "Mr Guise, I... I didn't mean to hurt your daughter, I swear it. She was done with her drink; she'd given it to her sister. Otherwise, I would never have—"

There it is again, that clicking tongue, now accentuated by Mardequai's wagging finger. "Now, you do not know that, dear, you do not know she was finished with that glass. Do not lie to me."

"Please, I'm not lying, I—"

Mardequai's face turns into a grimace of annoyance, his fingers moving toward his ears as if to pinch them closed. "There is no need to shout and scream, child. It is too late for excuses." He pivots away from Zara, his eyes landing on the gap in the wall I'm peering through. My muscles lock, my lungs seizing mid-breath, fearing I've been spotted.

"There is only one thing left to do now, Zara dearest," he says, and I release the breath I've been holding when his eyes keep wandering. "Can you guess what it might be?"

"What is it?" Zara asks, brushing her nose with the back of her hand.

"Fight," Mardequai announces. "I'm giving you the chance to fight for your life."

But his words only result in a fresh bout of sobs from Zara, her eyes darting around the stall, meeting the sneers of three witches years beyond her own experience level.

Mardequai follows her gaze. "What, them? No." He spreads his hands wide, his smile condescending. "What do you take me for? A bully? No, you won't be fighting *them* – you'll be fighting *me*. How does that sound?" He takes off his cloak, handing it to Orna.

I watch, entranced despite these gruesome games, wondering why he's doing this. He might be immortal, and Zara is a comparatively inexperienced witch. But still, I've seen her in action – she possesses the power to inflict damage, serious damage, maybe even flee if she plays her hand well.

"Come on, Zara." Mardequai widens his stance, like a baseball player preparing for a catch. "Show me what you got."

Then, out of nowhere, Zara jumps into action. Her body tenses, coiling like a spring, and in a flash, she's attacking. Lunging forward, a haunting note emerges from her lips, not quite singing, not quite screaming. The sound wave precedes her physical attack, disorienting Mardequai, and in that split second of confusion, Zara's hands thrust forward, channelling a burst of Anima directly into his chest – a devastating impact I can tell he didn't see coming.

Mardequai flies backward across the stall, crashing down hard on his back. The thud of his impact makes me wince. For a moment, everything is still, and I'm certain she's killed him – well, technically, anyway.

But only seconds later, Mardequai stirs, his body jerking as life comes back to him.

"Owww," he exclaims, holding his stomach in a mock gesture. "That was a good one, Zara. See, you *can* kill if you really put your mind to it."

Mardequai draws himself to full height. "*Again,*" he challenges, a cold command. Now Zara responds with desperate fury, unleashing another spell, her scream echoing off the walls, raw and desperate. But this time, Mardequai barely flinches – if he did die again just then, I missed it entirely. Zara's magic seems to have pearled off his body like rain, and he advances, unperturbed.

Each new spell she casts strikes him down, but only for a second. He collapses, then recovers with unnatural speed. Understanding dawns on me as I witness it. Mardequai has achieved what Kettering has thus far avoided: he has mastered the art of dying, honing his ability to return quickly from the land of the dead.

Now mere inches from Zara, he reaches out, fingers wrapping around her throat. Yet she fights on, blasting his chest, spell after desperate spell. It's a bizarre, horrifying spectacle – Mardequai repeatedly dying, only to revive and then resume his stranglehold on her. It's a macabre dance that buys Zara precious seconds, a fact I think she realises, but it also prolongs her torment.

Minutes crawl by, each one an eternity of struggle. But eventually, Zara's curses falter, and her resistance fades. As her body begins to sag, I tear my eyes away, my hand clamped over my mouth to stifle my sobs. I look around the stall, an idea forming, a plan to interfere somehow, to stop the man from killing the girl. My hand is already reaching for my coat pocket to retrieve the Celestial Stone, but Kettering stops me, laying his arm across my chest like a bar. My eyes find his, as I desperately try to communicate my need to help, to use my magic for a distraction, another decoy – anything. But the warning in Kettering's eyes brooks no dissent; if I reveal myself now, none of us will make it out of here.

And so, I sit, and I listen, horrified, as Zara meets her end. Yes, she had tried to kill me, but now I see her for what she truly was: another pawn in Mardequai's cruel game. She doesn't deserve this. Nobody deserves this.

When the gruesome deed is done, the two guard witches lift Zara's lifeless body, carrying her away into the night, limp feet scraping against the floor.

Heavily, I lean against the wood. In the sudden quiet, I strain to hear as the monster turns to address his remaining disciple. "Well, now that's out of the way, would you do me the honours, Orna dear, and finish what Zara could not?"

My heart seizes in my chest. For a terrifying moment, I'm certain he knows I'm hidden just behind this wall, waiting for them to finish me off.

"It would be my pleasure," Orna replies. "I'll depart for

London immediately."

"But no errors this time," warns Mardequai. "After all, this isn't *your* first failure in this matter, either."

A weighted pause, then: "I haven't mastered the ruse like you have, Mardequai. Indirect methods aren't my forte. Slipping the girl a Celestial Stone was a clever ploy, but it was your strategy, not mine. That's why I failed."

As these words reach us, Kettering's hand finds mine, pressing it tightly. I return the grip. There it is: my proof.

"You know, that is an excuse I still struggle to accept, not to mention the loss of the stone as a result." A muscle twitches along Mardequai's jawline as he inhales through flared nostrils, composing himself with visible effort before continuing. "Well, this time, you may do it in whatever way you see fit, as long as it gets done. Indeed, the current mayhem out there should come to your aid."

"May I ask one thing?" Orna's voice carries a note of trepidation as she ventures into what must be dangerous territory.

"You may."

"Why did you change your mind about the Chyulu Prophecy when—"

"Let me stop you right there," Mardequai interrupts. "I know where this is going. The prophecy spoke of twins – *two* sisters. As long as one of them perishes, it cannot come to pass."

"Are you sure about that?"

"My daughter will not be harmed," Mardequai snarls through clenched teeth. "And I won't hear mention of the prophecy again."

* * *

Kettering and I pass through the coal black darkness, feet squelching through the bog with each hurried step. Not a word has passed between us since we watched Mardequai and Orna depart the stable, then made our own escape from the castle. Only when I slip through the gap in the fence, do I allow myself a break, gasping for air as I sink onto a rock jutting from the moors.

"He killed her," I rasp, burying my face in my palms. "He murdered her because she failed to finish *me*."

"I know." Kettering lowers himself onto his haunches before me. His hands find my knees, rubbing gently, but his comfort does little, after the horrors we've just witnessed. "I'm so sorry you had to see that."

"He's a monster," I growl. "I knew it was him, I goddamn knew it was him who slipped me that stone. The entire time, every instinct told me!"

"You were right," Kettering agrees.

I lift my head, meeting his eyes. "What was Orna talking about? What prophecy?"

He sighs, nodding as if he realises whatever he knows about it cannot wait another second.

"It's... it's the proof you've been looking for," he says with a resigned smile. "The reason he wants you dead, although we still won't know why exactly, until you hear it for yourself."

"What do you mean?"

"Chyulu Prophecies are the most surefire, powerful prophecies a witch may cast. They are very much the definition of 'self-fulfilling', meaning that whatever the witch includes in her prophecy will eventually come to pass. *However* – it's very hard to be specific. The prophecy is fed with memories, emotions, thoughts, and wishes, so there's a lot of cosmic push and pull, a lot of room for the Universe to interpret the outcome, if you know what I mean."

I scratch my temple. "I have thoughts, but continue."

"Anyway, only those the prophecy concerns may receive it.

In this case, it seems that's Mardequai, you, and your sister." He lets that sink in, and I nod, signalling him to continue.

"Well, clearly, Mardequai has heard it, at what point in time we have no way of knowing. But you've surely pieced it together – the prophecy is the reason why he wants you dead. And his… *care* for your sister has led him to believe eliminating just you will suffice."

I picture Mardequai then, the patient predator, watching, waiting as entire centuries passed him by. In my mind, he's like one of those ancient crocodiles that lurk beneath murky waters, barely visible, seemingly part of the landscape itself. How many generations has he observed? How many witch twins has he tracked through the ages, poring over dusty records and following whispered rumours to their source?

I imagine him in countless guises throughout time, sometimes a nobleman, sometimes a vagrant, always with those same penetrating eyes that never reveal his true nature. Registry books, birth records, town gossip – all threads in his web, trembling with information. Each set of twins must have triggered the same methodical response: surveillance, assessment, and – if they matched some criteria in the prophecy – swift elimination. How many false alarms has he endured, how many twins has he disposed of unnecessarily, all to prevent whatever fate the prophecy has carved for him? And when he finally received word of us – did something change in those ancient eyes? Did he feel the culmination of his endless vigil approaching?

No, something about it doesn't add up.

"Why didn't he just do it? Why didn't he have me killed the moment he learnt I was still alive? Why invite me to the Assembly and all that?"

"I suppose that was his first mistake. He likely thought he could bide his time, find a more 'opportune' moment. Expose you to the Assembly, divide the community, *then* have you eliminated. Not to mention, your tragic passing would have distressed your sister at exactly the time he needed to use her as a pawn for the pre-empted Reveal."

"True. But he also didn't factor in that one of his own brothers would douse his efforts at every turn," I say, tapping his hand.

"And *that* was his second mistake. Now, come on, let's get you out of the cold." He helps me to my feet, but as we begin our cautious trek along the estate's perimeter, my mind still races.

"So, how can I hear that prophecy, then?" I ask.

"There's only one way, or better yet: one place."

"Where?"

"Kenya, of course." Kettering's says in a reverent tone. "The prophecies must be cast high in the cloud forests of the Chyulu Hills, infused into raindrops before they touch earth. Once grounded, they take centuries to resurface in a spring at the hills' base. It's a secret guarded by the mountains, and by time itself."

"When do we leave?"

"One step at a time," Kettering cautions. "First, we must clear your name. The authorities still think you're evil incarnate after what you did in that water chamber, and with everyone knowing who you are, there's no chance you'll leave the country without risking arrest."

"So how do I redeem myself?"

"Simple: bargaining power."

"Using what?"

"The Celestial Stone, of course. You still have it, right?"

"I do. It's right here in my..." But my words die in my throat when my fingers meet nothing but empty space in my pocket. I freeze, terror paralysing me.

"*What?* What is it?"

"The stone," I choke out, my head dizzying while I frantically search my other pockets. "It's... it's *gone*."

Chapter Thirty-Two

Ember embraces her sister as if it is the last time she'll ever be able to do so – which might well be true, considering what she's about to do.

Hugging tighter, she reaches inside Alva's coat pocket, where she knows her sister has stored the stone. Fingers curling around it, the smooth surface causes a ripple of power to shoot through her hand, which she quickly masks with words.

"Don't be mad at me," she pleads – in advance, knowing Alva will be furious once she finds out the truth.

The stone sinks into Ember's own pocket as she watches the driver pull her sister away, into the taxi, taking her away from here. This is, as ever, about keeping Alva safe. If only she wouldn't insist on making it so damn difficult.

It's best this way, Ember rationalises as the door clicks shut. The stone has brought Alva nothing but grief, and she's not remotely qualified to handle such a powerful weapon – which she's demonstrated, repeatedly. Ember, on the other hand, has three years of martial training at Chyulu under her belt.

"Was that really necessary?" Pippa asks, leaning against the doorway. "She worries about you, you know? We all do."

"Yeah, yeah, everybody worries about everyone. It's all very touching. You know, sometimes I wonder if it isn't all this worrying we do that gets us into these messes in the first place."

Ember retreats into her lair, slumping back down onto the couch.

"And what now?" Pippa inquires. "You just going to drink yourself into a coma?"

"Nope. Now we send a message to the puppet master," announces Ember, already typing out the words via the RN app.

Got news. Need to see you, she types, thinking for a beat before she adds: *Coming up to Dunmorrough.*

Mardequai might have cast her off in the eye of the public, but now Ember's got something in her possession she knows he'd desperately want. Indeed, the stone will ensure that, whatever future he envisions, she will be a crucial part of it.

The message sends, and to her surprise, it isn't met with the usual heavy pause, the calculated silence her foster father knows how to deploy so well.

No. Stay put. I do not want you here.

"Yeah, I bet you don't," Ember murmurs, tossing the phone on the table. She's become the face of this mess of a reveal, the rogue foster child who could not be contained. Naturally, he wouldn't want her by his side at Dunmorrough for his victory lap.

Indeed, he's got her exactly where he has always wanted her now, doesn't he? Cornered like a wild animal in a cage, entirely at the mercy of his good graces. How did she ever allow this to happen? When did it happen? She can't so much as buy a coffee without him knowing about it – she cannot even *afford* one without his credit cards. To the eyes of the world, Ember Wild is this fierce, independent rebel witch, but in truth, she's nothing but a puppet on a string, dancing at *his* whim.

Ember reaches for the remote, her fingers trembling slightly from the booze as she flicks through the channels. Each click brings a new blow:

Click. "Ember Wild: Public Enemy Number One," scrolls across the bottom of the screen. *Click.* A pundit gesticulates wildly: "She's single-handedly destabilised our society!" *Click.* "Witch Hunt: Search For Ember Wild Continues!" *Click.* Prime Minister Nigel Hall's pig face fills the screen. "Ember Wild is a disgrace to all women, and to all citizens of this nation. Her reckless actions have incited nothing but panic and fear. At this very moment, there are reports of innocent women – *innocent women* – being attacked in the streets by vigilantes who suspect them of witchcraft. That, Miss Wild, is on you. *You did this.*"

He leans forward, gripping the famous podium outside of Downing Street. "I am speaking to you directly, Ember Wild, and I'm imploring you to turn yourself in. Face the consequences of your actions. Every hour you remain in hiding, you put more lives at risk. The blood of any further victims will be on your hands."

A surge of rage courses through Ember, hot and vicious. Her free hand reaches for the Celestial Stone in her pocket, clenches into a fist around that unbridled power wanting to be used. And she imagines unleashing it right there, at Downing Street, showing Nigel Hall and the world what this witch is capable of. The urge to set the record straight, to make them understand – no, to make them *fear* her – is almost overwhelming.

But before she can act on her fury, her thumb instinctively hits the channel button once more when she simply cannot stand the face of that bloody chauvinist a second longer.

In the next report, the Millennium Bridge comes into view,

packed with people, mostly women, all dressed in pink. They're camping out, a defiant crowd, holding daring signs aloft:

"Hex the Patriarchy!"

"Our Magic, Our Legacy, Our Future!"

"Witches Rise, Misogynists Fall!"

Even the famous "We are the granddaughters of the witches you didn't burn!" made the cut.

The camera pans across the bridge, capturing passionate faces. Ember recognises witches from the Pink Cauldron among them, but the majority must be mortal women, standing in solidarity with her despite – or maybe because of – her witchcraft. The audio feed picks up a growing chant, voices rising in unison that make Ember's skin tingle.

"We stand with Ember Wild! We stand with Ember Wild!"

The chant grows louder, more insistent, an ocean of support spilling through the TV screen.

Ember rolls the Celestial Stone in her hand, its surface heating as she makes the call.

"*Pippa,*" she shouts into the hallway. "Get your tablet out, we've got work to do."

She adds, murmuring to herself, "It's time to buy some coffee."

Chapter Thirty-Three

"How can you be so sure your sister has it? What if you dropped it somewhere in the castle?" Kettering asks, a drizzle misting our faces as we walk back along the estate wall.

"I didn't drop the stone, alright? Sofia took it when she hugged me goodbye. I *know* she did. I just... didn't know it at the time."

"But how can you know now? It's not like you took great care of it, exactly."

I whirl around to him. "Are we really going to do that now? Fighting about something that can't be undone? – The stone is with Sofia. I did not lose it. Trust me on that one."

"Well, great. Another Hausmann witch about to meddle with a magical weapon she has no clue how to control."

"She may have *some* clue how to use it, actually," I say and continue walking.

"What do you mean?"

"She was at Chyulu Academy for three years. She's trained to use Celestial Stones."

Kettering stops. "I don't know if that's better or worse, actually," he says to the clouds.

In the distance, I finally spot my ride. Horace jumps out like an excited guard dog as soon as he spots me.

"Horace, ready the horses, it's back to London now."

"Heathrow, innit?" he notes, grabbing hold of my arm again, yanking me gently towards the back door.

"Actually, there will be another stop, I'm afraid. But don't worry: we'll get to Heathrow eventually."

"What is going on?" Kettering asks, his eyes wandering between Horace, the taxi, and me.

"Long story," I reply, rolling my eyes. "Basically, my sister hexed him into not leaving my side until he's dropped me off at Heathrow Airport."

"Charming," comments Kettering as he slides into the back-seat next to me. "Yeah, we can't have that," he murmurs as Horace rounds the car, settling behind the wheel.

"Horace, our next stop is just down the road," Kettering says through the glass separator. "I'll tell you when."

"Alrighty, love. Fasten your seatbelts, please," Horace replies cheerfully, starting the engine whilst humming yet another tune.

"*Don't* fasten your seatbelt. Get ready to jump when I tell you," Kettering instructs me as we pass a line of cars parked along the gravel road.

"Here we are, Horace, you can slow down now, please." The moment Horace hits the brakes, Kettering yanks open my car door. "*JUMP* – now!" he shouts, giving me a push, and I land in the mud – yet again.

"*Hey* – what the bloody hell are you doing, mate? The lady needs to get to Heathrow!"

I pull myself to my feet and circle around to the rear of the car. Just as I reach the back bumper, Kettering emerges from the other side, thumbing the fob on his key. His rental car responds with a flash of its lights and a double beep. I yank the door open, sliding into the passenger seat whilst simultaneously pressing the lock button, just as Horace slams into the metal. Thumping his fists against the window, his outcries are almost touching. "No! Please," he pleads, "I must take you to Heathrow, I…"

Kettering starts the engine, pulling out of the parking space in one smooth manoeuvre. The second Horace realises he has lost me, he jumps back into the taxi, making chase.

"Oh goodness, the poor fellow," I say, watching through the rearview mirror. "We cannot actually do this to him; he's going to get himself into an accident."

"Don't worry, I put a hole in his back tyre. He'll stop chasing us soon."

"But then he's going to look for me for the rest of his life…"

"Nah, the spell will wear off eventually. Just give it a couple of days."

Kettering steps on the gas, increasing the distance between us and Horace until I cannot see him anymore.

It's a shame, really. I was growing rather fond of him.

* * *

Somewhere past Northampton, the rental forces a rest stop on us as it needs time to charge its batteries. It's just past five o'clock in the morning; we've been taking turns driving all night. The motorways have been eerily quiet – too quiet, even for a night drive. Those vehicles we did pass often sported hastily made symbols or charms dangling in the windows or from rearview mirrors. The petrol station has posted handwritten signs: "No witches allowed inside" or "Brooms park at the back." At one point, we passed a field where a small group was gathered around a massive bonfire, performing what looked like a strange ritual at sunrise.

Even the radio has been different, with news bulletins instead of any music, reporting on the latest magical demonstrations or offering advice on how to identify suspected witches.

While the car is charging, both Kettering and I fall asleep. When I wake up, the clock on the dashboard informs me that it's just past seven in the morning. I reach over to Kettering, tapping him on the shoulder to wake him as well.

"What time is it?"

"Still early," I reply, switching on the radio.

"Breaking news from London this morning. Ember Wild, the controversial witch at the centre of the recent magical reveal, made a surprise appearance at the ongoing Millennium Bridge protest. Wild arrived shortly after dawn, bringing coffee and doughnuts for the women who have been camping out in the cold."

I meet Kettering's eyes, which mirror my own panic. Fumbling my phone from the glove box, I google her name, while Kettering turns up the volume.

"Armed forces have since secured the perimeter, encircling the protestors. Predominantly women, they insist they have organised peacefully. But witnesses report a tense standoff, with authorities maintaining a strong presence around the bridge. A spokesperson for the demonstrators stated, 'We are here to peacefully defend our right to exist as women and as witches. The heavy-handed response from authorities is unnecessary and provocative.' Meanwhile, Prime Minister Hall claims the measures are for public safety, citing concerns about potential magical incidents."

At last, my phone loads a video. "Here we go, turn it down, turn it down," I instruct Kettering, and he switches off the radio while I watch the live footage on my tiny screen with bated breath.

A pink truck, its back doors wide open, is parked at the

northern end of the famous bridge. My sister stands on the truck bed, handing out pink paper cups of coffee and doughnuts with a matching glaze. Her hair is twisted into a messy topknot, strands escaping to frame her face. She's wearing what I recognise is her own version of Taylor Swift's famous 'reputation outfit', one leg in black fishnet stockings, the other covered in a sensual snake print that effortlessly melts into a form-fitting bodysuit – hers, naturally, in daring pink.

As Sofia passes out the treats, she's chatting and laughing with the protesters. Despite the tense situation – armed forces are visible on both ends of the bridge – she seems at ease, as if hosting a casual garden party rather than standing at the centre of a global controversy.

Every so often, she pauses to wave at the cameras or give a cheeky salute to the encircling military, who cannot seem to get to her – thanks to a wall of protective wards, I'm sure, but also because the crowd simply will not *let* them.

Kettering has started his own internet search in the driver's seat, landing on a live video from the 'MYPINKCAULDRON' Instagram account, which offers a more intimate angle, showing my sister leaning her phone against the truck canvas while she snaps a hawker's tray around her waist, filled with more pink doughnuts. She picks up her phone, winking cheekily into the camera, then places it on the tray and steps off the truck bed, taking a bath in the crowd.

"Is she mad?" I gasp. "She's going to get arrested!"

"Well, I may not have quite believed you until now," Kettering murmurs, eyes still on the phone screen. "But as of this moment, I'm one hundred per cent certain she's got that Celestial Stone. And I don't think she has any plans of getting herself arrested..."

My blood runs cold as I picture the stone, stashed somewhere, waiting to be used. Where is she keeping it? Secured to the hawker's tray? Tucked in her bra? Hidden in her hair?

I turn my attention back to my own phone, which has switched to a drone shot. Horrified, I watch as the crowd on the bridge parts while Ember Wild strides down its centre, the dome of St. Paul's Cathedral perfectly framing her, heading straight for the military barricade on the other side. Armed to the teeth, the soldiers stand ready, forming an impenetrable barrier halfway across the Thames.

"Drive," I implore Kettering, gripping my phone so tight it might crack in my hand.

Chapter Thirty-Four

The crowd moves because Ember wills it to.

She has used this spell so many times before, it's child's play for her to create a path to the centre of the bridge. She's not remotely scared of the soldiers and their guns on the other side; she could direct them like marionettes, too, if she wanted to. Only she doesn't. She wants them to stay, wants them to witness what true power looks like.

Emboldened by the stone clasped in her palm, she moves through the crowd as hands reach out from all sides, touching her, filming her, shaking her hand now that she's set the hawker's tray down.

A quick glance downriver confirms her getaway ride. The water is swamped with police boats, but there, on the south bank, waits Pippa on one of Mardequai's sleek vessels. Once Ember completes her task, they'll run away together. A leap into the water, a stroke of luck, and they'll be gone – never to return, shedding their former lives. Ember has nothing left to lose, anyway.

But first things first: there's still work to be done.

Ember approaches the front line of soldiers, who raise their shields, ready to attack at a moment's notice. But with a jab of her arm and a muttered incantation, the soldiers freeze in place, their weapons still raised but useless. She turns her back on them, facing the crowd of women gathered behind her. Her eyes blaze with determination as her voice carries across the bridge:

"This one goes out to every woman who's ever swallowed her anger, who's smiled when she wanted to scream, who's been told to be smaller, to be quieter – to be *less*," she begins calmly, gesturing to the frozen soldiers behind her. "Look around you. Can you see what they fear? It's not magic. It's not witchcraft – it's us. All of us. They've always known our power. That's why they've tried so hard to contain it. But no more. No more."

Ember shakes her head, her posture straightening.

"We are *done* being polite. We are *done* being silent." Now her voice rises. "We are done waiting for permission to exist fully and wholly and unapologetically in this world. Because our rage? It is sacred. It is the fire that will forge a new world, a new era."

"Witch or not, we have powers they can only dream of. They cannot even *comprehend* them. Resilience. Compassion. Sisterhood. Fierce protection of those we love. Our power, our *strength* lies in every 'no' we have said, every boundary we have drawn, and every stand we have taken."

Ember scans the crowd, making eye contact with several women. "Your anger is not ugly. Your ambition is not selfish. Your fire is not something to be ashamed of. Embrace it. Use it. Let it fuel you."

"From now on, we stand together. Because a witch is a woman, and a woman is a witch. And we will use our magic, our hands, our voices, our votes – every tool in our arsenal – to remake this world, so that one day, our daughters won't have to fight the same battles we've fought. Mark this day, ladies.

Because this is the first day in a world where we *live* our magic, unapologetically. A world where we reign. And if it scares them, I say: let them be scared."

She raises her fist, her final words a battle cry: "Because they should be. We're not asking for our place in this world anymore – we are *claiming* it."

At that, Ember spins back around, a wicked grin splitting her face as the pink crowd breaks into uncontrolled cheers while the soldiers fume with determined rage, trying to get to her past the frozen front line.

She raises her arms, channelling her power to redirect a sudden gust of wind sweeping down the Thames. With a careful push, she guides the women back, creating a safe distance between them and the soldiers. She manoeuvres the gale, her hair whipping around her face.

Once she's secured enough space, Ember closes her fist around the Celestial Stone, its power pulsing against her skin. With a curl of her fingers, she releases the soldiers, and they stumble forward, quickly regaining their bearings and breaking into a sprint towards her.

Just as they approach, Ember harnesses the stone's power, pushing her fist down until it hits the ground. The bridge beneath her feet groans, a spiderweb of cracks spreading from where she stands, and in an instant, she's propelled upward, hovering above the astonished soldiers. Their faces fall open with disbelief as they gaze up at her, floating effortlessly in the air.

Ember turns, preparing to dive into the murky waters of the Thames and vanish. But then, a commotion below catches her attention. Her breath leaves her as she sees the soldiers, thwarted in their attempt to capture *her*, now redirecting their aggression towards the crowd of women. They advance menacingly, clubs raised high.

The demonstrators cry out in fear, some covering their heads while others scramble to escape. Panic spreads through the crowd like wildfire. Amidst the chaos below, one figure stands out, and the sight of her twists a cold knot in Ember's stomach – *Alva*. Her sister is pushing against the tide of fleeing women, desperately trying to reach her.

Ember's heart races. She can't leave now, not with Alva in danger – not with *all* of them in danger. She loosens her grip on the stone and then she descends back onto the bridge.

Chapter Thirty-Five

The rental car barely inches forward, caught in a line of honking vehicles. Kettering's knuckles are white on the steering wheel, his breath hissing out between gritted teeth while I can't tear my eyes away from the phone screen in my hand, where Sofia has just turned to face the people behind her. The camera pans, showing the crowd pressed together on the Millennium Bridge. An ocean of faces, all turned towards my sister, marvelling at her as she speaks. The camera cannot pick up her voice, but her facial expressions still deliver the message – she's pissed, but passionate.

"This is insane," Kettering grumbles, pressing the horn. Indeed, the street before us has practically turned into a parking lot. All around us, I spot people climbing out of their cars, leaving doors ajar as they run towards the Thames. A business-woman stumbles past my window, stilettos in her hands as she runs barefoot in the same direction.

"They're all heading to the bridge," I say, craning my neck out the window.

"We're never going to make it there," Kettering notes, peering through the windshield at the abandoned cars ahead.

"Fuck!" I blurt out, hitting the dashboard. "Alright, that's it, we've got to try our luck on foot."

Without waiting for Kettering's opinion, I leave the car and begin to run. He follows me, but even on foot we don't get far. Up ahead, a military barricade blocks the way. I can just about spot the roof of the pink truck behind them, but for the life of me, I cannot get there!

"You cannot save her, Alva," Kettering tries to reason with me. "Look at this – this is madness. She's in the eye of the storm over there with the stone, but everyone close to her will get whacked."

"...eagles always soar above the storm," I mutter then, struck by an idea. "Or *below!*"

"What are you talking about?"

"The Resonance Network," I exclaim, gripping his arm. "If we can get to that hidden courtyard where Klein dropped us, and then find our way back through those tunnels—"

"We'd get out at Blackfriars Pier," he finishes my thought.

My gaze meets his.

"It could work," he says.

"Let's go."

When we round the corner to the courtyard, the sound of the chaos behind us momentarily fades. We push through the dense foliage, and the heavy iron door appears before us, its hinges groaning as Kettering wrenches it open. And then we plunge back into the tunnels.

Kettering takes the lead, finding his way through this underground maze with surprising ease, while I struggle to keep up, my eyes straining to make out the cobbles right in front of me. As we hurry through the Resonance Network base, my heart sinks. I picture Effie Bell and all the other telepaths somewhere down here, operating those terrible switchboards. The setup here in London must be on a whole other level compared to what I witnessed in Scotland.

Finally, the sound of rushing water fills my ears, and we reach the water chamber, our footsteps echoing as we pass the walkway. Pushing through one more door, we rush down the last corridor, until we find ourselves back above ground, right in between the Blackfriars Bridge and the Millennium Bridge.

Here, the riverbank is free of the pedestrians and police that crowd the areas above, thanks to the protective wards. Without hesitation, I break into a run across the gravel beach, feet slipping on the wet stones. I barely hear Kettering's breathing behind me as we race up the stairs to the street level. My heart thrums in my ribcage; we're so close now.

I crane my neck, searching for Sofia. Time seems to warp as I sprint towards the bridge. Lungs burning and muscles throbbing, I fight my way through the sea of pink. But my blood turns to ice water as I watch Sofia slam her fist onto the bridge floor – undoubtedly clutching the stone. The whole structure shudders with a deep groan, and in a heartbeat, Sofia is airborne.

Partial spells spill from my lips, fuelled by my own desperation to get through to her. Most fizzle without doing anything, but a few do provide me with slivers of space, so that I can push further. If she uses that stone to harm anyone, I will never forgive myself. At last, I break through to the front row, where Sofia hovers above the bridge, her face triumphant as she looks down at the bewildered soldiers. But to my surprise – and my relief – she doesn't attack them. It would be so easy for her now, but she doesn't do it. I look up to her, then around, until my eyes land on a distant person on a boat, not far from Blackfriars Pier – Pippa.

Too late I realise, my sister never meant to use the stone for harm – only for show. I look up at her, desperate to communicate she should just go. The tension is now a hair's breadth from snapping.

And then it does.

One of the soldiers nearest to me makes what looks like a rash decision, his eyes hardening as they lock onto mine. Time slows to a crawl, but then he charges, his club raised high. The fierce roar tearing from his throat causes those soldiers around him to spring into action too, rallying the entire troop. The crowd around me shrieks, many women instantly scrambling backward – leaving me exposed at the front.

Panic claws at my insides because I might be the only witch left on the bridge to protect these innocents. My hands shake as I raise them, preparing a spell I'm not sure how to pull off. Desperate, I look up, turning to my sister in a plea for help.

Everything happens all at once, but when my eyes meet hers, understanding passes between us, and she releases her hold on the stone's power. She descends, and I can see the resolve in her eyes. The first soldier is mere feet away from me now, his club already in a downward arc.

Sofia lands beside me, making the bridge tremble, her hair wild and eyes blazing with fury. "Why the fuck do you never listen when I tell you to leave?" she snarls, even as her outstretched hand freezes the charging soldier mid-swing, inches from my face.

There's no time to reply, with more soldiers advancing towards us. I scan the crowd, relief washing over me as I spot more threads of Anima. We're not the only witches anymore. I spot Adanna, Saskia, and Eun-Ji, all three of them already busy casting protective shields around some of the women close to them.

But they're not the only ones. As I steel myself for the confrontation, a glint of silver catches my eye on the opposite side, and it makes my stomach drop. A group of women in sleek silver bodysuits advance with the military. I recognise them from Arcadia House, and with a sickening feeling, I realise that these witches aren't here as our allies – but *theirs*. The Arcadia witches are here to fight us because I guess nothing says 'we stand with humans' better than offering up their powers to capture Ember Wild herself.

But it gets worse. Like a nightmare made flesh, I see *her*: Orna Morrígan, parting the lines of soldiers as if they were nothing more than pawns in her game. Flanking her are the two witches from the Dunmorrough stables, their eyes trained on me with murderous thirst.

And now the bridge becomes a battleground, not just clubs and shields soaring through the air – but *Anima*. Witches on both sides hurl their magic, casting spells, the air shimmering with protective barriers and violent blasts. Adanna's water spell clashes with an Arcadia witch's fire, creating a hissing steam cloud. Saskia and Eun-Ji levitate debris to block incoming attacks.

Amidst this magical mayhem, the soldiers barely make a dent, their human weapons useless against the Anima at play. One charges at Sofia, only to be flung back by an invisible strike. Kettering fights like a man possessed, his fists slamming into jaws and ribs. I cry out when a witch's spell catches him at the temple, and he goes down hard. For a heart-stopping moment, he's still. But then, with a gasp, he stumbles back to his feet.

"Very inconvenient, this whole dying business," he mutters, more to himself, then dives back into the fray.

I try to keep track of him, but when a blast of Anima whizzes past my ear, singeing my hair, I duck. Narrowly avoiding the spell, I collide with a panicked protester, and we both tumble to the ground, the impact knocking all strength out of me.

Before I can regain my footing, an Arcadia witch looms over me, planting her boot aggressively on my chest, pinning me to the ground. Fear surges through me when I see her hands weaving a complex pattern, energy gathering at her fingertips. And the possibility of losing my own freedom – maybe even my life – lets something in me snap. A voice, dark and sinister, whispers in my mind: *Let me help. Let me protect us.*

It's Ruth. And the intensity of her presence shocks me. I'm not holding the Celestial Stone anymore, so how can she be this strong in me? But as I lay there, faced with certain defeat, I don't have the time to question her; all I can do is surrender my control to her.

My vision darkens, and I feel her power surging through me. My hands move of her accord, weaving spells I never even knew existed. Dark threads coalesce around my head like Medusa's snakes, lashing out at my attacker. The witch screams, stumbling back as my dark tendrils try to catch her legs.

Meanwhile, Sofia is locked in fierce combat with Orna, their powers colliding in harsh flashes. I stand by, ready to interfere, to take over should my sister need me.

"You can't win this, child," Orna snarls, hurling a bolt of Anima that Sofia deflects with ease.

"Watch me." Her grip tightens around the Celestial Stone, and with a fierce yell, she unleashes its magic, catapulting Orna backwards. The witch, stunned, tumbles end over end down the length of the bridge. Once again, the structure groans ominously, and new fissures spread across its pillars.

"What is *she* even doing here?" Sofia asks me breathlessly, wiping her forehead with her arm.

"She's here for me," I just about manage before a soldier lunges at me from behind, and Ruth's instincts take over once more. Anima surges through me as she reaches out, fingers curling into claws. The Thames responds to her call, a tendril of murky water rising high. With a vicious twist of the wrist, Ruth forces the stream straight down the soldier's throat. It's a shocking use of magic, yet I can't help but marvel at Ruth's creativity.

The soldier's eyes bulge in terror as he chokes and splutters. "I... I yield," he sputters but now fury scorches through me before I can stop it. Ruth and I revel in our display of power, and she urges me to go further, to crush this insignificant little ant who dared attack us.

Then, from the corner of my eye, I catch sight of Cornelis. The look on his face stops me cold: horror and shock and, beneath it all... disgust. He is watching me become the monster he always feared was there.

"Alva, stop! He's surrendering!" Sofia's voice pierces through the fog of my anger. She grabs my arm, and as soon as she does, I let go of the man, but not out of mercy – no, something else has drawn my attention: the stone in Sofia's hand, throbbing with energy. Just like in the water chambers with Gathoni, I feel myself unravelling, reaching for that celestial power with a hunger that terrifies me, a desperate, primal need. With a predatory hiss, I lunge at my own sister, hands clawing at her clothes as I try to grasp the stone.

"Alva, what are you doing?" Sofia cries out, struggling to keep the stone away from me. She's holding back, I can tell. She doesn't want to use the stone on me.

Seconds pass as we grapple on the bridge. Stretching her arm, she's keeping the stone away from me, and then, as I tear at her sleeve, it happens: almost as if in slow motion, the stone slips from Sofia's fingers, tumbling downward before plunging into the murky depths of the Thames below.

"What did you do?" Sofia screams.

Before I can even respond, a chilling sound pierces the air. Orna's voice rises in a dark, foreboding chant. I turn just in time to see the witch, eyes filled with fury, hands weaving Anima to accompany her spell. Suddenly, a blast erupts from her fingertips, a writhing mass of magic hurtling straight towards me.

Out of nowhere, Kettering shoves me aside. "Look out!" he yells, taking the brunt of the spell, and – dropping dead instantly. Still, a wisp of the dark Anima catches my shoulder, causing searing pain to lance through me, and I crumple to the ground next to the druid, my vision blurring.

Through the haze, I see Sofia. "Don't you dare," she roars, hurling her own Anima back towards Orna.

Orna's eyes widen in terror as Sofia's wrath barrels towards her. At the last second, she turns and leaps off the bridge, choosing the Thames as her last escape.

In the chaos, Sofia rushes to my side. "Hey, hey, are you—"

But her words are cut short by another groan from the bridge, which now shudders beneath us, more cracks spidering out from where we are, branching across the surface like strikes of lightning.

Kettering coughs himself back to life. He sits up, looks around, momentarily disoriented, before the impending danger registers. With impressive speed, he comes to his feet, just as a collective gasp from everyone around us pulls my attention back towards my sister. The world seems to slow as my eyes lock onto her, now surrounded by silvery figures weaving chains of Anima which snake towards Sofia like octopus arms.

The bridge groans again, even louder this time, paired with the sound of twisting metal and crumbling concrete.

"We need to move, *now*!" Kettering shouts, helping me up.

"No, Sofia!" I cry out, watching in terror as the Arcadia witches swarm around her, their Anima wrapping around her limbs. She fights back, but for every magical chain she breaks, two more take its place.

Kettering's grip around my waist pulls me backwards against my will. "Alva, we have to go! The bridge is collapsing!"

"No!" I thrash against him. "We can't leave her!"

"We don't have a choice!" He grunts, further tightening his hold on me. "They've got her! Alva – they've got her."

And then a deafening crack splits the air, as the section of bridge where we lay mere seconds ago collapses, plummeting into the river and creating a chasm between me and Sofia.

"NO!" I scream, my voice hoarse with fear as my sister's eyes meet mine. She mouths something, but I cannot hear her over the falling debris. The silver witches pull her away, disappearing into the crowds on the other side.

A scream tears from me as Kettering drags me back, the bridge crumbling to dust behind us.

At last, we reach safe ground, and Kettering lets go of me. My body racked with sobs, I collapse to my knees, but the curse from my shoulder spreads into my chest, my arms, my head. Darkness overcomes me, and I don't have any strength left to fight it off anymore.

Chapter Thirty-Six

When I wake, I keep my eyes closed, and for a blissful, drawn-out moment, I don't remember what happened. There's a weightlessness to my body, as if I'm suspended in a warm cocoon. My senses are still muted, my hearing not yet activated, the world around me not quite materialising. There's no sound, no sensation. Just a soft and peaceful silence. It's as if I'm still wrapped in the aftermath of a lovely dream, which lingers like a fading song just beyond my grasp. At last, my senses return one by one, and the world around me begins to take shape again. Sounds filter in; the low hum of an engine and the rattle of loose fittings tell me I'm on a plane before I even open my eyes.

When I do, I'm met with the sight of Kettering seated across from me, his face etched with worry. It's a small plane, with no more than eight seats. It's also undoubtedly the most luxurious space I've ever set foot in, all fine leather, polished wood, and plush carpets.

Panic grips me then, and images from the bridge wash over

me. *"Sofia,"* I gasp, trying to sit up despite the pounding in my head. "Where is she? What happened?"

Kettering's face grows grim. He leans forward, placing a gentle but firm hand on my arm to keep me from moving. "Alva, it's too late," he says with an urgency that stops me cold. "You cannot help her anymore."

"What? No!" I protest, my heart racing. "We have to go back. We have to rescue her!"

"Alva, it is *done*. They're..." He sighs, sitting back in his seat once more. "They're taking her to Saltholm, alright?"

"How do you even know that?" I demand, searching his face. "You cannot know that."

"I *know*," Kettering insists. "Trust me, I would not tell you if I wasn't certain."

Tears well up in my eyes, and a lump forms in my throat. My chest tightens with a crushing pain of desperation, helplessness, and overwhelming guilt. I blink, trying to hold back the tears, but they're coming no matter how much I try to fight them.

"So, what now?" I manage to choke out.

"Now we have to get you to a hospital," Kettering replies, his tone softening slightly at my visible distress.

I struggle to focus. "Where even are we?"

Kettering looks out the small oval window. "Right now, probably somewhere above the Mediterranean Sea."

The world seems to tilt and spin around me. I lean back against the headrest, closing my eyes against the dizziness.

"But – what about all my stuff?" The question sounds silly, trivial, considering everything that's happened.

"I fetched it from the hotel before we took off," Kettering answers.

I swallow, wincing at the stale taste in my mouth, my tongue feeling rough like sandpaper. "Where are we going?" I ask, touching my throbbing head.

"Kenya," Kettering says. The old coldness has returned to his voice and now I notice he's avoiding my gaze, as if afraid of what he might find lurking in my eyes. Suddenly, another memory flashes through my mind – the bridge, the soldier, and what I did to him.

Kettering saw it all.

But before I can dwell on this, the door to the cockpit swings open, and a man enters the confined space of the cabin. He's tall, probably in his late thirties, dressed in olive-green pants and a simple white button-down shirt.

"Ah, the patient is awake," the man notes, his eyes fixing on me with an almost doctor-like interest.

"Hi," I say, a little self-conscious because this man – whoever he is – clearly has done me a great kindness.

"Nice to meet you, Alva," he says, his back hunched under the low ceiling of the plane, reaching out a hand to me. "My name is Hannes Kettering."

I was about to thank him and all that, but the moment I hear his name, I'm too stunned to say anything at all. Baffled, I shake his hand.

"Well, you gave us all quite the fright," he says into my awkward silence. Moving toward a fancy bar set-up, he pours two cups of tea, handing me one of them.

"Thank you," I manage at last, taking the cup from him.

"Don't mention it. You'll still need thorough magical nursing, I'm afraid. But nothing they cannot fix at Chyulu."

"Ch-Chyulu?" I stammer. "Is that where we're going?"

"That is exactly right, yes," Hannes Kettering replies with a polite smile, then excuses himself and returns to the cockpit.

"Was that... is he your..." I keep stammering, my temples throbbing with a piercing headache.

"That would be my father, yes," Cornelis replies.

I put my tea down and get up from my seat, a hiss of pain escaping my lips. "Listen, about what you saw on that bridge..."

He continues to stare pointedly out the window. "A lot happened today, Alva. I cannot say I feel particularly up for a chat about it all at this point."

"But you see, it... it wasn't *me*," I insist. "You know that, right?"

"I do know that." At last, his eyes meet mine. "And that is exactly what frightens me. It was her. She still lives in you. I was so relieved when I found out you had a Celestial Stone. I truly thought your darkness was caused by it. But it's not, is it?" He searches my face, the old familiar inquiry – so desperate, so demanding, I cannot stand it a moment longer.

I turn away from him, sinking back into my seat. Shame consumes me as I stare into nothingness, knowing he is right. The stone may strengthen the grip Ruth has on me, but the truth is, she manages to take control even when I'm not under its influence. Some part of me already knew it – that first night in the rain, when Zara chased me after leaving the Pink Cauldron, I was wearing Dennis's jacket then, I *didn't* have the stone on me. And yet, Ruth awoke as soon as she saw a chance to destroy – to kill. And I don't know *why*. But some part of me—some dark part—*wants* the power she offers. And each time I use it, each time I let her magic flow through me, she grows stronger. More real. More... present.

"I think she's getting stronger," I whisper. "Every time she takes over, it's like she leaves a little more of herself behind. And I don't know how to stop it."

"You should try to sleep some more," Cornelis says, almost as if to cut me off. "We'll take you to the academy's medical wing once we reach Chyulu. But for now, rest is your best option."

"NO, I..." The words burst out of me, louder than intended. I take a breath, then try anew. "I'm sorry, but... if it's alright with you, I'd prefer to go directly to the spring. You know, to hear that prophecy."

His eyebrows knit together. "Are you certain you're up for that?"

"I've made it this far, haven't I?" I attempt a casual shrug, then wince inwardly at the pain, struggling to keep my face as neutral as possible.

"Alright, I'll inform the captain," Cornelis replies curtly as he stands, disappearing into the cockpit without another glance.

Left alone, I turn to the window, sipping on my tea. Outside, dusk settles in, and the clouds turn dark as a new world unfolds below.

A week ago, I was an herbalist, worried about not much more than if my deliveries would arrive on time, or if my shea butter was running low. Today, I'm an under-prepared witch in a world on fire because my kind has burst into the open. My sister is headed for the most dreaded prison on the planet, and an immortal nemesis wants me dead because of some ancient prophecy I have yet to hear.

But what frightens me most is not the storms howling all around me – it's the battle raging within my own mind.

Chapter Thirty-Seven

I've always wanted to see Kenya, the fabled land where magic first touched the earth.

Mama had been once, during a pilgrimage many witches undertake at least once in their lives. Sofia and I had grown up listening to her tales of the white-capped peak of Kilimanjaro, mighty African elephants striding across the open plains below, the secret cloud forests of the Chyulu Mountains... We'd always wanted to go together one day, as a family.

The plane descends onto this ancient land of lava and volcanic rock, red soil and lush green hills, and I'm overcome with deep awe as the bedtime stories from my childhood come to life before my eyes. Despite my shoulder throbbing with pain, my whole body tingles with excitement. Nose pressed against the window, my breath fogging up the screen, I watch the sun push above the horizon, this blood-red, ancient thing that has moulded everything in its light.

"Welcome to Tsavo National Park," announces a female voice through the speaker – the pilot, I gather.

I look over at Cornelis, my face a question he answers without me having to voice it out loud.

"Tsavo lies about twenty miles west of the Chyulu Hills. The Prophecy Spring is part of the Mzima Springs ecosystem. It'll be a bumpy drive from the airstrip. Are you sure you'll manage?"

My head dips in a nod, the fire to prove myself burning hot, fuelling my commitment to do what I can to help the good guys. Understanding Mardequai's game plan is crucial to that effort, and the sooner I know it, the better.

The jet slides to a stop on the rustic, unpaved airstrip, the rough landing causing my entire body to stiffen as I try to protect my shoulder.

"I suppose I don't have to worry about getting my passport stamped," I note as I press off my seat.

Hannes Kettering chuckles, slipping into a worn leather jacket. "We prefer to stay under the radar," he confirms and opens the plane door, which he pushes toward the outside.

"Then why did you worry about me not being allowed to leave the UK?" I mutter at Cornelis as we alight from the plane.

"Well, I hadn't planned on calling 'Daddy' for help until your sister blasted one of England's most cherished monuments, and you almost got yourself killed," he snaps, then bumps his head on the door frame.

Outside, a morning chill engulfs us, and we're met with a symphony of birdsong. Green acacia bushes frame the red, dusty runway. In the distance, silhouettes of imposing mountains tower against the morning sky, and under a simple thatched-roofed pergola stands a mustard yellow Land Rover.

"Hi Alva, I'm Bea," the pilot introduces herself and I shake her hand before she deftly approaches the Rover, casually using a levitation spell to produce the right key on her chain. Another witch, then. Dressed in olive green overalls, she might be in her late fifties, with wild salt-and-pepper locs falling loosely over her shoulder and mahogany eyes that complement her outfit.

We follow her towards the car, where she takes the driver's seat. The engine sputters to life as Hannes, Cornelis, and I take our seats on the open back on opposite benches. The leather upholstery is cracked with age, but at least it's thick and plush, allowing for some cushioning for my ailing body during the impending 'bumpy ride'.

"Here, you might need these," Bea announces, handing out thick, red-checkered Maasai blankets to everyone. "Gets quite chilly here during morning drives."

And then we're off, my head involuntarily shaking as I try to grasp how we even got here. "Who *are* you people?" I ask the two Dutch gentlemen sitting across from me.

Father and son exchange a long look, and their resemblance is hard to miss. Indeed, they could be brothers – a twisted spin on reality due to the fact that a druid's aging slows down with time.

"Well, I guess I'll take this one," Kettering senior finally says, his voice competing with the roar of the engine and the wind whipping past us. "The Chyulu Hills are the birthplace of magic, as I'm sure you already knew. So, naturally, these hills have long become the centre of magical governance. They're our equivalent to Whitehall, the Kremlin, Capitol Hill. The academy stands as its flagship, but there are *other* institutions nestled up in those cloud forests." Hannes's gaze drifts towards the rolling hills on the horizon, capped by the rising sun.

"And you work for one of those institutions?" I probe. The elder Kettering proves to be just as tight-lipped as his son. Now I know where Cornelis gets it from.

"Indeed, we do."

"Well, what is it?" I ask, my face grimacing in pain as we hit a particularly nasty pothole.

"One thing at a time, Miss Hausmann. One thing at a time," replies Hannes Kettering. "My son may have convinced me that your insights, especially regarding a possible prophetic revelation," – he nods at the gravel path ahead of us – "might be of great value. But you'll have to excuse my caution when it comes to trusting you. Your history, after all, is of concern to us, as I'm sure you've gathered by now."

I turn toward Cornelis. What else has he told his old man? But Kettering junior's eyes remain aimed at some point in the distance.

* * *

The sun-dappled waters of Mzima Springs emerge from the earth like a hushed secret, their clear waters an oasis in the rugged volcanic landscape that birthed them. The Land Rover bumps along a rough track, stirring plumes of dust, as smells of damp earth and lush jungle vegetation fill my nostrils.

The drive here has been nothing short of surreal. Zebras and antelopes crossed our path, so commonplace here yet so extraordinary to my own eyes. However, it was the sudden appearance of Kilimanjaro's snow-capped peak on the horizon that nearly undid me. A gasp caught in my throat as I beheld the impressive mountain I'd missed entirely from the plane as I was seated on the wrong side. The sight of that white crown throning above the savanna struck me more than I thought it would, reminding me of just how far from home I've come.

As we approach the springs, we're greeted by – there is no other way to say it – *life*, making itself known in a variety of motions and sounds. Hippos wallow in the shallows, their grunts reverberating off the water's surface like deep grandfather laughs. The scaled bodies of crocodiles slip silently into the depths, barely leaving ripples. Fish dart through the crystal waters, flashes of silver amid a sea of water lilies.

The Land Rover comes to a halt, and I step out, my senses overwhelmed by the wild beauty.

"The Prophecy Spring is a short walk from here," says Cornelis. "I'll take you, but you'll have to enter alone, otherwise your prophecy won't reveal itself."

"Enter what?" I ask, unable to hide my nerves. I'm not exactly keen on entering a pool of water where crocodiles might lurk.

"You'll see," answers Cornelis. "It's hard to explain."

I force myself upright and follow him, wondering if it's the surge of adrenaline or sheer necessity that's numbing the worst of my pain, leaving me oddly clear-headed as all my senses sharpen and we make our way through this wild oasis. A leopard or a lion could pounce on us from behind every bush, after all.

We approach a wonderful mother of a tree, her branches sprawling like protective arms, with hands dipping into the spring. Every once in a while, a ripe fig falls with a pleasant *plop*.

Cornelis leads the way toward the base of the tree, where a dark, gaping hole in the ground appears, the fig tree's white roots dripping down into the abyss like candle wax.

"The spring is down there. You'll need to climb down the roots, do you think you can manage that?"

I nod. "That's the least of my worries right now," I say, gazing down into the dark void.

"Don't worry, animals stay away from this spring."

"And I'm just going to take your word on that?"

"Your choice," replies the druid.

Still wary of me, I see.

"And what must I do once I get down there?"

"This is as far as I've ever been. You'll figure it out, I'm sure."

I take a breath of courage. "Right, I suppose we've come all this way. Help me, will you?"

I walk around the hole in the ground and sit down at its edge. Kettering comes down on his haunches behind me, reaching for a rope someone must have used before. Dread spills through me like a cold when I realise it might have been Mardequai.

Cornelis slings the rope around my waist, and I turn toward him. His eyes meet mine for a second before I step one foot onto a protruding root, lowering myself down. "Wish me luck," I sigh, my shoulder throbbing with pain as I descend into the cave.

"Luck," murmurs Kettering, giving more rope.

Down below, the air is damp and earthen, trickles echoing off the water surface, reflections dancing over the walls. It's a peaceful place, a quiet place, and I'm reminded of that feeling I had right before waking on the plane. I feel safe down here, shrouded in this secret hideout.

I take a seat beside the water's edge, hugging my knees to my chest, gazing at the surface, flat as a mirror, reflecting the tree crown above.

For a very long time nothing happens, and I wonder if I need to make my presence known somehow. Say my name, perhaps? Possibly even slide into the water?

I edge closer, extending my arm, carefully lowering my hand towards the water until the cool touch sends ripples outward.

Suddenly, I feel it – a gentle tug, an invitation pulling at my arm, urging me to reach further, to come lower. Despite the protest of my sore shoulder, I come to lie prone on the ground, instinctively knowing what's asked of me here. I draw in a deep breath through the mouth, then I lean forward, my face hovering over the edge. For a moment, I catch my own reflection mirrored on the surface before I lower my head underwater.

The cool liquid envelops my face, my forehead, my neck. I

keep my eyes open, marvelling at the clarity of the water, my hair floating around me like Anima threads.

The moment my head submerges, a wave of images – memories – floods my mind, and for a second, I think I'm back in Ruth's life. But then I notice other women by my side, and their attire tells me I've plunged much deeper into the past: coarse woollen dresses in simple earthy tones, with tight-fitting bodices and full skirts; some, like me, have linen coifs covering their hair.

We're huddled in a town square, our collective fear palpable as angry voices, shouting insults and accusations, rise around us. Suddenly, a rotten head of lettuce sails through the air, splattering against a woman's head close to me. More follow – cabbages, tomatoes gone to mush – as we flinch and try to shield ourselves.

Rough hands grab at us, and we're being pushed forward, marched across the square. Ahead, an iron doorway yawns at us, the stench of dirt and faeces wafting out. We're forced inside, and the door clangs shut behind us. Now I know with brutal clarity exactly *when* I am: I'm deep in medieval times, and I'm experiencing firsthand the terrors of the European witch hunts. The dark cell closes in around me, and with it, the injustice that countless women of that time had to suffer through.

I want to stay submerged, to see more, to understand what happened next, but my lungs begin to burn with desperate need. Reluctantly, I break the surface, gasping and gulping air. The moment I catch my breath, I plunge back down, the cool water rushing over my face once more. To my utter shock, none other than Mardequai himself suddenly swims into my view. At first, I barely recognise him; he's much younger, his face smooth and his hair a dark shade of brown. He, too, is dressed in medieval clothing: an emerald tunic, cinched at the waist with a simple cord, but the old familiar, charcoal cloak draped over his shoulders.

He passes through the crowd with confidence, his voice

rising above angry shouts. I can't make out his words, but I can see the effect they're having. The mob begins to disperse, then guards approach our huddled group, but instead of guiding us toward the pyres, they begin to unlock our chains.

With growing shock, I realise what's happening. Mardequai is *saving* us – rescuing us from the very fires that would have been our certain end. The relief spreads among the accused witches, some weeping with gratitude, others still wary and disbelieving as they thank the druid in their midst.

As he draws nearer, I can see the determination in Mardequai's eyes. He's playing the role of protector perfectly. An icy chill grips me when I realise, this is where his scheme began. But the witch whose mind I'm in doesn't know it. I'm horrified when, eyes shining with affection, he leans in to kiss her. Their lips meet and she practically lights up under the warm sun of their connection – two souls walking beside each other through many of her lifetimes, finding each other again and again in every single one.

Indeed, I understand now that her mind, just like my own, holds more than just this one life – only she can access *all* of them. Like magical threads, she sees all her past witch lives stretching back through the ages, and she has loved *him* in each one. Each life distinct yet connected to Mardequai. It's overwhelming, this totality of memory, this love so big, so eternal.

Once again, I have to come up for air, my lungs screaming. A few quick breaths, then I'm back under.

Now the witch is shouting at Mardequai, her voice rough like sandpaper, but beneath her fury, something in her is bleeding. "I hate you! I hate you! I will *never* forgive you for what you've done!" The pain tears through her like a blade as she faces the man she's loved across the ages, now a stranger she despises. His betrayal burns like acid: he never was the protector he claimed to be, but the cunning architect of the witch hunts, whispering lies into the ears of priests and mayors, even kings. He described women who know nature's ways as evil incarnate. With his poisoned words, he spun the tales that stoked the fires of fear and superstition among humankind, using his knowledge of the witches' ways against them, revealing their secrets to those who would use the knowledge to destroy them. From village squares to royal courts, druid lies spread like a thick fog, turning husband against wife, brother against sister. And for what? Power?

As she stares into the eyes of the druid she once trusted above all others, she cannot see him anymore. In his place stands a man of calculated ambition, a man who wields the fear of the unknown like an artist's brush. He has painted a world where Witch cowers from Man, seeking protection beneath the wings of druids. The bitter irony of it all leaves her numb as she realises just how thoroughly they've all been ensnared in Mardequai's web.

Another ripple, and now she's kneeling in a moonlit clearing. The earthy scent of damp wood fills the air; wind rustles the leaves above her. Her powerful mind stretches out, entering the realm where all witch memories reside. She wants to forget, wants to rid herself of all the lives she's lived with him, to end this vicious cycle of love and betrayal between them. But just as her own threads of memory start to unravel, Mardequai steals up on her from the shadows. Before she can stop him, he presses an object into her hand – a Celestial Stone, cold as ice against her palm. Just like I experienced in the water chamber, the stone's power interferes with her spell, only the effect is a thousand times stronger, causing a cataclysmic rebound.

Horrified, the witch watches as, instead of her own memories, the memories of every other witch who has ever lived begin to vanish. It's as if a great cosmic broom is wiping clean the base of their collective existence, leaving only hers – the spell-caster's

– intact. The pain of this loss is staggering, a chasm ripping open in the lives of witches – of *women* – where once there were vast fields of ancestral knowledge. And now she is left as the sole keeper of their truth, bearing the unbearable weight of being the last to remember. Her only hope is to come here, to make her way to Chyulu before Mardequai can stop her, stop her from casting a prophecy as her last resort to preserve the witches' memory, and maybe one day bring it back.

As I come up from the water, gasping for air, her voice resounds from the cave walls, desperate and eerily familiar – here it is, the prophecy, at last:

Remember, remember, sisters twain,
You shall bring back once more what he sought to drain.
Because the truth never burned, but lingered concealed,
And by my bones, the Witches' past shall be revealed.

The melody hits me with an intensity that nearly undoes me, the words so similar to the ones my sister always sang to me when we were kids. My whole body shivers when I realise it: the prophecy is the third verse to Sofia's lullaby.

And now, I know. I know what Mardequai knows – what he has done and what he came here to the spring to uncover. The implications are so grave, they stagger me. I stumble backwards, bracing myself against the cold cave wall. I breathe, eyes closed, begging my heart to stop racing.

My wet clothes cling to my skin as I climb up the fig's twisted roots, favouring my uninjured arm and trying to keep most of my weight off my damaged shoulder. The rope around my waist goes taut – Cornelis is pulling from above. With a final push, I haul myself over the lip of the hole, wincing as my shoulder protests with the sharpest pain.

"What happened? What did you see?" Cornelis asks, fumbling with the knot at my waist.

I roll over, still catching my breath, the peaceful sounds of the spring, birdsong, and crickets entirely at odds with the strife on my mind. I open my mouth, then close it, like a fish gasping after it's been caught in a net, struggling to put into words what I've just uncovered.

"My... my ability to remember my grandmother's life..."

"Yes?"

"You won't believe it but, once upon a time, *all* witches had it."

Cornelis's hands freeze on the rope. "Hang on, what?"

"Before the witch hunts, every witch remembered her past lives, and not just one but... *all* of them."

"What do you mean? Do you remember *all* of your past lives now, not just Ruth's?"

"No," I reply, running my fingers through my wet hair. "I'm still down to only my grandmother's, or at least I think so."

Cornelis comes down on his haunches, scratching the base of his neck. "So, but... why would witches not remember their past lives anymore? What happened?"

I nod, and then I swallow hard, still struggling to fathom the truth myself. "Mardequai stole them. He tricked a witch, a very powerful witch, into destroying that connection to our collective memory."

Cornelis is suddenly very still. "How?"

"A Celestial Stone, at the peak of the Solantha Comet's passing." The words feel ancient on my tongue, a silenced truth finally spoken out loud.

"Who was she? The witch?"

"I don't know." I shake my head. "I couldn't see her face."

"Well, no wonder Mardequai is hellbent on keeping that a secret." Cornelis leans against the tree trunk, arms crossed in front of his chest. "If this came out, it would render druid supremacy futile. Mardequai's whole claim to power rests on the fact that druids, well, *remember* – and witches don't."

"More than that." I push myself to my feet. "It means everything witches have come to believe for the past five hundred years was a lie. Druids didn't protect witches from the pyres." The anger in me spikes. "Druids *stacked* the pyres."

Now Cornelis lowers himself to the earth, picking up clumps of soil as he thinks. "But then... what was the prophecy? What does this have to do with you and your sister?"

I meet his eyes, awe and rage and utter disbelief all tangled in my mind. Even the tree seems to hold its breath, waiting for my answer.

"The prophecy said, we are destined to bring them back, the lost memories. My sister and I, we are the ones to make everyone remember."

With those words, the tangle inside me finally ignites, burning away everything else until only white-hot determination remains. Mardequai believes he erased the truth when he reduced our memory to ashes, but he had better watch for sparks.

Because this time, it's our turn to light the match.

Thank you for reading my story.

Writing it was a labour of love, full of late nights, endless cups of coffee, and moments where I wondered if I would ever get it right. But knowing it is now in your hands makes it all worth it. If you enjoyed it, would you take just a minute to leave a review? For self-published authors like me, every single review makes a world of difference, and your thoughts mean more to me than you might realise. So if you can, please share your feedback. I will be on the other side reading it with gratitude...

Acknowledgments

A book is never written by just one person. For this one, I'd like to thank the following people:

My husband Frank, who never tires of untangling my messy first drafts. My sister and my dad, the first two people to read and love this book. As always, a heartfelt thanks to my editor Kristen Tate for her keen eye in breaking down this story with me, encouraging me to do better and tackling topics I was afraid of. To Chris who believed in my story at a time when I doubted everything. And to you, the readers, who make this dream possible...

About the Author

Gisele Stein is an Australian author whose work explores witches, women, and the wild. Her urban fantasy series, The Pyre Song Trilogy, blends history and myth with the rawness of nature to tell a story about female power and memory. Through fantasy rooted in real landscapes, her witch novels ask what happens when we start listening again to the wild parts of ourselves. If you love stories steeped in wonder and witchcraft, with a strong dose of female badassery, she's your girl.

For updates, latest releases, and a free story sign up to join her Reader Group here:

www.giselestein.com/free-story